SNORRI STURLUSON

Born in Iceland, 1178. Law-speaker of the General Assembly, 1215–18, 1222–31. In Norway 1218–20, 1237–9. Accused of treason by the Norwegian king and murdered by a political enemy in 1241.

SNORRI STURLUSON

Heimskringla

PART ONE

The Olaf Sagas

IN TWO VOLUMES · VOLUME ONE

TRANSLATED BY
SAMUEL LAING

REVISED WITH AN INTRODUCTION
AND NOTES BY
JACQUELINE SIMPSON, M.A.

DENT: LONDON, MELBOURNE AND TORONTO
EVERYMAN'S LIBRARY
DUTTON: NEW YORK

© *Editing and Introduction,*
J. M. Dent & Sons Ltd, 1964
All rights reserved
Printed in Great Britain by
Biddles Ltd, Guildford, Surrey
and bound at the
Aldine Press · Letchworth · Herts
for
J. M. DENT & SONS LTD
Aldine House · Albemarle Street · London
This edition was first published in
Everyman's Library in 1914
Revised edition 1964
Last reprinted 1978

Published in the U.S.A. by arrangement
with J. M. Dent & Sons Ltd

No. 717 Hardback ISBN 0 460 00717 3
No. 1717 Paperback ISBN 0 460 01717 9

CONTENTS

VOLUME ONE

VOLUME TWO

INTRODUCTION

1. The Life of Snorri

SNORRI STURLUSON,[1] the author of the *Heimskringla*, is a figure
of outstanding interest in thirteenth-century Iceland, not only
for his literary achievements, but for the position he occupied
as chieftain and landowner, and for the part he played in the
politics of his time. He is often mentioned in contemporary
sources, the most important of which is the compilation *Sturlunga
Saga*, one section of which was written by Snorri's nephew,
Sturla Thordarson.

Snorri was born in 1178. His father, Sturla of Hvamm, was the
founder of a family whose members became so prominent that the
period from about 1200 to 1264 traditionally takes its name from
them and is called the Age of the Sturlungs. They were relative
newcomers among the chieftainly families of Iceland; Sturla,
whose career is the subject of one section of *Sturlunga Saga*, was
an ambitious, ruthless, shrewd and sharp-tongued man whose
power, though considerable, could not compare with that of
more established chieftains. On his mother's side he could claim
descent from notable men, but his father's ancestors were of less
importance; his wife, Gudny Bodvarsdottir, however, was a
chieftain's daughter and was descended from the famous tenth-
century poet Egil Skallagrimsson.

In 1180 Sturla was drawn into a lawsuit between his father-
in-law Bodvar and a priest of good family, Pall Solvason. At a
meeting between the various parties in the dispute Pall's wife
grew angry and stabbed Sturla in the cheek in an attempt to
blind him. This gave Sturla a legal advantage over Pall, so that
he was able to exact from him not only an agreement in Bodvar's
favour, but also a promise to pay whatever compensation for his
wound Sturla would demand. In due course Sturla claimed his
compensation; invoking the precedent of a great chieftain some
sixty years previously, he demanded a sum far in excess of the

[1] In the Introduction the spelling of proper names follows the conventions
now generally adopted for rendering Icelandic names into English. In the
body of the text, however, forms used by Laing and his editors are left
unchanged—*e.g.* Trygvesson for Tryggvason, Snorre for Snorri, etc.

legal penalty for such an injury. The arrogant demand was
rejected, and Pall found many strong supporters, including Jon
Loftsson of Oddi, the most influential chieftain of the period.
Sturla prudently agreed to let Jon judge the matter; Jon awarded
him a mere eighth of the sum claimed, but in order to soften the
blow of this defeat he offered to act as foster-father to Sturla's
son Snorri, then aged three. The offer was an honour that Sturla
willingly accepted, and so it came about that Snorri was brought
up at Oddi, where he remained till early manhood.

Oddi, in the South Quarter of Iceland, had been a centre of
culture and learning since the beginning of the twelfth century.[1]
Sæmund the Learned, Jon's grandfather, had studied in France
and had written a Latin work on the kings of Norway; he had
founded a school at Oddi, which still flourished in Jon's time.
Jon's mother was an illegitimate daughter of King Magnus
Bareleg, and this connection with the royal house of Norway must
have reinforced the interest of the Oddi family in historical and
genealogical knowledge. No account is given anywhere of Snorri's
education and early years, but one may reasonably suppose that
it was at Oddi that he laid the foundations of his knowledge of
history, genealogies, law, poetry and mythology. There too he
was among men born to a power far greater and more deeply
rooted than Sturla's; Jon's unquestioned authority among the
other chieftains (so great that one writer calls him the 'uncrowned
king of Iceland') cannot have failed to impress Snorri, and may
have helped to feed his own ambitions.

Sturla died in 1183, when Snorri was five, and his second son
Sigvat inherited the chieftainship. Snorri's share of the inherit-
ance was largely squandered by his mother, and so when Jon
Loftsson died in 1197 Snorri, then nineteen years old, had few
resources with which to build himself a position. Two years later,
however, his eldest brother Thord arranged for him to marry
Herdis, daughter of Bersi the Rich, owner of the farmstead of
Borg, which had been the home of Snorri's maternal ancestor
Egil Skallagrimsson. Snorri's mother gave him the estate of
Hvamm, and he lived partly there and partly at Oddi until 1202,
when Bersi died; he then moved to Borg and acquired a chieftainship, probably by inheritance from Bersi. He also shared another
chieftainship with his maternal uncle Thord Bodvarsson.

In about 1206 Snorri moved to Reykjaholt in the district of
Borgarfjord, a large estate whose owner was old and incapable

[1] See Halldór Hermannsson, *Sæmund Sigfússon and the Oddaverjar*
(*Islandica*, XXII; 1932).

of running it efficiently. Snorri took over the property in exchange for an undertaking to support the former owner and his family; the wealth he thus acquired led to a considerable increase in his power. His wife, however, remained behind at Borg, and their marriage appears to have broken up; they had had two children, a daughter named Hallbera, and a son, Jon Murt. Snorri had already begotten one illegitimate child, and from this period for many years he kept a series of mistresses, by whom he had several more children.

Snorri's influence was now beginning to make itself felt more widely; he was on good terms with his brothers Thord and Sigvat (who were also rapidly building up power by their accumulation of land and chieftainships), but his links with Oddi were now no longer so close. He played a part in several disputes and feuds, though his temperament was not that of a fighter, and his successes were due more to intelligence and to the support of his kinsmen than to any qualities of warlike leadership on his part. Despite his youth, he was chosen Law-speaker in 1213; this, the highest position in the Icelandic republic, required a thorough knowledge of the laws and the ability to judge and arbitrate in feuds and lawsuits. At about the same period he turned his thoughts to the possibility of winning favour from the rulers of Norway, and, following the well-established custom of ambitious young Icelanders, applied his poetic talent to that end. He composed and sent a poem of praise to Earl Hakon Galin; in return the earl sent him fine gifts and invited him to come to Norway, saying he would bestow great honours on him. This pleased Snorri greatly, but soon afterwards the earl died, so Snorri remained at home, though fully determined to go to Norway at some favourable opportunity.

The opportunity came in 1218. At this time the rulers of Norway were King Hakon Hakonarson, then aged fourteen, and Earl Skuli Bardarson, in whose hands lay most of the real power. Snorri was welcomed by Earl Skuli on his arrival in Norway, and received hospitality in his household. The following spring he went to the Swedish district of Gotland to visit Kristin, the widow of Hakon Galin, and bring her a poem written in her honour, for which she rewarded him with rich gifts. The knowledge of Gotland he gained on this journey is reflected in certain passages in *Heimskringla*. He then returned to Earl Skuli, with whom he stayed for the next year and a half; he accepted from the king and earl the title of *skutilsvein*, a rank of high honour in the Norwegian court, and thereby became their liegeman.

In the spring of 1220 Snorri intended to return home. It happened that at this time the Norwegians were so enraged with the Icelanders, and especially with the men of Oddi, that they meant to send a fleet to raid and plunder the country, and preparations for this expedition had already begun. The hostility had first arisen some years before, in a dispute between Sæmund Jonsson, head of the family of Oddi since his father's death, and some merchants from Bergen whose trade in Iceland he had restricted. Soon afterwards Sæmund's son Pall had visited Bergen, where he met with such mockery for his family pride and airs of grandeur that he set sail for home in a rage; his ship was wrecked, and all on board perished. Sæmund held that the men of Bergen were to blame, and in revenge seized goods of great value from other Norwegian merchants who were in Iceland at the time. They retaliated by killing Sæmund's brother Orm Jonsson, who was quite free from blame in the matter, and returned to Norway to demand even further vengeance for their losses.

Snorri now intervened, and convinced Earl Skuli that it would be better to win the friendship of the chief men of Iceland and induce them to give their allegiance to Norway. He said that his own arguments could soon bring this about, and that his brothers, the most powerful chieftains in Iceland apart from Sæmund Jonsson, would let themselves be guided by him. So the king was persuaded to forgo the intended raid, and he and the earl bestowed on Snorri the further title of *lendrmaðr*, on the understanding that he would use his influence on their behalf, and send them his son as proof of goodwill. Snorri sailed home that autumn, with many gifts.

His activities as peacemaker were much resented by the family at Oddi, who saw themselves deprived of the chance of avenging Orm; they mocked at his new honours, ridiculed a poem he had written on Earl Skuli, and seemed likely to avenge themselves on him. However, the family was itself divided by rivalries, and by playing on the hatred between two of its younger members Snorri helped to stir up a feud in which his most threatening enemy, Orm's son-in-law Bjorn, was killed. In due course Snorri sent his son Jon to Norway, but he never did anything to get his countrymen to accept Norwegian overlordship—perhaps because he had never seriously intended to do so, or perhaps because his own influence was not in fact strong enough for him to attempt it. Nor did the king try to press the point, and Jon was soon allowed home again.

In 1222 Snorri was re-elected Law-speaker, and held the

position till 1231. At the same time he set about extending
his power by various marriage alliances. In 1224 he gave his
daughter Ingibjorg to Gissur, son of Thorvald Gissurarson, the
head of the powerful Haukadal family; he gave another daughter,
Thordis, to Thorvald Snorrason of Vatnsfjord, a chieftain who
had formerly been his enemy. Snorri himself had hoped to marry
Solveig, daughter of Sæmund Jonsson of Oddi, but lost her to his
own nephew Sturla Sigvatsson; from the account in *Sturlunga
Saga* it seems as if personal affection as well as considerations of
rank and wealth had influenced his choice of Solveig, and his
reaction to the news of her marriage was noticeably bitter. He
then turned his attention to Hallveig (daughter of Orm Jonsson
of Oddi and widow of that Bjorn whose death he had helped to
bring about), although it is recorded that once, being with
Solveig and seeing Hallveig go by, he had made fun of her ostenta-
tious appearance. Nevertheless she was the richest woman in
Iceland. Snorri brought her to Reykjaholt and set up house with
her, arranging that they should hold all property in common and
that he should also take charge of the property of her two sons
by her first marriage. By this contract he became by far the
wealthiest man in Iceland. Finally, four years later, he gave his
eldest daughter, Hallbera, to Kolbein the Young, of the Asbirning
family, thus completing a series of alliances by which he might
well expect that his influence would be strongly reinforced.

Meanwhile he was trying to undermine the position of his
nephew Sturla Sigvatsson, with whom he was now on bad terms.
The two elder Sturlung brothers, Thord and Sigvat, had at one
time shared the family chieftainship, and Sigvat had passed his
share of it to his son Sturla; Snorri now urged Thord to claim this
share back, and from this arose a lengthy dispute, in the course
of which Snorri forced Sturla from his chieftainship and exacted
oaths of loyalty to himself from Sturla's former supporters. He
also gained authority in some areas of the north-west, for when
his son-in-law Thorvald Snorrason was slain in 1228, Snorri
claimed the inheritance on behalf of his own infant grandson.

Nevertheless Snorri's position was not as secure as might have
seemed probable. The marriage of Hallbera to Kolbein the Young
proved a failure, and in a legal dispute that arose from this
Snorri found himself unable to enforce a settlement made in his
favour. The marriage of Ingibjorg and Gissur Thorvaldsson also
ended in divorce. Nor was Snorri's relationship with his own
family harmonious; he refused to part with lands on which his
legitimate son Jon had hoped to set himself up, and later refused

a similar request from his bastard son Oraekja. He was on rather
cool terms with his brothers, though they might act in alliance
if circumstances demanded it; a reconciliation with Sturla Sigvatsson in 1230 proved shallow and short-lived. In a community
where a chieftain's authority was not merely a matter of birth
and wealth but of the ability to win and hold the loyalty of
kinsmen and followers, Snorri, despite many advantages, failed
to gain the position he sought. He had not the effortless superiority of character which had been the basis of Jon Loftsson's
unquestioned leadership, nor had he the aggressive ruthlessness
to maintain his power if it were seriously challenged.

Such a challenge came in 1235, when Sturla Sigvatsson
returned from a two-year journey to Norway and Rome. The
area of Sturla's present chieftainship was close to that which
Thorvald Snorrason had held and which Snorri had taken over
on behalf of his infant grandson. Sturla had therefore been displeased when, at about the time of his own departure, Snorri
handed over the authority over this area to his bastard son
Oraekja. Oraekja was by nature quarrelsome, overbearing and
violent; he misused his power, came into conflict with his uncle
Sigvat and raided the property of men who were followers of his
cousin Sturla, one of whom he killed. On his return to Iceland,
Sturla therefore joined with Sigvat in planning an attack on
Snorri, and gathered men for the purpose soon after Christmas
1236.

Snorri was warned of the plan, and sent for Oraekja, who
arrived with more than seven hundred men. He and others
urged Snorri to pit his strength openly against his kinsmen, but
Snorri preferred to send a message suggesting an attempt at
compromise, and so Oraekja's band was allowed to disperse.
In the week before Palm Sunday he learnt that Sigvat and
Sturla were about to attack in earnest, and without delay he
abandoned his farmstead and took refuge in the south, with the
result that Sturla was able to seize his lands and take over his
chieftainship unopposed. Next, Sturla entrapped Oraekja,
castrated him and drove him to exile in Norway. The following
year Snorri made a show of strength and came from the south
with four hundred men, his chief ally being his cousin on the
mother's side, Thorleif Thordarson; yet on learning of the
superiority of Sturla's forces he refused to risk an encounter, and
rode away again with only one companion. Thorleif remained and
did battle against Sturla, but was defeated and exiled to Norway;
shortly afterwards Snorri too set sail for Norway.

There the situation had changed since the time of Snorri's first visit. King Hakon now wielded power more firmly, and Skuli's influence over him had waned. Hakon had been on very friendly terms with Sturla during the latter's visit to Norway, and it was generally thought that they had agreed that Sturla should make himself the king's agent in bringing Iceland into subjection, and that in exchange the king would make him supreme chieftain there. Snorri therefore was no longer of use to King Hakon, and could expect no favours from him. Not surprisingly, therefore, he attached himself once more to Skuli, who had now risen to the rank of duke.

In the autumn of 1238 news reached Norway that Sigvat and Sturla had both been killed in battle by Kolbein the Young, who had opposed Sturla's ambitions and had now himself seized power over the whole North Quarter. Snorri was much grieved by Sigvat's death, and expressed his sorrow in a verse which he sent to one of Sigvat's two surviving sons. But he also realized that this gave him some hope of regaining his power and wealth, and in the following spring he made ready to return, together with Oraekja and Thorleif. He was on the point of leaving, and was in Nidaros to bid farewell to Duke Skuli, when he was brought a letter from King Hakon forbidding any Icelander to leave Norway that summer. It seems to have been Hakon's policy to keep influential Icelanders under his own eye till they would agree to fall in with his plans. In the present case he may also have feared that if Snorri were to further Norwegian interests at all, it would be on Skuli's behalf rather than on his own. On seeing the letter Snorri merely remarked: 'I am leaving.' He had a secret conference with Skuli before he went, at which only four other men were present; later it was said that on this occasion Skuli bestowed on him the title of earl, and though Sturla Thordarson writes of the matter as very doubtful, the probability is that such a title was in fact offered and accepted. Once again, as in 1220, Snorri had accepted honours that entailed a pledge of allegiance, and had thus committed himself to support Norwegian policy; once again, however, he did nothing to fulfil his implied pledge. A year later news reached Iceland that Duke Skuli was dead.

On their return Snorri, Thorleif and Oraekja claimed compensation from all who had helped Sturla Sigvatsson in his attacks on them, and obtained considerable sums; Snorri himself regained all his former chieftainships, and even increased his wealth. He also assisted Sigvat's surviving son, Tumi, to get

compensation for his father's death from Kolbein the Young, and
also from Gissur Thorvaldsson, who had also been a leader in the
battle where Sigvat and Sturla were killed. Gissur and Kolbein,
both formerly Snorri's sons-in-law, were now hostile to him,
though not yet openly so; both were personally ambitious, and
belonged to families of long-established power who must have
looked upon the Sturlungs as dangerous upstarts. Snorri was
now the chief representative of the Sturlungs, and Kolbein and
Gissur seemed resolved to prevent him from rebuilding his
position at their expense. During a meeting between Snorri and
Gissur at the General Assembly of 1241, Kolbein appeared with a
force of five hundred men, so that Snorri though it prudent to
withdraw for safety to the nearby church; nothing, however,
came of the threat, and the negotiations between Tumi, Snorri
and Gissur ended to the former's satisfaction.

Not long after this Snorri's wife, Hallveig, died suddenly, and
he had to face the disagreeable task of sharing out her valuable
estates with his two stepsons. They claimed a half share of all
that Snorri and Hallveig had jointly owned, but Snorri character-
istically raised difficulties, maintaining that several of the best
pieces of land had been his alone. A compromise was reached
whereby the movable property was shared out at once, but the
division of the lands was postponed. Since Hallveig's first
husband had been Gissur Thorvaldsson's brother, Gissur now
eagerly took up her sons' cause, seeing in it a welcome opportunity to pick a quarrel with Snorri. He prepared a plan of
attack in concert with Kolbein the Young, and gathered a group
of helpers, several of whom had formerly been friends of Snorri.
He then showed them a letter from King Hakon, in which the
king ordered Gissur to send Snorri willy-nilly back to Norway,
or, if this was impossible, to kill him, as penalty for the act of
treason he had committed in leaving Norway against the king's
command. Gissur told his allies that he felt bound to obey, and
that as Snorri would never go willingly they must go to Reykjaholt and capture him. Of Snorri's two stepsons, one went to
raise more men for Gissur, but the other refused to have any
part in the affair.

Gissur and his men reached Reykjaholt during the night of
22nd September 1241. They broke their way into the building
where Snorri was sleeping, but he evaded them and ran into a
small outhouse; then, on the advice of the priest of his household,
he took refuge in the cellar. Meanwhile Gissur was searching the
buildings; he found the priest, who denied knowing where Snorri

was. Gissur said there could be no hope of making peace if they could not even meet and discuss the matter. The priest then said that Snorri might be found if they would swear to spare his life. Thus they found out where Snorri was, and five of Gissur's men went down into the cellar. The chief of them, Gissur's servant Simon Knut, ordered one of the others to strike Snorri down. 'You must not strike,' said Snorri. Simon repeated his order. 'You must not strike,' said Snorri again. But the man struck him his death-blow.

So Snorri was killed defenceless, despite the promise of quarter, and without chance to parley or offer terms, or to accept Hakon's summons back to Norway. What the king's real intentions towards him had been remained unclear; on hearing the news of Snorri's death, Hakon declared that if he had submitted he would not have been severely treated. For Gissur the killing of Snorri was a necessary step in breaking the power of the Sturlungs and establishing himself as supreme in Iceland. It was Snorri's fate to live among men of ruthless ambition, himself having ambition enough to incur their hostility, but not the vigour and ferocity to counter it successfully. He aspired to play a leading part in the politics of his age, and indeed it was he who took the chief part in averting the danger that threatened Iceland in 1220. Nevertheless, except for that one instance, one can point to no occasion when his influence actively or decisively moulded the course of public events.

On the gravest issue of the times, Iceland's relationship with Norway, it is hard to assess Snorri's attitude. If one judges merely by *Sturlunga Saga*'s account of his actions, it is easy to conclude that by his explicit undertaking to King Hakon in 1220 and by his repeated acceptance of Norwegian titles he proved himself willing to barter Icelandic independence for personal aggrandizement, and that only unfavourable circumstances and the weakness of his own position prevented him from putting his undertakings into effect. Yet from his writings a different picture emerges. The most striking instance is the section in *St Olaf's Saga* (pp. 261–4) concerning Olaf's 'show of friendship' to the Icelanders, his request to be given one of their small offshore islands, Einar's exposition of the hidden danger in this request, and the warning that it was unwise for too many prominent chieftains to visit Norway, even for 'a journey of honour'. Every word in this passage could be, and doubtless was, read by Snorri's contemporaries as a direct warning to them to resist all Hakon's demands and promises. Nor does this passage stand alone; in

telling the story of Harald Gormsson's proposed raid on Iceland,
and how it was abandoned when his magician saw the warlike
'spirits of the land' ranged against him, Snorri is obviously
expressing joy in Iceland's ability to resist a foreign threat. Time
and again in *Heimskringla* we hear the protests of the regional
petty rulers against the claims of centralized kingship, an issue
closely similar to that of Iceland's independence; and in *Egil's
Saga*, if that work is Snorri's, we find a forceful expression of the
traditional view that it was Harald Fairhair's tyranny that drove
the proudest and most independent of his subjects to found the
free republic of Iceland. With such passages in mind some
historians, not surprisingly, have been led to speak of Snorri as
an outstanding patriot, and the chief obstacle to King Hakon's
plans.

In such a case it is not possible to justify unqualified judgments
either of praise or blame.   Nor is it even possible to reconcile the
inconsistencies by tracing a definite process of development in
Snorri's attitudes. Perhaps, however, this very uncertainty has a
significance, reflecting as it does the basic ambivalence in the
feelings of the Icelanders towards Norway. They cherished the
memory of their Norwegian ancestry, but also of the independence with which their forefathers had turned their backs on
Norway; their poets sought wealth and fame as eulogists in the
courts of kings and earls, but their saga-writers delighted in
stories to show how little these same poets were in awe of their
patrons; in many sagas the hero wins honour abroad in his
youth, but it is at home that he finds the duties and challenges
of maturity, by which his fate is shaped. It is fitting that Snorri,
the epitome of so much that is typically Icelandic, should have
hesitated before the power of Norway, uncertain whether it held
in greater degree a promise of glory or threat of tyranny.

2. SNORRI'S WRITINGS

Sturlunga Saga sets out to chronicle deeds of public importance,
so it is not surprising that it has almost nothing to say about
Snorri's literary interests and activities. Some of his poems are
mentioned, as he used them to win favour in Norway, and there
is a mention of books among the valuables he shared out with his
stepsons. As a sign of the reconciliation of Snorri and Sturla in
1230 it is said: 'Sturla stayed for a long time at Reykjaholt, and
took great interest in having copies made of the saga-books which

Snorri was writing.' For all further knowledge of Snorri's writings, we must turn to the works themselves.

(i) *Poetry*. For many generations Icelanders had composed eulogies for the kings and earls of Norway, using the rigid and intricate metres and ornate metaphors of scaldic verse.[1] Snorri is known to have written several such poems: one on Earl Hakon Galin, another (called *Andvaka*) on his wife Kristin, one on King Sverrir, one on King Ingi Bardarson, one on Earl Skuli. Of all these nothing has been preserved, except for the refrain of that on Skuli, which is quoted in *Sturlunga Saga* because Snorri's enemies parodied it. He also composed various occasional verses, and probably a poem on Bishop Gudmund Arason.

His chief surviving poem is the *Háttatál*, a long work in praise of King Hakon and Earl Skuli, which must, from the nature of its subject, have been composed between 1221 and 1223, and the most striking feature of which is indicated by its name, 'List of Metres'. Each of its 102 stanzas is composed in a different metre, so that it forms a compendium of all the types of verse used in scaldic poetry. The idea was not original, a similar *tour de force* having been composed by Earl Rognvald of Orkney and Hall Thorarinsson, but Snorri's work is even more exhaustive than theirs. The technical skill required is evidently great, and several passages in the poem itself express Snorri's pride in his achievement; nevertheless its merits as poetry are low, and it would probably have suffered the same fate as his other poems had he not incorporated it in his *Edda*.

(ii) *The Prose Edda*. The importance of scaldic poetry to Snorri is out of all proportion to the small surviving amount of his own work in that style. His knowledge of its contents is one of the main bases of his historical writings, and his interest in its style led him to write his *Edda*.[2]

This work is at the same time a handbook from which young scalds could learn their art, and a manual on Scandinavian mythology. Such a combination of interests is explained by one of the characteristics of scaldic poetry, its use of kennings— figurative expressions in which an object or person is not named but indirectly described by nature or function, or by allusion to an associated story. Many such expressions embodied mythological knowledge or referred to particular mythical episodes.

[1] For a description of scaldic technique, see *Sagas of the Norse Kings* (Everyman's Library, No. 847), Introduction, pp. viii–x.
[2] Trans. A. G. Brodeur, *The Prose Edda* (American-Scandinavian Foundation, 1916); the chief sections are also translated by J. Young, *The Prose Edda* (1954).

Thus, as Odin was the god of war, any battle could be called the 'storm of Odin', and for the sake of variation and metrical convenience, any of Odin's numerous names or titles could be substituted for his best-known name; as Odin's gold ring Draupnir produced other rings from itself, gold could be called 'drops' or 'shower' or 'rain of Draupnir'; as Odin once hanged himself, the gallows are his 'horse' and he himself is 'the burden of the gallows'. Hero legends also provide material for kennings; as Sigurd won the pile of gold on which the dragon Fafnir lay in his lair on Gnitaheid, and carried it away on his horse Grani, gold can be called 'Fafnir's bed', 'Fafnir's dwelling', 'metal of Gnitaheid' or 'burden of Grani'. Similar examples could be multiplied indefinitely; skill in handling them is essential to success in composing scaldic poetry. The knowledge of myths and heathen legends necessary to compose, or even to understand, the kennings had survived the Christianization of Iceland, but in Snorri's time it was in danger of disappearing, as a growing fashion for simpler, Europeanized verse-forms was rendering it superfluous. The *Prose Edda* is Snorri's reponse to that danger.

The meaning of the word *Edda* is not certain; it may be connected with *óðr*, 'poetry', and so mean 'poetic art'; or it might be derived from the place-name Oddi, perhaps implying the work was partly written there, perhaps as a tribute to Snorri's education there, or, most plausibly, because a manuscript of it was kept there and the name was later transferred from one manuscript to the work itself. Snorri's work is known as the *Prose* or *Younger Edda* to distinguish it from a collection of ancient poems on mythological and heroic subjects known as the *Poetic* or *Elder Edda*—a collection which in its present form dates from the mid thirteenth century, though almost all its poems are far older, and many of them were used by Snorri as the chief sources of his *Edda*. The precise date of Snorri's *Edda* cannot be fixed, though it is usually thought to be a comparatively early work; the work falls into three sections, the last of which comprises the *Háttatál* and can therefore be fairly accurately dated (see above, p. xvii), but whether the rest of the work was composed before or immediately after Snorri's visit to Norway in 1218–20 cannot be determined.

The first section is called *Gylfaginning*, 'The Tricking of Gylfi', and is devoted entirely to mythology, without any references to scaldic technique. It opens with a Prologue setting out Snorri's explanation of the origins of belief in heathen gods. Most medieval thinkers explained this as the devil's work, but Snorri

advances a considerably more sophisticated theory: after the
Flood most of Noah's descendants forgot the revelations of God,
but their amazement at the marvels of earth and sky, and at
growth, harvest and decay, led them to deify the earth and the
heavenly bodies. This theory seems to be Snorri's own, and is
remarkably modern in outlook. He supplements it by a more
common medieval theory, euhemerism, according to which 'gods'
were merely human beings. He declares that Thor and Odin were
kings in Asia, descended respectively from Priam of Troy and
from 'a wise woman named Sybil', and that Odin wandered as
far as the Scandinavian lands, where he and his sons became
rulers revered for their magical powers. The same argument is to
be found in the first chapters of *Heimskringla*. The *Gylfaginning*
proper tells how a Swedish king named Gylfi questioned these
magicians, who told him long stories about the gods and tricked
him into repeating them to all mankind in such a way that men
identified these magicians with the gods in their stories.

These 'stories' are, of course, the traditional Scandinavian
myths. Snorri's knowledge of them is drawn chiefly from many
poems of the *Elder Edda* and from other poems, now lost, of the
same type; partly from scaldic poems with rich mythological
content, and partly from oral tradition. He quotes freely from the
poems he has used. The material is systematically arranged,
beginning with creation myths, passing to accounts of the
attributes, homes and adventures of the various gods, and
finally foretelling the death of Balder, the last battle of the gods
against the monsters of evil, and the destruction of the gods and
the world. Thus Snorri binds his varied and often contradictory
material into a coherent whole, while deploying all the resources
of his art to make each story effective.

The second section of the *Edda* is called *Skáldskaparmál*,
'Language of Poetry'. It too is set out as a dialogue, not this time
between Gylfi and the magician-gods, but between the god of
the sea and the god of poetry; the subject of their dialogue is the
nature and characteristics of scaldic poetry, and the supposed
protagonists are soon forgotten. Snorri's method here is to
define various types of kenning and to compile a list of those
used for such constantly recurrent concepts as 'warrior', 'ship',
'gold', 'weapon', 'king', and so forth. At the same time he
retells whatever myth or legend must be known in order to understand the kenning quoted. Many details of mythology that would
overload the scheme of the *Gylfaginning* find place here, as also
do legends about Germanic heroes. Snorri is sometimes willing to

stretch the limits of this scheme in order to include, as a coherent narrative, the whole of a legend that is of importance to poets, even if only part of it is relevant to the kenning under discussion; thus the question, 'Why is gold called "Blood-money for the Otter"?' is the starting-point for a summary of the whole cycle of legends concerning the Rhine Gold, Sigurd the Volsung, Brynhild, Gudrun, Gunnar, Hogni, Atli the Hun and Jormunrekk. On the whole, however, the arrangement of *Skáldskaparmál* is closely related to the primary task of recording and interpreting the kennings; here more than four hundred stanzas or fragments of stanzas are quoted, as against sixty-seven in *Gylfaginning*, and this profusion of examples, together with the fact that the stories are often rather baldly summarized, makes this section less attractive than the first, great as is the interest of its material.

The third section is purely technical; it consists of the poem *Háttatál* (see above, p. xvii), together with a detailed running commentary on the metrical peculiarities of each stanza.

In so far as Snorri hoped to save the scaldic style from falling into disuse, he failed; he did, however, provide such ample guidance for all future readers and commentators that he saved it from becoming incomprehensible, as might well have happened, and preserved many verses that would otherwise have been lost. Still more important is his contribution to mythological knowledge; not only to do his paraphrases of ancient poems cast light on their obscurities, but several of his best stories are not known from any other sources. His versions are quite free from the moralizings and explicitly Christian presentation by which all non-Icelandic and many Icelandic writers of this period would have destroyed the artistic effectiveness and lessened the scientific value of such a work. And if it is true, as some have thought, that the manuscript of the *Elder Edda* itself would never have been written if Snorri had not revived his countrymen's interest in their ancient heritage of mythological and heroic poetry, then the debt we owe to his work is incalculable.

Snorri's literary skill is often to be seen at its most attractive in the *Edda*. The stories are vividly and entertainingly told; the style is brisk, flexible and frequently humorous, and can rise to considerable heights of dramatic power when the subject requires it, as in the description of Balder's death and of the Doom of the Gods. In writing of the latter he quotes at length from his source, the *Vǫluspá*, the noblest and most impressive poem of pagan Iceland, and it is perhaps the greatest tribute to the art of

Snorri's prose that it can form an acceptable setting for that masterpiece, and not suffer in the juxtaposition.

(iii) *The Saga of Egil Skallagrimsson*.[1] The attribution of this work to Snorri is a conjecture supported by many modern scholars. Egil, the central figure of the saga, was a maternal ancestor of Snorri, and was the greatest of all scaldic poets, both for his technical mastery and—a rarer quality in scalds—for the passionate intensity of feeling in his finest poems. Snorri's interest in poetry would certainly have led him to study Egil's works, passages from which he quotes in the *Prose Edda,* while at the same time Egil's personality and career make him a tempting subject for a saga. Moreover, Egil's home, Borg, was also Snorri's home for several years, so that he would be well placed to glean all surviving traditions about him; the saga does in fact show signs of having been written by someone familiar with that area. The literary quality of the saga shows it to be the work of a practised author; the interests, outlook and range of knowledge revealed in it correspond well with Snorri's, and it is generally accepted that the narrative technique is close to his. No really convincing argument against his authorship has been brought forward, and it is now usually thought to be one of the works of Snorri's early maturity. There is nothing to show whether it was written before or after the *Separate Saga of St Olaf,* but for the present survey it will be more convenient to discuss it first.

In writing a poet's life Snorri was reflecting an interest already present in Icelandic literature. The earliest sagas had been biographies of Norwegian kings, the material for which was drawn partly from verses of court poets; it was natural that anecdotes about Icelandic poets should find place in the lives of their royal patrons. In the first decades of the thirteenth century a new form of saga arose, the 'Family Saga' or 'Saga of Ice-landers', taking as subject stories of Icelanders of the tenth or early eleventh century; the dating of such sagas is a controversial matter, but of the five which can with most probability be assigned to a period before or contemporary with that of *Egil's Saga,* four have poets for their heroes.

The relationship of Egil to King Eric Bloody-axe is central to the saga, though it is far from being that of court poet to patron.

[1] Trans: W. C. Green, *The Story of Egil Skalagrimson* (1893); by E. R. Eddison, *Egil's Saga* (1930); and Gwyn Jones, *Egil's Saga* (American-Scan-dinavian Foundation, 1960). The arguments in favour of Snorri's author-ship are fully set out in the introduction to the last-named translation.

The story hinges upon their bitter enmity, whose roots go back to the previous generation and to Harald Fairhair's attempt to subordinate the power of the independent chieftains to his own central authority. Egil's grandfather, father and uncle were such chieftains, and the first part of the saga tells of their repeated clashes with King Harald which forced Egil's father to emigrate to Iceland. Throughout the saga the Norwegian kings are seen as harsh, vengeful, covetous and wily; the portrayal of Harald Fairhair in particular is unlike the favourable picture of him in *Heimskringla*, where his ambition is presented as praiseworthy and the crushing of his rivals as a necessary step in forming the kingdom of Norway.

This discrepancy has been used as an argument against Snorri's authorship of *Egil's Saga*, but it is readily explicable on artistic grounds. *Heimskringla* is a history of Norway, in which the discontent that drove many of Harald's subjects overseas is a marginal matter needing only a brief mention. In *Egil's Saga* it is central; the pressures which, in the traditional Icelandic view, caused the colonization of that country, are here shown acting upon a particular family with whose point of view the author identifies himself. The two works are different in emphasis, but not wholly opposed in outlook; the kings in *Egil's Saga* may be harsh and overbearing, but they have their full measure of royal dignity; the kings in *Heimskringla* are never presented as faultless, and the opinions of their enemies are often given powerful expression. The preference for complex characters and issues rather than mere black and white is one of the basic qualities of saga-writers, and one which Snorri possessed in full measure.

Almost all of the surviving examples of Egil's poetry are to be found in this saga, and many of its episodes are designed to explain the circumstances in which they were composed. Much information is drawn from the poems themselves, with the same care for detail as can be seen in the *Prose Edda* and in *Heimskringla*. Yet, as a saga of this type is more concerned with the imaginative re-creation of a past era than with the scrupulous disentanglement of historical truth, Snorri does not limit himself to what may be deduced from the poems themselves. Egil's three long poems are given in full: one in praise of Eric Bloody-axe, one a lament for the deaths of two of his sons and one in memory of his friend Arinbjorn. The first two, according to the saga, were composed in intensely dramatic circumstances; in the first case Egil, inexplicably lured into the power of his royal enemy, saved his life by making up the poem in less than one night and persuading the king to hear it before putting him to death; in the second case Egil had resolved to starve himself to death for grief, but was tricked by his daughter into breaking his fast, whereupon he agreed to live, and eased his sorrow in poetry. These episodes are justly famous for their dramatic vividness, but cannot be supported by evidence from the poems themselves. They may be traditional stories developed and transmitted by Egil's descendants, or they may, though this is less likely, be invented largely by Snorri himself; in either case it is their artistic quality that is important, not the problem of their factual reliability.

The same thing may be said of this saga as a whole, despite the great historical interest not only of the Norwegian episodes but of the account of Egil's visits to England and his part in a battle which is probably that of Brunanburh (A.D. 937). Historical knowledge is indeed so well handled in this saga that one must conclude that if it is not Snorri's then Snorri must have learnt much by studying it; yet it is not in the presentation of history that its greatest achievement lies. It is a masterpiece of character drawing, more mature, subtle and complex than can be found in any preceding saga (unless, as is possible, Snorri's *Separate Saga of St Olaf* is earlier than this). Egil's grim, unscrupulous, avaricious and deeply emotional nature is presented in such a way that the reader remains, throughout the work, divided between admiration and dislike; so realistic, objective and convincing a portrait justly ranks among the most memorable achievements of the Family Sagas.

(iv) *The (Separate) Saga of St Olaf.* Snorri's *Saga of St Olaf* is found both as the central section of *Heimskringla* and as a separate work, and it was in the latter form that he first wrote it. The chief difference between the two versions is that the separate work opens with a brief summary of the history of Norway from the time of Harald Fairhair, and concludes with a few chapters on events after Olaf's death, and in particular on the growth of his cult during subsequent reigns. These sections naturally were removed when the work was incorporated in the larger scheme, but the main body of the saga was left unchanged; for the purposes of the present discussion *St Olaf's Saga* as separately written can be treated as identical with the work as found in *Heimskringla*. It is probable that Snorri wrote it some time after his return from Norway in 1220 and that it was among the sagas already in existence when Sturla visited him in 1230.

It is not surprising that Snorri should have chosen the life of

St Olaf for his first attempt at the biography of a Norwegian king, for there was much material available to draw on, and yet the picture that emerged from it was sufficiently contradictory and paradoxical to offer a challenge to Snorri's interpretative powers.[1] The facts of history showed a strange reversal in the attitude of Olaf's subjects towards him. He had met considerable hostility during much of his reign, and had eventually been first driven from the country and then slain in battle by his own former liegemen; yet within a few months of his death he was revered as a saint, miracles were ascribed to him and the popular acclaim which had never been his in life was lavished upon him. Moreover, many of his recorded acts showed him to be ambitious, cruel, proud, unforgiving and unchaste, so that the tales of his piety and miracles were hard to reconcile with the impression given by his life. The explanation of this paradox given in the older accounts was not such as could satisfy Snorri, whose *Saga of St Olaf* is evidently intended not only to be more reliable as history than those of his predecessors, but also deeper as analysis of Olaf's personality and his relations with his subjects.

The earliest source for any life of Olaf would naturally be the verses composed in his lifetime by his own court poets, and these Snorri used to the full. As is to be expected of such poetry, they give valuable information on Olaf's battles, but say little about his personality beyond conventional praise of his courage and generosity to his retainers. Nevertheless it is clear that at least one of Olaf's poets, Sigvat Thordsson, felt strong personal affection for the king and mourned sincerely for his death.[2] It is poets also who provide the earliest evidence for the belief in Olaf's sanctity. The *Glælognskviða* of Thorarin Loftunga (pp. 390–1) was written about 1032, two years after Olaf's death; it already speaks of the signs of his holiness, of his uncorrupted corpse with hair and nails still growing, of bells ringing of themselves around his bier, of miracles of healing at his tomb. Sigvat too, in a *Memorial Lay* composed *c.* 1043, speaks of Olaf's uncorrupted corpse and of miracles of healing. Snorri evidently attached much importance to such contemporary testimony.

In 1153 the poet Einar Skulason composed and publicly recited a long poem in praise of St Olaf, as part of the ceremonies

[1] For a general survey of Icelandic historical writings before Snorri, see *Sagas of the Norse Kings*, Introduction, pp. x–xx. Here only sources of major importance for the *Saga of St Olaf* will be mentioned.
[2] See the verses quoted in the *Saga of Magnus the Good*, chap. viii (*Sagas of the Norse Kings*, pp. 132–4).

celebrating the establishment of an archbishop's see at Nidaros.
It is entitled *Geisli*, 'Sunbeam', for it compares Olaf to a ray of
light emitted by the Heavenly Sun, which is God; Olaf is also the
Christ of the North, at whose death the sun was darkened as at
the Crucifixion. Many posthumous miracles are here ascribed to
him; some are of healing, as in the earlier poems, and some are
miraculous victories attributed to his protection.

Tales of Olaf's miracles must also have been circulating orally
in Norway ever since the 1030's, and it is possible that accounts
of them began to be recorded in writing, in Latin, even before
the end of that century. In the next century, at any rate, such
writings certainly existed. In about 1170 Archbishop Eystein
Erlendsson of Nidaros wrote the *Passio et Miraculi Beati Olavi*
(or *Acta Sancti Olavi*), of which several versions survive; as well
as miracle stories, it contains a brief biography, in which Olaf's
opponents are represented as devil-inspired villains wantonly
resisting the king's holy work.

At about the same time the first saga on St Olaf (indeed, as
far as is known, the first saga of Icelandic literature) was written
to provide a full-scale biography on him. Of this work, known as
the *Oldest Saga of St Olaf*, only short fragments survive; it was
followed by a revised version, the *Middle Saga*, written *c*. 1200
and now wholly lost; and this in turn was used as basis for a
later work, the *Legendary Saga of St Olaf*, known in a Norwegian
manuscript of *c*. 1250. The *Legendary Saga* follows the *Oldest
Saga* sufficiently closely to serve as a guide to its contents.
Drawing on the verses of the court poets, it gives a fairly accurate
account of Olaf's wars and campaigns, but interlards them with
numerous stories of miracles and marvels—not only the posthumous ones, but many said to have been worked by Olaf in his
lifetime. It ascribes the opposition to him to relentless hostility
on the part of almost all of the powerful men of Norway,
among whom the king seems isolated and friendless. All such
hostility is regarded as utterly unjustified, and though the
Legendary Saga does list certain grievances against him—'They
called him hard and domineering, severe and spiteful, close-
fisted and covetous, fierce and quarrelsome, ambitious and proud,
and in every way a worldly chieftain'—the author dismisses
these charges as quite baseless.

Another life of St Olaf was written, about 1220, by Styrmir
Karason the Learned, who was a close friend of Snorri. Styrmir's
version was based on the *Middle Saga*; it does not survive as a
whole, but parts of it are to be found incorporated in various

later works. This saga was Snorri's main source, but it is never possible to see directly how he modified it, since the extant fragments of Styrmir's work are all episodes which do not correspond to anything in Snorri; indeed, it is precisely because they thus supplement Snorri's work that they have been preserved. As far as can be seen, Styrmir's version seems to have been as pious and eulogistic as the *Legendary Saga*, with an equally fervent taste for miracles and edifying anecdotes.

Biographies such as these must have seemed pitifully inadequate to Snorri, not merely because of their uncritical acceptance of implausible tales, but because their naïve partisanship and shallow psychology could give no convincing picture either of Olaf himself or of the attitude of his subjects towards him. Space does not here allow of any detailed study of the omissions, additions and alterations by which Snorri built up from such sources a saga so effective that it supplanted all previous versions, but certain of the chief trends in his work can be examined.

The most immediately striking difference is in the treatment of Olaf's sanctity. In reading Snorri's work we are always conscious of Olaf's character as ruler and warrior, but only rarely of his personal holiness. One factor contributing to this effect is that Snorri, with characteristic care of detail, never calls Olaf 'the Holy' during his lifetime, but always either simply 'King Olaf' or 'Olaf Digri';[1] another factor is Snorri's drastic re-handling of the edifying and miraculous tales so abundant in his sources. All those relating to Olaf's early years have been eliminated or rationalized. Thus previous sagas said that at the time of his viking raids he once was helped by a band of warrior-angels, and on another occasion escaped from the Swedes by splitting the land between Lake Mælare and the sea by the fervour of his prayers. Snorri omits the first incident, and invents a rational, though unlikely, explanation for the second (pp. 119–20). The miracles of his years as ruler are also omitted, except for the breaking of the dice (pp. 217–18), and one case of healing, which Snorri apparently regarded as natural (p. 313; *cf.* p. 347). It is only after Olaf is driven into exile that miracles, prophecies and visions are frequently mentioned, that an aura of martyrdom begins to encircle him, and that saintly traits appear in his behaviour. With uncharacteristic gentleness he refrains from burning the farmsteads of his enemies, though these tactics

[1] Laing translates this nickname as 'The Thick', but it can also mean 'the Haughty', and this seems to have been its sense when applied to Olaf—see pp. 118, 160.

might have won him his final battle. Snorri clearly implies that this leniency (the motives for which were partly practical and partly religious) cost him his life (see pp. 357–8). Olaf's holiness thus is presented as a gradual development in his character, springing from his experience of adversity; all his life, says Snorri, the king had been pious and zealous in prayer, but only when freed from the responsibilities of power did he have leisure to 'turn all his mind to God's service' (p. 338).

It would seem from this last phrase that Snorri did not regard Olaf's forcible conversion of his subjects to the true faith as being purely a matter of 'God's service'. The Christianization of Norway was of course a highly important aspect of Olaf's reign, and Snorri gives an ample account of it; at the same time he sees the issue as being as much political as religious, since it was so closely linked with the crushing of semi-independent chieftains and the establishment of Olaf as sole and unquestioned ruler. Thus the revolt of the Upland Kings is provoked by Olaf's forcible conversion of their followers, but the arguments by which they justify it (pp. 180–1) are purely political; this passage, which is original to Snorri, shows how far he regarded the conflict as a secular one, dominated by considerations of power and policy. Time and again Olaf's suppression of heathen customs in a particular district is mentioned in the same breath as his demand to be accepted as its ruler.

Moreover Snorri stresses the brutality of Olaf's methods, especially his use of mutilation (a practice which the Icelanders abhorred); where the *Legendary Saga* has only one sentence on the fate of the blinded King Hrœrek (Rörek), Snorri devotes several powerfully written chapters to him, making this one of the most memorable episodes in the saga. The unfavourable impression of Olaf produced by such passages must be part of Snorri's deliberate intention, one aspect of the complexity in his interpretation of Olaf. His own Christianity was never fanatical; his comment on the attachment of the Norwegians to their heathen customs—'When the common man is left to himself, the faith which he has been taught in his childhood is that which has the strongest hold over his inclinations'—shows the same readiness to attribute reasonable motives to heathen believers as does the Prologue to the *Prose Edda*.

In presenting the political aspects of Olaf's reign Snorri gives ample proof of his clear grasp of wide issues. It is well exemplified by the lengthy speeches in which Olaf and his stepfather, Sigurd Syr, discuss the wisdom of Olaf's claim to the throne, and those in which the Upland Kings debate whether to accept this claim; these speeches are Snorri's own, and are characteristic of his methods: they set the particular political decision against the whole background of history from the time of Harald Fairhair (Haarfager), describe the forces ranged for and against Olaf, and show that his claim must involve him in strife with Olaf of Sweden and Canute of Denmark. Olaf's conflict with his Swedish namesake is a major theme in the first part of the saga, as is the part played by Canute in his overthrow in the second; both conflicts are more clearly set out and motivated in Snorri's version than in that of his predecessors.

Snorri's saga also deals more fully with Olaf's efforts to impose his authority on the Orkneys, Faeroes and Iceland; indeed, Olaf's message to Iceland is not mentioned at all in any earlier work, and Snorri's source for it is unknown. For material concerning the other two territories, he drew on the *Orkneyinga saga* and the *Færeyinga saga*,[1] which are now extant only as sections in later manuscripts; in the case of the former, all sections used by Snorri have been replaced in the extant text by passages transcribed from Snorri's text, making it impossible to tell what changes he made in his treatment of this source. The *Færeyinga Saga* may also be a revised version—not that which Snorri knew; the extant version is explicitly hostile to Thrand of Gata, the leader of the Faeroese opposition to Olaf's claims, whereas Snorri seems less so. If this is indeed a change made by Snorri, it corresponds well with his attitude to Olaf's request to the Icelanders. The importance he gives to such episodes springs partly from their obvious relevance to the political situation of his own times, partly from a wish to relate the events of Olaf's reign to the wider history of the other Scandinavian lands, and partly from their value as illustrations of Olaf's character as a ruler seeking further extensions of his power.

The central theme in the *Olaf's Saga* is the king's internal policy, his relationship with the lendermen and other chieftains whose eventual revolt is his downfall. Basing himself on some verses of Sigvat's, Snorri gives one general explanation of the hostility of the lendermen: that Olaf, by laws that were just but harsh, had tried to suppress the ancient custom whereby such men thought themselves free to live by plundering others (pp. 339–40). However, he is more usually concerned to trace the individual reasons for each chieftain's revolt; in so doing he

[1] Trans. A. B. Taylor, *The Orkneyinga Saga* (1938); trans. M. A. C. Press, *The Saga of the Fåroe Islanders* (1934).

covers, to a large extent, the same ground as his predecessors, but with more subtlety in drawing the characters of the king's enemies and interpreting their motives.

These characters and motives are interestingly varied: Erling Skjalgsson, who resents the curtailment of his power and the advancement of men of low birth; Thorir (Thore) Hund, for whom revolt against Olaf is a bitter personal blood-feud in which he avenges the death of his nephew Asbjorn; Einar Tambarskelve, ambitious for power and wealth, and gambling on receiving more from Canute than from Olaf; Harek of Thjotta, offended by the loss of half his sheriffdom, but cunning enough to hide his resentment till Canute's power outweighs Olaf's; Kalf Arneson, who like Thorir has a kinsman to avenge, yet remains partly loyal until Olaf retreats before Earl Hakon, joins Canute unwillingly, and even at Stiklestad itself tries to suggest a reconciliation. The wish to explain the personal motives of these and other actors in the story will often lead Snorri to include episodes that may at first sight seem digressions, but the relevance of which is gradually made plain; one of the basic assumptions of his work is that events are brought about by the interaction of ordinary human personalities, not by some superhuman clash of the forces of good and evil.

One of the most interesting sections in the work is Snorri's attempt to answer the question; 'Why did men accept Olaf as a saint?' For the earlier biographers this was no problem; God had vouched for Olaf's sanctity by miracles, and thus men's eyes were opened. There is no reason to think that Snorri disbelieved in the miracle stories, many of which were supported by ancient sources and some by almost contemporary verses. Yet the mere fact that miracles occurred could be only a partial explanation, since unless men had willingly believed in them and repeated tales about them, they would not have become so widely known as to change the country's opinion of its dead king. The problem thus becomes one of personal motives and of the public mood. Having told of one or two miracles, therefore, Snorri turns to the harsh taxes and unjust laws imposed by the Danish rulers; these cause a revulsion of feeling among the Norwegians in favour of Olaf, which finds expression in rumours of his miracles that spread among the common people. The chieftains accept these rumours, for characteristic reasons of their own: the ambitious Einar, because the earldom promised by Canute had not been given him; Kalf, because he too was deceived by Canute's promises, and also because of his wish to be reconciled to his brothers, who were loyal to Olaf; Thorir Hund, a man of strong emotions and inclined to superstition, because of an experience on the battle-field itself which he later interprets as a miracle, so that he accepts Olaf's sanctity as whole-heartedly as he once had accepted his duty of revenge. Belief in Olaf's holiness becomes a mark of Norwegian patriotism, both among the chieftains and the people, and when Olaf's son Magnus is recalled from exile to his father's throne the cult of Olaf becomes an official part of Norwegian Christianity.

The majority of Snorri's additions to and changes in the material provided by his sources can be accounted for either by his deeper interest in political forces or by his desire to clarify the motives of individuals who had a determining influence on the course of history. Nevertheless it seems that certain episodes attracted him by their intrinsic interest, so that he gave more space and careful art to the telling of them than the rigorous standards of an historian would justify. Such are the accounts of Sigvat's journey to Gotland, of Thormod's death at Stiklestad, of the blinded Hrœrek (Rörek), of Asbjorn's feud with Thorir Sel and of Thorir Hund's expedition to Bjarmaland. All these do have a relevance to the saga as a whole, but they are treated with a zest and an amplitude of detail that reveal a fondness for tales of personal courage, honour and vengeance, and for adventurous journeys in comparatively little-known regions. Most remarkable of all is the inclusion of the story of Thorodd Snorrason's meeting with Arnljot Gellini; the mere fact of Arnljot's presence at Stikle-stad can hardly justify so elaborate an introduction for him, so it must be assumed that this colourful anecdote, with its folk-tale elements, seemed to Snorri to deserve inclusion for its own sake. The saga is thus enriched by several vivid and entertaining episodes which, even if not wholly relevant by the most austere historical standards, contribute to the effective variety of the saga as a whole.

The artistic merit of the *Saga of St Olaf* is not, however, merely a matter of the effectiveness of particular episodes. Its firm mastery of construction is also outstanding, for no previous writer had undertaken to weave so many strands into a unified work. Snorri moves with ease from one aspect of his story to the next, interlocking them with such skill that the orderly pro-gression of chronological narrative is never disturbed, nor are connections of each part to the whole obscured. The methods of presentation are varied; opinions and attitudes are sometimes made explicit in formal speeches, sometimes revealed in flashes in the apparently casual remarks of lifelike dialogue; some events are narrated in brief but clear summary, others treated in ample detail; often Snorri will let facts speak for themselves, but also at intervals he will pause to reflect on the history he is recording and interpose his own interpretations of it. The result is a work of firmly organized structure and rich variety, in which scholarship and imaginative insight combine to create a subtle, well-balanced and completely convincing portrait of Olaf Haraldsson, king and saint.

(v) *Heimskringla*. It is generally thought that this, the most elaborately conceived of Snorri's works, was completed before his second journey to Norway in 1235. In it he surveys the whole course of Norwegian history, beginning with the legendary period of the Yngling dynasty, and then giving biographies of all the rulers of Norway, whether kings or earls, from the time of Halfdan the Black (died *c.* 880) to that of Magnus Erlingsson, who became king in about 1162 and died in 1184. *Heimskringla* actually ends in 1177, just before the beginning of the struggle between Magnus and his eventual successor Sverrir; Sverrir's rise to power and his reign had already been treated in a work written with accuracy and considerable literary skill, the *Saga of Sverrir*, whose author, Karl Jonsson, began the work under Sverrir's own direction. The existence of a saga of such merit and authority must have been the determining factor in Snorri's choice of a terminal date for *Heimskringla*.

In order to cover so extensive a period, Snorri drew material not only from the scaldic poems but from a wide range of written works;[1] some of these were biographies of individual kings, while others were more summary surveys covering several reigns, and others again were accounts of particular families, communities or countries whose histories were to some extent linked with that of Norway. In addition to written works, he made use of oral traditions, not only those current in Iceland, but also those which he gathered during his journeys in Norway and Sweden. His indebtedness to such sources is naturally less easy to estimate than that to written works, but their importance to him is reflected by the fact that when, in his Preface to *Heimskringla*, he discusses his sources, his first reference is to stories 'as I have heard them told by intelligent people'.

From these sources Snorri selected his material, skilfully blending it so as to avoid repetitions and inconsistencies, and imposing upon the whole the unity of his personal tone and

[1] See *Sagas of the Norse Kings*, Introduction, pp. x–xx.

outlook. His handling of the sources is varied and discriminating. Occasionally he transcribes passages almost verbatim, usually those whose artistry is already of high standard; more frequently he condenses and rephrases them, aiming always at greater clarity, terseness and vigour, or rearranges the sequence of events so as to achieve stronger dramatic impact; implausible episodes are omitted, or more convincing explanations of them supplied; episodes that were inadequately treated are amplified, enriched, and their implications brought to light; characters who were only sketchily presented or distorted by prejudice are reinterpreted more vividly and objectively. Furthermore, the elements drawn from diverse sources are unified by the fact that they are presented from a consistent point of view and shaped to form a harmonious pattern of historical interpretation.

In order to appreciate the full narrative and structural qualities of *Heimskringla* it would be necessary to consider its various sections in the order in which they were designed to be read, *i.e.* with the sagas of Olaf Tryggvason and of Olaf the Saint coming between that of Earl Hakon and that of King Magnus the Good (*Sagas of the Norse Kings*, p. 127). The *Saga of Olaf Tryggvason* in particular suffers from being dissociated from the foregoing sections. Unlike the *Saga of St Olaf*, it was never designed as a separate work, and so takes for granted a knowledge of events of previous reigns; moreover, Olaf's dealings with Earl Hakon and his son Earl Eric are seen as only one episode in the long story of the relationship between the descendants of Harald Fairhair and the Earls of Hladir (Lade). Nevertheless, brief as was the reign of Olaf Tryggvason, its importance as the period of the conversion of Norway and the particularly dramatic nature of Olaf's life and death had made it a subject for previous writers, and Snorri himself devotes considerable space to it. It is thus possible to consider at least certain aspects of the *Saga of Olaf Tryggvason* in isolation from the rest of *Heimskringla*.

The life of Olaf Tryggvason, like that of his saintly namesake, early attacted the attention of biographers in ecclesiastical circles. Although he had not been declared a saint, he was yet honoured as a hero of Christendom, the driving force in a movement which brought about the conversion not only of Norway but of Iceland and other Scandinavian settlements. The first 'Life of Olaf Tryggvason' was written in Latin, *c.* 1190, by Odd Snorrason, who was a monk of the Benedictine monastery of Thingeyrar in northern Iceland; the Latin text is lost, but an Icelandic translation made early in the thirteenth century survives in three versions. Odd must have known the *Oldest Saga of St Olaf*, and may have been directly stimulated by it to compose his own work. He begins by a Prologue in which he compares the two namesakes and claims that Olaf Tryggvason too was a holy man, though no miracles had occurred to prove this; he played the part of John the Baptist to St Olaf's 'Northern Christ', paving the way for his greater successor's work, and indeed baptizing him.[1] The historical side of Odd's biography is based largely on scaldic verses; he also used such written works as were available to him. In addition he included many stories imitated from foreign saints' lives, or drawn from popular tradition; some of these concern the adventures of Olaf's early years, and others, of considerable interest as folklore, tell of the attempts of trolls, heathen gods and magicians to oppose the conversion of Norway. Odd's work is lively and entertaining, and many passages show that his powers as a story-teller were not negligible; it is the chief source used by Snorri for this section of *Heimskringla*.

About 1200 another monk of Thingeyrar, Gunnlaug Leifsson, wrote a second Latin 'Life of Olaf Tryggvason', which was likewise soon translated into Icelandic; the work as a whole is lost, but considerable portions of it have been incorporated into later texts. From the examination of these it is possible to see that Gunnlaug's work was based on Odd's, but was more detailed, included even more legendary and hagiographical episodes, had a strongly edifying and moralistic tone, and was written in a style of pompously inflated verbiage. Long speeches abound in it, but, unlike those that Snorri invents for his characters, their length is almost always due to empty rhetoric. The most influential and valuable part of the work was its account of the conversion of Iceland by missionaries sent by Olaf. Snorri knew Gunnlaug's book and took certain details from it, but it was too much lacking in historical reliability to be of more than occasional use to him.

Snorri's *Saga of Olaf Tryggvason* is, as has been said, based largely on Odd's work. In addition he made ample use of other sources, one of the most important being the *Ágrip af Nóregs konunga sögum* (*Compendium of the Histories of the Kings of Norway*), a Norwegian work dating from about 1190. For the sections on Earl Hakon the Great he drew upon the *Saga of the Earls of Hlaðir*, a work now wholly lost; for those on the Jomsburg Vikings, on a version of the *Jómsvíkinga Saga* earlier than

[1] This is probably not historically true, but was generally believed in Iceland; see p. 58, and p. 129, n. 5.

any redaction now extant. He naturally also made full use of the scaldic verses relevant to this period.

The changes made by Snorri in composing this saga from its various sources are less fundamental than those in his *Saga of St Olaf*, but several are of the same general type. The distaste for anecdotes of a specifically religious tone is even more marked here than in the earlier work, probably because here there were no contemporary or near-contemporary sources attesting to them; as a result, the stories of Olaf's youth, though still un-realistic, have been stripped of the hagiographical elements often to be seen in Odd. Certain marvels are eliminated; thus, Gunnlaug ascribes the verbal paralysis of the bonders of Roga-land (pp. 54–5) to a miraculous intervention of St Martin, but Snorri offers no explanation. Odd says that when Thorir Hjort was struck down, a hart sprang from his body but was killed by the dog Vigi; Snorri rationalizes the incident, although it is quite possible that Odd's story, reflecting as it does popular superstitions, may be an old folk-tradition without any such basis in fact as Snorri assumes. There are far fewer of the tales of trolls and magic in which Odd delighted, and Snorri makes plain (p. 71) that their omission is his deliberate policy; nevertheless, some of them do find a place in his work. Similarly, he is aware of the 'many tales' alleging that Olaf escaped from the battle of Svold and ended his days in some monastery in Greece, Syria or the Holy Land—tales which Odd had been inclined to believe, and which Gunnlaug enthusiastically accepted and elaborated. Snorri, however, though realizing that Hallfred's poetry proves such tales to have been current almost immediately after the battle itself, shares Hallfred's own attitude of scepticism towards them.

Other characteristics of Snorri's art reappear in this saga. His interest in the unscrupulous intrigues of great men, and his ability to unfold their motives in dialogue, are seen in the chapters describing how Earl Hakon exploited the rivalries between Gold Harald, King Harald Gormsson and Harald Greyskin to win Norway for himself. His skill in presenting an unbiased picture of one towards whom most of his predecessors had been markedly hostile is seen in his study of Earl Hakon. Many passages are strongly dramatic, notably the chapters on the expedition of the Jomsburg Vikings, the description of Earl Hakon's death and the account of the battle of Svold. Often in such cases Snorri's sources already gave clear and effective narratives, but he is always at pains to prune and rearrange his material so as to intensify its effect. Here, as in so much of his work, Snorri has a threefold aim: to reconstruct as truthful a picture of the past as the best sources available to him will allow; to enrich that picture by the interpretations which his experience and clear insight may suggest; and to present it lucidly, powerfully and with all the resources of his artistry. The value of *Heimskringla* as history may be judged less highly in the light of modern researches, but the increased understanding of the literary tradition in which Snorri was working and of the modifications he himself brought to it will ensure that his literary achievements will meet with increased recognition and appreciation.

3. THE PRESENT TRANSLATION

Samuel Laing's translation of the *Heimskringla*, in three volumes, was published in London in 1844; it was republished in the Everyman series in two volumes in 1914 and 1930 respectively, with Introductions and Notes by John Beveridge. Laing's translation was based upon an edition by Gerhard Schøning and Skúli Thorlaicus which appeared in Copenhagen in 1777–83; the textual peculiarities of this edition, together with the relationships of the chief manuscripts, are described by Mr P. Foote in the Introduction to *Sagas of the Norse Kings*, pp. xxviii–xxxi. In the text of *The Olaf Sagas* interpolations are less frequent than in that of the companion volume; the most extensive are the following: 21^{20-8}, 72^{13-43}, 84^{13}–85^{36}, 86^{6-28}, 129^{16-19}, 130^{15-21}, 161^{17-25}, 313^{10-14} (where an abridged version has been substituted for the true text, which will be found in Appendix I) and 378^{17-25}. Minor interpolations and omissions will be found listed in Appendices II and III.

The present edition is a reprint from plates, so that only limited revision of the text has been possible; nevertheless I hope that the chief errors have been rectified, either in the text itself, in Appendix I or in the footnotes. The verses have been much revised (though in such a way as to preserve the style of Laing's couplets), since a more accurate rendering was often essential if Snorri's handling of these primary sources was to be appreciated. The majority of the footnotes have been wholly or partly rewritten, and textual appendices and a greatly enlarged Index have been provided.

JACQUELINE SIMPSON.

SELECT BIBLIOGRAPHY

FULL bibliographies will be found in two works by Halldór Hermannsson: *Bibliography of the Sagas of the Kings of Norway and related Sagas and Tales* (*Islandica*, III; 1910) and *The Sagas of the Kings and the Mythical-Heroic Sagas: Two Bibliographical Supplements* (*Islandica*, XXVI; 1937).

The standard critical edition of the *Heimskringla* is by Finnur Jónsson (*Samfund til Udgivelse af Gammel Nordisk Litteratur*, XXIII; 1893-1900). The best general edition, also of value for textual criticism, is by Bjarni Aðalbjarnarson (*Íslenzk Fornrit*, XXVI–XXVIII; 1941-51).

The following short list is restricted to works in English dealing with the historical and literary background: G. Vigfusson and F. York Powell, *Corpus Poeticum Boreale* (2 vols.), 1883; A. Mawer, *The Vikings*, 1913; K. Gjerset, *History of the Norwegian People* (2 vols.), 1915 and *History of Iceland*, 1925; A. Walsh, *Scandinavian Relations with Ireland during the Viking Period*, 1922; M. Olsen, *Farms and Fanes of Ancient Norway*, 1928; A. W. Brøgger, *Ancient Emigrants*, 1929; T. D. Kendrick, *A History of the Vikings*, 1930; A. Olrik, *Viking Civilization*, 1930; H. Hermannsson, *Sæmund Sigfússon and the Oddaverjar* (*Islandica*, XXII; 1932); L. M. Larson, *The Earliest Norwegian Laws*, 1935; H. Shetelig, H. Falk and E. V. Gordon, *Scandinavian Archaeology*, 1937; H. Shetelig, ed., *Viking Antiquities in Great Britain and Ireland*, 1-6, 1940–54; F. M. Stenton, *Anglo-Saxon England*, 1943; L. M. Hollander, *The Skalds*, 1945; K. Larsen, *A History of Norway*, 1948; A. W. Brøgger and H. Shetelig, *The Viking Ships*, 1951; E. O. Sveinsson, *The Age of the Sturlungs* (*Islandica*, XXXVI; 1953); G. Turville-Petre, *The Heroic Age of Scandinavia*, 1951; *Origins of Icelandic Literature*, 1953; T. K. Derry, *A Short History of Norway*, 1957; J. Brøndsted, *The Vikings*, 1960; H. Arbman, *The Vikings*, 1961; P. H. Sawyer, *The Age of the Vikings*, 1962; G. Jones, *A History of the Vikings*, 1968; P. G. Foote and D. M. Wilson, *The Viking Achievement*, 1970.

KING OLAF TRYGVESSON'S SAGA[1]

(968-1000)

CHAPTER I. OLAF TRYGVESSON'S BIRTH [968].—King Trygve Olafsson had married a wife who was called Astrid. She was a daughter of Eric Biodaskalde, a great man, who dwelt at Ofrostad. But after Trygve's death Astrid fled, and privately took with her all the loose property she could. Her foster-father, Thoralf Lusiskiæg, followed her, and never left her, and others of her faithful followers spied about to discover her enemies, and where they were. Astrid was pregnant with a child of King Trygve, and she went to a lake, and concealed herself in a holm or small island in it with a few men. Here her child was born, and it was a boy; and water was poured over it, and it was called Olaf after the grandfather. Astrid remained all summer here in concealment; but when the nights became dark, and the day began to shorten and the weather to be cold, she was obliged to take to the land, along with Thoralf and a few other men. They did not seek for houses, unless in the night time, when they came to them secretly; and they spoke to nobody. One evening, towards dark, they came to Ofrostad, where Astrid's father Eric dwelt, and privately sent a man to Eric to tell him; and Eric took them to an out-house, and spread a table for them with the best of food. When Astrid had been here a short time her travelling attendants left her, and none remained behind with her but two servant girls, her child Olaf, Thoralf Lusiskiæg, and his son Thorgils, who was six years old; and they remained all winter.

[1] Olaf Tryggvason reigned from A.D. c. 995 to 1000. His father Tryggvi was a petty king of two districts in Norway, and was a grandson of Harald Fairhair. He was treacherously killed by Gudrod, one of the sons of Eric Bloody-axe and Gunnhild; at this time Gudrod was ruling Norway jointly with his brothers Harald Greyskin (Greycloak), Erling, Ragnfrid, and Sigurd (Sleva). (See *Sagas of the Norse Kings*, pp. 112 ff.)

CHAPTER II. OF GUNHILD'S SONS.—After Trygve Olafsson's murder, Harald Greyskin and his brother Gudrod went to the farm which he owned; but Astrid was gone, and they could learn no tidings of her. A loose report came to their ears that she was pregnant to King Trygve; but they went away northwards to Drontheim. As soon as they met their mother Gunhild, they told her all that had taken place. She inquired particularly about Astrid, and they told her the report they had heard; but as Gunhild's sons the same harvest and winter after had bickerings with Earl Hakon, they did not seek after Astrid and her son that winter.

CHAPTER III. ASTRID'S JOURNEY [969].—The spring after Gunhild sent spies to the Uplands, and all the way down to Viken, to spy what they could about Astrid; and her men came back, and could only tell her that Astrid must be with her father Eric, and it was probable was bringing up her infant, the son of Trygve. Then Gunhild, without delay, sent off men well furnished with arms and horses, and in all a troop of thirty; and as their leader she sent a particular friend of her own, a powerful man called Hakon. Her orders were to go to Ofrostad to Eric, and take King Trygve's son from thence, and bring the child to her; and with these orders the men went out. Now when they were come to the neighbourhood of Ofrostad, some of Eric's friends observed the troop of travellers, and about the close of the day brought him word of their approach. Eric immediately, in the night, made preparation for Astrid's flight, gave her good guides, and sent her away eastward to Sweden, to his good friend Hakon Gamle, who was a powerful man there. Long before day they departed, and towards evening they reached a district called Skon.[1] Here they saw a large mansion, towards which they went and begged a night's lodging. For the sake of concealment they were clad in mean clothing. There dwelt here a bonder [2] called Biorn Edderquise, who was very rich, but very inhospitable. He drove them away; and therefore, towards dark, they went to another village close by that was called Vizkar.[3] Thorstein was the name of the bonder; and he gave them lodging, and took good care of them, so that they slept well, and were well entertained.

Early that morning Hakon with Gunhild's men had come to

---

[1] There are several districts of this name east of the mountains.
[2] A freeholder, yeoman.
[3] This place is unknown.

Ofrostad, and inquired for Astrid and her son. As Eric told them she was not there, they searched the whole house, and remained till late in the day before they got any news of Astrid. Then they rode after her the way she had taken, and late at night they came to Biorn Edderquise in Skon, and took up their quarters there. Hakon asked Biorn if he knew anything about Astrid, and he said some people had been there in the evening wanting lodgings; "but I drove them away, and I suppose they have gone to some of the neighbouring houses." Thorstein's labourer was coming from the forest, having left his work at nightfall, and called in at Biorn's house because it was in his way; and finding there were guests come to the house, and learning their business, he comes to Thorstein and tells him of it. As about a third part of the night was still remaining, Thorstein wakens his guests, and orders them in an angry voice to go about their business; but as soon as they were out of the house upon the road, Thorstein tells them that Gunhild's messengers were at Biorn's house, and are upon the trace of them. They entreat of him to help them, and he gave them a guide and some provisions. He conducted them through the forest to a lake, in which there was an islet overgrown with reeds. They waded out to the islet, and hid themselves among the reeds. Early in the morning Hakon rode away from Biorn's into the township, and wherever he came he asked after Astrid; and when he came to Thorstein's he asked if she had been there. He said that some people had been there; but as soon as it was daylight they had set off again, eastwards, to the forest. Hakon made Thorstein go along with them, as he knew all the roads and hiding-places. Thorstein went with them; but when they were come into the woods, he led them right across the way Astrid had taken. They went about and about the whole day in searching, but they could find no trace of her; so they turned back to tell Gunhild the end of their travel. Astrid and her friends proceeded on their journey, and came to Sweden, to Hakon Gamle (the Old), where she and her son remained a long time, and had friendly welcome.[1]

CHAPTER IV. HAKON'S EMBASSY TO SWEDEN.—When Gunhild, the mother of the kings, heard that Astrid and her son

---

[1] In describing Olaf's childhood adventures Snorri draws mainly on the *Agrip* and on Odd's *Life of Olaf*, (*vide* Introduction, p. xxxii); but he omits the latter's many pious touches, and the former's statement that Astrid fled first to the Orkneys before going to Sweden.

Olaf were in the kingdom of Sweden, she again sent Hakon, with a good attendance, eastward, to Eric king of Sweden, with presents and messages of friendship. The ambassadors were well received and well treated. Hakon, after a time, disclosed his errand to the king, saying that Gunhild had sent him with the request that the king would assist him in getting hold of Olaf Trygvesson, to conduct him to Norway, where Gunhild would bring him up. The king gave Hakon people with him, and he rode with them to Hakon the Old, where Hakon desired, with many friendly expressions, that Olaf should go with him. Hakon the Old returned a friendly answer, saying that it depended entirely upon Olaf's mother. But Astrid would on no account listen to the proposal; and the messengers had to return as they came, and to tell King Eric how the matter stood. The ambassadors then prepared to return home, and asked the king for some assistance to take the boy, whether Hakon the Old would or not. The king gave them again some attendants; and when they came to Hakon the Old, they again asked for the boy, and on his refusal to deliver him they used high words and threatened violence. But one of the slaves, Burste by name, attacked Hakon, and was going to kill him; and they barely escaped from the thralls without a cudgelling, and proceeded home to Norway to tell Gunhild their journey, and that they had only seen Olaf.

CHAPTER V. OF SIGURD ERICSSON [971].—Astrid had a brother called Sigurd, a son of Eric Biodaskalde, who had long been abroad in Russia with King Valdemar,[1] and was there in great consideration. Astrid had now a great inclination to travel to her brother there. Hakon the Old gave her good attendants, and what was needful for the journey, and she set out with some merchants. She had then been two years with Hakon the Old, and Olaf was three years of age. As they sailed out into the Baltic they were attacked by vikings of Esthonia, who made booty both of the people and goods, killing some, and dividing others as slaves. Olaf was separated from his mother, and an Esthonian man called Klerkon got him as his share along with Thoralf and Thorgils. Klerkon thought that Thoralf was too old for a slave, and that there was not much work to be got out of him, so he killed him; but took the boys with him,

---

[1] It appears that Valdemar was not king when Olaf arrived in Russia. Sigurd probably had been with Valdemar before he ascended the throne in 980, as Vladimir the Great (980–1014). He was Grand Duke in Kiev (not Novgorod, as Snorri says,) in 972.

and sold them to a man called Klerk for a stout and good ram. A third man, called Reas, bought Olaf for a good cloak. Reas had a wife called Rekon, and a son by her whose name was Rekone. Olaf was long with them, was treated well, and was much beloved by the bonder. Olaf was six years in Esthonia in this banishment.

CHAPTER VI. OLAF IS SET FREE IN ESTHONIA [977].—Sigurd, the son of Eric (Astrid's brother), came into Esthonia from Novgorod, on King Valdemar's business to collect the king's taxes and rents. Sigurd came as a man of consequence, with many followers and great magnificence. In the market-place he happened to observe a remarkably handsome boy; and as he could distinguish that he was a foreigner, he asked him his name and family. He answered him, that his name was Olaf; that he was a son of Trygve Olafsson; and Astrid, a daughter of Eric Biodaskalde, was his mother. Then Sigurd knew that the boy was his sister's son, and asked him how he came there. Olaf told him minutely all his adventures, and Sigurd told him to guide him to the peasant Reas'. When he came there he bought both the boys, Olaf and Thorgils, and took them with him to Novgorod. But, for the first, he made nothing known of Olaf's relationship to him, but treated him well.

CHAPTER VII. KLERKON KILLED BY OLAF.—Olaf Trygvesson was one day in the market-place, where there was a great number of people. He recognised Klerkon again, who had killed his foster-father Thoralf Lusiskiæg. Olaf had a little axe in his hand, and with it he clove Klerkon's skull down to the brain, and ran home to his lodging, and told his friend Sigurd what he had done. Sigurd immediately took Olaf to Queen Allogia's[1] house, told her what had happened, and begged her to protect the boy. She replied that the boy appeared far too comely to allow him to be slain; and she ordered her people to be drawn out fully armed. In Novgorod, the sacredness of peace is so respected, that it is law there to slay whoever puts a man to death except by judgment of law; and, according to this law and usage, the whole people stormed and sought after the boy. It was reported that he was in the queen's house, and that there was a number of armed men there. When this was told to the king, he went there with his people, but would allow no fighting. The king brought about a truce and a settlement; he named

[1] She is otherwise unknown; the whole episode may well be fiction.

the fine for the murder; and the queen paid it. Olaf remained afterwards with the queen, and was much beloved. It is a law at Novgorod that no man of a royal descent shall stay there without the king's permission. Sigurd therefore told the queen of what family Olaf was, and for what reason he had come to Russia; namely, that he could not remain with safety in his own country: and begged her to speak to the king about it. She did so, and begged the king to help a king's son whose fate had been so hard; and in consequence of her entreaty the king promised to assist him, and accordingly he received Olaf into his court, and treated him nobly, and as a king's son. Olaf was nine years old when he came to Russia, and he remained nine years more with king Valdemar. Olaf was the handsomest of men, very stout and strong, and in all bodily exercises he excelled every Northman that ever was heard of.

CHAPTER VIII. OF HAKON EARL OF LADE.—Earl Hakon, Sigurd's son, was with the Danish king, Harald Gormson, the winter after he had fled from Norway before Gunhild's sons. During the winter the earl had so much care and sorrow that he took to bed, and passed many sleepless nights, and ate and drank no more than was needful to support his strength. Then he sent a private message to his friends north in Drontheim, and proposed to them that they should kill King Erling, if they had an opportunity; adding, that he would come to them in summer. The same winter the Drontheim people accordingly, whilst he was at a feast, killed King Erling. There was great friendship between Earl Hakon and Gold Harald, and Harald told Hakon all his intentions. He told him that he was tired of a ship-life, and wanted to settle on the land; and asked Hakon if he thought his uncle King Harald would agree to dividing the kingdom with him if he asked it. " I think," replied Hakon, " that the Danish king would not deny thy right; but the best way to know is to speak to the king himself. I know for certain so much, that you will not get a kingdom if you don't ask for it." Soon after this conversation Gold Harald spoke to the king about the matter, in the presence of many great men who were friends to both; and Gold Harald asked King Harald to divide the kingdom with him in two equal parts, to which his royal birth and the custom of the Danish monarchy gave him right. The king was highly incensed at this demand, and said that no man had asked his father Gorm to be king over half of Denmark, nor yet his grandfather King Hordeknut, or Sigurd Orm, or Ragnar

Lodbrok; and he was so exasperated and angry that nobody ventured to speak of it to him.

CHAPTER IX. OF GOLD HARALD.—Gold Harald was now worse off than before; for he had got no kingdom, and had got the king's anger by proposing it. He went as usual to his friend Hakon, and complained to him of his fate, and asked for good advice, and if he could help him to get his share of the kingdom; saying that he would rather try force, and the chance of war, than give it up.

Hakon advised him not to speak to any man so that this should be known; "for," said he, "it concerns thy life: and rather consider with thyself what thou art man enough to undertake; for to accomplish such a purpose requires a bold and firm man, who will neither stick at good nor evil to do that which is intended; for to take up great resolutions, and then to lay them aside, would only end in dishonour."

Gold Harald replies,—"I will so carry on what I begin, that I will not hesitate to kill Harald with my own hands, if I can have the chance, for he denies me the kingdom which is mine by right." And so they separated.

Now King Harald comes also to Earl Hakon, and tells him the demand on his kingdom which Gold Harald had made, and also his answer, and that he would upon no account consent to diminish his kingdom. "And if Gold Harald persists in his demand, I will have no hesitation in having him killed; for I will not trust him if he does not renounce it."

The Earl answered,—"My thoughts are, that Harald has carried his demand so far that he cannot now let it drop, and I expect nothing but war in the land; and that he will be able to gather a great force, because his father was so beloved. And then it would be a great enormity if you were to kill your relation; for, as things now stand, all men would say that he was innocent. But I am far from saying, or advising, that you should make yourself a smaller king than your father Gorm was, who in many ways enlarged, but never diminished his kingdom."

The king replies,—"What then is your advice,—if I am neither to divide my kingdom, nor to get rid of my fright and danger?"

"Let us meet again in a few days," said Earl Hakon, "and I will then have considered the matter well, and will give you my advice upon it."

The king then went away with his people.

CHAPTER X. COUNCILS HELD BY EARL HAKON AND KING HARALD.—Earl Hakon had now great reflection, and many opinions to weigh, and he let only very few be in the house with him. In a few days King Harald came again to the earl to speak with him, and ask if he had yet considered fully the matter they had been talking of.

" I have," said the earl, " considered it night and day ever since, and find it most advisable that you retain and rule over the whole of your kingdom just as your father left it; but that you obtain for your relation Harald another kingdom, that he also may enjoy honour and dignity."

" What kind of kingdom is that," said the king, " which I can give to Harald, that I may possess Denmark entire? "

" It is Norway," said the earl. " The kings who are there are oppressive to the people of the country, so that every man is against them who has tax or service to pay."

The king replies,—" Norway is a large country, and the people fierce, and not good to attack with a foreign army. We found that sufficiently when Hakon defended that country; for we lost many people, and gained no victory. Besides, Harald the son of Eric is my foster-son, and has sat on my knee."

The earl answers,—" I have long known that you have helped Gunhild's sons with your force, and a bad return you have got for it; but we shall get at Norway much more easily than by fighting for it with all the Danish force. Send a message to your foster-son Harald, Eric's son, and offer him the lands and fiefs which Gunhild's sons held before in Denmark. Appoint him a meeting, and Gold Harald will soon conquer for himself a kingdom in Norway from Harald Greyskin."

The king replies, that it would be called a bad business to deceive his own foster-son.

" The Danes," answered the earl, " will rather say that it was better to kill a Norwegian viking than a Danish, and your own brother's son."

They spoke so long over the matter, that they agreed on it.

CHAPTER XI. KING HARALD GORMSSON'S MESSAGE TO NORWAY.—Thereafter Gold Harald had a conference with Earl Hakon; and the earl told him he had now advanced his business so far that there was hope a kingdom might stand open for him in Norway. " We can then continue," said he, " our ancient friendship, and I can be of the greatest use to you in Norway. Take first that kingdom. King Harald is now very old, and has but one son, and cares but little about him, as he is but the son of a concubine."

The earl talked so long to Gold Harald that the project pleased him well; and the king, the earl, and Gold Harald often talked over the business together. The Danish king then sent messengers north to Norway to Harald Greyskin, and fitted them out magnificently for their journey. They were well received by Harald. The messengers told him that Earl Hakon was in Denmark, but was lying dangerously sick, and almost out of his senses. They then delivered from Harald, the Danish king, the invitation to Harald Greyskin, his foster-son, to come to him, and receive investiture of the fiefs he and his brothers before him had formerly held in Denmark; and appointing a meeting in Jutland. Harald Greyskin laid the matter before his mother and other friends. Their opinions were divided. Some thought that the expedition was not without its danger, on account of the men with whom they had to deal; but the most were in haste to begin the journey, for at that time there was such a famine in Norway that the kings could scarcely feed their men-at-arms: and on this account the fjord, on which the kings resided, usually got the name of Hardanger (Hard-acre).[1] In Denmark, on the other hand, there had been tolerably good crops; so that people thought that if King Harald got fiefs, and something to rule over there, they would get some assistance. It was therefore concluded, before the messengers returned, that Harald should travel to Denmark to the Danish king in summer, and accept the conditions King Harald offered.

CHAPTER XII. TREACHERY OF KING HARALD AND EARL HAKON TOWARDS GOLD HARALD [974].—Harald Greyskin went to Denmark in summer with three long-ships; and Herse Arenbiorn [2] from the Fjords district, commanded one of them. King Harald sailed from Viken over to Lymfjord in Jutland, and landed at Hals [3] where the Danish king was expected. Now when Gold Harald heard of this, he sailed there with nine ships which he had fitted out before for a viking cruise. Earl Hakon had also his war force on foot; namely, twelve large ships, all ready, with which he proposed to make an expedition. When Gold Harald had departed, Earl Hakon says to the king, " Now

---

[1] Hardanger. Snorri is wrong. *Hard* refers to a clan, and *anger* means bay or fjord; therefore Hardanger is the bay or fjord of the Hards.
[2] Foster-brother of Eric Bloody-axe; a major character in *Egil's Saga*.
[3] Viken is the Oslo fjord; Lymfjord runs into Jutland from the Baltic, and Hals is at its mouth.

I don't know if we are not sailing on an expedition, and yet are to pay the penalty [1] of not having joined it. Gold Harald may kill Harald Greyskin, and get the kingdom of Norway; but you must not think he will be true to you, although you do help him to so much power, for he told me in winter that he would take your life if he could find opportunity to do so. Now I will win Norway for you, and kill Gold Harald, if you will promise me a good condition under you. I will be your earl; swear an oath of fidelity to you, and, with your help, conquer all Norway for you; hold the country under your rule; pay you the scatt and taxes; and you will be a greater king than your father, as you will have two kingdoms under you." The king and the earl agreed upon this, and Hakon set off to seek Gold Harald.

CHAPTER XIII. HARALD GREYSKIN FALLS AT THE NECK OF LAND AT LYMFJORD [976].—Gold Harald came to Hals at Lymfjord, and immediately challenged Harald Greyskin to battle; and although Harald had fewer men, he went immediately ashore, prepared for battle, and drew up his troops. Before the lines came together Harald Greyskin urged on his men, and told them to draw their swords. He himself advanced the foremost of the troop, hewing down on each side. So says Glum Geirason, in Greyskin's lay:—

> " Brave were thy words in battle-field,
> Thou stainer of the snow-white shield!—
> Thou gallant war-god! With thy voice
> Thou couldst the dying man rejoice:
> The cheer of Harald could impart
> Courage and life to every heart.
> While swinging high the blood-smeared sword,
> By arm and voice we knew our lord."

There fell Harald Greyskin. So says Glum Geirason:—

> " The king who once so strongly plied
> The shields that deck the vessel's side
> Now lies (fine horseman was our lord!)
> On the broad shore of Eylimfjord.
> The generous ruler of the land
> Fell at Hals upon the sand;
> The prince's foe by cunning talk
> Is guilty of this bloody work."

The most of King Harald's men fell with him. There also fell Herse Arenbiorn.

[1] Those who absented themselves from an expedition or arrived at the wrong time or place had to pay a fine.

This happened fifteen years [1] after the death of Hakon Athelstan's foster-son, and thirteen years after that of Sigurd earl of Lade. The priest Are Frode says that Earl Hakon was thirteen years earl over his father's dominions in Drontheim district before the fall of Harald Greyskin; but, for the last six years of Harald Greyskin's life, Are Frode says the Earl Hakon and Gunhild's sons fought against each other, and drove each other out of the land in turns.

CHAPTER XIV. GOLD HARALD'S DEATH.—Soon after Harald Greyskin's fall, Earl Hakon came up to Gold Harald, and the earl immediately gave battle to Harald. Hakon gained the victory, and Harald was made prisoner; but Hakon had him immediately hanged on a gallows. Hakon then went to the Danish king, and no doubt easily settled with him for the killing his relative Gold Harald.

CHAPTER XV. DIVISION OF THE COUNTRY.—Soon after King Harald Gormson ordered a levy of men over all his kingdom, and sailed with 600 ships.[2] There were with him Earl Hakon, Harald Grænske a son of King Gudrod, and many other great men who had fled from their udal estates in Norway on account of Gunhild's sons. The Danish king sailed with his fleet from the south to Viken, where all the people of the country surrendered to him. When he came to Tunsberg swarms of people joined him; and King Harald gave to Earl Hakon the command of all the men who came to him in Norway, and gave him the government over Rogaland, Hordaland, Sogn, Fjords district, South Möre, Raumsdal, and North Möre. These seven districts gave King Harald to Earl Hakon to rule over, with the same rights as Harald Haarfager gave with them to his sons; only with the difference, that Hakon should there, as well as in Drontheim, have the king's land-estates and land-tax, and use the king's money and goods according to his necessities whenever there was war in the country. King Harald also gave Harald Grænske Vingulmark, Westfold, and Agder all the way to the Naze,[3] together with the title of king; and let him have these dominions with the same rights as his family in former times had held them,

[1] These datings were probably taken from the first version (not now extant) of Ari's *Book of the Icelanders* (see *Sagas of the Norse Kings*, pp. x–xii and 4–6). It makes Harald Greyskin's death fall *c.* 976, but this may well be several years too late.

[2] Reckoned by the "long hundred," *i.e.* 120; therefore 600 = 720.

[3] *Liðandisness*—Lindesnes in the extreme south of Norway.

and as Harald Haarfager had given with them to his sons. Harald Grænske was then eighteen years old, and he became afterwards a celebrated man. Harald king of Denmark returned home thereafter with all his army.

CHAPTER XVI. GUNHILD'S SONS LEAVE THE COUNTRY.— Earl Hakon proceeded northwards along the coast with his force; and when Gunhild and her sons got the tidings they proceeded to gather troops, but were ill off for men. Then they took the same resolution as before, to sail out to sea with such men as would follow them away to the westward. They came first to the Orkney Islands, and remained there a while. There were in Orkney then the Earls Lodve, Arnvid, Liod, and Skule, the sons of Thorfin Hausakliff.

Earl Hakon now brought all the country under him, and remained all winter in Drontheim. Einar Skalaglam speaks of his conquests in Vellekla [1]:—

> " Norway's great watchman, Hakon, now
> May bind the silk snood on his brow—
> Seven provinces he seized. The realm
> Prospers with Hakon at the helm."

As Hakon the earl proceeded this summer along the coast subjecting all the people to him, he ordered that over all his dominions the temples and sacrifices should be restored, and continued as of old. So it is said in the Vellekla:—

> " Hakon the earl, so good and wise,
> Let all the ancient temples rise;—
> Thor's temples, which all men had known,
> And shrines of gods, lay overthrown
> Until with strong shield in his hand
> Hakon returned into the land
> And fought his way from sea to hill—
> The gods protect this warrior well!
> The helping gods return once more
> To taste the sacrifice of gore;
> The shield-bearer in Hlakka's game [2]
> Has thus won glory for his name;
> Now the earth grows green once more
> As she was wont in days of yore,
> Since Hakon bids men sit again
> Joyfully in the gods' fane.
> The earl has conquered with strong hand
> All that lies north of Viken land:
> In battle storm, and iron rain,
> Hakon spreads wide his sword's domain."

[1] The title of this sequence of verses means " Gold Dearth "; presumably he hoped it would win him a rich reward from Earl Hakon.
[2] Warfare; Hlakka was one of the valkyries.

The first winter that Hakon ruled over Norway the herrings
set in everywhere through the fjords to the land, and the corn
had grown that autumn wherever it had been sown. The
people, therefore, laid in seed for the next year, and got their
lands sowed, and had hope of good times.

CHAPTER XVII. EARL HAKON'S BATTLE WITH RAGNFRID
[977-978].—King Ragnfrid and King Gudrod, both sons of
Gunhild and Eric, were now the only sons of Gunhild remaining
in life. So says Glum Geirason in Greyskin's lay:—

> " When in the battle's bloody strife
>   The sword took noble Harald's life,
>   Half of my fortunes with him fell:
>   But his two brothers, I know well,
>   My loss would soon repair, should they
>   Again in Norway bear the sway,
>   And to their promises should stand,
>   If they return to rule the land."

Ragnfrid began his course in the spring after he had been a
year in the Orkney Islands. He sailed from thence to Norway,
and had with him fine troops, and large ships. When he came
to Norway he learnt that Earl Hakon was in Drontheim; therefore he steered northwards around Stad, and plundered in South
Möre. Some people submitted to him; for it often happens,
when parties of armed men scour over a country, that those who
are nearest the danger seek help where they think it may be
expected. As soon as Earl Hakon heard the news of disturbance in Möre, he fitted out ships, sent the war-token through
the land, made ready in all haste, and proceeded out of the fjord.
He had no difficulty in assembling men. Ragnfrid and Earl
Hakon met at the north corner of Möre; and Hakon, who had
most men, but small ships, began the battle. The combat was
severe, but heaviest on Hakon's side; and, as the custom then
was, they fought bow to bow, and there was a current in the
sound which drove all the ships in upon the land. The earl
ordered to row with the oars to the land where landing seemed
easiest. When the ships were all grounded, the earl with all
his men left them, and drew them up so far that the enemy
might not launch them down again, and then drew up his men
on a grass field, and challenged Ragnfrid to land. Ragnfrid
and his men laid their vessels in along the land, and they shot
at each other a long time; but upon the land Ragnfrid would
not venture: and so they separated. Ragnfrid sailed with his
fleet southwards around Stad; for he was much afraid the whole

forces of the country would swarm around Hakon. Hakon, on his part, was not inclined to try again a battle, for he thought the difference between their ships in size was too great; so in harvest he went north to Drontheim, and stayed there all winter. King Ragnfrid consequently had all the country south of Stad at his mercy; namely, Fjords district, Hordaland, Sogn, Rogaland; and he had many people about him all winter. When spring approached he ordered out the people, and collected a large force. By going about the districts he got many men, ships, and warlike stores sent as he required.

CHAPTER XVIII. ANOTHER BATTLE BETWEEN EARL HAKON AND RAGNFRID IN SOGN.—Towards spring Earl Hakon ordered out all the men north in the country, and got many people from Halogaland and Naumadal; so that from Byrda [1] to Stad he had men from all the sea coast. It was said for certain that he had men from four great districts, and that seven earls followed him, and a matchless number of men. So it is said in the Vellekla:—

> " Hakon, defender of the land,
>   Armed in the North his warrior-band;
>   To Sogne's shore [2] his force he led,
>   And from all quarters thither sped
>   War-ships and men; and haste was made
>   By the young god of the sword-blade,
>   The hero-viking of the wave,
>   His wide domain from foes to save.
>   With shining keels seven kings sailed on
>   To meet this raven-feeding one.
>   When the clash came, the stunning sound
>   Was heard in Norway's farthest bound;
>   And sea-borne corpses, floating far,
>   Brought round the Naze news from the war."

Earl Hakon sailed then with his fleet southwards around Stad; and when he heard that King Ragnfrid with his army had gone towards Sogn, he turned there also with his men to meet him: and there Ragnfrid and Hakon met. Hakon came to the land with his ships, marked out a battle-field with hazel branches for King Ragnfrid,[3] and took ground for his own men in it. So it is told in the Vellekla:—

---

[1] Probably the headland between North Möre and Maumadal.
[2] Sognefjord.
[3] In the Norse form of single combat (*hólmganga*) the fighting area was marked out by stakes called *hǫslur*, " hazels." Figuratively the phrase means " challenged to battle at a fixed spot."

" In the fierce battle Ragnfrid then
  Met the grim foe of Vendland men; [1]
  And many a hero of great name
  Fell in the sharp sword's bloody game.
  The wielder of the shield's fell foe [2]
  Bade his oarsmen shoreward row.
  He laid his war-ships on the strand,
  And ranged his warriors on the land."

There was a great battle; but Earl Hakon, having by far the most people, gained the victory. It took place on the Tinganess where Sogn and Hordaland meet.[3]

King Ragnfrid fled to his ships, after 300 of his men had fallen. So it is said in the Vellekla:—

" Sharp was the battle-strife, I ween,—
  Deadly and close it must have been,
  Before, upon the bloody plain,
  Three hundred corpses of the slain
  Were stretched for the black raven's prey;
  And when the conquerors took their way
  To the sea-shore, they had to tread
  O'er piled-up heaps of foemen dead."

After this battle King Ragnfrid fled from Norway; but Earl Hakon restored peace to the country, and allowed the great army which had followed him in summer to return home to the north country, and he himself remained in the south that harvest and winter.

CHAPTER XIX. EARL HAKON'S MARRIAGE.—Earl Hakon married a girl called Thora, a daughter of the powerful Skage Skoptason, and very beautiful she was. They had two sons, Swend and Heming, and a daughter called Bergliot, who was afterwards married to Einar Tambarskielve. Earl Hakon was much addicted to women, and had many children; among others a daughter Ragnhild, whom he married to Skopte Skagason, a brother of Thora. The Earl loved Thora so much, that he held Thora's family in higher respect than any other people, and Skopte his brother-in-law in particular; and he gave him many great fiefs in Möre. Whenever they were on a cruise together, Skopte must lay his ship nearest to the earl's, and no other ship was allowed to come in between.

[1] Earl Hakon; there were Vends (Wends) among the forces he defeated in the battle at the Danavirke (vide pp. 24–6).
[2] i.e. an axe or sword; the warrior in question is Hakon.
[3] Things were generally held on nesses or points accessible by water, as roads were not formed. This Tinganess is now Dingenes on the south side of the entrance to the Sognefjord. It has been a part of Sogn since 1773.

CHAPTER XX. SKOPTE THE NEWSMAN'S DEATH.—One summer that Earl Hakon was on a cruise, there was a ship with him of which Thorleif the Wise was steersman. In it was also Eric, Earl Hakon's son, then about ten or eleven years old. Now in the evenings, as they came into harbour, Eric would not allow any ship but his to lie nearest to the earl's. But when they came to the south, to Möre, they met Skopte, the earl's brother-in-law, with a well-manned ship; and as they rowed towards the fleet, Skopte called out that Thorleif should move out of the harbour to make room for him, and should go to the roadstead. Eric in haste took up the matter, and ordered Skopte to go himself to the roadstead. When Earl Hakon heard that his son thought himself too great to give place to Skopte, he called to them immediately that they should haul out from their berth, threatening them with chastisement if they did not. When Thorleif heard this, he ordered his men to slip their land-cable, and they did so; and Skopte laid his vessel next to the earl's, as he used to do. When they came together, Skopte brought the earl all the news he had gathered, and the earl communicated to Skopte all the news he had heard; and Skopte was therefore called the Newsman. The winter after Eric was with his foster-father Thorleif, and early in spring he gathered a crew of followers, and Thorleif gave him a boat of fifteen benches of rowers, with ship furniture, tents, and ship provisions; and Eric set out from the fjord, and southwards to Möre. Newsman Skopte happened also to be going with a fully manned boat of fifteen rowers' benches from one of his farms to another, and Eric went against him to have a battle. Skopte was slain, but Eric granted life to those of his men who were still on their legs. So says Eyolf Dadaskald in the Banda lay:—[1]

> " When young, he went at close of day
> In warship to the battle-play,
> And equal forces both men led
> When Eric there left Skopte dead.
> To ravening wolf and bird of prey
> Eric gave welcome food that day!
> Eric (from whose hands gold doth flow)
> Laid Hakon's dearest liegeman low
> When they two met in battle's strife—
> Yea, thou didst take great Skopte's life,
> Didst leave there dead upon the field
> One who rejoiced in clash of shield,
> O warrior with the threatening steel!
> *This land he rules by the gods' will.*"

[1] *Banda* means " of the gods "; the word occurs in one of the lines of the refrain incorporated into certain stanzas (here italicized, *cf.* pp. 78–9.)

Eric sailed along the land and came to Denmark, and went to King Harald Gormson, and stayed with him all winter. In spring the Danish king sent him north to Norway, and gave him an earldom, and the government of Vingulmark [1] and Raumarike, on the same terms as the small scatt-paying kings had formerly held these domains. So says Eyolf Dadaskald:—

> " South through ocean's spray
> His sea-snake sailed away,
> And there some years lived he—
> (Mine is the mead of poesy!)
> Until men set in his true place
> This youth of noble race
> Where, shield and sword in hand,
> He would aye defend his land."

Eric became afterwards a great chief.

CHAPTER XXI. OLAF TRYGVESSON'S JOURNEY FROM RUSSIA. —All this time Olaf Trygvesson was in Russia, and highly esteemed by King Valdemar, and beloved by the queen. King Valdemar made him chief over the men-at-arms whom he sent out to defend the land. So says Hallarstein:—

> " The hater of the niggard hand,[2]
> The chief who loves the Northman's land,
> Was only twelve years old when he
> His Russian war-ships put to sea.
> The wain that ploughs the sea was then
> Loaded with war-gear by his men—
> With swords, and spears, and helms; and deep
> Out to the sea his good ships sweep."

Olaf had several battles, and was lucky as a leader of troops. He himself kept a great many men-at-arms at his own expense out of the pay the king gave him. Olaf was very generous to his men, and therefore very popular. But then it came to pass, what so often happens when a foreigner is raised to higher power and dignity than men of the country, that many envied him because he was so favoured by the king, and also not less so by the queen. They hinted to the king that he should take care

---

[1] This contradicts chap. xv. (p. 15) which says that Harald Grænske got Vingulmark. Perhaps the mistake is in chap. xv., for according to chap. xliii. Harald was king only in Vestfold.

[2] The original figure of expression is " hater of the fire of the bow's seat: " viz. the seat of the bow is the hand; the fire of the hand the gold rings worn on the fingers; the hater of this fire is he who does not care for it, but parts with it readily—the generous man.

not to make Olaf too powerful,—"for such a man may be dangerous to you, if he were to allow himself to be used for the purpose of doing you or your kingdom harm; for he is extremely expert in all exercises and feats, and very popular. We do not, indeed, know what it is he can have to talk of so often with the queen." It was then the custom among great monarchs that the queen should have half of the court attendants, and she supported them at her own expense out of the scatt and revenue provided for her for that purpose. It was so also at the court of King Valdemar that the queen had an attendance as large as the king, and they vied with each other about the finest men, each wanting to have such in their own service. It so fell out that the king listened to such speeches, and became somewhat silent and blunt towards Olaf. When Olaf observed this, he told it to the queen; and also that he had a great desire to travel to the Northern land, where his family formerly had power and kingdoms, and where it was most likely he would advance himself. The queen wished him a prosperous journey, and said he would be found a brave man wherever he might be. Olaf then made ready, went on board, and set out to sea in the Baltic.

As he was coming from the east he made the island of Bornholm, where he landed and plundered. The country people hastened down to the strand, and gave him battle; but Olaf gained the victory, and a large booty.

CHAPTER XXII. OLAF TRYGVESSON'S MARRIAGE [987].—While Olaf lay at Bornholm there came on bad weather, storm, and a heavy sea, so that his ships could not lie there; and he sailed southward under Vendland,[1] where they found a good harbour. They conducted themselves very peacefully, and remained some time. In Vendland there was then a king called Burislaf,[2] who had three daughters,—Geyra, Gunhild, and Astrid. The king's daughter Geyra had the power and government in that part where Olaf and his people landed, and Dixin was the name of the man who most usually advised Queen Geyra. Now when they heard that unknown people were come to the country, who were of distinguished appearance, and conducted themselves peaceably, Dixin repaired to them with a message from Queen Geyra, inviting the strangers to take up their winter abode with

---

[1] *Vindland*—the land of the Vindr (Vends or Wends), the Slavonic people who then occupied the coast from the Vistula to Holstein.

[2] Boleslav. Snorri confused Miesco of Poland (964–92) with his son Boleslav I (992–1025); the former is meant here, the latter on pp. 34 ff.

her; for the summer was almost spent, and the weather was severe and stormy. Now when Dixin came to the place he soon saw that the leader was a distinguished man, both from family and personal appearance, and he told Olaf the queen's invitation with the most friendly message. Olaf willingly accepted the invitation, and went in harvest to Queen Geyra. They liked each other exceedingly, and Olaf courted Queen Geyra; and it was so settled that Olaf married her the same winter, and was ruler, along with Queen Geyra, over her dominions.

Halfred Vandrædaskald tells of these matters in the lay he composed about King Olaf:—

> " Why should the deeds the hero did
> In Bornholm and the East be hid?
> His deadly weapon Olaf bold
> Dyed red: why should not this be told? "

CHAPTER XXIII. EARL HAKON PAYS NO SCATT.—Earl Hakon ruled over Norway, and paid no scatt; because the Danish king gave him all the scatt revenue that belonged to the king in Norway, for the expense and trouble he had in defending the country against Gunhild's sons.

CHAPTER XXIV. KING HARALD'S LEVY TO OPPOSE THE EMPEROR OTTO'S DEMAND TO INTRODUCE CHRISTIANITY IN HIS KINGDOM.—The Emperor Otto was at that time in the Saxon [1] country, and sent a message to King Harald, the Danish king, that he must take on the true faith and be baptized, he and all his people whom he ruled; " otherwise," says the emperor, " we will march against him with an army." The Danish king ordered the land defence to be fitted out, the Danish wall [2] to be well fortified, and his ships of war rigged out. He sent a message also to Earl Hakon in Norway to come to him early in spring, and with as many men as he could possibly raise. In spring Earl Hakon levied an army over the whole country which was very numerous, and with it he sailed to meet the

---

[1] There is confusion here. Otto II (973–83) invaded Denmark in the late autumn of 974 (not 988, as Snorri reckons), to punish Harald for raiding territories under his rule. Harald had long been converted (*vide* p. 26, n. 3), and though Adam attributes this to an invasion by Otto I (936–73), the latter never did attack Denmark.

[2] *Danavirki*, " The Danes' Rampart," a series of fortifications first raised by Godfred in 808–10 to check the incursions of Charlemagne, and extended by later kings. It ran from the head of the Sle (Schlei) fjord to the Treene, a tributary of the Eider. (See J. Brøndsted, *The Vikings*, 1960, pp. 155–60.)

Danish king. The king received him in the most honourable
manner. Many other chiefs also joined the Danish king with
their men, so that he had gathered a very large army.

CHAPTER XXV. TRYGVESSON'S WAR EXPEDITION [988].—
Olaf Trygvesson had been all winter in Vendland, as before
related, and went the same winter to the baronies in Vendland
which had formerly been under Queen Geyra, but had withdrawn
themselves from obedience and payment of taxes. There Olaf
made war, killed many people, burnt out others, took much
property, and laid all of them under subjection to him, and then
went back to his castle. Early in spring Olaf rigged out his
ships and set off to sea. He sailed to Scania,[1] and made a landing.
The people of the country assembled, and gave him battle;
but King Olaf conquered, and made a great booty. He then
sailed eastward to the island of Gotland, where he captured a
merchant vessel belonging to the people of Jemteland.[2] They
made a brave defence; but the end of it was that Olaf cleared the
deck, killed all the men, and took all the goods. He had a third
battle in Gotland, in which he also gained the victory, and made
a great booty. So says Halfred Vandrædaskald:—

> " The king, all heathendom's fierce foe,
>   To battle 'gainst the Vends did go:
>   The Gotlanders must tremble next;
>   And Scania's shores are sorely vexed
>   By the sharp pelting arrow shower
>   The hero and his warriors pour;
>   And then the Jemtland men must fly,
>   Lest they should in his onslaught die."

CHAPTER XXVI. THE EMPEROR OTTO AND EARL HAKON
HAVE A BATTLE AT THE DANISH DYKE IN SLESWICK.—The
Emperor Otto assembled a great army from Saxonland,[3]
Frankland,[4] Friesland,[5] and Vindland.[6] King Burislaf followed
him with a large army, and in it was his son-in-law, Olaf

---

[1] *Skáni* or *Skáney* (modern Skaane), the province that forms the eastern
tip of Sweden, belonged at this period to the kingdom of Denmark.
[2] *Jämtland*, an inland province of Sweden; its inhabitants are unlikely to
have been sea-going merchants. Snorri is trying to account for the mention
of " Jemtland men " in the next verse; it is more likely that Halfred there
alludes to some raid on the Bothnian coast of Sweden and mistakenly
supposes that Jämtland included the coastal regions.
[3] *Saxland*, North Germany.   [4] *Frankland*, " Land of the Franks."
[5] The coast of North Holland.   [6] *Vindland*; *vide* note on p. 22.

Trygvesson.[1] The emperor had a great body of horsemen, and still greater of foot people, and a great army from Holstein.[2] Harald, the Danish king, sent Earl Hakon with the army of Northmen that followed him southwards to the Danish wall, to defend his kingdom on that side. So it is told in the Vellekla:—

> " Over the foaming salt sea spray
>   The Norse sea-horses took their way,
>   Racing across the ocean-plain
>   Southwards to Denmark's green domain.
>   The gallant chief of Hordaland [3]
>   Sat at the helm with steady hand,
>   In casque and shield, his men to bring
>   From Dovre [3] to his friend the king.
>   Harald, the prince of generous mood,
>   Who ruled to Jutland's boundary wood,
>   Desired to prove that warrior's worth
>   Who came to aid him from the north;
>   The monarch straightway gave command
>   To Hakon, with his sword in hand,
>   To man the Dane-work's rampart stout,
>   And keep the foreign foemen out."

The Emperor Otto came with his army from the south to the Danish wall, but Earl Hakon defended the rampart with his men. The Danevirke was constructed in this way:—Two fjords run into the land, one on each side; and in the farthest bight of these fjords the Danes had made a great wall of stone,[4] turf, and timber, and dug a deep and broad ditch in front of it, and had also built a castle over each gate of it. There was a hard battle there, of which the Vellekla speaks:—

> " Thick the storm of arrows flew,
>   Loud was the din, black was the view
>   When th' emperor came from southern lands
>   With Frankish, Vend and Frisian bands.
>   No easy conflict for one man!
>   Yet loud the cry might be heard then
>   Of Norway's brave sea-roving son—
>   'On 'gainst the foe! on! lead us on!'"

[1] It is unhistoric that Boleslav (or Miesco, *vide* p. 22) proceeded with the emperor to Danevirke; nor was Olaf Tryggvason there, for in 974 he was not grown up.

[2] *Holtsettaland* is Holstein.

[3] Literally the poet here calls Hakon " lord of the *Horðar* and *Dofrar*. The former is the group name for inhabitants of the Hordaland district; it is not certain whether the latter is also a group name or merely the name of the Dovre district itself.

[4] The Danevirke did not in fact stretch from coast to coast (*vide* p. 23, n. 2), nor was there everywhere a ditch in front of it; there was probably only one gate through it.

Earl Hakon drew up his people in ranks upon all the gate-towers of the wall, but the greater part of them he kept marching along the wall to make a defence wheresoever an attack was threatened. Many of the emperor's people fell without making any impression on the fortification, so the emperor turned back without farther attempt at an assault on it. So it is said in the Vellekla:—

> " They who the eagle's feast provide
> In ranked line fought side by side,
> 'Gainst lines of war-men under shields
> Close packed together on the fields.
> Earl Hakon drives by daring deeds
> These Saxons to their ocean-steeds;
> And the young hero saves from fall
> The Danevirke—the people's wall."

After this battle Earl Hakon went back to his ships, and intended to sail home to Norway; but he did not get a favourable wind, and lay for some time outside at Lymfjord.

CHAPTER XXVII. KING HARALD AND EARL HAKON ARE BAPTIZED.—The Emperor Otto turned back with his troops to Sleswick, collected his ships of war, and crossed the fjord of Sle [1] into Jutland. As soon as the Danish king heard of this he marched his army against him, and there was a battle, in which the emperor at last got the victory. The Danish king fled to Lymfjord, and took refuge in the island Morsey.[2] By the help of mediators who went between the king and the emperor, a truce and a meeting between them were agreed on. The Emperor Otto and the Danish king met upon Mors Isle. There Bishop Poppo instructed King Harald in the holy faith; and thereafter King Harald allowed himself to be baptized, and also the whole Danish army.[3] King Harald, while he was in Mors Isle, had sent a message to Hakon that he should come to his succour; and the earl had just reached the island when the king had received baptism. The king sends word to the earl to come to him, and when they met the king forced the earl to allow himself also to be baptized. So Earl Hakon and all the men who were with him were baptized; and the king gave them priests and other learned men [4] with them, and ordered

---

[1] The fjord now called Schlei runs up to the town of Schleswig.

[2] Morsey is now called Mors, an island in the Lymfjord.

[3] The part played by Poppo in converting King Harald is also mentioned by Widukind, *Res Gestæ Saxonicæ* III. 65. His conversion must have been between 953 and 965, and was quite unconnected with Otto II.'s invasion.

[4] Learned men, *i.e.*, church-learned men, therefore belonging to the clerical order.

that the earl should make all the people in Norway be baptized. On that they separated; and the earl went out to sea, there to wait for a wind.

CHAPTER XXVIII. EARL HAKON RENOUNCES THE CHRISTIAN FAITH AND PLUNDERS IN GOTLAND.—When a wind came with which he thought he could get clear out to sea, he put all the learned men on shore again, and set off to the ocean; but as the wind came round to south-west, and at last to west, he sailed eastward, out through Ore Sound,[1] ravaging the land on both sides. He then sailed eastward along Scania, plundering the country wherever he came. When he got east to the skerries of East Gotland, he ran in and landed, and made a great blood-sacrifice. There came two ravens flying which croaked loudly; and now, thought the earl, the blood-offering has been accepted by Odin, and he thought that this would be an auspicious day for him to go into battle. Then he set fire to his ships, landed his men, and went over all the country with armed hand. Earl Ottar, who ruled over Gotland, came against him, and they held a great battle with each other; but Earl Hakon gained the day, and Earl Ottar and a great part of his men were killed. Earl Hakon now drove with fire and sword over both the Gotlands, until he came into Norway; and then he proceeded by land all the way north to Drontheim. The Vellekla tells about this:—

> " The victor of many a battle-field,
> In viking garb, with axe and shield,
> Asks his question; valkyries tell
> On which day war will turn out well.[2]
> Two ravens, flying from the east,
> Come croaking to the bloody feast:
> The warrior knows what they foreshow—
> The days when Gotland blood will flow.
> A viking-feast Earl Hakon kept,
> The land with viking fury swept,
> Harrying the land far from the shore
> Where foray ne'er was known before.
> None further marched from ocean's side,
> He ranged through Gotland far and wide,—
> Led many a gold-decked viking shield
> O'er many a peaceful inland field.
> Bodies on bodies Odin found
> Heaped high upon each battle ground:
> 'Tis Hakon's doing; well may he,
> Son of the gods, cry victory!
> Who doubts now that the gods do guide
> Hakon, the breaker of kings' pride?
> I say the mighty gods delight
> To add yet more to Hakon's might."

[1] *Eyrarsund*, the Baltic Straits.
[2] Ravens were associated with valkyries as well as with Odin.

CHAPTER XXIX. THE EMPEROR OTTO RETURNS HOME.—
The Emperor Otto went back to his kingdom in the Saxon land,
and parted in friendship with the Danish king. It is said that
the Emperor Otto stood godfather to Swend, King Harald's
son, and gave him his name; so that he was baptized Otto
Swend.[1] King Harald held fast by his Christianity to his
dying day.

King Burislaf went to Vendland, and his son-in-law King
Olaf went with him. This battle is related also by Halfred
Vandrædaskald in his song on Olaf [2]:—

> " He who through the foaming surges
> His white-winged ocean-coursers urges,
> Hewed from the Danes, in armour dressed,
> The iron bark off mail-clad breast."

CHAPTER XXX. OLAF'S JOURNEY FROM VENDLAND [990].—
Olaf Trygvesson was three years in Vendland when Geyra his
queen fell sick, and she died of her illness. Olaf felt his loss so
great that he had no pleasure in Vendland after it. He provided himself, therefore, with war-ships, and went out again a
plundering, and plundered first in Friesland, next in Saxland,
and then all the way to Flanders. So says Halfred Vandrædaskald:—

> " Olaf's broad axe of shining steel
> For the shy wolf left many a meal.
> At length the Saxon corpses lay
> Heaped up, the witch-wife's horses' [3] prey.
> The steeds that she-trolls ride by night
> Lap up the blood that's spilt in fight;
> Our well-loved prince poured out for them
> Brown blood of many Friesland men.
> The mighty lord of warlike strife
> Gave to the Valkers [4] death for life,
> Left Flemish flesh for raven's joy—
> Thus Olaf doth his foes destroy."

CHAPTER XXXI. KING OLAF TRYGVESSON'S FORAYS [991–
994].—Thereafter Olaf Trygvesson sailed to England, and
ravaged wide around in the land. He sailed all the way north
to Northumberland, where he plundered; and thence to Scotland,
where he marauded far and wide. Then he went to the Hebrides,

---

[1] This was Swend, or Svein, afterwards the conqueror of England, and
father of Canute the Great.
[2] This poem probably refers to another battle, for Olaf was at that time
in Russia.
[3] Wolves, on which valkyries, here called witches, rode.
[4] Men from the district of Walcheren in Holland.

where he fought some battles; and then southwards to Man, where he also fought. He ravaged far around in Ireland, and thence steered to Bretland,[1] which he laid waste with fire and sword, and also the district called Cumberland. He sailed southward from thence to Valland,[2] and marauded there. When he left the south, intending to sail to England, he came to the islands called the Scilly Isles, lying westward from England in the ocean. Thus tells Halfred Vandrædaskald of these events:—

> " The brave young king, who ne'er retreats,
> The Englishman in England beats.
> Death through Northumberland is spread
> From battle-axe and broad spear-head.
> Through Scotland with his spears he rides;
> To Man his glancing ships he guides:
> Feeding the wolves where'er he came,
> The young king drove a bloody game.
> The gallant bowman in the isles
> Slew foemen, who lay heaped in piles.
> The Irish fled at Olaf's name—
> Fled from a young king seeking fame.
> In Bretland, and in Cumberland,
> People against him could not stand:
> Thick on the fields their corpses lay,
> To ravens and howling wolves a prey."

Olaf Trygvesson had been four years on this cruise from the time he left Vendland till he came to the Scilly Islands.

CHAPTER XXXII. KING OLAF IS BAPTIZED IN THE SCILLY ISLANDS [994].[3]—While Olaf Trygvesson lay in the Scilly Isles he heard of a seer, or fortune-teller, on the islands, who could tell beforehand things not yet done, and what he foretold many believed was really fulfilled. Olaf became curious to try this man's gift of prophecy. He therefore sent one of his men, who was the handsomest and strongest, clothed him magnificently, and bade him say he was the king; for Olaf was known in all countries as handsomer, stronger, and braver than all others, although, after he had left Russia, he retained no more of his name than that he was called Ole, and was Russian. Now when the messenger came to the fortune-teller, and gave himself out for the king, he got the answer, " Thou art not the king, but I advise thee to be faithful to thy king." And more he would not say to that man. The man returned and told Olaf, and his

[1] *Bretland*, the " Land of Britons," is Wales.
[2] Valland is the west coast of France, from the Seine to the Loire.
[3] Snorri took this episode from the *Ágrip*; its ultimate source is an anecdote about St. Benedict and Totila the Goth in the *Dialogues* of Gregory the Great. The same story is told of St. Olaf and a hermit.

desire to meet the fortune-teller was increased; and now he had no doubt of his being really a fortune-teller. Olaf repaired himself to him, and, entering into conversation, asked him if he could foresee how it would go with him with regard to his kingdom, or of any other fortune he was to have. The hermit replies in a holy spirit of prophecy: "Thou wilt become a renowned king, and do celebrated deeds. Many men wilt thou bring to faith and baptism, and both to thy own and others' good; and that thou mayst have no doubt of the truth of this answer, listen to these tokens: When thou comest to thy ships many of thy people will conspire against thee, and then a battle will follow in which many of thy men will fall, and thou wilt be wounded almost to death, and carried upon a shield to thy ship; yet after seven days thou shalt be well of thy wounds, and immediately thou shalt let thyself be baptized." Soon after Olaf went down to his ships, where he met some mutineers and people who would destroy him and his men. A fight took place, and the result was what the hermit had predicted, that Olaf was wounded, and carried upon a shield [1] to his ship, and that his wound was healed in seven days. Then Olaf perceived that the man had spoken truth,—that he was a true fortune-teller, and had the gift of prophecy. Olaf went once more to the hermit, and asked particularly how he came to have such wisdom in foreseeing things to be. The hermit replied, that the Christian's God himself let him know all that he desired; and he brought before Olaf many great proofs of the power of the Almighty. In consequence of this encouragement Olaf agreed to let himself be baptized, and he and all his followers were baptized forthwith. He remained here a long time, took the true faith, and got with him priests and other learned men.

CHAPTER XXXIII. OLAF MARRIES GYDA.—In autumn Olaf sailed from Scilly to England, where he put into a harbour, but proceeded in a friendly way; for England was Christian, and he himself had become Christian.[2] At this time a summons to a Thing went through the country, that all men should come to hold a Thing. Now when the Thing was assembled a queen

---

[1] The shield of the Norsemen was narrow and oblong.
[2] *The Anglo-Saxon Chronicle* speaks of Olaf (*Anlaf*) coming to England in 994 with Swein (Swend) of Denmark and ravaging many districts, till he made peace with King Ethelred, who stood sponsor to him at confirmation. Olaf is probably also the *Anlaf* who led the viking raids of 991 and defeated Byrtnoth at Maldon.

called Gyda came to it, a sister of Olaf Kvaran,[1] who was king of Dublin in Ireland. She had been married to a great earl in England, and after his death she was at the head of his dominions. In her territory there was a man called Alfin, who was a great champion and single-combat man. He had paid his addresses to her; but she gave for answer, that she herself would choose whom of the men in her dominions she would take in marriage; and on that account the Thing was assembled, that she might choose a husband. Alfin came there dressed out in his best clothes, and there were many well-dressed men at the meeting. Olaf had come there also; but had on his bad-weather clothes, and a coarse over-garment, and stood with his people apart from the rest of the crowd. Gyda went round and looked at each, to see if any appeared to her a suitable man. Now when she came to where Olaf stood she looked at him straight in the face, and asked " what sort of man he was ? "

He said, " I am called Ole; and I am a stranger here."

Gyda replies, " Wilt thou have me if I choose thee? "

" I will not say no to that," answered he; and he asked what her name was, and her family, and descent.

" I am called Gyda," said she; " and am daughter of the king of Ireland, and was married in this country to an earl who ruled over this territory. Since his death I have ruled over it, and many have courted me, but none to whom I would choose to be married."

She was a young and handsome woman. They afterwards talked over the matter together, and agreed, and Olaf and Gyda were betrothed.

CHAPTER XXXIV. KING OLAF AND ALFIN'S DUEL.—Alfin was very ill pleased with this. It was the custom then in England, if two strove for anything, to settle the matter by single combat; and so now Alfin challenges Olaf Trygvesson to fight about this business. The time and place for the combat were settled, and that each should have twelve men with him. When they met, Olaf told his men to do exactly as they saw him do. He had a large axe; and when Alfin was going to cut at him with his sword, he hewed away the sword out of his hand, and with the next blow struck down Alfin himself. He then bound him fast. It went in the same way with all Alfin's men.

[1] Olaf Kvaran Sigtrygsson died as an old man in 980; it is unlikely that any sister of his could be young enough to marry Olaf Tryggvason, and the details of this episode are more like folk-tale than history. Nor do Snorri and Odd (his source here) explain what became of Gyda, if she ever existed.

They were beaten down, bound, and carried to Olaf's lodging. Thereupon he ordered Alfin to quit the country, and never appear in it again; and Olaf took all his property. Olaf in this way got Gyda in marriage, and lived sometimes in England and sometimes in Ireland.[1]

CHAPTER XXXV. KING OLAF GETS HIS DOG VIGE.—While Olaf was in Ireland he was once on an expedition which went by sea. As they required to make a foray for provisions on the coast, some of his men landed, and drove down a large herd of cattle to the strand. Now a peasant came up, and entreated Olaf to give him back the cows that belonged to him. Olaf told him to take his cows, if he could distinguish them; "but don't delay our march." The peasant had with him a large house-dog, which he put in among the herd of cattle, in which many hundred head of beasts were driven together. The dog ran into the herd, and drove out exactly the number which the peasant had said he wanted; and all were marked with the same mark, which showed that the dog knew the right beasts and was very sagacious. Olaf then asked the peasant if he would sell him the dog. "I would rather give him to you," said the peasant. Olaf immediately presented him with a gold ring in return, and promised him his friendship in future. This dog was called Vige, and was the very best of dogs, and Olaf owned him long afterwards.[2]

CHAPTER XXXVI. OF KING HARALD GORMSON, AND HIS EXPEDITION AGAINST ICELAND.—The Danish king, Harald Gormson, heard that Earl Hakon had thrown off Christianity, and had plundered far and wide in the Danish land. The Danish king levied an army, with which he went to Norway; and when he came to the country which Earl Hakon had to rule over he laid waste the whole land, and came with his fleet to some islands called Sulen Isles. Only five houses were left standing in Lœrdal; but all the people fled up to the fjelds, and into the forest, taking with them all the movable goods they could carry with them. Then the Danish king proposed to sail with his fleet to Iceland, to avenge the mockery and scorn all the Icelanders had shown towards him; for they had made a law in Iceland that they should make as many lampoons

[1] The Tryggvi who laid claim to Norway in 1033 called himself son of Olaf and Gyda (*vide* pp. 393-4); perhaps the whole story of this marriage was invented by him.
[2] *Vide* also p. 69. According to Odd, Vige died of grief for Olaf's fall.

against the Danish king as there were persons in that country; and the reason was, because a vessel which belonged to certain Icelanders was stranded in Denmark, and the Danes took all the property, and called it wreck. One of the king's bailiffs called Birger was to blame for this; but the lampoons were made against both. In the lampoons were the following lines:—

> " Harald, well known for murders rank,
> Once kicked against a fat mare's flank;
> Himself was changed to stallion's form
> And grew to be, like wax, full warm.
> And there did feeble Birger stand
> (Hateful to spirits of the land)
> Changed to the likeness of a mare—
> And at this sight did all men stare! "

CHAPTER XXXVII. KING HARALD SENDS A WARLOCK IN A TRANSFORMED SHAPE TO ICELAND.—King Harald told a warlock to hie to Iceland in some altered shape, and to try what he could learn there to tell him: and he set out in the shape of a whale. And when he came near to the land he went to the west side of Iceland, north around the land, where he saw all the mountains and hills full of land-spirits,[1] some great, some small. When he came to Vapnafjord [2] he went in towards the land, intending to go on shore; but a huge dragon rushed down the dale against him with a train of serpents, paddocks, and vipers, that blew poison towards him. Then he turned to go westward around the land as far as Eyafjord,[3] and he went into the fjord. Then a bird flew against him, which was so great that its wings stretched over the mountains on either side of the fjord, and many birds, great and small, with it. Then he swam farther west, and then south into Breidefjord.[4] When he came into the fjord a large grey bull ran against him, wading into the sea, and bellowing fearfully, and he was followed by a crowd of land-spirits. So from there he went round by Reikaness,[5] and wanted to land at Vikarskeid,[6] but there came down a hill-giant against him with an iron staff in his hands. He was a head higher than the mountains, and many other giants followed him. He then swam eastward along the land, and there was

---

[1] *Landvættir*, local protective beings living in hillocks, waterfalls, or woods; little is known of the beliefs and cult concerning them. The parallel between dragon, bird, bull, and giant and the four chieftains named on p. 34 suggests that Snorri has blended the conception of the *landvættr* with that of the *fylgja*, a man's " external soul " which might sometimes manifest itself in an appropriate animal form.

[2] On the east coast.   [3] In the north country.
[4] The great bay on the west of Iceland.   [5] The south-west corner.
[6] Now Skeid, a flat stretch of sand in the south country.

nothing to see, he said, but sand and vast deserts, and, without the skerries, high-breaking surf; and the ocean between the countries was so wide that a long-ship could not cross it. At that time Brod-helge dwelt in Vapnafjord, Eyolf Valgerdson in Eyafjord, Thord Gelle in Breidefjord, and Thorodd gode in Olfus. Then the Danish king turned about with his fleet, and sailed back to Denmark.

Hakon the earl settled habitations again in the country that had been laid waste, and paid no scatt as long as he lived to Denmark.

CHAPTER XXXVIII. HARALD GORMSON'S DEATH.—Swend, King Harald's son, who afterwards was called Tweskiæg (forked beard), asked his father King Harald for a part of his kingdom; but now, as before, Harald would not listen to dividing the Danish dominions, and giving him a kingdom. Swend collected ships of war, and gave out that he was going on a viking cruise; but when all his men were assembled, and the Jomsburg viking Palnatoke had come to his assistance, he ran into Sealand to Isefjord, where his father had been for some time with his ships ready to proceed on an expedition. Swend instantly gave battle, and the combat was severe. So many people flew to assist King Harald, that Swend was overpowered by numbers, and fled. But King Harald received a wound which ended in his death: and Swend was chosen King of Denmark. At this time Sigvald was earl over Jomsburg [1] in Vendland. He was a son of King Strut-Harald, who had ruled over Scania. Heming, and Thorkel the Tall, were Sigvald's brothers. Bue the Thick from Bornholm, and Sigurd his brother, were also chiefs among the Jomsburg vikings: and also Vagn, a son of Aake and Thorgunna, and a sister's son of Bue and Sigurd. Earl Sigvald had taken King Swend prisoner, and carried him to Vendland, to Jomsburg, where he had forced him to make peace with Burislaf, the king of the Vends, and to take him as the peace-maker between them. Earl Sigvald was married to Astrid, a daughter of King Burislaf; and told King Swend that if he did not accept of his terms, he would deliver him into the hands of the Vends. The king knew that they would torture him to death, and therefore agreed to accept the earl's mediation. The earl delivered this judgment between them—that King Swend should marry Gunhild, King Burislaf's daughter; and King Burislaf again Thyre, a daughter

[1] A fortified market town on the Isle of Wollin by the mouths of the Oder (see *The Saga of the Jomsvikings*, ed. N. F. Blake, 1962).

of Harald, and King Swend's sister; but that each party should retain their own dominions, and there should be peace between the countries. Then King Swend returned home to Denmark with his wife Gunhild. Their sons were Harald - and Knut (Canute) the Great. At that time the Danes threatened much to bring an army into Norway against Earl Hakon.

CHAPTER XXXIX. THE SOLEMN VOW OF THE JOMSBURG VIKINGS [994].—King Swend made a magnificent feast, to which he invited all the chiefs in his dominions; for he would give the succession-feast, or the heirship-ale, after his father Harald. A short time before, Strut-Harald in Scania, and Vesete in Bornholm, father to Bue the Thick and to Sigurd, had died; and King Swend sent word to the Jomsburg vikings that Earl Sigvald, and Bue, and their brothers, should come to him, and drink the funeral-ale for their fathers in the same feast the king was giving. The Jomsburg vikings came to the festival with their bravest men, eleven ships of them from Vendland, and twenty ships from Scania. Great was the multitude of people assembled. The first day of the feast, before King Swend went up into his father's high seat, he drank the bowl to his father's memory, and made the solemn vow, that before three winters were past he would go over with his army to England, and either kill King Adalred (Ethelred),[1] or chase him out of the country. This heirship bowl all who were at the feast drank. Thereafter for the chiefs of the Jomsburg vikings was filled and drunk the largest horn to be found, and of the strongest drink. When that bowl was emptied, all men drank Christ's beaker; and again the fullest measure and the strongest drink were handed to the Jomsburg vikings. The third bowl was to the memory of Saint Michael, which was drunk by all. Thereafter Earl Sigvald emptied a remembrance bowl to his father's honour, and made the solemn vow, that before three winters came to an end he would go to Norway, and either kill Earl Hakon, or chase him out of the country. Thereupon Thorkel the Tall, his brother, made a solemn vow to follow his brother Sigvald to Norway, and not flinch from the battle so long as Sigvald would fight there. Then Bue the Thick vowed to follow them to Norway, and not flinch so long as the other Jomsburg vikings fought. At last Vagn Aakeson vowed that he would go with them to Norway, and not

[1] Swend first attacked England in 994; in 1014 he drove Ethelred out. The custom of making vows at a feast is also described in *Sagas of the Norse Kings*, pp. 34, 94; Christian toasts here replace heathen ones.

return until he had slain Thorkel Leire, and gone to bed to his daughter Ingebjorg without her friends' consent. Many other chiefs made solemn vows about different things. Thus was the heirship-ale drunk that day; but the next morning, when the Jomsburg vikings had slept off their drink, they thought they had spoken more than enough. They held a meeting to consult how they should proceed with their undertaking, and they determined to fit out as speedily as possible for the expedition; and without delay ships and men-at-arms were prepared, and the news spread quickly.

CHAPTER XL. EARL ERIC AND EARL HAKON PREPARE A WAR LEVY.—When Earl Eric, the son of Hakon, who at that time was in Raumarike, heard the tidings, he immediately gathered troops, and went to the Uplands, and thence over the Fjelds to Drontheim, and joined his father Earl Hakon. Thord Kolbeinson [1] speaks of this in the lay of Eric:—

> " News from the south are flying round;
> The bonder comes with look profound,
> Bad news of bloody battles bringing,
> Of steel-clad men, of weapons ringing.
> I hear that in the Danish land
> Long-sided ships slide down the strand,
> And, floating with the rising tide,
> The ocean-coursers soon will ride."

The earls Hakon and Eric had war-arrows split up and sent round the Drontheim country; and despatched messages to both the Möres, North Möre and South Möre, and to Raumsdal, and also north to Naumadal and Halogaland. They summoned all the country to provide both men and ships. So it is said in Eric's lay:—

> " The scald must now a war-song raise,—
> The gallant active youth must praise,
> Who o'er the ocean's field spreads forth
> Ships, cutters, boats, from the far north.
> His mighty fleet comes sailing by,—
> From headlands many a mast we spy:
> The valiant Eric, shield in hand,
> Comes to defend his father's land."

Earl Hakon set out immediately to the south, to Möre, to reconnoitre and gather people: and Earl Eric gathered an army from the north to follow.

CHAPTER XLI. THE EXPEDITION OF JOMSBURG VIKINGS TO NORWAY.—The Jomsburg vikings assembled their fleet in

---

[1] An Icelander, prominent in *The Saga of Bjorn, the Hitdale champion.*

Lymfjord, from whence they went to sea with sixty sail of vessels. When they came under the coast of Agder, they steered northwards to Rogaland with their fleet, and began to plunder when they came into the earl's territory; and so they sailed north along the coast, plundering and burning. A man, by name Geirmund, sailed in a light boat with a few men northwards to Möre, and there he fell in with Earl Hakon, stood before his dinner table, and told the earl the tidings of an army from Denmark having come to the south end of the land. The earl asked if he had any certainty of it. Then Geirmund stretched forth one arm, from which the hand was cut off, and said, "Here is the token that the enemy is in the land." Then the earl questioned him particularly about his army. Geirmund says it consists of Jomsburg vikings, who have killed many people, and plundered all around. "And hastily and hotly they pushed on," says he, "and I expect it will not be long before they are upon you." On this the earl rowed into every fjord, going in along the one side of the land and out at the other, collecting men; and thus he drove along night and day. He sent spies out upon the upper ridges,[1] and also southwards into the Fjords; and he proceeded north to meet Eric with his men. This appears from Eric's lay:—

> "The earl, well skilled in war to speed
> O'er the wild wave the viking-steed,
> Now launched the high stems from the shore,
> Which death to Sigvald's vikings bore.
> Rollers beneath the ships' keels crash,
> Oar-blades loud in the grey sea splash,
> And they who give the ravens food
> Row fearless through the curling flood."

Eric hastened southwards with his forces the shortest way he could.

CHAPTER XLII. OF THE JOMSBURG VIKINGS AND THEIR EXPEDITION.—Earl Sigvald steered with his fleet northwards around Stad, and came to the land at Herö Islands.[2] Although the vikings fell in with the country people, the people never told the truth about what the earl was doing; and the vikings went on pillaging and laying waste. They laid to their vessels at the outer end of Had Island,[3] landed, plundered, and drove both men and cattle down to the ships, killing all the men able to bear arms.

[1] Possibly modern Maunseid.   [2] Islands west of Hareidland.
[3] Now Hareidland.

As they were going back to their ships, came a bonder, walking near to Bue's troop, who said to them, " Ye are not doing like true warriors, to be driving cows and calves down to the strand, while ye should be giving chase to the bear, since ye are coming near to the pit where ye may trap him."

" What says the old man? " asked some. " Can he tell us anything about Earl Hakon? "

The peasant replies, " The earl went yesterday into the Horunder fjord[1] with one or two ships, certainly not more than three, and then he had no news about you."

Bue ran now with his people in all haste down to the ships, leaving all the booty behind. Bue said, " Let us avail ourselves now of this news we have got of the earl, and be the first to the victory." When they came to their ships they rowed off from the land. Earl Sigvald called to them, and asked what they were about. They replied, " The earl is in the fjord "; on which Earl Sigvald with the whole fleet set off, and rowed north about the island Had.

CHAPTER XLIII. BEGINNING OF THE BATTLE WITH THE JOMSBURG VIKINGS.—The earls Hakon and Eric lay in Halkels-wick,[2] where all their forces were assembled. They had 150 ships, and they had heard that the Jomsburg vikings had come in from sea, and lay at the island Had; and they, in consequence, rowed out to seek them. When they reached a place called Hiörungavaag[3] they met each other, and both sides drew up their ships in line for an attack. Earl Sigvald's banner was displayed in the midst of his army, and right against it Earl Hakon arranged his force for attack. Earl Sigvald himself had 20 ships, but Earl Hakon had 60. In Earl Hakon's army were these chiefs,—Thore Hiort from Halogaland, and Styrkar from Gimsar. In the wing of the opposite array of the Jomsburg vikings was Bue the Thick, and his brother Sigurd, with 20 ships. Against him Earl Eric laid himself with 60 ships; and with him were these chiefs,—Gudbrand Huite from the Uplands, and Thorkel Leire from Viken. In the other wing of the Jomsburg vikings' array was Vagn Aakeson with 20 ships; and against him stood Swend the son of Hakon, in whose division was

---

[1] North-east of Had Island.   [2] South of Had Island.
[3] A long inlet running north-east of Had (now Liavaag). Snorri assigns this battle to A.D. 994, but Saxo says it was an attack on Norway ordered by Harald Gormsson, who died c. 986. The most probable date for the battle is between 974 and 983. (See The Saga of the Jomsvikings.)

Skiegge of Yria at Uphaug, and Rognvald of Arvig at Stad, with
60 ships. It is told in the Earl Eric's lay thus:—

> " The bonders' ships along the coast
> Sailed on to meet the foremen's host;
> The stout earl's ships, with eagle flight,
> Rushed on the Danes in bloody fight.
> The Danish ships, of rich men full,
> Were cleared of men,—and many a hull
> Was driving empty on the main,
> With the warm corpses of the slain."

Eyvind Skaldaspiller says also in the Haleygia-tal:—

> " That meeting at the dawn of day
> Brought grief to foes of Yngve Frey,[1]
> For then the rulers of this land
> Sped out in long ships to withstand
> Those who came their realm to ravage;
> Yea, and there the swordsman savage
> Steered his wave-bestriding horse
> From the south against their force."

Then the fleets came together, and one of the sharpest of
conflicts began. Many fell on both sides, but the most by far
on Hakon's side; for the Jomsburg vikings fought desperately,
sharply, and murderously, and shot right through the shields.
So many spears were thrown against Earl Hakon that his armour
was altogether split asunder, and he threw it off. So says Tind
Halkelson:—

> " There was no gold-decked lady there
> Who might with her own hand prepare
> A bed for Hakon—nay, not so,
> But clashing, flashing swords now glow!
> His mailshirt now away he flings,
> Since all too few are now its rings; [2]
> The armoured men are driven back
> And swept from off the sea-steed's deck.
> The earl's strong shirt of iron links
> Is split apart, and down it sinks,
> Hurled far away on sandy shore;
> The marks of this the good earl bore."

CHAPTER XLIV. EARL SIGVALD'S FLIGHT.—The Jomsburg
vikings had larger and higher-sided ships; and both parties
fought desperately. Vagn Aakeson laid his ship on board of

[1] Probably merely " warriors," who are the foes of Frey because he is
a god of peace; but the allusion might also be to Danish Christianity.
[2] *Hringfár*, applied to Hakon's mailshirt, may mean either " having few
rings " or " of the gleaming rings." Snorri clearly took it to mean the
former. The first lines can also be interpreted as: " That which a gold-
decked lady had sewn for the earl with her own hand (*i.e.* the shirt of
ringmail) proved to be of no avail."

Swend Earl Hakon's son's ship, and Swend allowed his ship to give way, and was on the point of flying. Then Earl Eric came up, and laid his ship alongside of Vagn, and then Vagn gave way, and the ships came to lie in the same position as before. Thereupon Eric goes to the other wing, which had gone back a little, and Bue had cut the ropes, intending to pursue them. Then Eric laid himself, board to board, alongside of Bue's ship, and there was a severe combat hand to hand. Two or three of Eric's ships then laid themselves upon Bue's single vessel. A thunderstorm came on at this moment, and such a heavy hail-storm that every hailstone weighed an öre.[1] The Earl Sigvald cut his cable, turned his ship round, and took flight. Vagn Aakeson called to him not to fly; but as Earl Sigvald paid no attention to what he said, Vagn threw his spear at him, and hit the man at the helm. Earl Sigvald rowed away with 35 ships, leaving 25 of his fleet behind.

CHAPTER XLV. BUE DIGRE THROWS HIMSELF OVERBOARD.—
Then Earl Hakon laid his ship on the other side of Bue's ship, and now came heavy blows on Bue's men. Vigfus,[2] a son of Vigaglum, took up an anvil with a sharp end, which lay upon the deck, and on which a man had welded the hilt to his sword just before, and being a very strong man cast the anvil with both hands at the head of Aslak Holmskalle, and the end of it went into his brains. Before this no weapon could wound this Aslak, who was Bue's foster-father, and forecastle commander, although he could wound right and left. Another man among the strongest and bravest was Haavard Huggende.[3] In this attack Eric's men boarded Bue's ship, and went aft to the quarter-deck where Bue stood. There Thorstein Midlang cut at Bue across his nose, so that the nose-piece of his helmet was cut in two, and he got a great wound; but Bue, in turn, cut at Thorstein's side, so that the sword cut the man through. Then Bue lifted up two chests full of gold, and called aloud, " Overboard all Bue's men," and threw himself overboard with his two chests. Many of his people sprang overboard with him. Some fell in the ship, for it was of no use to call for quarter. Bue's ship was cleared of people from stem to stern, and afterwards all the others, the one after the other.

[1] The öre weighed 26·7 grammes, or rather less than 1¾ ounces. There was a tradition that this storm was raised by magic.
[2] An Icelander, son of a famous chieftain (see *Viga-Glúms Saga*).
[3] *Hǫggvandi*, " the Hewer "; the *Jomsvikings Saga* says he saw, by second sight, the ogresses fighting for Hakon.

CHAPTER XLVI. THE JOMSBURG VIKINGS BOUND TOGETHER IN ONE CHAIN.—Earl Eric then laid himself alongside of Vagn's ship, and there was a brave defence; but at last this ship too was cleared, and Vagn and thirty men were taken prisoners, and bound, and brought to land. Then came up Thorkel Leire, and said, "Thou madest a solemn vow, Vagn, to kill me; but now it seems more likely that I will kill thee." Vagn and his men sat all upon a log of wood together. Thorkel had an axe in his hands, with which he cut at him who sat outmost on the log. Vagn and the other prisoners were bound so that a rope was fastened on their feet, but they had their hands free. One of them said, "I will stick this belt-knife that I have in my hand into the earth, if it be so that I know anything, after my head is cut off." His head was cut off, but the belt-knife fell from his hand. There sat also a very handsome man with long hair, who twisted his hair over his head, put out his neck, and said, "Don't make my hair bloody." A man took the hair in his hands and held it fast. Thorkel hewed with his axe; but the viking twitched his head so strongly that he who was holding his hair fell forwards, and the axe cut off both his hands, and stuck fast in the earth. Then Earl Eric came up, and asked, "Who is that handsome man?"

He replies, "I am called Sigurd, and am said to be Bue's son. Not all the Jomsburg vikings are dead yet!"

Eric says, "Thou art certainly Bue's son. Wilt thou now take life and peace?"

"That depends," says he, "upon who it is that offers it."

"He offers who has the power to do it—Earl Eric."

"That will I," says he, "from his hands." And now the rope was loosened from him.

Then said Thorkel Leire, "Although thou should give all these men life and peace, earl, Vagn Aakeson shall never come from this with life." And he ran at him with uplifted axe; but the viking Skarde swung himself in the rope, and let himself fall just before Thorkel's feet, so that Thorkel fell over him, and Vagn caught the axe and gave Thorkel a death-wound. Then said the earl, "Vagn, wilt thou accept life?"

"That I will," says he, "if you give it to all of us."

"Loose them from the rope," said the earl; and it was done. Eighteen were killed, and twelve got their lives.

CHAPTER XLVII. DEATH OF GISSUR OF VALDERS.—Earl Hakon, and many with him, were sitting upon a piece of wood, and a bow-string twanged from Bue's ship, and the arrow struck Gissur from Valders, who was sitting next to the earl, and was clothed splendidly. Thereupon the people went on board, and found Haavard Huggende standing on his knees at the ship's railing, for his feet had been cut off, and he had a bow in his hand. When they came on board the ship Haavard asked, " Who fell by that shaft? "

They answered, " A man called Gissur."

" Then my luck was less than I wished," said he.

" Great enough was the misfortune," replied they; " but thou shalt not make it greater." And they killed him on the spot.

The dead were then ransacked, and the booty brought all together to be divided; and there were twenty-five ships of the Jomsburg vikings in the booty. So says Tind Halkelson:—

> " He who raven flocks befriends
> Has left his sword-mark on the Vends;
> That blade that snarled against the shield
> Bit at men's legs on battlefield,
> Till he who there that swordblade bore
> Cleared five-and-twenty ships of war:
> A proof that in the furious fight
> None can withstand the Norsemen's might."

Then the army dispersed. Earl Hakon went to Drontheim, and was much displeased that Earl Eric had given quarter to Vagn Aakeson. It was said that at this battle Earl Hakon had sacrificed for victory his son, young Erling, to the gods;[1] and instantly came the hail-storm, and then was heavier loss among the Jomsburg vikings.

Earl Eric went to the Uplands, and eastward by that route to his own kingdom, taking Aakeson with him. Earl Eric married Vagn to Ingebjorg [p. 36], a daughter of Thorkel Leire, and gave him a good ship of war and all belonging to it, and a crew; and they parted the best of friends. Then Vagn went home south to Denmark, and became afterwards a man of great consideration, and many great people are descended from him.

CHAPTER XLVIII. KING HARALD GRÆNSKE'S DEATH [994–995].—Harald Grænske, as before related [p. 15], was king in

[1] " To the gods " is not in the text; the sacrifice was to the goddess (or ogress) Thorgerd Holgabrud and her sister Irpa. She was particularly associated with the district of Halogaland and with Earl Hakon, who had a temple with her image; she and Irpa are said to have raised the hailstorm. (See Saga of the Jomsvikings, pp. 36–8 and Appendix III.)

Westfold, and was married to Aasta, a daughter of Gudbrand Kula. One summer Harald Grænske made an expedition to the Baltic to gather property, and he came to Sweden. Olaf the Swede was king there, son of Eric the Victorious and Sigrid, a daughter of Skogul Toste. Sigrid was then a widow, and had many and great estates in Sweden. When she heard that her foster-brother was come to the country a short distance from her, she sent men to him to invite him to a feast. He did not neglect the invitation, but came to her with a great attendance of his followers, and was received in the most friendly way. He and the queen sat in the high seat, and drank together towards the evening, and all his men were entertained in the most hospitable manner. At night, when the king went to rest, a bed was put up for him with a hanging of fine linen around it, and with costly bed-clothes; but in the lodging-house there were few men. When the king was undressed, and had gone to bed, the queen came to him, filled a bowl herself for him to drink, and was very kind, and pressed him to drink. The king was drunk above measure, and, indeed, so were they both. Then he slept, and the queen went away, and laid herself down also. Sigrid was a woman of the greatest understanding, and too clever in many things. In the morning there was also the most excellent entertainment; but then it went on as usual when people have drunk too much, that next day they take care not to exceed. The queen was very gay, and she and the king talked of many things with each other; among other things she valued her property, and the dominions she had in Sweden, as nothing less than his kingdom and property in Norway. With that observation the king was nowise pleased; and he found no pleasure in anything after that, but made himself ready for his journey in an ill humour. On the other hand, the queen was remarkably gay, and made him many presents, and followed him out to the road. Now Harald returned about harvest to Norway, and was at home all winter; but was very silent, and cast-down.

In summer he went once more to the Baltic with his ships, and steered to Sweden. He sent a message to Queen Sigrid that he wished to have a meeting with her, and she rode down to meet him. They talked together, and he soon brought out the proposal that she should marry him. She replied, that this was foolish talk for him, who was so well married already that he might think himself well off. Harald says, "Aasta is a good and clever woman; but she is not so well born as I am." Sigrid replies, "It may be that thou art of higher birth, but I think she is now pregnant with both your fortunes."[1] They exchanged but few words more before the queen rode away. King Harald was then somewhat heavy-hearted, and prepared himself again to ride up the country to meet Queen Sigrid. Many of his people dissuaded him; but nevertheless he set off with a great attendance, and came to the house in which the queen dwelt. The same evening came another king, called Visavald,[2] from Russia, likewise to pay his addresses to Queen Sigrid. Lodging was given to both the kings, and to all their people, in a great old room of an outbuilding, and all the furniture was of the same character; but there was no want of drink in the evening, and that so strong that all were drunk, and the watch, both inside and outside, fell fast asleep. Then Queen Sigrid ordered an attack on them in the night, both with fire and sword. The house was burnt, with all who were in it, and those who slipped out were put to the sword. Sigrid said that she would make these small kings tired of coming to court her. She was afterwards called Sigrid the Haughty.

CHAPTER XLIX. BIRTH OF KING OLAF, SON OF KING HARALD GRÆNSKE.—This happened the winter after the battle of the Jomsburg vikings at Hiörunga-Vaag. When Harald went up the country after Sigrid, he left Rane behind with the ships to look after the men. Now when Rane heard that Harald was cut off, he returned to Norway the shortest way he could, and told the news. He repaired first to Aasta, and related to her all that had happened on the journey, and also on what errand Harald had visited Queen Sigrid. When Aasta got these tidings she set off directly to her father to the Uplands, who received her well; but both were enraged at the design which had been laid in Sweden, and that King Harald had intended to set her in a single condition. In summer Aasta, Gudbrand's daughter, was confined, and had a boy-child, who had water poured over him, and was called Olaf. Rane himself poured water over him, and the child was brought up at first in the house of Gudbrand and his mother Aasta.

CHAPTER L. ABOUT EARL HAKON.—Earl Hakon ruled over the whole outer part of Norway that lies on the sea, and had thus sixteen districts under his sway. The arrangement

[1] This refers to Saint Olaf, Aasta's son by Harald.
[2] i.e. Vsevolod; no such king is mentioned in Russian sources.

introduced by Harald Haarfager, that there should be an
earl in each district, was afterward continued for a long
time; and thus Earl Hakon had sixteen earls under him. So
says the Vellekla:—

> " Who before has ever known
> Sixteen earls' realms held by one?
> Who has seen all Norway's land
> Conquered by one brave hero's hand?
> Let the host whose lord he is
> Ponder in their hearts on this.
> The praise of warlike Hakon's worth
> Fills the four corners of the earth."

While Earl Hakon ruled over Norway there were good crops
in the land, and peace was well preserved in the country among
the bonders. The earl, for the greater part of his lifetime, was
therefore much beloved by the bonders; but it happened, in the
course of time, that the earl became very intemperate in his
intercourse with women, and even carried it so far that he made
the daughters of people of consideration be carried away, and
brought home to him; and after keeping them a week or two as
concubines, he sent them home. He drew upon himself the
indignation of the relations of these girls; and the bonders
began to murmur loudly, as the Drontheim people have the
custom of doing when anything goes against their judgment.

CHAPTER LI. THORE KLAKKE'S JOURNEY TO DISCOVER
OLAF TRYGVESSON.—Earl Hakon, in the meantime, hears some
whisper that to the westward, over the North Sea, was a man
called Ole, who was looked upon as a king. From the conversation of some people, he fell upon the suspicion that he must
be of the royal race of Norway. It was, indeed, said that this
Ole was from Russia; but the earl had heard that Trygve
Olafsson had had a son called Olaf, who in his infancy had gone
east to Russia, and had been brought up by King Valdemar.
The earl had carefully inquired about this man, and had his
suspicion that he must be the same person who had now come
to these western countries. The earl had a very good friend
called Thore Klakke, who had been long upon viking expeditions,
—sometimes also upon merchant voyages; so that he was well
acquainted all around. This Thore Earl Hakon sends over the
North Sea, and told him to make a merchant voyage to Dublin,
as many were in the habit of doing, and carefully to discover
who this Ole was. Provided he got any certainty that he was
Olaf Trygvesson, or any other of the Norwegian royal race, then

Thore should endeavour to ensnare him by some deceit, if he could do so.

CHAPTER LII. OLAF TRYGVESSON COMES TO NORWAY.—On this Thore sails westward to Ireland, and hears that Ole is in Dublin with his wife's father [1] King Olaf Kvaran. Thore, who was a plausible man, immediately got acquainted with Ole; and as they often met, and had long conversations together, Ole began to inquire about news from Norway, and above all of the Upland kings and great people,—which of them were in life, and what dominions they now had. He asked also about Earl Hakon, and if he was much liked in the country. Thore answers him, " The earl is such a powerful man that no one dares to speak otherwise than he would like; but that comes from there being nobody else in the country to look up to. Yet, to say the truth, I know it to be the mind of many brave men, and of whole communities, that they would much rather see a king of Harald Haarfager's race come to the kingdom. But we know of no one suited for this, especially now that it is proved how vain every attack on Earl Hakon must be." As they often talked together in the same strain, Ole disclosed to Thore his name and family, and asked him his opinion, and whether he thought the bonders would take him for their king if he were to appear in Norway. Thore encouraged him very eagerly to the enterprise, and praised him and his talents highly. Then Olaf's inclination to go to the heritage of his ancestors became strong. Olaf sailed accordingly, accompanied by Thore, with five ships; first to the Hebrides,[2] and from there to the Orkneys. At that time Earl Sigurd, Lodve's son, lay in Osmundswall,[3] in the island South Ronaldsa, with a ship of war, on his way to Caithness. Just at the same time Olaf was sailing with his fleet from the westward to the islands, and ran into the same harbour, because Pentland Firth was not to be passed at that tide. When the king was informed the earl was there, he made him be called; and when the earl came on board to speak with the king, after

---

[1] This is Laing's rendering of *mágr*, " kinsman by marriage," since he thought it chronologically more likely that Gyda was Olaf Kvaran's daughter rather than his sister; Snorri, however, must mean it as " brother-in-law " (*vide* p. 31).

[2] *Suðreyjar*, " Southern Isles "—so called in contrast to the other Norse colonies in the Orkneys and Faroes and in Iceland.

[3] Snorri here makes a slip, for really Osmundswall is the name of a harbour on that part of the island of Hoy which is now called Walls, opposite to (not in) South Ronaldshay, still used for waiting a tide favourable for crossing Pentland Firth.

a few words only had passed between them, the king says the earl must allow himself to be baptized, and all the people of the country also, or he should be put to death directly; and he assured the earl he would lay waste the islands with fire and sword, if the people did not adopt Christianity. In the position the earl found himself, he preferred becoming Christian, and he and all who were with him were baptized. Afterwards the earl took an oath to the king, went into his service, and gave him his son, whose name was Whelp, or Dog, as a hostage; and the king took Whelp to Norway with him. Thereafter Olaf went out to sea to the eastward, and made the land at Möster Island,[1] where he first touched the ground of Norway. He had high mass sung in a tent, and afterwards on the spot a church was built. Thore Klakke said now to the king, that the best plan for him would be not to make it known who he was or to let any report about him get abroad, but to seek out Earl Hakon as fast as possible and fall upon him by surprise. King Olaf did so, sailing northward day and night, when wind permitted, and did not let the people of the country know who it was that was sailing in such haste. When he came north to Agdaness,[2] he heard that the earl was in the fjord, and was in discord with the bonders. On hearing this, Thore saw that things were going in a very different way from what he expected; for after the battle with the Jomsburg vikings all men in Norway were the most sincere friends of the earl on account of the victory he had gained, and of the peace and security he had given to the country; and now it unfortunately turns out that a great chief has come to the country at a time when the bonders are in arms against the earl.

CHAPTER LIII. EARL HAKON'S FLIGHT.—Earl Hakon was at a feast in Medalhus in Guldal, but his ships lay out at Vigg.[3] There was a powerful bonder, by name Orm Lyrgia, who dwelt in Buness, who had a wife called Gudrun, a daughter of Bergthor of Lunde. She was called the Lunde-sun; for she was the most beautiful of women. The earl sent his slaves to Orm, with the errand that they should bring Orm's wife, Gudrun, to the earl. The thralls tell their errand, and Orm bids them first seat themselves for a supper; but before they had done eating, many people from the neighbourhood, to whom Orm had sent notice,

[1] In Söndhorland.
[2] Agdaness, the south point of the mouth of Trondheim fjord.
[3] Vigg, now Viggen in Börsen district on the Orkedalsfjord.

had gathered together: and now Orm declared he would not send Gudrun with the messengers. Gudrun told the thralls to tell the earl that she would not come to him, unless he sent Thora of Rimol [1] after her. Thora was a woman of great influence, and one of the earl's best beloved. The thralls say that they will come another time, and both the bonder and his wife would be made to repent of it; and they departed with many threats. Orm, on the other hand, sent out a message-token to all the neighbouring country, and with it the message to attack Earl Hakon with weapons and kill him. He sent also a message to Haldor in Skirdingsted,[2] who also sent out his message-token. A short time before, the earl had taken away the wife of a man called Bryniolf, and there had very nearly been an insurrection about that business. Having now again got this message-token, the people made a general revolt, and set out all to Medalhus. When the earl heard of this, he left the house with his followers, and concealed himself in a deep glen, now called Earl's Dale. Later in the day, the earl got news of the bonders' army. They had beset all the roads; but believed the earl had escaped to his ships, which his son Erlend, a remarkably handsome and hopeful young man, had the command of. When night came the earl dispersed his people, and ordered them to go through the forest roads into Orkedal; " for nobody will molest you," said he, " when I am not with you. Send a message to Erlend to sail out of the fjord, and meet me in Möre. In the meantime I will conceal myself from the bonders." Then the earl went his way with one thrall or slave, called Kark, attending him. There was ice upon the river of Guldal, and the earl drove his horse upon it, and left his cloak behind him there. They then went to a cave, since called the Earl's Hole, where they slept. When Kark awoke he told his dream,—that a black threatening man had come past the cave, and he was afraid lest this man should enter it; and that the man had said, " Ulle is dead." The earl said that his son Erlend must be killed. Kark slept again, and was again disturbed in his sleep; and when he awoke he told his dream,—that the same man had again appeared to him, and bade him tell the earl that all the Sounds were closed. From this dream the earl began to suspect that it betokened a short life to him. They stood up, and went to the house of Rimol. The earl now sends Kark to Thora, and begs of her to come

---

[1] Now Romol on the west bank of the river Gul opposite Melhus.
[2] Now Skerdingstad, south of Melhus.

secretly to him. She did so, and he took it very kind of her, and begged her to conceal him for a few nights until the army of the bonders had dispersed. "Here about my house," said she, "you will be hunted after, both inside and outside; for many know that I would willingly help you if I can. There is but one place about the house where they could never expect to find such a man as you, and that is the swine-stye." When they came there the earl said, "Well, let it be made ready for us; as to save our life is the first and foremost concern." The slave dug a great hole in it, bore away the earth that he dug out, and laid wood over it. Thora brought the tidings to the earl that Olaf Trygvesson had come from sea into the fjord, and had killed his son Erlend. Then the earl and Kark both went in the hole. Thora covered it with wood, and threw earth and dung over it, and drove the swine upon the top of it. The swine-stye was under a great stone.

CHAPTER LIV. ERLEND'S DEATH.—Olaf Trygvesson came from sea into the fjord with five long-ships, and Erlend, Earl Hakon's son, rowed towards him with three ships. When the vessels came near to each other, Erlend suspected they might be enemies, and turned towards the land. When Olaf and his followers saw long-ships coming in haste out of the fjord, and rowing towards them, they thought Earl Hakon must be here; and they put out all oars to follow them. As soon as Erlend and his ships got near the land they rowed aground instantly, jumped overboard, and took to the land; but at the same instant Olaf's ship came up with them. Olaf saw a remarkably handsome man swimming in the water, and laid hold of a tiller and threw it at him. The tiller struck Erlend, the son of Hakon the earl, on the head, and clove it to the brain; and there left Erlend his life. Olaf and his people killed many; but some escaped, and some were made prisoners, and got life and freedom that they might go and tell what had happened. They learned then that the bonders had driven away Earl Hakon, and that he had fled, and his troops were all dispersed.

CHAPTER LV. EARL HAKON'S DEATH.—The bonders then met Olaf, to the joy of both, and they made an agreement together. The bonders took Olaf to be their king, and resolved, one and all, to seek out Earl Hakon. They went up Guldal; for it seemed to them likely that if the earl was concealed in any house it must be at Rimol, for Thora was his dearest friend in that valley. They come up, therefore, and search everywhere, outside and inside the house, but could not find him. Then Olaf held a House Thing or council out in the yard, and stood upon a great stone which lay beside the swine-stye, and made a speech to the people, in which he promised to enrich the man with rewards and honours who should kill the earl. This speech was heard by the earl and the thrall Kark. They had a light in there with them.

" Why art thou so pale," says the earl, " and now again black as earth? Thou hast not the intention to betray me? "

" By no means," replies Kark.

" We were born on the same night," says the earl, " and the time will be short between our deaths."

King Olaf went away in the evening. When night came the earl kept himself awake; but Kark slept, and was disturbed in his sleep. The earl woke him, and asked him, " what he was dreaming of? "

He answered, " I was at Lade, and Olaf Trygvesson was laying a gold ring about my neck."

The earl says, " It will be a red ring Olaf will lay about thy neck if thou meetest him. Take care of that! From me thou shalt enjoy all that is good, therefore betray me not."

They then kept themselves awake both; the one, as it were, watching upon the other. But towards day the earl suddenly dropped asleep; but his sleep was so unquiet that he drew his heels under him, and raised his neck, as if going to rise, and screamed dreadfully high. On this Kark, dreadfully alarmed, drew a large knife out of his belt, stuck it in the earl's throat, and cut it across, and killed Earl Hakon. Then Kark cut off the earl's head, and ran away. Late in the day he came to Lade, where he delivered the earl's head to King Olaf, and told all these circumstances of his own and Earl Hakon's doings. Olaf had him taken out and beheaded.

CHAPTER LVI. EARL HAKON'S HEAD.—King Olaf, and a vast number of bonders with him, then went out to Nidarholm,[1] and had with them the heads of Earl Hakon and Kark. This holm was used then for a place of execution of thieves and ill-doers, and there stood a gallows on it. He had the heads of the earl and of Kark hung upon it, and the whole army of the bonders cast stones at them, screaming and shouting that the one worthless fellow had followed the other. They then sent up to

[1] Now Munkholm, opposite to the town of Tr ndheim.

Guldal for the earl's dead body. So great was the enmity of the Drontheim people against Earl Hakon, that no man could venture to call him by any other name than Hakon the Bad; and he was so called long after those days. Yet, sooth to say of Earl Hakon, he was in many respects fitted to be a chief: first, because he was descended from a high race; then because he had understanding and knowledge to direct a government; also manly courage in battle, and good luck in victories and in killing his enemies. So says Thorleif Raudfeldson:—

> " In Norway's land was never known
> A braver earl than the brave Hakon.
> Under the sky, the moon's highway,
> No braver man e'er sought the fray.
> Nine kings to Odin's wide domain
> Were sent, by Hakon's right hand slain!
> So well the raven-flocks were fed—
> And thus thy power fills men with dread."

Earl Hakon was very generous; but the greatest misfortunes attended even such a chief at the end of his days: and the great cause of this was that the time was come when heathen sacrifices and idolatrous worship were doomed to fall, and the holy faith and good customs to come in their place.

CHAPTER LVII. OLAF TRYGVESSON ELECTED KING AT A GENERAL THING [996].—Olaf Trygvesson was chosen at Drontheim by the General Thing to be the king over the whole country, as Harald Haarfager had been. The whole public and the people throughout all the land would listen to nothing else than that Olaf Trygvesson should be king. Then Olaf went round the whole country, and brought it under his rule, and all the people of Norway gave in their submission; and also the chiefs in the Uplands and in Viken, who before had held their lands as fiefs from the Danish king, now became King Olaf's men, and held their lands from him. He went thus through the whole country during the first winter and the following summer. Earl Eric, the son of Earl Hakon, his brother Swend, and their friends and relations, fled out of the country, and went east to Sweden to King Olaf the Swede, who gave them a good reception. So says Thord Kolbeinson:—

> " O thou that huntest outlaw bands,
> How swiftly once did treason's hands
> Take Hakon's life! Thus destined fate
> Can rule men's lives; its power is great.
> When the host came from out the west
> Came Trygve's son among the rest,
> Seeking the land which Hakon's might
> Had won and held in every fight."

And again:—

> " Eric has more upon his mind,
> Against the new Norse king designed,
> Than by his words he seems to show—
> And truly it may well be so.
> Stubborn and stiff are Drontheim men,
> But Drontheim's earl in wrath has gone
> To seek advice from Sweden's king;
> No man can turn him from this thing."

CHAPTER LVIII. LODEN'S MARRIAGE.—Loden was the name of a man from Vigg who was rich and of good family. He went often on merchant voyages, and sometimes on viking cruises. It happened one summer that he went on a merchant voyage with much merchandise in a ship of his own. He directed his course first to Esthonia, and was there at a market in summer. To the place at which the market was held many merchant goods were brought, and also may thralls or slaves for sale. There Loden saw a woman who was to be sold as a slave; and on looking at her he knew her to be Astrid, Eric's daughter, who had been married to King Trygve. But now she was altogether unlike what she had been when he last saw her; for now she was pale, meagre in countenance, and ill clad. He went up to her, and asked her how matters stood with her. She replied, " It is heavy to be told; for I have been sold as a slave, and now again I am brought here for sale." After speaking together a little Astrid knew him, and begged him to buy her, and bring her home to her kinsmen. " On this condition," said he, " I will bring thee home to Norway,—that thou wilt marry me." Now as Astrid stood in great need, and moreover knew that Loden was a man of high birth, rich, and brave, she promised to do so for her ransom. Loden accordingly bought Astrid, took her home to Norway with him, and married her with her kinsmen's consent. Their children were Thorkel Nefia, Ingerid, and Ingegerd. Ingebjorg and Astrid were daughters of Astrid by King Trygve. Eric Biodaskalle's sons were Sigurd Karlshoved, Jostein, and Thorkel Dyrdel, who were all rich and brave people who had estates east in the country. In Viken, in the east, dwelt two brothers, rich and of good descent; one called Thorgeir, and the other Hyrning; and they married Loden and Astrid's daughters, Ingerid and Ingegerd.

CHAPTER LIX. KING OLAF BAPTIZES THE COUNTRY OF VIKEN. — When Harald Gormson, king of Denmark, had adopted Christianity, he sent a message over all his kingdom that all people should be baptized, and converted to the true faith. He himself followed his message, and used power and violence where nothing else would do. He sent two earls, Urguthriot and Brimiskjar, with many people to Norway, to proclaim Christianity there. In Viken, which stood directly under the king's power, this succeeded, and many were baptized of the country folk. But when Swend Forked-beard, immediately after his father King Harald's death, went out on war expeditions in Saxonland, Friesland, and at last in England, the Northmen who had taken up Christianity returned back to heathen sacrifices, just as before; and the people in the north of the country did the same. But now that Olaf Trygvesson was king of Norway, he remained long during the summer in Viken, where many of his relatives and some of his brothers-in-law were settled, and also many who had been great friends of his father; so that he was received with the greatest affection. Olaf called together his mother's brothers, his stepfather Loden, and his brothers-in-law Thorgeir and Hyrning, to speak with them, and to disclose with the greatest zeal the business which he desired they should undertake with him, and support with all their power; namely, proclaiming Christianity over all his kingdom. He would, he declared, either bring it to this, that all Norway should be Christian, or die. "I shall make you all," said he, "great and mighty men in promoting this work; for I trust to you most, as blood relations or brothers-in-law." All agreed to do what he asked, and to assist him in what he desired. King Olaf immediately made it known to the public that he recommended Christianity to all the people in his kingdom, which message was well received and approved of by those who had before given him their promise; and these being the most powerful among the people assembled, the others followed their example, and all the inhabitants of the east part of Viken allowed themselves to be baptized. The king then went to the north part of Viken, and invited every man to accept Christianity; and those who opposed him he punished severely, killing some, mutilating others, and driving some into banishment. At length he brought it so far, that all the kingdom which his father King Trygve had ruled over, and also that of his relation Harald Grænske, accepted of Christianity; and during that summer and the following winter all Viken was made Christian.

CHAPTER LX. OF THE HORDALAND PEOPLE [997].—Early in spring King Olaf set out from Viken with a great force westwards to Agder, and proclaimed that every man should be baptized. And thus the people received Christianity, for nobody dared oppose the king's will, wheresoever he came. In Hordaland, however, were many bold and great men of Horda-Kaare's race. He, namely, had left four sons,—the first Thorleif Spaake; the second, Ogmund father of Thorolf Skialg, who was father of Erling of Sole;[1] the third was Thord, father of Herse Klyp who killed Sigurd Sleve Gunhild's son; and lastly, Olmod[2] father of Askel, whose son was Aslak Fitiaskalle; and that family branch was the greatest and most considered in Hordaland. Now when this family heard the bad tidings, that the king was coming along the country from the eastward with a great force, and was breaking the ancient law of the people, and imposing punishment and hard conditions on all who opposed him, the relatives appointed a meeting to take counsel with each other, for they knew the king would come down upon them at once; and they all resolved to appear in force at the Gula Thing, there to hold a conference with King Olaf Trygvesson.

CHAPTER LXI. ROGALAND BAPTIZED. — When King Olaf came to Rogaland, he immediately summoned the people to a Thing; and when the bonders received the message-token for a Thing, they assembled in great numbers well armed. After they had come together, they resolved to choose three men, the best speakers of the whole, who should answer King Olaf, and argue with the king; and especially should decline to accept of anything against the old law, even if the king should require it of them. Now when the bonders came to the Thing, and the Thing was formed, King Olaf arose, and at first spoke good-humouredly to the people; but they observed he wanted them to accept Christianity, with all his fine words: and in the conclusion he let them know that those who should speak against him, and not submit to his proposal, must expect his displeasure and punishment, and all the ill that it was in his power to inflict. When he had ended his speech, one of the bonders stood up, who was considered the most eloquent, and who had been chosen as the first who should reply to King Olaf. But when he would begin to speak such a cough seized him, and such a difficulty of breathing, that he could not bring out a word, and had to sit down again. Then another bonder stood up,

[1] Now Kirkesole in the district of Haaland south of Stavanger.
[2] Probably the same man as Olmod the Old.

resolved not to let an answer be wanting, although it had gone
so ill with the former; but he stammered so badly that he could
not find a word to say, and all present set up a laughter, amid
which the bonder sat down again. And now the third stood up
to make a speech against King Olaf's; but when he began he
became so hoarse and husky in his throat, that nobody could
hear a word he said, and he also had to sit down. There was
none of the bonders now to speak against the king, and as
nobody answered him there was no opposition; and it came to
this, that all agreed to what the king had proposed. All the
people of the Thing accordingly were baptized before the Thing
was dissolved.

CHAPTER LXII. ERLING SKIALGSSON'S WOOING.—King Olaf
went with his men-at-arms to the Gula Thing; for the bonders
had sent him word that they would reply there to his speech.
When both parties had come to the Thing, the king desired first
to have a conference with the chief people of the country; and
when the meeting was numerous the king set forth his errand,—
that he desired them, according to his proposal, to allow themselves to be baptized. Then said Olmod the Old, "We relations
have considered together this matter, and have come to one
resolution. If thou thinkest, king, to force us who are related
together to such things as to break our old law or to bring us
under thyself by any sort of violence, then will we stand against
thee with all our might: and be the victory to him to whom
fate ordains it. But if thou, king, wilt advance our relations'
fortunes, then thou shalt have leave to do as thou desirest, and
we will all serve thee with zeal in thy purpose."

The king replies, "What do ye propose for obtaining this
agreement?"

Then answers Olmod, "The first is, that thou wilt give
thy sister Astrid in marriage to Erling Skialgsson, our relation,
whom we look upon as the most hopeful young man in all
Norway."

King Olaf replied, that this marriage appeared to him also
very suitable; "as Erling is a man of good birth, and a good-
looking man in appearance: but Astrid herself must answer to
this proposal."

Thereupon the king spoke to his sister. She said, "It is but
of little use that I am a king's sister, and a king's daughter, if I
must marry a man who has no high dignity or office. I will
rather wait a few years for a better match."

CHAPTER LXIII. HORDALAND BAPTIZED.—King Olaf took a falcon that belonged to Astrid, plucked off all its feathers, and then sent it to her. Then said Astrid, " Angry is my brother." And she stood up, and went to the king, who received her kindly; and she said, that she left it to the king to determine her marriage. " I think," said the king, " that I must have power enough in this land to raise any man I please to high dignity." Then the king ordered Olmod and Erling to be called to a conference, and all their relations; and the marriage was determined upon, and Astrid betrothed to Erling. Thereafter the king held the Thing, and recommended Christianity to the bonders; and as Olmod, and Erling, and all their relations, took upon themselves the most active part in forwarding the king's desire, nobody dared to speak against it; and all the people were baptized, and adopted Christianity.

CHAPTER LXIV. ERLING SKIALGSSON'S WEDDING.—Erling Skialgsson held his wedding in summer, and a great many people were assembled at it. King Olaf was also there, and offered Erling an earldom. Erling replied thus: " All my relations have been hersers only, and I will take no higher title than they have; but this I will accept from thee, king, that thou makest me the greatest of that title in the country." The king consented; and at his departure the king invested his brother-in-law Erling with all the land north of the Sogn fjord, and east to the Lidandisness,[1] on the same terms as Harald Haarfager had given land to his sons,[2] as has been written already.

CHAPTER LXV. RAUMSDAL AND THE FJORDS BAPTIZED. —The same harvest King Olaf summoned the bonders to a Thing of the four districts at Dragseid, in Stad; and there the people from Sogn, the Fjords district, South Möre, and Raumsdal were summoned to meet. King Olaf came there with a great many people who had followed him from the eastward, and also with those who had joined him from Rogaland and Hordaland. When the king came to the Thing, he proposed to them there, as elsewhere, Christianity; and as the king had such a powerful host with him, they were frightened. The king offered them two conditions,—either to accept Christianity, or to fight. But the bonders saw they were in no condition

---

[1] *i.e.* the Naze of Norway, Lindesnes (*vide* p. 15, n. 3). The region Erling got was Hordaland, Rogaland, and the west portion of Agder.
[2] See *Sagas of the Norse Kings*, p. 76.

to fight the king, and resolved, therefore, that all the people should agree to be baptized. The king proceeded afterwards to North Möre, and baptized all that district. He then sailed to Lade, in Drontheim; had the temple there razed to the ground; took all the ornaments and all property out of the temple, and from the gods in it; and among other things the great gold ring which Earl Hakon had ordered to be made, and which hung in the door of the temple; and then had the temple burnt. But when the bonders heard of this, they sent out a war-arrow as a token through the whole district, ordering out a warlike force, and intended to meet the king with it. In the meantime King Olaf sailed with a war-force out of the fjord along the coast northward, intending to proceed to Halogaland, and baptize there. When he came north to Björnör,[1] he heard from Halogaland that a force was assembled there to defend the country against the king. The chiefs of this force were Harek of Thiotto,[2] Thore Hiort from Vaage,[3] and Eyvind Kinnrif. Now when King Olaf heard this, he turned about and sailed southwards along the land; and when he got south of Stad proceeded at his leisure, and came early in winter all the way east to Viken.

CHAPTER LXVI. KING OLAF PROPOSES MARRIAGE TO QUEEN SIGRID THE HAUGHTY.—Queen Sigrid in Sweden, who had for surname the Haughty, sat in her mansion, and during the same winter messengers went between King Olaf and Sigrid to propose his courtship to her, and she had no objection; and the matter was fully and fast resolved upon. Thereupon King Olaf sent to Queen Sigrid the great gold ring he had taken from the temple door of Lade, which was considered a distinguished ornament. The meeting for concluding the business was appointed to be in spring on the frontier, at the Gotha river. Now the ring which King Olaf had sent Queen Sigrid was highly prized by all men; yet the queen's goldsmiths, two brothers, who took the ring in their hands, and weighed it, spoke quietly to each other about it, and so then the queen had them summoned, and asked why they sneered at the ring. But they would not say a word, and she commanded them to say what it was they had discovered. Then they said the ring was false. Upon this she ordered the ring to be broken in pieces, and it

---

[1] Now Roan, the most northerly district in Nordmore.
[2] Now Töjttö south of Alstahaug in Helgeland.
[3] Now Vaagan on the island of Vaag in Lofoten.

was found to be copper inside. Then the queen was enraged, and said that Olaf would deceive her in more ways than this one. In the same year King Olaf went into Ringerike, and there the people also were baptized.

CHAPTER LXVII. OLAF HARALDSSON BAPTIZED.—Aasta, the daughter of Gudbrand, soon after the fall of Harald Grænske married again a man who was called Sigurd Syr,[1] who was a king in Ringerike. Sigurd was a son of Halfdan, and grandson of Sigurd Rise, who was a son of Harald Haarfager. Olaf, the son of Aasta and Harald Grænske, lived with Aasta, and was brought up from childhood in the house of his stepfather, Sigurd Syr. Now when King Olaf Trygvesson came to Ringerike to spread Christianity, Sigurd Syr and his wife allowed themselves to be baptized, along with Olaf her son; and Olaf Trygvesson was godfather to Olaf, the stepson of Harald Grænske. Olaf was then three years old.[2] King Olaf returned from thence to Viken, where he remained all winter. He had now been three years king in Norway.

CHAPTER LXVIII. MEETING OF KING OLAF AND SIGRID THE HAUGHTY AT KONGHELLE [998].—Early in spring King Olaf went eastwards to Konghelle to have a meeting with Queen Sigrid; and when they met the business was considered about which the winter before they had held communication, namely, their marriage; and the business seemed likely to be concluded. But when Olaf insisted that Sigrid should let herself be baptized, she answered thus:—" I must not part from the faith which I have held, and my forefathers before me; and, on the other hand, I shall make no objection to your believing in the god that pleases you best." Then King Olaf was enraged, and answered in a passion, " Why should I care to have thee, an old faded woman, and a heathen bitch? " and therewith struck her in the face with his glove which he held in his hands, rose, and then they parted. Sigrid said, " This may well be thy death." The king set off to Viken, the queen to Sweden.

CHAPTER LXIX. THE BURNING OF WARLOCKS.—Then the king proceeded to Tunsberg, and held a Thing, at which he

[1] Syr, i.e. Sow. He was so called because he " nosed about and rooted up the ground," i.e. was a farmer. Vide also p. 138.
[2] This is not historic. Olaf the Saint was first baptized as a full-grown man in Normandy (vide St. Olaf's Saga, chap. xix., p. 129). The " pouring of water " mentioned on p. 44 was a heathen, not a Christian, ceremony.

declared in a speech that all the men of whom it should be
known to a certainty that they dealt with evil spirits, or in
witchcraft, or were sorcerers, should be banished forth of the
land. Thereafter the king had all the neighbourhood ransacked
after such people, and called them all before him; and when
they were brought to the Thing there was a man among them
called Eyvind Kellda, a grandson of Rognvald Rettilbein,[1]
Harald Haarfager's son. Eyvind was a sorcerer, and particularly knowing in witchcraft. The king let all these men be
seated in one room, which was well adorned, and made a great
feast for them, and gave them strong drink in plenty. Now
when they were all very drunk, he ordered the house to be set
on fire, and it and all the people within it were consumed, all
but Eyvind Kellda, who contrived to escape by the smoke-hole
in the roof. And when he had got a long way off, he met some
people on the road going to the king, and he told them to tell
the king that Eyvind Kellda had slipped away from the fire,
and would never come again in King Olaf's power, but would
carry on his arts of witchcraft as much as ever. When the
people came to the king with such a message from Eyvind, the
king was ill pleased that Eyvind had escaped death.

CHAPTER LXX. EYVIND KELLDA'S DEATH.—When spring
came King Olaf went out to Viken, and was on visits to his great
farms. He sent notice over all Viken that he would call out
an army in summer, and proceed to the north parts of the
country. Then he went west to Agder; and when Lent was
almost over he took the road to Rogaland with 300 (*i.e.* 360)
men, and came on Easter Saturday north to Augvaldsness, in
Kormt Island, where an Easter feast was prepared for him.
That same night came Eyvind Kellda to the island with a well-
manned long-ship, of which the whole crew consisted of sorcerers,
and other dealers with evil spirits. Eyvind went from his ship
to the land with his followers, and there they put forth the
powers of their witchcraft. Eyvind clothed them with caps
of darkness, and so thick a mist that the king and his men could
see nothing of them; but when they came near to the house of
Augvaldsness, it became clear day. Then it went differently
from what Eyvind had intended; for now there came just such a
darkness over him and his comrades in witchcraft as they had
made before, so that they could see no more from their eyes than

[1] Rognvald was a wizard, and son of a Lapland witch; his own father
burnt him to death (*Sagas of the Norse Kings*, pp. 69–70, 77).

from the back of their heads, but went round and round in a circle upon the island. When the king's watchmen saw them going about, without knowing what people these were, they told the king. Thereupon he rose up with his people, put on his clothes, and when he saw Eyvind with his men wandering about he ordered his men to arm, and examine what folk these were. The king's men discovered it was Eyvind, took him and all his company prisoners, and brought them to the king. Eyvind now told all he had done on his journey. Then the king ordered them all to be taken out to a skerry which was under water in flood tide, and there to be left bound. Eyvind and all with him left their lives on this rock, and the skerry is still called the Skerry of Warlocks.[1]

CHAPTER LXXI. OF KING OLAF AND ODIN'S APPARITION.—It is related that once on a time King Olaf was at a feast at this Augvaldsness, and one eventide there came to him an old man very gifted in words, and with a broad-brimmed hat upon his head. He was one-eyed, and had something to tell of every land. He entered into conversation with the king; and as the king found much pleasure in the guest's speech, he asked him concerning many things, to which the guest gave good answers: and the king sat up late in the evening. Among other things, the king asked him if he knew who the Augvald had been who had given his name both to the ness and to the house. The guest replied, that this Augvald was a king, and a very valiant man, and that he made great sacrifices to a cow which he had with him wherever he went, and considered it good for his health to drink her milk. "This same King Augvald had a battle with a king called Varen, in which battle Augvald fell. He was buried under a mound close to the house; and memorial stones set up; and in another spot close by the cow was buried." Such and many other things he told, about kings, or about ancient events. Now when the king had sat late into the night, the bishop reminded him that it was time to go to bed, and the king did so. But after the king was undressed, and had laid himself in bed, the guest sat upon the footstool before the bed, and still spoke long with the king; for after one tale was ended, he still wanted a new one. Then the bishop observed to the king it was time to go to sleep, and the king did so; and the guest went out. Soon after the king awoke, asked for the guest, and ordered him to be called; but the guest was not to be found. The morning after, the king

[1] *Skrattasker*; the place has not been identified.

ordered his cook and cellar-master to be called, and asked if any strange person had been with them. They said, that as they were making ready the meat a man came to them, and observed that they were cooking very poor meat for the king's table; whereupon he gave them two thick and fat pieces of beef, which they boiled with the rest of the meat. Then the king ordered that all the meat should be thrown away, and said this man can be no other than the Odin whom the heathen have so long worshipped; and added, " but Odin[1] shall not deceive us."

CHAPTER LXXII. THE THING IN DRONTHEIM.—King Olaf collected a great army in the east of the country towards summer, and sailed with it north to Nidaros[2] in the Drontheim country. From thence he sent a message-token over all the fjord, calling the people of eight different districts to a Thing at Froste ; but the bonders changed the Thing-token into a war-token,[3] and called together all men, free and unfree,[4] in all the Drontheim land. Now when the king met the Thing, the whole people came fully armed. After the Thing was seated, the king spoke, and invited them to adopt Christianity; but he had only spoken a short time when the bonders called out to him to be silent, or they would attack him and drive him away. " We did so," said they, " with Hakon foster-son of Athelstan, when he brought us the same message, and we held him in quite as much respect as we hold thee." When King Olaf saw how incensed the bonders were, and that they had such a war force that he could make no resistance, he turned his speech as if he would give way to the bonders, and said, " I wish only to be in a good understanding with you as of old; and I will come to where ye hold your greatest sacrifice-festival, and see your customs, and thereafter we shall consider which to hold by, and all agree on this. " And as the king spoke mildly and friendly with the bonders, their anger was appeased, and their conference

---

[1] This description of Odin disguised as a wanderer recurs in many stories; the word *gestr* (" stranger," " guest ") is itself one of his many names. The disguised Odin often challenges his host to compete in knowledge of myths and legends; defeat may entail death. This motif probably originates in Odin's ancient role as god of the Underworld, of magic and esoteric lore, and of initiation rites; in later sources it becomes a mere framework for story-telling, riddle contests, and the like. Snorri seems to imply that the meat Odin brings is taboo to a Christian; perhaps it is sacrificial meat.

[2] The mouth of the river Nid. Nidaros is the old name for Trondhjem.

[3] Arrows were sent round to summon men to a Thing (Assembly), or to war; only in the latter case would they bring arms. The difference between Thing-token and war-arrow may have been a cord, tied to the latter.

[4] *Þegn ok þræll*; here *þegn* means any free man, landowner (*bondi*) or not.

with the king went off peacefully. At the close of it a mid-summer sacrifice was fixed to take place in Mære,[1] and all chiefs and great bonders were to attend it as usual. The king was to be at it.

CHAPTER LXXIII. OF SKIÆGGE, OR IRON BEARD.—There was a great bonder called Skiægge, and sometimes Iron Skiægge, or Iron Beard, who dwelt in Ophaug in Yriar.[2] He spoke first at the Thing to Olaf; and was the foremost man of the bonders in speaking against Christianity. The Thing was concluded in this way for that time,—the bonders returned home, and the king went to Lade.

CHAPTER LXXIV. THE FEAST AT LADE.—King Olaf lay with his ships in the river Nid, and had thirty vessels, which were manned with many brave people; but the king himself was often at Lade with his court attendants. As the time now was approaching at which the sacrifices should be made at Mære, the king prepared a great feast at Lade, and sent a message to the districts of Strind, Guldal, and out to Orkadal, to invite the chiefs and other great bonders. When the feast was ready, and the chiefs assembled, there was a handsome entertainment the first evening, at which plenty of liquor went round, and the guests were made very drunk. The night after they all slept in peace. The following morning, when the king was dressed, he had matins and mass sung before him; and when the mass was over, ordered to sound the trumpets for a House Thing; upon which all his men left the ships to come up to the Thing. When the Thing was seated, the king stood up, and spoke thus:—
" We held a Thing at Froste, and there I invited the bonders to allow themselves to be baptized; but they, on the other hand, invited me to offer sacrifice to their gods, as King Hakon, Athelstan's foster-son, had done; and thereafter it was agreed upon between us that we should meet at Mære, and there make a great sacrifice. Now if I, along with you, shall turn again to making sacrifice, then will I make the greatest of sacrifices that are in use; and I will sacrifice men. But I will not select slaves or malefactors for this, but will take the greatest men only to be offered to the gods; and for this I select Orm Lygra of Medalhus, Styrkar of Gimsar, Kaare of Gryting, Asbiorn Thorbergson of

---

[1] At Mære, the site of the ancient temple in the Drontheim district, a large mound still remains with the name Mære.
[2] Orlandet at the entrance to the Trondhjemfjord.

Varness, Orm of Ljoxa, Haldor of Skirdingsted;" and besides these he named five others of the principal men. All these, he said, he would offer in sacrifice to the gods for peace and a fruitful season; and ordered them to be laid hold of immediately. Now when the bonders saw that they were not strong enough to make head against the king, they asked for peace, and submitted wholly to the king's pleasure. So it was settled that all the bonders who had come there should be baptized, and should take an oath to the king to hold by the right faith, and to renounce sacrifice to the gods. The king then kept all these men as hostages who came to his feast, until they sent him their sons, brothers, or other near relations.

CHAPTER LXXV. OF THE THING IN DRONTHEIM.—King Olaf went in with all his forces into the Drontheim country; and when he came to Mære, all among the chiefs of the Drontheim people who were most opposed to Christianity were assembled, and had with them all the great bonders who had before made sacrifice at that place. There was thus a greater multitude of bonders than there had been at the Froste Thing. Now the king let the people be summoned to the Thing, where both parties met armed; and when the Thing was seated the king made a speech, in which he told the people to go over to Christianity. Jern Skiægge (Iron Beard) replies on the part of the bonders, and says that the will of the bonders is now, as formerly, that the king should not break their laws. "We want, king," said he, "that thou shouldst offer sacrifice, as other kings before thee have done." All the bonders applauded his speech with a loud shout, and said they would have all things according to what Jern Skiægge said. Then the king said he would go into the temple of their gods with them, and see what the practices were when they sacrificed. The bonders thought well of this proceeding, and both parties went to the temple.

CHAPTER LXXVI. THE DRONTHEIM PEOPLE BAPTIZED.— Now King Olaf entered into the temple with some few of his men and a few bonders; and when the king came to where their gods were, Thor, as the most considered among their gods, sat there adorned with gold and silver. The king lifted up his gold-inlaid axe which he carried in his hands, and struck Thor so that the image rolled down from its seat. Then the king's men turned to and threw down all the gods from their seats; and while the king was in the temple, Jern Skiægge was killed outside of the temple doors, and the king's men did it. When the king came forth out of the temple he offered the bonders two conditions,—that all should accept of Christianity forthwith, or that they should fight with him. But as Jern Skiægge was killed, there was no leader in the bonders' army to raise the banner against King Olaf; so they took the other condition, to surrender to the king's will and obey his order. Then King Olaf had all the people present baptized, and took hostages from them for their remaining true to Christianity; and he sent his men round to every district, and no man in the Drontheim country opposed Christianity, but all people took baptism.

CHAPTER LXXVII. OF THE BUILDING OF THE TOWN IN THE DRONTHEIM COUNTRY.—King Olaf with his people went out to Nidaros, and made houses on the flat side of the river Nid, which he raised to be a merchant town, and gave people ground to build houses upon. The king's house he had built just opposite Skipakroken;[1] and he transported to it, in harvest, all that was necessary for his winter residence, and had many people about him there.

CHAPTER LXXVIII. KING OLAF'S MARRIAGE.—King Olaf appointed a meeting with the relations of Jern Skiægge, and offered them the compensation or penalty for his bloodshed; for there were many bold men who had an interest in that business. Jern Skiægge had a daughter called Gudrun; and at last it was agreed upon between the parties that the king should take her in marriage. When the wedding-day came King Olaf and Gudrun went to bed together. As soon as Gudrun, the first night they lay together, thought the king was asleep, she drew a knife, with which she intended to run him through; but the king saw it, took the knife from her, got out of bed, and went to his men, and told them what had happened. Gudrun also took her clothes and went away along with all her men who had followed her thither. Gudrun never came into the king's bed again.

CHAPTER LXXIX. BUILDING OF THE SHIP CRANE.—The same autumn King Olaf laid the keel of a great long-ship out on the strand at the river Nid. It was a snække;[2] and he employed

[1] A small creek on the west bank of the river Nid at the end of the present Strandgade (Shore Street) in Trondhjem.
[2] Snekkja, a smaller and faster type of long-ship, as contrasted with the dreki, " dragon."

many carpenters upon her, so that early in winter the vessel was ready. It had thirty benches for rowers, was high in stem and stern, but was not broad. The king called this ship the Crane. After Jern Skiægge's death his body was carried to Yriar, and lies there in the Skiægge mound on Austraatt.[1]

CHAPTER LXXX. THANGBRAND THE PRIEST GOES TO ICELAND [997].—When King Olaf Trygvesson had been two years king of Norway, there was a Saxon priest in his house who was called Thangbrand, a passionate, ungovernable man, and a great man-slayer; but he was a good scholar, and a clever man. The king would not have him in his house upon account of his misdeeds; but gave him the errand to go to Iceland, and bring that land to the Christian faith.[2] The king gave him a merchant vessel; and, as far as we know of this voyage of his, he landed first in Iceland at Ostfjord, in the southern Alptafjord, and passed the winter in the house of Hall of Sida.[3] Thangbrand proclaimed Christianity in Iceland, and on his persuasion Hall and all his house-people, and many other chiefs, allowed themselves to be baptized; but there were many more who spoke against it. Thorvald Veile and Veterlide the scald composed a satire about Thangbrand; but he killed them both outright.[4] Thangbrand was two years in Iceland, and was the death of three men before he left it.

CHAPTER LXXXI. OF SIGURD AND HAUK.—There was a man called Sigurd, and another called Hauk, both of Halogaland, who often made merchant voyages. One summer they had made a voyage westward to England; and when they came back to Norway they sailed northwards along the coast, and at North Möre they met King Olaf's people. When it was told the king that some Halogaland people were come who were heathen, he ordered the steersmen to be brought to him, and he asked them if they would consent to be baptized; to which they replied, no.

---

[1] The present farm Östraat; two mounds near it are both so named.

[2] Thangbrand's mission is described in Ari's *Íslendingabok* (*The Book of the Icelanders*, Halldór Hermannsson, *Islandica*, XX; 1930), in *Njáls Saga* (*The Story of Burnt Njal*), and elsewhere. An earlier attempt to convert Iceland had been made between 981 and 985 by a German, Bishop Frederick, and an Icelander named Thorvald whom he had converted abroad. Olaf himself had already sent one unsuccessful missionary in 996.

[3] Hall was one of the leading chieftains; he lived at Thvatta in Alptafjord, but is always named after his earlier home, Sida.

[4] A satire or lampoon (*nið*) was not merely a grave insult, but was thought to cause actual harm to its victim by magical means.

The king spoke with them in many ways, but to no purpose. He then threatened them with death and torture; but they would not allow themselves to be moved. He then had them laid in irons, and kept them in chains in his house for some time, and often conversed with them, but in vain. At last one night they disappeared, without any man being able to conjecture how they got away. But about harvest they came north to Harek of Thiotto, who received them kindly, and with whom they stopped all winter, and were hospitably entertained.

CHAPTER LXXXII. OF HAREK OF THIOTTO.—It happened one good-weather day in spring that Harek was at home in his house with only few people, and time hung heavy on his hands. Sigurd asked him if he would row a little for amusement. Harek was willing; and they went to the shore, and drew down a six-oared skiff; and Sigurd took the mast and rigging belonging to the boat out of the boathouse, for they often used to sail when they went for amusement on the water. Harek went out into the boat to hang the rudder. The brothers Sigurd and Hauk, who were very strong men, were fully armed, as they were used to go about at home among the peasants. Before they went out to the boat they threw into her some butter-kits and a bread-chest, and carried between them a great keg of ale. When they had rowed a short way from the island the brothers hoisted the sail, while Harek was seated at the helm; and they sailed away from the island. Then the two brothers went aft to where Harek the bonder was sitting; and Sigurd says to him, " Now thou must choose one of these conditions,—first, that we brothers direct this voyage; or, if not, that we bind thee fast and take the command; or, third, that we kill thee." Harek saw how matters stood with him. As a single man, he was not better than one of those brothers, even if he had been as well armed; so it appeared to him wisest to let them determine the course to steer, and bound himself by oath to abide by this condition. On this Sigurd took the helm, and steered south along the land, the brothers taking particular care that they did not encounter people. The wind was very favourable; and they held on sailing along until they came south to Drontheim and to Nidaros, where they found the king. Then the king called Harek to him, and in a conference desired him to be baptized. Harek made objections; and although the king and Harek talked over it many times, sometimes in the presence of other people, and sometimes alone, they could not agree upon it.

At last the king says to Harek, " Now thou mayst return home, and I will do thee no injury; partly because we are related together, and partly that thou mayst not have it to say that I caught thee by a trick: but know for certain that I intend to come north next summer to visit you Halogalanders, and ye shall then see if I am not able to punish those who reject Christianity." Harek was well pleased to get away as fast as he could. King Olaf gave Harek a good boat of ten or twelve pair of oars, and let it be fitted out with the best of everything needful; and besides he gave Harek thirty men, all lads of mettle, and well appointed.

CHAPTER LXXXIII. EYVIND KINNRIF'S DEATH.—Harek of Thiotto went away from the town as fast as he could; but Hauk and Sigurd remained in the king's house, and both took baptism. Harek pursued his voyage until he came to Thiotto. He sent immediately a message to his friend Eyvind Kinnrif, with the word that he had been with King Olaf; but would not let himself be cowed down to accept Christianity. The message at the same time informed him that King Olaf intended coming to the north in summer against them, and they must be at their posts to defend themselves; it also begged Eyvind to come and visit him, the sooner the better. When this message was delivered to Eyvind, he saw how very necessary it was to devise some counsel to avoid falling into the king's hands. He set out, therefore, in a light vessel with a few hands as fast as he could. When he came to Thiotto he was received by Harek in the most friendly way, and they immediately entered into conversation with each other behind the house. When they had spoken together but a short time, King Olaf's men, who had secretly followed Harek to the north, came up, and took Eyvind prisoner, and carried him away to their ship. They did not halt on their voyage until they came to Drontheim, and presented themselves to King Olaf at Nidaros. Then Eyvind was brought up to a conference with the king, who asked him to allow himself to be baptized, like other people; but Eyvind decidedly answered he would not. The king still, with persuasive words, urged him to accept Christianity, and both he and the bishop used many suitable arguments; but Eyvind would not allow himself to be moved. The king offered him gifts and great fiefs, but Eyvind refused all. Then the king threatened him with tortures and death, but Eyvind was steadfast. Then the king ordered a pan of glowing coals to be placed upon

Eyvind's belly, which burst asunder. Eyvind cried, "Take away the pan, and I will say something before I die," which also was done. The king said, "Wilt thou now, Eyvind, believe in Christ?" "No," said Eyvind, "I can take no baptism; for I am an evil spirit put into a man's body by Lapland sorcery, because in no other way could my father and mother have a child." With that died Eyvind, who had been one of the greatest sorcerers.

CHAPTER LXXXIV. HALOGALAND MADE CHRISTIAN [999].—The spring after King Olaf fitted out and manned his ships, and commanded himself his ship the Crane. He had many and smart people with him; and when he was ready, he sailed northwards with his fleet past Byrd Isle, and to Halogaland. Wheresoever he came to the land, or to the islands, he held a Thing, and told the people to accept the right faith, and to be baptized. No man dared to say anything against it, and the whole country he passed through was made Christian. King Olaf was a guest in the house of Harek of Thiotto, who was baptized with all his people. At parting Harek gave the king good presents; and he entered into the king's service, and got fiefs, and the privileges of lenderman from the king.

CHAPTER LXXXV. THORE HIORT'S DEATH.—There was a bonder, by name Raud the Strong, who dwelt in Godö Isle in Salten fjord. Raud was a very rich man, who had many house servants; and likewise was a powerful man, who had many Laplanders in his service when he wanted them. Raud was a great idolater, and very skilful in witchcraft, and was a great friend of Thore Hiort, before spoken of [p. 57]. Both were great chiefs. Now when they heard that King Olaf was coming with a great force from the south to Halogaland, they gathered together an army, ordered out ships, and they too had a great force on foot. Raud had a large ship, with a gilded head formed like a dragon, which ship had thirty rowing benches, and even for that kind of ship was very large. Thore Hiort had also a large ship. These men sailed southwards with their ships against King Olaf, and as soon as they met gave battle. A great battle there was, and a great fall of men; but principally on the side of the Halogalanders, whose ships were cleared of men, so that a great terror came upon them. Raud rowed with his dragon out to sea, and set sail. Raud had always a fair wind wheresoever he wished to sail, which came from his arts of witchcraft; and, to make a short story, he came home to Godö. Thore Hiort fled from the ships up to the land; but King Olaf landed people, followed those who fled, and killed them. Usually the king was the foremost in such skirmishes, and was so now. When the king saw where Thore Hiort, who was quicker on foot than any man, was running to, he ran after him with his dog Vige. The king said, "Vige! Vige! catch Hiorten."[1] Vige ran straight in upon him; on which Thore halted, and the king threw a spear at him. Thore struck with his sword at the dog, and gave him a great wound; but at the same moment the king's spear flew under Thore's arm, and went through and through him, and came out at his other side. There Thore left his life; but Vige was carried wounded to the ships.

CHAPTER LXXXVI. KING OLAF'S VOYAGE TO GODÖ.—King Olaf gave life and freedom to all the men who asked it and agreed to become Christian. King Olaf sailed with his fleet northwards along the coast, and baptized all the people among whom he came; and when he came north to Salten fjord,[2] he intended to sail into it to look for Raud, but a dreadful tempest and storm was raging in the fjord. They lay there a whole week, in which the same weather was raging within the fjord; while without there was a fine brisk wind only, fair for proceeding north along the land. Then the king continued his voyage north to Omd, in Hind island, where all the people submitted to Christianity. Then the king turned about and sailed to the south again; but when he came to the north side of Salten fjord, the same tempest was blowing, and the sea ran high out from the fjord, and the same kind of storm prevailed for several days while the king was lying there. Then the king applied to Bishop Sigurd, and asked him if he knew any counsel about it; and the bishop said he would try if God would give him power to conquer these arts of the Devil.

CHAPTER LXXXVII. OF BISHOP SIGURD, AND OF RAUD'S BEING TORTURED.—Bishop Sigurd took all his mass robes and

[1] Hiorten signifies the deer or hart. "Vige! Vige! catch the hart!"
[2] The Salten fjord is more celebrated in the north of Norway, and more dreaded, than the famous Maelstrom. It is a large fjord within; but the throat through which the vast mass of water has to run in and out at flood and ebb is so narrow that it makes a very heavy and dangerous race or roost for many miles out in the sea, especially in ebb, when the whole body of water is returning to the ocean. The stream can only be crossed during a few minutes at still water, when flood or ebb has not begun to run, unless at a great distance from the jaws of this singular gulf.

went forward to the bow of the king's ship; ordered tapers to be lighted, and incense to be brought out. Then he set the crucifix upon the stem of the vessel, read the Gospel and many prayers, besprinkled the whole ship with holy water, and then ordered the ship-tent to be stowed away, and to row into the fjord. The king ordered all the other ships to follow him. Now when all was ready on board the Crane to row, she went into the fjord without the rowers finding any wind; and the sea was curled about their keel track like as in a calm, so quiet and still was the water; yet on each side of them the waves were lashing up so high that they hid the sight of the mountains. And so the one ship followed the other in the smooth sea track; and they proceeded this way the whole day and night, until they reached Godö. Now when they came to Raud's house his great ship, the dragon, was afloat close to the land. King Olaf went up to the house immediately with his people; made an attack on the loft in which Raud was sleeping, and broke it open. The men rushed in: Raud was taken and bound, and of the people with him some were killed and some made prisoners. Then the king's men went to a lodging in which Raud's house-servants slept, and killed some, bound others, and beat others. Then the king ordered Raud to be brought before him, and offered him baptism. "And," says the king, "I will not take thy property from thee, but rather be thy friend, if thou wilt make thyself worthy to be so." Raud exclaimed with all his might against the proposal, saying he would never believe in Christ, and making his scoff of God. Then the king was wroth, and said Raud should die the worst of deaths. And the king ordered him to be bound to a beam of wood, with his face uppermost, and a round pin of wood to be set between his teeth to force his mouth open. Then the king ordered an adder to be stuck into the mouth of him; but the serpent would not go into his mouth, but shrunk back when Raud breathed against it. Now the king ordered a hollow branch of an angelica root to be stuck into Raud's mouth; others say the king put his horn into his mouth, and forced the serpent to go in by holding a red-hot iron before the opening. So the serpent crept into the mouth of Raud and down his throat, and gnawed its way out of his side; and thus Raud perished. King Olaf took here much gold and silver, and other property of weapons, and many sorts of precious effects; and all the men who were with Raud he either had baptized, or if they refused had them killed or tortured. Then the king took the dragon-ship which Raud had owned, and steered it himself; for it was a much larger and handsomer vessel than the Crane. In front it had a dragon's head, and aft a crook, which turned up, and ended with the figure of the dragon's tail. The two necks [1] and 'the whole of the stem were gilded. This ship the king called the Serpent. When the sails were hoisted they represented, as it were, the dragon's wings; and the ship was the handsomest in all Norway. The islands on which Raud dwelt were called Gylling and Hæring; but the whole islands together were called Godö Isles, and the current between the isles and the mainland the Godö Stream. King Olaf baptized the whole people of the fjord, and then sailed southwards along the land; and on this voyage happened much and various things, which are set down in tales and sagas,— namely, how witches and evil spirits tormented his men, and sometimes himself; but we will rather write about what occurred when King Olaf made Norway Christian, or in the other countries in which he advanced Christianity. The same autumn Olaf with his fleet returned to Drontheim, and landed at Nidaros, where he took up his winter abode.

What I am now going to write about concerns the Icelanders.

CHAPTER LXXXVIII. OF THE ICELANDERS [999].—Kjartan Olafsson, a son's son of Hoskuld, and a daughter's son of Egil Skallagrimson, came the same autumn from Iceland to Nidaros, and he was considered to be the most agreeable and hopeful man of any born in Iceland.[2] There was also Haldor, a son of Gudmund of Modrovald; and Kolbein, a son of Thord, Frey's gode, and a brother's son of Brennu-Flose;[3] together with Sverting, a son of the gode Runolf. All these were heathens; and besides them there were many more,—some men of power, others common men of no property. There came also from Iceland considerable people, who, by Thangbrand's help, had been made Christians; namely, Gissur White, a son of Teit Ketilbiornson; and his mother was Aalov, daughter of Herse Bodvar who was the viking Kaare's son. Bodvar's brother was Sigurd, father of Eric Biodaskalde, whose daughter Astrid was King Olaf's mother. Hialte Skeggiason was the name of another Iceland man, who was married to Vilborg, Gissur White's daughter. Hialte was also a Christian; and King Olaf was very friendly to his relations Gissur and Hialte, who

[1] The " necks " (svírar) were probably the elongated part of the prow below the actual dragon-head, and the corresponding part of the stern.
[2] Hero of the Laxdæla Saga (see C. M. Fox, The Men of Laxdale, 1929).
[3] i.e. Flosi the Burner; leader of those who burnt Njal to death.

lived with him. But the Iceland men who directed the ships, and were heathens, tried to sail away as soon as the king came to the town of Nidaros, for they were told the king forced all men to become Christians; but the wind came stiff against them, and drove them back to Nidarholm. They who directed the ships were Thorarin Nefiulfson, the scald Halfred Ottarson, Brand the Generous, and Thorleik Brand's son. It was told the king that there were Icelanders with ships there, and all were heathen, and wanted to fly from a meeting with the king. Then the king sent them a message forbidding them to sail and ordering them to bring their ships up to the town, which they did, but without discharging the cargoes.

[They carried on their dealings and held a market at the king's pier. In spring they tried three times to slip away, but never succeeded; so they continued lying at the king's pier. It happened one fine day that many set out to swim for amusement, and among them was a man who distinguished himself above the others in all bodily exercises. Kiartan challenged Halfred Vandrædaskald to try himself in swimming against this man, but he declined it. " Then will I make a trial," said Kiartan, casting off his clothes, and springing into the water. Then he set after the man, seizes hold of his foot, and dives with him under water. They come to the surface, and without speaking a word dive again, and are much longer under water than the first time. They come up again, and without saying a word dive a third time, until Kiartan thought it was time to come up ; this, however, he could in no way accomplish, which showed sufficiently the difference in their strength. They were under water so long that Kiartan was almost drowned. They then came up, and swam to land. This Northman asked what the Icelander's name was. Kiartan tells his name.

He says, " Thou art a good swimmer; but art thou expert also in other exercises? "

Kiartan replied, that such expertness was of no great value.

The Northman asks, " Why dost thou not inquire of me such things as I have asked thee about? "

Kiartan replies, " It is all one to me who thou art, or what thy name is."

" Then will I," says he, " tell thee: I am Olaf Trygvesson."

He asked Kiartan much about Iceland, which he answered generally, and wanted to withdraw as hastily as he could; but the king said, " Here is a cloak which I will give thee, Kiartan." And Kiartan took the cloak with many thanks.]

CHAPTER LXXXIX. OF THE BAPTISM OF THE ICELANDERS [999].—When Michaelmas came (September 29), the king had high mass sung with great splendour. The Icelanders went there, and listened to the fine singing and the sound of the bells; and when they came back to their ships every man told his opinion of the Christian man's worship. Kiartan expressed his pleasure at it, but most of the others scoffed at it; and it went according to the proverb, " the king has many ears," for this was told to the king. He sent immediately that very day a message to Kiartan to come to him. Kiartan went to the king with some men, and the king received him kindly. Kiartan was a very stout and handsome man, and of ready and agreeable speech. After the king and Kiartan had conversed a little, the king asked him to adopt Christianity. Kiartan replies, that he would not say no to that, if he thereby obtained the king's friendship; and as the king promised him the fullest friendship, they were soon agreed. The next day Kiartan was baptized, together with his relation Bolle Thorlakson, and all their fellow-travellers. Kiartan and Bolle were the king's guests as long as they were in their white baptismal clothes,[1] and the king had much kindness for them. Wherever they came they were looked upon as people of distinction.

CHAPTER XC. HALFRED THE SCALD BAPTIZED.—As King Olaf one day was walking in the street [2] some men met him, and he who went the foremost saluted the king. The king asked the man his name, and he called himself Halfred.

" Art thou the scald? " said the king.

" I can compose poetry," replied he.

" Wilt thou then adopt Christianity, and come into my service? " asked the king.

" If I am baptized," replies he, " it must be on one condition,— that thou thyself art my godfather; for no other will I have."

The king replies, " That I will do." And Halfred was baptized, the king holding him during the baptism.

Afterwards the king said, " Wilt thou enter into my service? "

Halfred replied, " I was formerly in Earl Hakon's court; but now I will neither enter into thine nor into any other service, unless thou promise me it shall never be my lot to be driven away from thee."

[1] These were worn for a week after baptism.

[2] i.e. Lang-gaden, Long Street, along the river Nid; the present Kram-bodgade is a remnant of it.

" It has been reported to me," said the king, " that thou art neither so prudent nor so obedient as to fulfil my commands."

" In that case," replied Halfred, " put me to death."

" Thou art a scald who composes difficulties," says the king; " but into my service, Halfred, thou shalt be received."

Halfred says, " If I am to be named the composer of difficulties,[1] what dost thou give me, king, on my name-day? "

The king gave him a sword without a scabbard, and said, " Now compose me a song upon this sword, and let the word sword be in every line of the verses." Halfred sang thus:—

> " This sword of swords is my reward.
> For him who knows to wield a sword,
> And with his sword to serve his lord,
> Yet wants a sword, his lot is hard.
> I would I had my good lord's leave
> For this good sword a sheath to choose:
> I'm worth three swords where men swords use,
> But for the sword-sheath now I grieve."

Then the king gave him the scabbard [,observing that the word sword was wanting in one line of his strophe. " But there are three swords at least in two other lines," says Halfred. " So it is," replies the king[2]]. Out of Halfred's lays we have taken the most of the true and faithful accounts that are here related about Olaf Trygvesson.

CHAPTER XCI. THANGBRAND THE PRIEST RETURNS FROM ICELAND.—The same harvest Thangbrand the priest came back from Iceland to King Olaf, and told the ill success of his journey; namely, that the Icelanders had made lampoons about him; and that some even sought to kill him, and there was little hope of that country ever being made Christian. King Olaf was so enraged at this, that he ordered all the Icelanders to be assembled by sound of horn, and was going to kill all who were in the town; but Kiartan, Gissur, and Hialte, with the other Icelanders who had become Christians, went to him, and said, " King, thou must not fall from thy word,—that however much any man may

---

[1] *Vandræðaskáld*, " troublesome poet," by analogy with *vandræðamaðr*, " a man troublesome to deal with." It does not imply that his verses were unusually difficult to understand. The story of Halfred's somewhat reluctant and regretful conversion and of his friendship with King Olaf is the main theme of *Hallfredar Saga*, which may have been used by Snorri.

[2] Scaldic verse was governed by a system of rigid and intricate rules of metre, assonance, alliteration, and rhyme; the king's stipulation was a severe challenge to Halfred's skill. For a brief account of scaldic verse and Snorri's use of it see *Sagas of the Norse Kings*, pp. viii–x; see also L. M. Hollander, *The Skalds*, 1945; G. Turville-Petre, *Origins of Icelandic Literature*, 1953, pp. 26–47.

irritate thee, thou wilt forgive him if he turn from heathenism and become Christian. All the Icelanders here are willing to be baptized; and through them we may find means to bring Christianity into Iceland: for there are many amongst them, sons of considerable people in Iceland, whose friends can advance the cause; but the priest Thangbrand proceeded there as he did here in the court, with violence and manslaughter, and such conduct the people there would not submit to." The king hearkened to these remonstrances; and all the Iceland men who were there were baptized.

CHAPTER XCII. OF KING OLAF'S FEATS.—King Olaf was more expert in all exercises than any man in Norway whose memory is preserved to us in sagas; and he was stronger and more agile than most men, and many stories are written down about it. One is, that he ascended the Smalsar Horn,[1] and fixed his shield upon the very peak. Another is, that one of his followers had climbed up the peak after him, until he came to where he could neither get up nor down; but the king came to his help, climbed up to him, took him under his arm, and bore him to the flat ground. King Olaf could run across the oars outside of the vessel while his men were rowing the Serpent. He could play with three daggers, so that one was always in the air, and he took the one falling by the handle. He could walk all round upon the ship's rails, could strike and cut equally well with both hands, and could cast two spears at once. King Olaf was a very merry frolicsome man; gay and social; was most eager in everything; was very generous; stood out clearly among other men; in battle he exceeded all in bravery. He was distinguished for cruelty when he was enraged, and tortured many of his enemies. Some he burnt in fire; some he had torn in pieces by mad dogs; some he had mutilated, or cast down from high precipices. On this account his friends were attached to him warmly, and his enemies feared him greatly; and thus he made such a fortunate advance in his undertakings, for some obeyed his will out of the friendliest zeal, and others out of dread.

CHAPTER XCIII. OF THE BAPTISM OF LIEF ERICSSON.—Leif, a son of Eric the Red, who first settled in Greenland, came this summer from Greenland to Norway; and as he met King Olaf he adopted Christianity, and passed the winter with the king.

[1] Now called Hornelen,—an inaccessible peak or needle on the summit of a mountain in Bremanger.

CHAPTER XCIV. FALL OF GUDROD, THE LAST OF ERIC'S AND GUNHILD'S SONS [999].—Gudrod, a son of Eric Bloodyaxe and Gunhild the Mother of Kings, had been ravaging in the western countries ever since he fled from Norway before the Earl Hakon. But the summer before mentioned, when King Olaf Trygvesson had ruled four years over Norway, Gudrod came to the country, and had many ships of war with him. He had sailed from England; and when he thought himself near to the Norway coast, he steered south along the land, to the quarter where it was least likely King Olaf would be. Gudrod sailed in this way south to Viken; and as soon as he came to the land began to plunder, to subject the people to him, and to demand that they should accept of him as king. Now as the country people saw that a great army was come upon them, they desired peace and terms. They offered King Gudrod to send a Thing-message over all the country, and to accept of him at the Thing as king, rather than suffer from his army; but they desired some period of respite, while the token of the Thing's assembling was going round through the land. The king demanded maintenance during the time this delay lasted. The bonders preferred entertaining the king as a guest, by turns, as long as he required it; and the king accepted of the proposal to go about with some of his men as a guest from place to place in the land, while others of his men remained to guard the ships. When King Olaf's relations, Hyrning and Thorgeir, heard of this, they gathered men, fitted out ships, and went northwards to Viken. They came in the night with their men to a place at which King Gudrod was living as a guest, and attacked him with fire and weapons; and there King Gudrod fell, and most of his followers. Of those who were with his ships some were killed, some slipped away and fled to great distances; and now were all the sons of Eric and Gunhild dead.

CHAPTER XCV. THE BUILDING OF THE SHIP LONG SERPENT [1000].—The winter after King Olaf came from Halogaland, he had a great vessel built at Ladehammer,[1] which was larger than any ship in the country, and of which the ship stocks are still to be seen. The length of keel that rested upon the grass was seventy-four ells. Thorberg Skafhogg was the man's name who was the master-builder of the ship; but there were many others besides,—some to fell wood, some to shape it, some to make

---

[1] Ladehammer,—the knob or point of land below the house of Lade, still known by the same name. Lade is close to Trondhjem.

nails, some to carry timber; and all that was used was of
the best. The ship was both long and broad and high-sided,
and strongly timbered. While they were planking the ship, it
happened that Thorberg had to go home to his farm upon some
urgent business; and as he remained there a long time, the ship
was planked up on both sides when he came back. In the
evening the king went out, and Thorberg with him, to see how
the vessel looked, and everybody said that never was seen so
large and so beautiful a ship of war. Then the king returned
to the town. Early next morning the king returns again to the
ship, and Thorberg with him. The carpenters were there before
them, but all were standing idle with their arms across. The
king asked "what was the matter?" They said the ship was
all spoilt; for somebody had gone from stem to stern, and cut
one deep notch after the other down the one side of the planking.
When the king came nearer he saw it was so, and said, with an
oath, that that man should die if the king learnt who had spoilt the
vessel from sheer malice—"and I shall bestow a great reward on
whoever can tell me about this."

"I can tell you, king," says Thorberg, "who has done this
piece of work."

"I don't think," replies the king, "that any one is so likely
to find it out as thou art."

Thorberg says, "I will tell you, king, who did it. I did it
myself."

The king says, "Thou must restore it all to the same condition
as before, or thy life shall pay for it."

Then Thorberg went and chipped the planks until the deep
notches were all smoothed and made even with the rest; and
the king and all present declared that the ship was much handsomer on the side of the hull which Thorberg had chipped, and
bade him shape the other side in the same way, and gave him
great thanks for the improvement.[1] Afterwards Thorberg was
the master-builder of the ship until she was entirely finished.
The ship was a dragon, built after the one the king had captured
in Halogaland; but this ship was far larger, and more carefully
put together in all her parts. The king called this ship the
Long Serpent, and the other the Short Serpent. The Long

[1] Thorberg's nickname, "Smoothing Stroke," evidently arose from this
incident. His objection to the planking seems to have been that it was
unnecessarily thick, owing to the inexperience of the other workmen; by
paring the ship's sides he gave her greater lightness and speed. On
viking ships see J. Brøndsted, *The Vikings*, 1960, pp. 130–7; A. Binns,
Introduction to H. Arbmann, *The Vikings*, 1962.

Serpent had thirty-four benches for rowers. The head and the arched tail were both gilt, and the bulwarks were as high as in sea-going ships. This ship was the best and most costly ship ever made in Norway.

CHAPTER XCVI. OF EARL ERIC, THE SON OF HAKON [995].— Earl Eric, the son of Earl Hakon, and his brother, with many other valiant men their relations, had left the country after Earl Hakon's fall. Earl Eric went eastward to Sweden, to Olaf the Swedish king, and he and his people were well received. King Olaf gave the earl peace and freedom in the land, and great fiefs; so that he could support himself and his men well. Thord Kolbeinsson speaks of this in the verses before given.[1] Many people who fled from the country on account of King Olaf Trygvesson came out of Norway to Earl Eric; and the earl resolved to fit out ships and go a-plundering, in order to get property for himself and his people. First he steered to Gotland, and lay there long in summer watching for merchant vessels sailing towards the land, or for vikings. Sometimes he landed and ravaged all round upon the sea-coasts. So it is told in the "Banda-drapa":—

> "Eric, as we have lately heard,
> Has waked the song of shield and sword,—
> Has waked the slumbering storm of shields.
> *Power in this land Eric wields.*
> From Gotland's lonely shore he's gone
> Far up the land, and battle won;
> And o'er the sea his name is spread.
> *In peace, most mild; in battles, dread.*"

Afterwards Earl Eric sailed south to Vendland, and at Stauren[2] found some viking ships, and gave them battle. Eric gained the victory, and slew the vikings. So it is told in the "Banda-drapa":—

> "The chieftain who leads men to war
> Turned his prow towards Stauren's shore;
> It was our prince who made the choice.
> *Ever in strife he doth rejoice.*
> The gulls that love blood-welling gash
> Tore at the slaughtered vikings' flesh
> After the bitter battle's end.
> *Earl of the land the gods defend.*"[3]

CHAPTER XCVII. EARL ERIC'S FORAY ON THE BALTIC COASTS [996–997].—Earl Eric sailed back to Sweden in autumn, and

[1] In the verses given on p. 51.
[2] Possibly Staver, the south-east point of Femern Island.
[3] The italicized lines are part of a refrain (*vide* p. 20, n. 1).

stayed there all winter; but in spring he fitted out his war force again, and sailed up the Baltic. When he came to Valdemar's dominions he began to plunder and kill the inhabitants, and burn the dwellings everywhere as he came along, and to lay waste the country. He came to Aldeigioburg,[1] and besieged it until he took the castle; and he killed many people, broke down and burned the castle, and then carried destruction all around far and wide in Russia. So it is told in the " Banda-drapa ":—

> " The generous earl, brave and bold,
> Who scatters his bright shining gold,
> Eric, with fire-scattering hand,
> Wasted the Russian monarch's land,—
> With arrow-shower, and storm of war,
> Wasted the land of Waldemar.
> Aldeigio burns, and Eric's might
> Scours through all Russia by its light."

Earl Eric was five years in all on this foray; and when he returned from Russia he ravaged all Adalsyssel and Eysyssel,[2] and took there four viking ships from the Danes, and killed every man on board. So it is told in the " Banda-drapa ":—

> " He that slakes his sword in gore
> (I heard the tale) once more made war;
> The Sounds were then his battlefields.
> *Power in this land Eric wields.*
> He cleared four Danish ships of men
> (We heard the story once again);
> His gold with generous hand he shed.
> *In peace, most mild; in battles, dread.*
> O thou that steer'st thy ship aright,
> 'Gainst Gotland men thou then didst fight,
> And warriors ran to save their life.
> *Ever he doth rejoice in strife.*
> And then the valiant hero bore
> Through all the Syssels shield of war,
> And where he came did all peace end.
> *Earl of the land the gods defend.*"

When Eric had been a year in Sweden he went over to Denmark to King Swend the Forked-bearded, the Danish king, and courted his daughter Gyda. The proposal was accepted, and Earl Eric married Gyda; and a year after they had a son, who was called Hakon. Earl Eric was in the winter in Denmark, or sometimes in Sweden; but in summer he went a-plundering.

[1] Aldeigioburg is the town at Aldagen or Ladoga which then lay on the river Volkhov which flows into Lake Ladoga.
[2] Estland was the country along the Gulf of Finland, as far west as the Vistula; and Eysyssel was the district of the islands of Osel and others along this coast. Adalsyssel was the district on the mainland opposite to Eysyssel.

CHAPTER XCVIII. KING SWEND'S MARRIAGE.—The Danish king, Swend Forked Beard, was married to Gunhild, a daughter of Burislaf king of the Vends. But in the times we have just been speaking of it happened that Queen Gunhild fell sick, and died.[1] Soon after King Swend married Sigrid the Haughty,[2] a daughter of Skogul Toste, and mother of the Swedish King Olaf; and by means of this relationship there was great friendship between the kings and Earl Eric, Hakon's son.

CHAPTER XCIX. KING BURISLAF'S MARRIAGE. — Burislaf,[3] the king of the Vends, complained to his son-in-law, Earl Sigvald, that the agreement was broken which Sigvald had made between King Swend and King Burislaf, by which Burislaf was to get in marriage Thyre, Harald's daughter, a sister of King Swend: but that marriage had not proceeded, for Thyre had given a positive " no " to the proposal to marry her to an old and heathen king. " Now," said King Burislaf to Earl Sigvald, " I must have the promise fulfilled." And he told Earl Sigvald to go to Denmark, and bring him Thyre as his queen. Earl Sigvald loses no time, but goes to King Swend of Denmark; explains to him the case; and brings it so far by his persuasion that the king delivered his sister Thyre into his hands. With

[1] There is disagreement on the question of Swend Forked Beard's marriages. Icelandic sources state that he married Gunhild, daughter of King Burislaf (Boleslav I of Poland), that she bore him two sons, Harald and Canute the Great, and that when she died he married Sigrid the Haughty, widow of King Eric the Victorious of Sweden. But continental sources (Adam of Bremen, Thietmar of Merseburg, the *Gesta Cnutonis*) give him only one wife, in whom characteristics of Gunhild and Sigrid are blended; she is said to be sister of Boleslav, widow of Eric and mother of Harald and Canute. Her name is not given; presumably it was Slavonic. Thietmar says that Swend divorced her and sent her home to Vendland, whence her sons, after Swend's death in 1014, brought her back to Denmark.

[2] There has been much dispute over whether or not Sigrid the Haughty ever existed, and no conclusive proof or disproof is forthcoming. She is not mentioned in any continental sources, nor in scaldic verses, nor in the Norwegian synoptic histories. It is at any rate obvious that even if the Icelandic writers did not entirely invent her, they exaggerated her importance and made of her a strikingly dramatic character. It has been suggested that the story of her vengeful hatred for Olaf after the breaking of their betrothal was influenced by the legend of Brynhild and Sigurd (with Swend and Thyre corresponding to Gunnar and Gudrun). Snorri and the author of the *Legendary Saga of St. Olaf* also associate her with the story of St. Olaf, in that it was her ambition to become the mother of that saint, whose birth she could foresee; hence her attempt to seduce Harald Grænske, St. Olaf's destined father, and her vengeance when she fails (see pp. 42–4). Her son by Eric the Victorious was the Olaf, King of Sweden, who was so bitterly hostile to St. Olaf (see p. 168).

[3] Boleslav I of Poland (992–1025); *cf.* pp. 34–5 and p. 22, n. 2.

her went some female attendants, and her foster-father, by name Ossur Aageson, a man of great power, and some other people. In the agreement between the king and the earl, it was settled that Thyre should have in property the possessions which Queen Gunhild had enjoyed in Vendland, besides other great properties as bride-gifts. Thyre wept sorely, and went very unwillingly. When the earl came to Vendland, Burislaf held his wedding with Queen Thyre, and received her in marriage; but as long as she was among heathens she would neither eat nor drink with them, and this lasted for seven days.

CHAPTER C. KING OLAF GETS THYRE IN MARRIAGE [999–1000].—It happened one night that Queen Thyre and Ossur ran away in the dark, and into the woods, and, to be short in our story, came at last to Denmark. But there Thyre did not dare to remain, knowing that if her brother King Swend heard of her, he would send her back directly to Vendland. She went on, therefore, secretly to Norway, and never stayed her journey until she fell in with King Olaf, by whom she was kindly received. Thyre related to the king her sorrows, and entreated his advice in her need, and protection in his kingdom. Thyre was a well-spoken woman, and the king had pleasure in her conversation. He saw she was a handsome woman,[1] and it came into his mind that she would be a good match; so he turns the conversation that way, and asks if she will marry him. Now, as she saw that her situation was such that she could not help herself, and considered what a luck it was for her to marry so celebrated a man, she bade him to dispose himself of her hand and fate; and, after nearer conversation, King Olaf took Thyre in marriage. This wedding was held in harvest, after the king returned from Halogaland; and King Olaf and Queen Thyre remained all winter at Nidaros. The following spring Queen Thyre complained often to King Olaf, and wept bitterly over it, that she who had so great property in Vendland had no goods or possessions here in the country that were suitable for a queen; and sometimes she would entreat the king with fine words to get her property restored to her, and saying that King Burislaf was so great a friend of King Olaf that he would not deny King Olaf anything if they were to meet. But when King Olaf's friends heard of such speeches, they dissuaded him from any such expedition. It is related that the king one day early in spring was walking in the street, and met a man in the market

---

[1] She was the widow of Styrbjorn the Strong; *vide* p. 176. n. 3.

with many and, for that early season, remarkably large angelica roots. The king took a great stalk of the angelica in his hand, and went home to Queen Thyre's lodging. Thyre sat in her room weeping as the king came in. The king said, " See here, queen, is a great angelica stalk, which I give thee." She struck it aside with her hand and said " Harald Gormson gave greater presents; and he was less afraid to go out of the land and take his own. That was shown when he came here to Norway, and laid waste the greater part of the land, and seized on all the scatt and revenues; and thou darest not go across the Danish dominions for this brother of mine, King Swend." As she spoke thus, King Olaf sprang up, and answered with a loud oath, " Never shall I go in fear of thy brother King Swend; and if we meet he shall give way before me! "

CHAPTER CI. OLAF'S LEVY FOR WAR.—Soon after the king convoked a Thing in the town, and proclaimed to all the public that in summer he would go abroad upon an expedition out of the country, and would raise both ships and men from every district; and at the same time fixed how many ships he would have from the whole Drontheim fjord. Then he sent his message-token south and north, both along the sea coast and up in the interior of the country, to let an army be gathered. The king ordered the Long Serpent to be put into the water, along with all his other ships both small and great. He himself steered the Long Serpent. When the crews were taken out for the ships, they were so carefully selected that no man on board the Long Serpent was older than sixty or younger than twenty years, and all were men distinguished for strength and courage. Those who were Olaf's bodyguard were in particular chosen men, both of the country and foreigners,[1] and the boldest and strongest.

CHAPTER CII. THE CREW ON BOARD OF THE LONG SERPENT.— Ulf Röde was the name of the man who bore King Olaf's banner and was in the forecastle of the Long Serpent; and with him was Kolbiorn the marshal, and Thorstein Oxfoot,[1] and Vikar of Tiundaland, a brother of Arnliot Gelline.[2] By the bulkhead next to the forecastle were Vak Elfske Raumason, Berse Bollason the Strong, Ann Skytte from Jemteland, Thrand Ramme from

---

[1] So called, according to *þorsteins þáttr uxafóts*, because at Olaf's request he tore off the leg of a huge ox worshipped by a man in Thrandheim.

[2] For Arnliot see pp. 295-7, 365, 373.

Thelemark, and his brother Uthyrme. Besides these were, of Halogaland men, Thrand Skialge and Ogmund Sande, Lodve Lange from Saltvig, and Harek Huase; together with these Drontheim men—Ketel Höie, Thorfin Eisle, Haavard and his brothers from Orkedal. The following were in the fore-hold: Biorn from Studla, Bork from the Fjords, Thorgrim Thiodolfson from Hvin, Asbiorn and Orm, Thord from Nardarlög, Thorstein White from Oprostad, Arnor from Mære, Halstein and Hauk from the Fjords district, Eyvind Snaka, Bergtor Bestill, Halkel from Fialer, Olaf Dreng, Arnfin from Sogn, Sigurd Bild, Einar from Hordaland, and Fin and Ketel from Rogaland, and Griotgard the Brisk. The following were in the hold next the mast: Einar Tambarskelve, who was not reckoned as fully experienced, being only eighteen years old; Halstein Hlifarson, Thorolf, Ivar Smette, and Orm Skoganef. Many other valiant men were in the Serpent, although we cannot tell all their names. In every half division of the hold were eight men, and each and all chosen men; and in the fore-hold were thirty men. It was a common saying among people, that the Long Serpent's crew was as distinguished for bravery, strength, and daring, among other men, as the Long Serpent was distinguished among other ships. Thorkel Nefia, the king's brother, commanded the Short Serpent; and Thorkel Dyrdel and Jostein, the king's mother's brothers, had the Crane; and both these ships were well manned. King Olaf had eleven large ships from Drontheim, besides vessels with twenty rowers' benches, smaller vessels, and provision-vessels.[1]

CHAPTER CIII. ICELAND BAPTIZED.—When King Olaf had nearly rigged out his fleet in Nidaros, he appointed men over the Drontheim country in all districts and communities. He also sent to Iceland Gissur White and Hialte Skeggiason to proclaim Christianity there; and sent with them a priest called Thormod, along with several men in holy orders. But he retained with him, as hostages, four Icelanders whom he thought the most important; namely, Kiartan Olafsson, Haldor Gudmundsson, Kolbein Thordsson, and Sverting Runalfsson. Of Gissur and Hialte's progress, it is related that they came to Iceland before the All-thing, and went to the Thing; and in that Thing Christianity was introduced by law into Iceland, and in the course of the summer all the people were baptized.

[1] Snorri took this list of names from Odd.

CHAPTER CIV. GREENLAND BAPTIZED [1000].—The same
spring King Olaf also sent Leif Ericsson to Greenland to proclaim
Christianity there, and Leif went there that summer. In the
ocean he took up the crew of a ship which had been lost, and who
were clinging to the wreck. He also found Vinland [1] the Good;
arrived in summer in Greenland; and brought there with him a
priest and other teachers, with whom he went to Brattalid to
lodge with his father Eric. People called him afterwards Leif
the Lucky: but his father Eric said that his luck and ill luck
balanced each other; for if Leif had saved a wreck in the ocean,
he had brought a hurtful fellow [2] with him to Greenland, and
that was the priest. [3]

CHAPTER CV. EARL ROGNVALD SENDS MESSENGERS TO KING
OLAF.—The winter after King Olaf had baptized Halogaland, he
and Queen Thyre were in Nidaros; and the summer before Queen
Thyre had brought King Olaf a boy-child, which was both stout
and promising, and was called Harald, after its mother's father.
The king and queen loved the infant exceedingly, and rejoiced
in the hope that it would grow up and inherit after its father;
but it lived barely a year after its birth, which both took much
to heart. In that winter were many Icelanders and other clever
men in King Olaf's house, as before related. His sister Ingeborg,
Trygve's daughter, was also at the court at that time. She was
beautiful in appearance, modest and frank with the people,
had a steady manly judgment, and was beloved of all. She was
very fond of the Icelanders who were there, most of all Kiartan
Olafsson, for he had been longer than the others in the king's
house; and he found it always amusing to converse with her,
for she had both understanding and cleverness in talk. The
king was always gay and full of mirth in his intercourse with

---

[1] *Vinland,* "Wine-Land," the name given by the Norsemen of Greenland
to a land they discovered to the south-west, in part of which vines were
growing wild. It must have been somewhere along the east coast of North
America (*vide* pp. 100–16, and references there given).

[2] *Skémaðr, skimaðr,* is a rendering of "hypocrite" in certain religious
writings, and that may be the meaning here; it may, however, mean
"evil wizard," since *ski* (itself a rare word) apparently denotes some form
of deceptive spell.

[3] There are eight chapters here in Peringskiöld's edition of the *Heimskringla* which relate to the discovery of Vinland, and are taken from the
Codex Flateyensis, but are not in the manuscripts of the *Heimskringla.*
They are certainly an interpolation unconnected with Snorri's work; they
will be found below, pp. 100–16. When separately edited these chapters
are called *Grœnlendinga pattr* or *Grœnlendinga Saga—The Tale* (or *The
Saga*) *of the Greenlanders.*

the people; and often asked about the manners of the great men and chiefs in the neighbouring countries, when strangers from Denmark or Sweden came to see him. The summer before Halfred Vandrædaskald had come from Gotland, where he had been with Earl Rognvald, Ulf's son, who had lately come to the government of Wester Gotland. Ulf, Rognvald's father, was a brother of Sigrid the Haughty; so that King Olaf the Swede and Earl Rognvald were brother and sister's children. Halfred told Olaf many things about the earl: he said he was an able chief, excellently fitted for governing, generous with money, brave, and steady in friendship. Halfred said also that the earl desired much the friendship of King Olaf, and had spoken of making court to Ingeborg, Trygve's daughter. The same winter came ambassadors from Gotland, and fell in with King Olaf in the north, in Nidaros, and brought the message which Halfred had spoken of,—that the earl desired to be King Olaf's entire friend, and wished to become his brother-in-law by obtaining his sister Ingeborg in marriage. Therewith the ambassadors laid before the king sufficient tokens in proof that in reality they came from the earl on this errand. The king listened with approbation to their speech; but said that Ingeborg herself must determine on his assent to the marriage. The king then talked to his sister about the matter, and asked her opinion about it. She answered to this effect,—" I have been with you for some time, and you have shown brotherly care and tender respect for me ever since you came to the country. I will agree therefore to your proposal about my marriage, provided that you do not marry me to a heathen man." The king said it should be as she wished. The king then spoke to the ambassadors; and it was settled before they departed that in summer Earl Rognvald should meet the king in the east parts of the country, to enter into the fullest friendship with each other, and when they met they would settle about the marriage. With this reply the earl's messengers went westward, and King Olaf remained all winter in Nidaros in great splendour, and with many people about him.

CHAPTER CVI. KING OLAF BEGINS HIS EXPEDITION TO VENDLAND.—King Olaf proceeded in summer with his ships and men southwards along the land, and past Stad. With him were Queen Thyre and Ingeborg, Trygve's daughter, the king's sister. Many of his friends also joined him, and other persons of consequence who had prepared themselves to travel with the king. The first man among these was his brother-in-law, Erling Skialgsson, who had with him a large ship of thirty benches of rowers, and which was in every respect well equipt. His brothers-in-law Hyrning and Thorgeir also joined him, each of whom for himself steered a large vessel; and many other powerful men besides followed him. With all this war-force he sailed southwards along the land; but when he came south as far as Rogaland he stopped there, for Erling Skialgsson had prepared for him a splendid feast at Sole. There Earl Rognvald, Ulf's son, from Gotland, came to meet the king, and to settle the business which had been proposed in winter in the messages between them, namely, the marriage with Ingeborg the king's sister. Olaf received him kindly; and when the matter came to be spoken of, the king said he would keep his word, and marry his sister Ingeborg to him, provided he would accept the true faith, and make all his subjects he ruled over in his land be baptized. The earl agreed to this, and he and all his followers were baptized. Now was the feast enlarged that Erling had prepared, for the earl held his wedding there with Ingeborg the king's sister. King Olaf had now married off all his sisters. The earl, with Ingeborg, set out on his way home; and the king sent learned men with him to baptize the people in Gotland, and to teach them the right faith and morals. The king and the earl parted in the greatest friendship.

CHAPTER CVII. KING OLAF'S EXPEDITION TO VENDLAND.— After his sister Ingeborg's wedding, the king made ready in all haste to leave the country with his army, which was both great and made up of fine men. When he left the land and sailed southwards he had sixty ships of war, with which he sailed past Denmark, and in through the Sound, and on to Vendland. He appointed a meeting with King Burislaf; and when the kings met, they spoke about the property which King Olaf demanded, and the conference went off peaceably, as a good account was given of the properties which King Olaf thought himself entitled to there. He passed here much of the summer, and found many of his old friends.

CHAPTER CVIII. CONSPIRACY OF THE KINGS OF SWEDEN AND DENMARK AND EARL ERIC AGAINST KING OLAF.—The Danish king, Swend Forked Beard, was married, as before related [p. 80], to Sigrid the Haughty. Sigrid was King Olaf Trygvesson's greatest enemy; the cause of which, as before said [p. 58], was that King Olaf had broken off with her, and had struck her in the face. She urged King Swend much to give battle to King Olaf Trygvesson; saying that he had reason enough, as Olaf had married his sister Thyre without his leave, " and that your predecessors would not have submitted to." Such persuasions Sigrid had often in her mouth; and at last she brought it so far that Swend resolved firmly on doing so. Early in spring King Swend sent messengers eastward into Sweden, to his kinsman-in-law, Olaf, the Swedish king, and to Earl Eric; and informed them that King Olaf of Norway was levying men for an expedition, and intended in summer to go to Vendland. To this news the Danish king added an invitation to the Swedish king and Earl Eric to meet King Swend with an army, so that all together they might make an attack on King Olaf Trygvesson. The Swedish king and Earl Eric were ready enough for this, and immediately assembled a great fleet and an army through all Sweden, with which they sailed southwards to Denmark, and arrived there after King Olaf Trygvesson had sailed to the eastward. Haldor the Unchristian tells of this in his lay on Earl Eric:—

> " The king-subduer raised a host
> Of warriors on the Swedish coast.
> The brave went southwards to the fight,
> Who love the sword-storm's gleaming light;
> The brave, who fill the wild wolf's mouth,
> Followed bold Eric to the south;
> And there at sea the birds of prey
> Found blood to quench their thirst that day."

The Swedish king and Earl Eric sailed to meet the Danish king, and they had all when together an immense force.

CHAPTER CIX. EARL SIGVALD'S TREACHEROUS PLANS.— At the same time that King Swend sent a message to Sweden for an army, he sent Earl Sigvald to Vendland to spy out King Olaf Trygvesson's proceedings, and to bring it about by cunning devices that King Swend and King Olaf should fall in with each other. So Sigvald sets out to go to Vendland. First, he came to Jomsburg, and then he sought out King Olaf Trygvesson. There was much friendship in their conversation, and the earl got himself into great favour with the king. Astrid, the earl's wife, King Burislaf's daughter, was a great friend of King Olaf Trygvesson, particularly on account of the connection which had been between them when Olaf was married to her sister Geira. Earl Sigvald was a prudent, ready-minded man; and as he had got a voice in King Olaf's council, he put him off much from sailing homewards, finding various reasons for delay. Olaf's people were in the highest degree dissatisfied with this; for the men were anxious to get home, and they lay ready to sail, and there was a good wind. At last Earl Sigvald got a secret message from Denmark that the Swedish king's army was arrived from the east, and that Earl Eric's also was ready; and that all these chiefs had resolved to sail eastwards to Vendland, and wait for King Olaf at an island which is called Svold.[1] They also desired the earl to contrive matters so that they should meet King Olaf there.

CHAPTER CX. KING OLAF'S VOYAGE FROM VENDLAND.— There came first a flying report to Vendland that the Danish king, Swend, had fitted out an army; and it was soon whispered that he intended to attack King Olaf. But Earl Sigvald says to King Olaf, " It never can be King Swend's intention to venture with the Danish force alone to give battle to thee with such a powerful army; but if thou hast any suspicion that evil is on foot, I will follow thee with my force (at that time it was considered a great matter to have Jomsburg vikings with an army), and I will give thee eleven manned ships." The king accepted this offer; and as the light breeze of wind that came was favourable, he ordered the ships to get under weigh, and the war-horns to sound the departure. The sails were hoisted; and all the small vessels, sailing fastest, got out to sea before the others. The earl, who sailed nearest to the king's ship, called to those on board to tell the king to sail in his keel-track: " For I know where the water is deepest between the islands and in the sounds, and you need it with these large ships." Then the earl sailed first with his eleven ships, and the king followed with his large ships, also eleven in number; but the whole of the rest of the fleet sailed out to sea. Now when Earl Sigvald came sailing close under the island Svold, a skiff rowed out to inform the earl that the Danish king's army was lying in the harbour before them. Then the earl ordered the sails of his vessels to be struck, and they rowed in under the island. Haldor the Unchristian says:—

> " From out the south the king is come
> With seventy ships of war and one,
> To dye his sword in bloody fight,
> Riding his wave-steed swift and light.

[1] The site is uncertain; Skuli's verse on p. 92 speaks of a " mouth," as of a river or creek; Halldor's on p. 94 mentions an island.

For now the earl hath made request
That Scania's men should give the best
Of their tall ships to him. Yea, peace
Is broken now, and now must cease."

It is said here that King Olaf and Earl Sigvald had seventy sail of vessels and one more, when they sailed from the south.

CHAPTER CXI. THE CONSULTATION OF THE KINGS [1000].—
The Danish king Swend, the Swedish king Olaf, and Earl Eric were there with all their forces. The weather being fine and clear sunshine, all these chiefs, with a great suite, went out on the isle to see the vessels sailing out at sea, and many of them crowded together; and they saw among them one large and stately ship. The two kings said, "That is a large and very beautiful vessel: that will be the Long Serpent."

Earl Eric replied, "That is not the Long Serpent." And he was right; for it was a ship belonging to Eindride of Gimsar.

Soon after they saw another vessel coming sailing along much larger than the first; then says King Swend, "Olaf Trygvesson must be afraid, for he does not venture to sail with the figure-head of the dragon upon his ship."

Says Earl Eric, "That is not the king's ship yet; for I know that ship by the coloured stripes of cloth in her sail. That is Erling Skialgsson. Let him sail; for it is the better for us that this ship is away from Olaf's fleet, so well equipt as she is."

Soon after they saw and knew Earl Sigvald's ships, which turned in and laid themselves under the island. Then they saw three ships coming along under sail, and one of them very large. King Swend ordered his men to go to their ships, "for there comes the Long Serpent."

Earl Eric says, "Many other great and stately vessels have they besides the Long Serpent. Let us wait a little."

Then said many, "Earl Eric will not fight and avenge his father; and it is a great shame that it should be told that we lay here with so great a force, and allowed King Olaf to sail out to sea before our eyes."

But when they had spoken thus for a short time, they saw four ships coming sailing along, of which one had a large dragon-head richly gilt. Then King Swend stood up, and said, "That dragon shall carry me this evening high, for I shall steer it."

Then said many, "The Serpent is indeed a wonderfully large and beautiful vessel, and it shows a great mind to have built such a ship."

Earl Eric said so loud that several persons heard him, "If King Olaf had no other vessels but only that one, King Swend would never take it from him with the Danish force alone."

Thereafter all the people rushed on board their ships, took down the tents,[1] and in all haste made ready for battle.

While the chiefs were speaking among themselves as above related, they saw three very large ships coming sailing along, and at last after them a fourth, and that was the Long Serpent. Of the large ships which had gone before, and which they had taken for the Long Serpent, the first was the Crane; the one after that was the Short Serpent; and when they really saw the Long Serpent all knew, and nobody had a word to say against it, that it must be Olaf Trygvesson who was sailing in such a vessel; and they went to their ships to arm for the fight.

An agreement had been concluded among the chiefs, King Swend, King Olaf the Swede, and Earl Eric, that they should divide Norway among them in three parts, in case they succeeded against Olaf Trygvesson; but that he of the chiefs who should first board the Serpent should have her, and all the booty found in her, and each should have the ships he cleared for himself. Earl Eric had a large ship of war [2] which he used upon his viking expeditions; and there was an iron beard or comb above on both stem and stern, and below it a thick iron plate as broad as the stem, which went down quite to the waterline.

CHAPTER CXII. OF KING OLAF'S PEOPLE. — When Earl Sigvald with his vessels rowed in under the island, Thorkel Dyrdel of the Crane, and the other ship commanders who sailed with him, saw that he turned his ships towards the isle, and thereupon let fall the sails, and rowed after him, calling out and asking why he sailed that way. The earl answered, that he was waiting for King Olaf as he feared there were enemies in the way. They lay upon their oars until Thorkel Nefia came up with the Short Serpent and the three ships which followed him. When they told them the same they too struck sail, and let the ships drive, waiting for King Olaf. But when the king sailed in towards the isle, the whole enemies' fleet came rowing within them out to the Sound. When they saw this they begged the

[1] The ship-tents or tilts, under which the crews appear to have lived when not under sail.

[2] A *barði*, a ship with strengthened prow. The central sections of the tall prow and stern were both called *barð*, and were often covered with iron plates to protect the ship when lashed to others in fighting. The "beard or comb" (*skegg*) seems to have been a set of spikes for use in ramming.

king to hold on his way, and not risk battle with so great a force. The king replied, high on the quarterdeck where he stood, "Strike the sails; never shall men of mine think of flight. I never fled from battle. Let God dispose of my life, but flight I shall never take." It was done as the king commanded. Halfred tells of it thus:—

> " And far and wide the saying bold
> Of the brave warrior shall be told.
> The king, in many a fray well tried,
> To his brave champions round him cried,
> ' My men shall never learn from me
> From the dark weapon-cloud to flee.'
> Nor were the brave words spoken then
> Forgotten by his faithful men."

CHAPTER CXIII. KING OLAF'S SHIPS ARE CLOSED UP FOR BATTLE.—King Olaf ordered the war-horns to sound for all his ships to close up to each other. The king's ship lay in the middle of the line, and on one side lay the Little Serpent, and on the other the Crane; and as they made fast the stems together,[1] the Long Serpent's stem and the Short Serpent's were made fast together; but when the king saw it he called out to his men and ordered them to lay the larger ship more in advance, so that its stern should not lie so far behind in the fleet.

Then says Ulf the Red, "If the Long Serpent is to lie as much more ahead of the other ships as she is longer than them, we shall have hard work of it here on the forecastle."

The king replies, "I did not think I had a forecastle man afraid as well as red."[2]

Says Ulf, "Defend thou the quarterdeck as I shall the forecastle."

The king had a bow in his hands, and laid an arrow on the string, and aimed at Ulf.

Ulf said, "Shoot another way, king, where it is more needful: my work is thy gain."

CHAPTER CXIV. OF KING OLAF.—King Olaf stood on the Serpent's quarter-deck, high over the others. He had a gilt

---

[1] The mode of fighting in sea battles appears, from this and many other descriptions, to have been for each party to bind together the stems and sterns of their own ships, forming them thus into a compact body as soon as the fleets came within fighting distance, or within spears'-throw. They appear to have fought principally from the forecastles; and to have used grappling-irons for dragging a vessel out of the line, or within boarding distance.

[2] The words *rauðr*, " red," and *ragr*, " cowardly," are sufficiently similar by their alliteration to give the impression of a fragment of verse or proverb. This is the same Ulf as is mentioned on p. 82 as Ulf Röde.

shield, and a helmet inlaid with gold; over his armour he had a short red coat, and was easy to be distinguished from other men. When King Olaf saw that the scattered forces of the enemy gathered themselves together under the banners of their ships, he asked, " Who is the chief of the force right opposite to us? "

He was answered, that it was King Swend with the Danish army.

The king replies, " We are not afraid of these soft Danes, for there is no bravery in them; but who is the chief fighting under those standards out on the right wing? "

He was answered, that it was King Olaf with the Swedish forces.

" Better it were," says King Olaf, " for these Swedes to be sitting at home licking their sacrificial bowls,[1] than to be venturing under our weapons from the Long Serpent. But who owns the large ships on the larboard side of the Danes? "

" That is Earl Eric Hakonson," say they.

The king replies, " He, methinks, has good reason for meeting us; and we may expect the sharpest conflict with these men, for they are Norsemen like ourselves."

CHAPTER CXV. THE BATTLE BEGINS.—The kings now laid out their oars and prepared to attack. King Swend laid his ship against the Long Serpent. Outside of him Olaf the Swede laid himself, and set his ship's stem against the outermost ship of King Olaf's line; and on the other side lay Earl Eric. Then a hard combat began. Earl Sigvald held back with the oars on his ships, and did not join the fray. So says Skule Thorsteinson, who at that time was with Earl Eric:—

> " I followed Sigvald in my youth,
> And gallant Eric; and in truth,
> Tho' now I am grown stiff and old,
> In the spear-song I once was bold.
> I wielded swordblade in the south
> In battle there at Svolde's mouth,
> And stood amidst the loudest clash
> When swords on shields made fearful crash."

And Halfred also speaks of these events:—

> " In truth, I think the gallant king,
> Midst such a foeman's gathering,
> Would be the better of some score
> Of his tight Drontheim lads, or more;

[1] Blótbollar, bowls to receive the blood of animals slain as sacrifices. He is referring to the Swedes being still heathen.

For many a chief has run away,
And left our brave king in the fray,
Two great kings' power to withstand,
And one great earl's, with his small band.
The scald who tells this glorious deed
Himself wins honour for his meed."

CHAPTER CXVI. FLIGHT OF KING SWEND AND KING OLAF THE SWEDE.—This battle [1] was one of the severest told of, and many were the people slain. The forecastle men of the Long Serpent, the Little Serpent, and the Crane threw grapplings and anchors into King Swend's ship, and used their weapons well against the people standing below them, for they cleared the decks of all the ships they could lay fast hold of; and King Swend, and all the men who escaped, fled to other vessels, and laid themselves out of bow-shot. It went with this force just as King Olaf Trygvesson had foreseen. Then King Olaf the Swede laid himself in their place; but when he came near the great ships it went with him as with them, for he lost many men and some ships, and was obliged to get away. But Earl Eric laid the Iron Beard side by side with the outermost of King Olaf's ships, thinned it of men, cut the cables, and let it drive. Then he laid alongside of the next, and fought until he had cleared it of men also. Now all the people who were in the smaller ships began to run into the larger, and the earl cut them loose as fast as he cleared them of men. The Danes and Swedes laid themselves now within shooting distance all around Olaf's ship; but Earl Eric lay always close alongside of the ships, and used his swords and battle-axes, and as fast as people fell in his vessel others, Danes and Swedes, came in their place. So says Haldor:—

" Sharp was the clang of shield and sword,
And shrill the song of spears on board,
And whistling arrows thickly flew
Against the Serpent's gallant crew
And still fresh foemen, it is said,
Earl Eric to her long side led;
Whole armies of his Danes and Swedes,
Wielding on high their blue sword-blades."

Then the fight became most severe, and many people fell. But at last it came to this, that all King Olaf Trygvesson's ships were cleared of men except the Long Serpent, on board of which all who could still carry their arms were gathered. Then Iron

---

[1] The battle took place in September 1000; some sources assign it to the 9th, some to the 10th or 11th. Snorri's silence on the point probably means that he found the evidence too slight to justify a mention.

Beard lay side by side with the Serpent, and the fight went on with battle-axe and sword. So says Haldor:—

> " Hard pressed on every side by foes,
> The Serpent reels beneath the blows;
> Crash go the shields around the bow!
> Breast-plates and breasts pierced thro' and thro'!
> In the sword-storm the Holm beside,
> The Iron Beard lay alongside
> The king's Long Serpent [1] of the sea—
> Fate gave the earl the victory."

CHAPTER CXVII. OF EARL ERIC.—Earl Eric was in the fore-hold of his ship, where a cover of shields [2] had been set up. In the fight, both hewing weapons, sword and axe, and the thrust of spears had been used; and all that could be used as weapon for casting was cast. Some used bows, some threw spears with the hand. So many weapons were cast into the Serpent, and so thick flew spears and arrows, that the shields could scarcely receive them; for on all sides the Serpent was surrounded by war ships. Then King Olaf's men became so mad with rage, that they ran on board of the enemies' ships, to get at the people with stroke of sword and kill them; but many did not lay themselves so near the Serpent, in order to escape the close encounter with battle-axe or sword; and thus the most of Olaf's men went overboard and sank under their weapons, thinking they were fighting on plain ground. So says Halfred:—

> " The daring lads shrink not from death,—
> O'erboard they leap, and sink beneath
> The Serpent's keel: all armed they leap,
> And down they sink five fathoms deep.
> And though the Serpent sail again,
> Though kings may steer her 'cross the main,
> Though long she sail, whate'er the seas,
> She ne'er shall find such lads as these."

CHAPTER CXVIII. OF EINAR TAMBARSKELVE.[3]—Einar Tambarskelve, one of the sharpest of bow-shooters, stood by the mast, and shot with his bow. Einar shot an arrow at Earl Eric, which hit the tiller-end just above the earl's head so hard that it entered the wood up to the arrow-shaft. The earl looked that way, and asked if they knew who had shot; and at the same moment another arrow flew between his hand and his side, and

---

[1] Literally, "fearsome Fafnir"—Fafnir being a famous dragon.

[2] Both in land and sea fights the commanders appear to have been protected from missile weapons,—stones, arrows, spears,—by a shieldburg; that is, by a party of men bearing shields surrounding them in such a way that the shields were a parapet, covering those within the circle.

[3] þambarskelfir, " he who twangs the gut-string (of the bow)."

into the head board,[1] so that the barb stood far out on the other side. Then said the earl to a man called Fin,—but some say he was of Finn (Laplander) race, and was a superior archer,— " Shoot that tall man by the mast." Fin shot; and the arrow hit the middle of Einar's bow just at the moment that Einar was drawing it, and the bow was split in two parts.

" What is that," cried King Olaf, " that broke with such a noise? "

" Norway, king, from thy hands," cried Einar.

" No! not quite so much as that," says the king; " take my bow, and shoot," flinging the bow to him.

Einar took the bow, and drew it over the head of the arrow. " Too weak, too weak," said he, " for the bow of a mighty king! " and, throwing the bow back to him, he took a sword and shield, and fought.

CHAPTER CXIX. OLAF GIVES HIS MEN SHARP SWORDS.— The king stood on the gangways of the Long Serpent, and shot the greater part of the day; sometimes with the bow, sometimes with the spear, and always throwing two spears at once. He looked down over the ship's side, and saw that his men struck briskly with their swords, and yet wounded but seldom. Then he called aloud, " Why do ye strike so gently that ye seldom cut? " One among the people answered, " The swords are blunt and full of notches." Then the king went down into the fore-hold, opened the chest under the throne, and took out many sharp swords, which he handed to his men; but as he stretched down his right hand with them, some observed that blood was running down under his steel glove, but no one knew where he was wounded.

CHAPTER CXX. THE SERPENT BOARDED. — Desperate was the defence in the Serpent, and there was the heaviest destruction of men done by the forecastle crew, and those of the fore-hold, for in both places the men were chosen men, and the ship was highest; but in the middle of the ship the people were thinned. Now when Earl Eric saw there were but few people remaining beside the ship's mast, he determined to board; and he entered the Serpent with fourteen men. Then came Hyrning, the king's brother-in-law, and some others against him, and there was the most severe combat; and at last the earl was forced to leap back, on board the Iron Beard again, and some who

[1] The board behind the steersman's head when he is sitting at the rudder.

had accompanied him were killed, and others wounded. Thord
Kolbeinsson alludes to this:—

> " Grasping a shield, all wet with blood,
> The helm-adorned hero stood;
> And gallant Hyrning honour gained,
> Clearing all round with sword deep stained.
> The high heavens themselves shall fall,
> Ere men forget this to recall."

Now the fight became hot indeed, and many men fell on board
the Serpent; and the men on board of her began to be thinned
off, and the defence to be weaker. The earl resolved to board
the Serpent again, and again he met with a warm reception.
When the forecastle men of the Serpent saw what he was doing,
they went aft and made a desperate fight; but so many men
of the Serpent had fallen, that the ship's sides were in many
places quite bare of defenders; and the earl's men poured in all
around into the vessel, and all the men who were still able to
defend the ship crowded aft to the king, and arrayed themselves
for his defence. So says Haldor the Unchristian, telling how
Earl Eric urged his men forward:—

> " Eric cheers on his men,—
> ' On to the charge again! '
> The gallant few
> Of Olaf's crew
> Must refuge take
> On the quarter-deck.
> Around the king
> They stand in ring;
> Their shields enclose
> The king from foes,
> The clash of steel draws near
> To him whom all Vends fear." [1]

CHAPTER CXXI. THE SERPENT'S DECKS CLEARED.—Kolbiorn
the marshal, who had on clothes and arms like the king's, and
was a remarkably stout and handsome man, went up to the king
on the quarter deck. The battle was still going on fiercely even
in the forehold.[2] But as many of the earl's men had now got
into the Serpent as could find room, and his ships lay all round
her, and few were the people left in the Serpent for defence
against so great a force; and in a short time most of the Serpent's

[1] Literally, " the murderer of Vends," which in the context probably
means Olaf (the same kenning is applied to him elsewhere). This may
allude to his early raids on Vendland (p. 24), or else may imply that some
of Earl Sigvald's Vendland men were taking part in the fighting.

[2] *Fyrirrúm*, the area of the hold just below the " quarter-deck " (*lypting*);
such vessels were decked fore and aft only.

men fell, brave and stout though they were. King Olaf and Kolbiorn the marshal both sprang overboard, each on his own side of the ship; but the earl's men had laid out boats around the Serpent, and killed those who leaped overboard. Now when the king had sprung overboard, they tried to seize him with their hands, and bring him to Earl Eric; but King Olaf threw his shield over his head, and sank beneath the waters. Kolbiorn held his shield behind him to protect himself from the spears cast at him from the ships which lay round the Serpent, and he fell so upon his shield that it came under him, so that he could not sink so quickly. He was thus taken and brought into a boat, and they supposed he was the king. He was brought before the earl; and when the earl saw it was Kolbiorn, and not the king, he gave him his life. At the same moment all of King Olaf's men who were in life sprang overboard from the Serpent; and Halfred says that Thorkel Nefia, the king's brother, was the last of all the men who sprang overboard.

> " Both the Serpents and the Crane
> Drifted unmanned upon the main;
> This the generous warrior saw
> (Gladly he'd reddened spears in war),
> So then the daring Thorketel—
> Fearless where metal rings on metal—
> Wise warrior—leapt from the ship's side,
> And swam away on ocean's tide." [1]

CHAPTER CXXII. OF THE REPORT AMONG THE PEOPLE OF THE ISLAND.—Earl Sigvald, as before related, came from Vendland, in company with King Olaf, with ten ships; but the eleventh ship was manned with the men of Astrid, the king's daughter, the wife of Earl Sigvald. Now when King Olaf sprang overboard, the whole army raised a shout of victory; and then Earl Sigvald and his men put their oars in the water and rowed towards the battle. Haldor the Unchristian tells of it thus:—

> " From far the Vendland vessels come
> Into the fight; the iron tongue
> Of shield-destroying axe in strife
> Now reaches out to taste men's life.
> The clash of swords rings o'er the waves;
> The eagle tears what wolf too craves;
> The chieftain whom his men hold dear
> Slays many; many flee in fear." [2]

But the Vendland cutter, in which Astrid's men were, rowed back to Vendland; and the report went immediately abroad,

---

[1] Odd also quotes this, but applies it to Thorkel Dyrdel, not Thorkel Nefia.

[2] It is not clear why Snorri thought this verse relevant here.

and was told by many, that King Olaf had cast off his coat
of mail under water, and swam, diving under the long-ships,
until he came to the Vendland cutter, and that Astrid's men had
conveyed him to Vendland: and many tales have been made
since about the adventures of Olaf the king.[1] Halfred speaks
thus about it:—

> " When I praise him who ravens fed,
> Praise I a live man?   Or one dead?
> I scarcely know what I should say,
> For many tell the tale each way.
> This I can say, nor fear to lie,
> That he was wounded grievously,—
> But more than this is hard to tell,
> For no news comes, nor good nor ill."

But however this may have been, King Olaf Trygvesson never
came back again to his kingdom of Norway.   Halfred Vandrædaskald speaks also thus about it:—

> " A noble warrior tells this thing:
> That Trygve's son, our gallant king,
> Is still alive; and others say
> That Olaf 'scaped from that fell fray.
> But oh, their tale is far from true,
> And greater sorrow we must rue.
> It never was the will of Fate
> That Olaf, from such perilous strait,
> Should safely come, when warrior horde
> Fought hard to reach our valiant lord.
> 'Tis but a guess.   Yet some still say
> He was but wounded there that day,
> And that when east across the sea
> The weapons clashed, he came off free.
> More true are tales that tell his death—
> I 'll not rust idle rumour's breath."

CHAPTER CXXIII. OF EARL ERIC, THE SON OF HAKON.—
By this victory Earl Eric Hakonson became owner of the Long
Serpent, and made a great booty besides; and he steered the
Serpent from the battle.   So says Haldor;—

> " Olaf, with glittering helmet crowned,
> Had steered the Serpent battle-bound;
> To where the swords in warfare meet—
> Her crew the picked men of the fleet.
> But in that fight on southern sea
> Hemming's great brother gallantly
> His blue sword in red life-blood stained,
> And bravely Olaf's long-ship gained."

---

[1] Gunnlaug Leifsson wrote several chapters on this theme in his Latin
Life of Olaf (*c.* 1200), saying that Olaf went on pilgrimage to the Holy
Land and lived there for many years as a monk.   Odd too is inclined to
believe that Olaf escaped, and became a monk in Greece or Syria.

Swend, a son of Earl Hakon, and Earl Eric's brother, was engaged at this time to marry Holmfrid, a daughter of King Olaf the Swedish king. Now when Swend the Danish king, Olaf the Swedish king, and Earl Eric divided the kingdom of Norway between them, King Olaf got four districts in the Drontheim country, and also the districts of Möre and Raumsdal; and in the east part of the land he got Ranrige, from the Gotha river to Svinesund. Olaf gave these dominions into Earl Swend's hands, on the same conditions as the sub-kings or earls had held them formerly from the over-king of the country. Earl Eric got four districts in the Drontheim country, and Halogaland, Naumadal, the Fjords districts, Sogn, Hordaland, Rogaland, and North Agder, all the way to the Naze. So says Thord Kolbeinson:—

> " All chiefs within our land
> On Eric's side now stand:
> Erling alone, I know,
> Remains Earl Eric's foe.
> All praise our generous earl,—
> He gives, and is no churl:
> All men are well content
> Fate such a chief has sent.
> From Veg [1] to Agder they,
> Well pleased, the earl obey;
> And all will by him stand.
> To guard the Norsemen's land.
> And now the news is spread
> That mighty Swend is dead,
> His lands lie drear and waste;
> Luck always ends at last."

The Danish king Swend retained Viken as he had held it before, but he gave Raumarike and Hedemark to Earl Eric. Swend Hakonson got the title of earl from Olaf the Swedish king. Swend was one of the handsomest men ever seen. The earls Eric and Swend both allowed themselves to be baptized, and took up the true faith; but as long as they ruled in Norway they allowed every one to do as he pleased in holding by his Christianity. But, on the other hand, they held fast by the old laws, and all the old rights and customs of the land, and were excellent men and good rulers. Earl Eric had most to say of the two brothers in all matters of government.

[1] Veiga or Vega, an island in the south of Halogaland.

THE TALE OF THE GREENLANDERS

THE following section, although included in Peringskiöld's edition of *Heimskringla* (1697) and in Schøning's (1777–83), has no connection at all with Snorri's work. It is a tale found inserted in the manuscript called *Flateyjarbók* (*Codex Flateyensis*), in that manuscript's long and diffuse *Greatest Saga of Olaf Tryggvason*. It is usually known as *The Tale of the Greenlanders* (*Grœnlendinga páttr*); the part of *Flateyjarbók* which contains it is known to have been written shortly before 1388, but how much older than that the *Tale* may be is a matter of controversy.

The story of the discovery of America by the Norsemen is known from three main sources: brief historical notices, such as that by Snorri on p. 84 above, ascribing the discovery to Leif the Lucky; the *Tale of the Greenlanders*, ascribing it to Bjarni and telling of four other expeditions that reached Vinland; and the *Saga of Eric the Red* (sometimes called *Thorstein Karlsefni's Saga*), giving first credit to Leif, but far more concerned with an expedition led by Thorfinn Karlsefni, the only other successful voyage to Vinland to be mentioned there. This saga has been translated by Gwyn Jones, *Eirik the Red and Other Icelandic Sagas*, 1961.

There are numerous points of difference between the *Tale* and the *Saga of Eric the Red*, and commentators have been led to widely different conclusions in considering their respective value as sources and in constructing a factual account of Norse explorations in America on the basis of one or both of them. G. M. Gathorne-Hardy (*The Norse Discoverers of America*, 1921) harmonizes the two accounts wherever possible; where he cannot do so, he gives preference to the *Tale*.

The opposite point of view is held by Halldór Hermannsson (*The Problem of Wineland, Islandica*, XXV, 1921; *The Vinland Sagas, Islandica*, XXX, 1944); in a powerfully destructive analysis of the *Tale* he argues that it is a chaotic mixture of motifs borrowed from *Eric the Red* and from garbled popular tradition, containing only a few details of value (e.g. the *eyktarstað* measurement, p. 105). He assigns it to the fourteenth century, and allows it no real importance as a source.

More recently, Jón Jóhannesson has argued in favour of the *Tale* as an old and valuable source ("The Date of Composition of the *Saga of the Greenlanders*", *Saga-Book* XVI: i. 1962). He considers that the very fact that it contradicts passages in *Heimskringla* and other historical works (all associated with Olaf Tryggvason and all derivable from Gunnlaug's Latin life of him) by ascribing the first discovery to Bjarni, not Leif, shows that it has preserved an older and truer tradition. As Gunnlaug's work is from *c.* 1200, the *Tale* must be yet older to have escaped Gunnlaug's influence; this would make it one of the oldest of the sagas. The relationship between it and the *Saga of Eric the Red* would then be that the latter used it as a source, but deviated from it by following the tradition stemming from Gunnlaug, and also by transposing and rearranging various episodes; the importance of the *Tale* would be much increased by this early dating.

Accuracy of detail in judging the geography of the Vinland voyages cannot be reached while the relationship and relative value of the two most detailed sources remain in dispute. On the data given in the *Tale*, Helluland is probably Labrador, Markland either Nova Scotia or Newfoundland, and Vinland an area well south of 50°, perhaps the coast of Massachusetts.

On the Greenland colony itself, see Poul Nørlund, *Viking Settlers in Greenland*, 1930; G. J. Marcus, "The Course for Greenland," *Saga-Book of the Viking Society*, XIV, 1–2, 1953–5; G. Jones, *The Norse Atlantic Saga*, 1964; K. J. Krogh, *Viking Greenland*, 1967.

CHAPTER I. OF THE VOYAGE OF BIARNE THE SON OF HERIULF.
—Heriulf was a son of Baard Heriulfsson, who was a relation of
Ingolf the landnaman.[1] Ingolf gave Heriulf land between Vog
and Reikaness. Heriulf dwelt first at Dropstock. His wife
was called Thorgird, and their son was called Biarne. He was a
promising young man. In his earliest youth he had a desire
to go abroad, and he soon gathered property and reputation;
and he was by turns a year abroad, and a year with his father.
Biarne was soon possessor of a merchant ship of his own. The
last winter, while he was in Norway, Heriulf prepared to go to
Greenland with Eric, and gave up his dwelling. There was a
Christian man belonging to the Hebrides along with Heriulf,
who composed the lay called the Hafgerding [2] Song, in which
is this refrain:—

> " I pray to God, Purest of all,
>   Tester of monks, my journey aid!
>   O Lord who rules earth's lofty hall,
>   Hold still Thy hand above my head! "

Heriulf settled at Heriulfsness,[3] and became a very distinguished man. Eric Red took up his abode at Brattalid,
and was in great consideration, and honoured by all. These
were Eric's children,—Leif, Thorvald, and Thorstein; and his
daughter was called Freydis. She was married to a man called
Thorvald; and they dwelt at Gardar, which is now a bishop's
seat. She was a haughty proud woman; and he was but a
mean man. She was much given to gathering wealth. The
people of Greenland were heathen at this time.

Biarne came to Eyrar [4] in his ship in the summer of the
same year when his father sailed abroad in spring. He was much
struck with the news, and would not unload his vessel. When
his crew asked him what he intended to do, he replied that
he was resolved to follow his old custom of taking up his winter

---

[1] *Landnámamaðr*, one of the first settlers of Iceland.

[2] *Hafgerðingar*, " Sea Walls "; according to the *Konungs Skuggsjá*, this
" strange feature of the Greenland seas " was three vast waves, steep and
high as crags, filling the whole area of the sea. This description would fit
the tidal waves of an underwater earthquake or eruption; perhaps the more
common occurrence of waves set up by capsizing icebergs is also meant.

[3] Heriulfsness, Brattalid and Gardar are in Greenland, which was
colonised by Eric the Red in A.D. 986. The Greenland sites have been
excavated (see Poul Nørlund, *Viking Settlers in Greenland*, 1930), and further
excavations are in progress at present (1962).

[4] *i.e. Eyrarbakki* in South Iceland.

abode with his father. "So I will steer for Greenland, if ye will go with me." They one and all agreed to go with him. Biarne said, "Our expedition will be thought foolish, as none of us have ever been on the Greenland sea before." Nevertheless they set out to sea as soon as they were ready, and sailed for three days, until they lost sight of the land they had left. But when the wind failed, a north wind with fog set in, and they knew not where they were sailing to; and this lasted many days. At last they saw the sun, and could distinguish the quarters of the sky; so they hoisted sail again, and sailed for one day and night,[1] when they made land. They spoke among themselves about what this land could be, and Biarne said that, in his opinion, it could not be Greenland. On the question if he should sail nearer to it, he said, "It is my advice that we sail close up to this land." They did so; and they soon saw that the land was without mountains, that it was covered with wood, and that there were small hills inland. They left the land on the larboard side, and had their sheet on the land side. Then they sailed two days and nights before they got sight of land again. They asked Biarne if he thought this would be Greenland; but he gave his opinion that this land was no more Greenland than the land they had seen before. "For on Greenland, it is said, there are great snow-mountains." [2] They soon came near to this land, and saw it was flat and covered with trees. Now, as the wind fell, the ship's people talked of its being advisable to make for the land; but Biarne would not agree to it. They thought they would need wood and water; but Biarne said, "Ye are not in want of either." And the men blamed him for this. He ordered them to hoist the sail, which was done. They now turned the ship's bow from the land, and kept the sea for three days and nights with a fine breeze from south-west. Then they saw a third land, which was high and mountainous, and with snowy mountains. Then they asked Biarne if he would land here; but he refused altogether. "For in my opinion this land is not of use to us." Now they let the sails stand, and kept along the land, and saw it was an island. Then they turned from the land, and stood out to sea with the same breeze; but the gale increased, and Biarne ordered a reef to be taken in, and not to sail harder than the ship and her tackle could easily

---

[1] *Dægr* could mean a period, either a period of twelve hours or of twenty-four, and could also be a measure of distance at sea, 150 miles.

[2] Here and on pp. 104 and 106 the word rendered as "snow (snowy) mountains (ridges)" and "snow-covered mountain-range" is simply *jokull* ("glacier").

bear. After sailing four days and nights they made, the fourth time, land; and when they asked Biarne if he thought this was Greenland or not, Biarne replies, " This is most like what has been told me of Greenland; and here we shall take to the land." They did so, and came to the land in the evening under a ness, where they found a boat. On this ness dwelt Biarne's father Heriulf; and from that it is Heriulfsness. Biarne went to his father's, gave up seafaring, and dwelt with his father Heriulf as long as he lived; and after his father's death continued to dwell there.

CHAPTER II. OF LIEF ERICSSON'S DISCOVERY OF LAND.[1]—It is next to be told that Biarne Heriulfsson came over from Greenland to Norway on a visit to Earl Eric, who received him well. Biarne tells of this expedition of his, on which he had discovered unknown lands; and people thought he had not been very curious to get knowledge, as he could not give any account of those countries, and he was somewhat blamed on this account. Biarne was made a court-man of the earl, and the summer after he went over to Greenland; and afterwards there was much talk about discovering unknown lands. Leif, a son of Eric Red of Brattalid, went over to Biarne Heriulfsson, and bought the ship from him, and manned the vessel, so that in all there were thirty-five men on board. Leif begged his father Eric to go as commander of the expedition, but he excused himself; saying he was getting old, and not so able as formerly to undergo the hardships of a sea voyage. Leif insisted that he among all their relations was the most likely to have good luck on such an expedition: and Eric consented and rode from home with Leif when they had got all ready for sea; but when they were coming near to the ship the horse on which Eric was riding stumbled, and he fell from the horse and hurt his foot. " It is not des- tined," said Eric, " that I should discover more lands than this of Greenland, on which we dwell and live; and now we will not go forward together." Eric accordingly returned home to Brattalid; but Leif, with his comrades, in all thirty-five men, rigged out their vessel. There was a man from Germany who was called Tyrker with the expedition. They put the ship in order, and went to sea when they were ready. They first

[1] In *Flateyjarbók* this section follows the account of Olaf Tryggvason's death; Earl Eric ruled Norway 1000–14, so Bjarni's visit to him must have been in 1001 or later, and Leif's voyage no earlier than 1002 or 1003. But according to Snorri (*vide* p. 84) and the *Saga of Eric the Red*, Leif discovered Vinland in A.D. 1000.

came to the land which Biarne had last discovered, sailed up to it, cast anchor, put out a boat, and went on shore; but there was no grass to be seen. There were huge snowy mountains up the country; but all the way from the sea up to these snowy ridges the land was one slab of stone, and it appeared to them a country of no advantages. Leif said, " It shall not be said of us, as it was of Biarne, that we did not come upon the land; for I will give the country a name, and call it Helleland." [1] Then they went on board again, put to sea, and found another land. They sailed in towards it, cast anchor, put out a boat, and landed. The country was flat and overgrown with wood; and wide white sands wherever they went, and a gentle slope towards the sea. Then Leif said, " We shall give this land a name according to its kind, and call it Markland." [2] Then they hastened on board, and put to sea again with an on-shore wind from north-east, and were out for two days, and made land. They sailed towards it, and came to an island which lay on the north side of the land, where they landed to wait for good weather. There was dew upon the grass; and having accidentally got some of the dew upon their hands and put it to their mouths, they thought they had never tasted anything so sweet as it was.[3] Then they went on board, and sailed into a sound that was between the island and a ness which went out northwards from the land, and sailed west past the ness. There was very shallow water on ebb-tide, so that their ship lay dry; and there was a long way between their ship and the water. They were so desirous to get to the land that they would not wait till their vessel floated, but ran to the land, to a place where a river comes out of a lake. As soon as their ship was afloat, they took the boats, rowed to the ship, towed her up the river, and from thence into the lake, where they cast anchor, carried their beds out of the ship, and set up their tents. They resolved to put things in order for wintering there, and they erected a large house. They did not want for salmon, both in the river and in the lake; and they thought the salmon larger than any they had ever seen before. The country appeared to them of so good a kind, that it would not be necessary to gather fodder for the cattle for the winter. There was no frost in winter, and the grass was not much withered. Day and night were more equal than in Green-

[1] *i.e.* " Land of Flint Stone."
[2] *i.e.* " Forest Land."
[3] This passage is influenced by legends of " honey-dew " and manna.

land or Iceland; for on the shortest day the sun was in the sky between the Eyktarstad and the Dagmalastad.[1] Now when they were ready with their house-building, Leif said to his fellow-travellers, " Now I will divide the crew into two divisions and explore the country: half shall stay at home and do the work, and the other half shall search the land; but so that they do not go farther than that they can come back in the evening, and that they do not wander from each other." This they continued to do for some time. Leif changed about, sometimes with them, and sometimes with those at home. Leif was a stout and strong man, and of manly appearance; and he was besides a prudent sagacious man in all respects.

CHAPTER III. LEIF WINTERS IN THIS COUNTRY AND CALLS IT VINLAND; THEN SAILS HOME TO GREENLAND, AND RESCUES SHIPWRECKED MEN.—It happened one evening that a man of the party was missing; and it was the man from Germany, Tyrker. Leif was very sorry for it; because Tyrker had been long with him and his father, and had loved Leif much as a child. Leif blamed his comrades very much, and prepared to go with twelve men on an expedition to find him; but they had gone only a short way from the station before Tyrker came to meet them, and he was joyfully received. Leif soon perceived that his foster-father was merry. Tyrker had a high forehead, sharp eyes, and a small face, and was little in size and ugly; but was very dexterous in all crafts. Leif said to him, " Why art thou so late, my foster-father? and why didst thou leave they comrades? " He spoke at first in German,[2] rolled his eyes, and knit his brows; but they could not make out what he was saying. After a while and some delay, he said in Norse, " I did not go much farther than they; and yet I have something altogether new to relate, for I found vines and grapes." " Is that true, my foster-father? " said Leif. " Yes, true it is," answered he; " for I was born where there is no scarcity of vines and grapes." Now they slept all night, and next morning Leif said to his men,

---

[1] *i.e.* between 9.0 a.m. (*dagmál*) and 3.0 or 3.30 p.m. (*eykt*). Many attempts have been made to calculate the latitude of Vinland from this; it must have been farther south than 50°, but how much farther is debatable. A latitude of about 40° fits best with other indications, *e.g.* the presence of salmon and wild grapes. The absence of frost must be an exaggeration.
[2] The passage may imply that Tyrker was drunk, or merely that he was excited. Legends of berries that are intoxicating even when freshly picked are known in oriental and Irish tales, and may have influenced this account.

"Now we have two occupations to follow, on alternate days; namely, to gather grapes or cut vines, and to fell wood in the forest to load our vessel." And this advice was followed. It is related that their stern-boat was filled with grapes, and then a cargo of wood was hewn for the vessel. In spring they made ready and sailed away; and Leif gave the country a name from its productions, and called it Vinland.[1] They put to sea, and had a favourable breeze until they came in sight of Greenland and the fjelds below the snow-covered mountain range. Then one of the men said to Leif, "Why do you bear away so much?" Leif replied, "I mind my helm, but I attend to other things too: do you see nothing strange?" He answered that he saw nothing to speak of. "I don't know," said Leif, "whether it be a ship or a rock I see there." Then they all looked, and said it was a rock. But he saw so much sharper than they did, that he could distinguish people upon the rock. "Now I will put the vessel before the wind," says Leif, "so that we may get close to them, in case they are people who want to meet us and need our help; and if they are not men of peace, it is in our power to do as we please, and not in theirs." Now they came up to the rock, let down the sail, cast anchor, and put out another little boat which they had with them. Then Tyrker hailed them, and asked who was the commander of these people. He called himself Thore, and said he was a Norwegian. "And what," said he, "is your name?" Leif told his name. "Are you a son of Eric Red of Brattalid?" Leif replied it was so. "And now," said Leif, "I invite you all to come on board my ship, with all your goods that the vessel can stow." They accepted the offer; and then they sailed to Ericsfjord, and until they came to Brattalid, where they discharged the cargo. Leif offered Thore and his wife Gudrid, and three others, lodging with himself, and found lodging elsewhere for the rest of the people, both of Thore's crew and his own. Leif took fifteen men from the rock, and was thereafter called Leif the Lucky.[2] After that time Leif advanced greatly in wealth and consideration. That winter a sickness came among Thore's people, and he himself and a great part of his crew died.[3] The same winter Eric Red also died. This expedition to Vinland was much talked of; and

---

[1] *i.e.* "Wine-Land."

[2] *Vide* also p. 84 and *The Saga of Eric the Red*, chap. 5.

[3] The date of Eric's death is uncertain; one manuscript of his saga says he was alive in 1006–7. That he died before Greenland was Christianized (p. 108) is certainly an error.

Leif's brother Thorvald thought that the country had not been explored enough in different places. Then Leif said to Thorvald, "You may go, brother, in my ship to Vinland, if you like; but I will first send the ship for the timber which Thore left upon the rock." And so it was done.

CHAPTER IV. OF THORVALD ERICSSON, LEIF'S BROTHER; AND OF THE SKRÆLINGER.—Now Thorvald made ready for his voyage with thirty men, after consulting his brother Leif. They rigged their ship, and put to sea. Nothing is related of this expedition until they came to Vinland, to the booths put up by Leif, where they secured the ship and tackle, and remained quietly all winter, and lived by fishing. In spring Thorvald ordered the vessel to be rigged, and that some men should proceed in the long-boat westward along the coast, and explore it during the summer. They thought the country beautiful and well wooded, the distance small between the forest and the sea, and the strand full of white sand. There were also many islands, and very shallow water. They found no abode for man or beast; but upon an island far towards the west they found a corn-barn constructed of wood. They found no other trace of human work, and came back in autumn to Leif's booths. The following spring Thorvald with his merchant ship proceeded eastward, and towards the north along the land. Opposite to a cape they met bad weather, and drove upon the land and broke their keel, and remained there a long time to repair the vessel. Thorvald said to his comrades, "We will stick up the keel here upon the ness, and call the place Keelness;" and so they did. Then they sailed away eastward along the country, which was everywhere covered with wood. They moored the vessel to the land, laid out gangways to the shore, and Thorvald with all his ship's company landed. He said, "Here it is beautiful, and I would willingly set up my farm here." They afterwards went on board, and saw three specks upon the sand within the point, and went to them, and found these were three skin-boats, with three men under each boat.[1] They divided their men, and took all of them prisoners except one man, who escaped with his boat. They killed eight of them, and then went to the point and looked about them. Within this fjord they saw several eminences, which they took to be habitations. Then a heavy drowsiness came upon them, and they could not keep themselves awake, but all of them fell asleep. A sudden scream

[1] See note, p. 111.

came to them, and they all awoke; and mixed with the scream they thought they heard the words, "Awake, Thorvald, with all thy comrades, if ye will save your lives. Go on board your ship as fast as you can, and leave this land without delay." In the same moment an innumerable multitude from the interior of the fjord came in skin-boats, and laid themselves alongside. Then said Thorvald, "We shall put up our war-screens along the gunwales, and defend ourselves as well as we can; but not use our weapons much against them." They did so accordingly. The Skrælinger[1] shot at them for a while, and then made off as fast as they could wherever they saw the way was open to fly. Then Thorvald asked if any one was wounded, and they said nobody was hurt. He said, "I have got a wound under the arm. An arrow flew between the gunwale and the shield under my arm: here is the arrow, and it will be my death-wound. Now I advise you to make ready with all speed to return; but ye shall carry me up to the point which I thought would be so convenient for a dwelling. It may be that it was true what I said, that here I would dwell for a while. Ye shall bury me there, and place a cross at my head and another at my feet, and call the place Crossness." Christianity had been established in Greenland at this time; but Eric Red was dead before Christianity was introduced. Now Thorvald died, and they did everything as he had ordered. Then they went away in search of their fellow-travellers; and they related to each other all the news. They remained in their dwelling all winter, and gathered vines and grapes, and put them on board their ships. Towards spring they prepared to return to Greenland, where they arrived with their vessel, and landed at Ericsfjord, bringing heavy tidings to Leif.

CHAPTER V. OF THORSTEIN ERICSSON, LEIF'S BROTHER, AND HIS VOYAGE TO VINLAND.—In the meantime it had happened in Greenland that Thorstein of Ericsfjord had married, and taken to wife Gudrid, the daughter of Thorbiorn, who had been married, as before related, to Thore the Northman. Thorstein Ericsson bethought him now that he would go to Vinland for his brother Thorvald's body. He rigged out the same vessel, and chose an able and stout crew. He had with him twenty-five men, and his wife Gudrid; and as soon as they were ready he put to sea, and they lost sight of land. They drove about on

---

[1] See note, p. 111.

the ocean the whole summer, without knowing where they were; and in the first week of winter [1] they landed at Lysefjord in Greenland, in the Western Settlement. Thorstein looked for lodgings for his men, and got his whole ship's crew accommodated, but not himself and his wife; so that for some nights they had to sleep on board. At that time Christianity was but young in Greenland. One day, early in the morning, some men came to their tent, and the leader asked them what people were in the tent. Thorstein replies, "Two: who is it that inquires?" "Thorstein," was the reply; "and I am called Thorstein the Black, and it is my errand here to offer thee and thy wife lodging beside me." Thorstein said he would speak to his wife about it; and as she gave her assent, he agreed to it. "Then I shall come for you to-morrow with my team, for I do not lack means to entertain you; but few care to live in my house, for I and my wife live lonely, and I am very self-willed. I have also a different religion from yours, although I think the one you have is the best." Now the following morning he came for them with horses; and they took up their abode with Thorstein Black, who was very friendly towards them. Gudrid had a good outward appearance, and was knowing, and understood well how to behave with strangers. Early in winter a sickness prevailed among Thorstein Ericsson's people, and many of his fellow-travellers died. He ordered that coffins should be made for the bodies of the dead, and that they should be brought on board, and stowed carefully. "For I will transport all the bodies to Ericsfjord in summer." It was not long before sickness broke out also in Thorstein Black's house; and his wife, who was called Grimhild, fell sick first. She was very sturdy, and as strong as a man, but yet she could not bear up against the illness. Soon after Thorstein Ericsson also fell sick, and they both lay ill in bed at the same time; but Grimhild, Thorstein Black's wife, died first. When she was dead Thorstein went out of the room for a skin to lay over the corpse. Then Gudrid said, "My dear Thorstein, be not long away;" which he promised. Then said Thorstein Ericsson, "Our good-wife is wonderful; for she raises herself up with her elbows, moves herself forward over the bed-frame, and is feeling for her shoes." In the same moment Thorstein the goodman came back, and instantly Grimhild laid herself down, so that it made every beam that was in the house crack. Thorstein now made a

---

[1] The Icelanders reckoned winter from the first Saturday after the 14th of October.

coffin for Grimhild's corpse, removed it outside, and buried it. He was a stout and strong man, but it required all his strength to remove the corpse from the house. Now Thorstein Ericsson's illness increased upon him, and he died, which Gudrid his wife took with great grief. They were all in the room, and Gudrid had set herself upon a stool before the bench on which her husband Thorstein's body lay. Now Thorstein the goodman took Gudrid from the stool in his arms, and set himself with her upon a bench just opposite to Thorstein's body, and spoke much with her. He consoled her, and promised to go with her in summer to Ericsfjord, with her husband Thorstein's corpse, and those of his fellow-travellers. " And," said he, " I shall take with me many servants to console and assist." She thanked him for this. Thorstein Ericsson then raised himself up and said, " Where is Gudrid? " And thrice he said this; but she was silent. Then she said to Thorstein the goodman, " Shall I give answer or not? " He told her not to answer. Then went Thorstein the goodman across the room, and sat down in a chair, and Gudrid set herself on his knee; and Thorstein the goodman said, " What do you want, namesake? " After a while the corpse replies, " I wish to tell Gudrid her fate beforehand, that she may be the better able to bear my death; for I have come to a blessed resting-place. And this I have now to tell thee, Gudrid, that thou wilt be married to an Iceland man, and ye will live long together; and from you will descend many men, brave, gallant, and wise, and a well-pleasing race of posterity. Ye shall go from Greenland to Norway, and from thence to Iceland, where ye shall dwell. And long will ye live together, but thou wilt survive him; and then thou shalt go abroad, and go southward,[1] and shalt return to thy home in Iceland. And there must be a church built, and thou must remain there, and be consecrated a nun, and there end thy days." And then Thorstein sank backwards, and his corpse was put in order and carried to the ship. Thorstein the goodman held all that he had promised. He sold in spring his land and cattle, and went with Gudrid and all her goods; made ready the ship, got men for it, and then went to Ericsfjord. The body was buried at the church. Gudrid went to Leif's at Brattalid; and Thorstein the Black took his abode in Ericsfjord, and dwelt there as long as he lived; and he was reckoned an able man.

CHAPTER VI. OF THORFINN KARLSEFNE. HOW HE WENT TO

[1] *i.e.* on pilgrimage to Rome.

VINLAND; AND OF THE SKRÆLINGER.[1]—That same summer came a ship from Norway to Greenland. The man was called Thorfinn Karlsefne who steered the ship. He was a son of Thord Hesthöfde, a son of Snorre Thordarson from Hofda. Thorfinn Karlsefne was a man of great wealth, and was in Brattalid with Leif Ericsson. Soon he fell in love with Gudrid and courted her, and she referred to Leif to answer for her. Afterwards she was betrothed to him, and their wedding was held the same winter. At this time, as before, much was spoken about a Vinland voyage; and both Gudrid and others persuaded Karlsefne much to that expedition. Now his expedition was resolved upon, and he got ready a crew of sixty men and five women; and then they made the agreement, Karlsefne and his people, that each of them should have equal share in what they made of gain. They had with them all kinds of cattle,[2] having the intention to settle in the land if they could. Karlsefne asked Leif for his houses in Vinland, and he said he would lend them, but not give them. Then they put to sea with the ship,

[1] The etymology of the name *Skrælingar* is uncertain; it may mean either "Screechers" or "Flinchers"—the latter presumably referring to the cowardice of these people, about which there are anecdotes here and in the *Saga of Eric the Red*. The name was applied by the Greenland settlers both to the Eskimos, of whose artefacts they had found traces there, and to the natives whom they encountered in Vinland. It is indeed plain from the earliest mention of Skrælings (in Ari's *Íslendingabók*) that they thought the natives of Greenland and those of Vinland to be of the same race. However, it is unlikely that Eskimos would come as far south as the regions described here, and there are several details in the accounts of the Skrælings of Vinland which point rather to their having been Red Indians, probably Algonquins. Their "skin-boats" (p. 107) might well be birch-bark canoes; certain Indian tribes are known to have slept habitually under their canoes. On the whole the encounters with Skrælings described here and in the *Saga of Eric the Red* seem plausible and factual, but occasionally a note of supernatural mystery has crept in, as in the episode of the uncanny woman seen by Gudrid (pp. 112–13). The point of this incident is obscure; perhaps this, and the other supernatural stories associated with Gudrid, are intended to emphasise her spiritual importance as the ancestress of three bishops (see p. 116), or possibly she was in actual fact liable to hallucinations and psychic experiences, about which stories were circulated among her descendants.

[2] There is no improbability in this statement; the doubts expressed in the previous editor's note on the passage are unfounded, for archaeological evidence shows that cattle flourished in the Greenland settlement, where their bones, together with those of sheep and pigs, are commonly found in deposits of this period. The climate of Greenland was then far milder. The most recent investigations, those of the Danish National Museum expedition in 1962, show that the pastures of Eric the Red's farm were extensive and well irrigated, and that his cow-stalls could accommodate forty animals; other farms in the Brattalid area seem also to have been well stocked. (See Gwyn Jones, "Where Norse Swords Became Ploughs," *The Times*, 4th August 1962.)

and came to Leif's houses safe, and carried up their goods. They soon had in hand a great and good prize; for a whale had driven on shore, both large and excellent. They went to it and cut it up, and had no want of food. Their cattle went up into the land; but soon they were unruly, and gave trouble to them. They had one bull with them. Karlsefne let wood be felled and hewed for taking away, and had it laid on a rock to dry. They had all the good of the products of the land which were there,— both grapes, and wood, and other products. After that first winter, and when summer came, they were aware of Skrælinger being there; and a great troop of men came out of the woods. The cattle were near to them, and the bull began to bellow and roar very loud, and with that the Skrælinger were frightened, and made off with their bundles,—and these were of furs, and sables, and all sorts of skins; and they turned to Karlsefne's habitation, and wanted to go into the houses, but Karlsefne defended the doors. Neither party understood the language of the other. Then the Skrælinger took their bundles and opened them, and offered them, and wanted to have weapons in exchange for them; but Karlsefne forbade his men to sell weapons. And then he took this plan with them, that he told the women to bear out milk and dairy products to them; and when they saw these things they would buy them, and nothing else. And now the trade for the Skrælinger was such that they carried away their winnings in their stomachs; and Karlsefne and his comrades got both their bags and skin-goods, and so they went away. And now it is to be told that Karlsefne let a good strong fence be made round the habitation, and strengthened it for defence. At this time Gudrid, Karlsefne's wife, lay in of a male child, and the child was called Snorre. In the beginning of the next winter came the Skrælinger again to them, and in much greater numbers than before, and with the same kind of wares. Then said Karlsefne to the women, " Now ye shall carry out the same kind of food as was best liked the last time, and nothing else." And when they saw that, they threw their bundles in over the fence: and Gudrid sat in the door within, by the cradle of Snorre her son. Then came a shadow to the door, and a woman went in with a black kirtle on, rather short, with a ribbon round her head; light brown hair; pale; with large eyes, so large that no one ever saw such eyes in a human head. She went to where Gudrid was sitting, and said, " What art thou called? " ", I am called Gudrid; and what art thou called? " " I am called

Gudrid," said she. Then the goodwife Gudrid put out her hand to her, that she might sit down beside her. And at the same time Gudrid heard a great noise, and the woman had vanished; and at the same moment one of the Skrælinger was killed by one of Karlsefne's housemen, because he was about to take one of their weapons; and they made off as fast as possible, leaving behind them clothes and goods. No one had seen this woman but Gudrid. "Now," says Karlsefne, "we must be cautious, and take counsel; for I think they will come the third time with hostility and many people. We shall now take the plan that ten men go out to that ness and show themselves there, and the rest of our men shall go into the woods, and make a clearance for our cattle against the time the enemy comes out of the forest; and we shall take the bull before us, and let him go in front." And it happened so that at the place they were to meet there was a lake on the one side and the forest on the other. The plan which Karlsefne had laid down was adopted. The Skrælinger came to the place where Karlsefne proposed to fight; and there was a battle there, and many of the Skrælinger fell. There was one stout and handsome man among the Skrælinger people, and Karlsefne thought that he must be their chief. One of the Skrælinger had taken up an axe and looked at it a while, and wielded it against one of his comrades, and cut him down, so that he fell dead instantly. Then the stout man took the axe, looked at it a while, and threw it into the sea as far as he could. They then fled to the forest as fast as they could, and so closed the battle. Karlsefne remained there with his men the whole winter; but towards spring he made known that he would not stay there longer, and would return to Greenland. Now they prepared for their voyage, and they took much goods from thence,—vines, grapes, and skin wares. They put to sea, and their ship came safe to Ericsfjord, and they were there for the winter.

CHAPTER VII. OF FREYDIS, ERIC'S DAUGHTER, AND HER VOYAGE TO VINLAND, AND HER MISDEEDS.—Now the conversation began again to turn upon a Vinland voyage, as the expedition was both gainful and honourable. The same summer that Karlsefne returned from Vinland, a ship arrived in Greenland from Norway. Two brothers commanded the ship, Helge and Finboge; and they remained that winter in Greenland. The brothers were of Icelandic descent, from Eastfjord. It is now to be told that Freydis, Eric's daughter, came home from Gardar,

and went to the abode of Helge and Finboge, and proposed to
them that they should go to Vinland with their vessel, and have
half with her of all the goods they could get there. They agreed
to this. Then she went to the abode of her brother Leif and
asked him to give her the houses he had built in Vinland; and
he answered as before, that he would lend, but not give the
houses. It was agreed upon between the brothers and Freydis
that each should have thirty fighting men, besides women. But
Freydis broke this, and had five men more, and concealed them;
and the brothers knew nothing of this until they arrived in
Vinland. They went to sea, and had agreed beforehand that
they should sail in company, if they could do so: and the
difference was but little, although the brothers came a little
earlier, and had carried up their baggage to Leif's houses. And
when Freydis came to the land, her people cleared the ship, and
carried her baggage also up to the house. Then said Freydis,
"Why are ye carrying your things in here?" "Because we
thought," said they, "that the whole of the agreement with us
should be held." She said, "Leif lent the house to me, not to
you." Then said Helge, "In evil we brothers cannot match
with thee;" and bore out their luggage, and made a shed, and
built it farther from the sea on the borders of a lake, and set all
about it in good order. Freydis let trees be cut down for her
ship's cargo. Now winter set in, and the brothers proposed
to have some games for amusement, and to pass the time. So
it was done for a time till discord came among them, and the
games were given up, and none went from the one house to the
other; and things went on so during a great part of the winter.
It happened one morning that Freydis got out of her berth,
and put on her clothes, but not her shoes; and the weather
was such that much dew had fallen. She took the cloak of her
husband over her, and went out, and went to the house of the
brothers, and to the door. A man had gone out a little before,
and left the door behind him half shut. She opened the door,
and stood in the doorway a little, and was silent. Finboge lay
the farthest inside in the hut, and was awake. He said, "What
wilt thou have here, Freydis?" She said, "I want thee to get
up and go out with me, for I would speak with thee." He did
so. They went to a tree that was lying under the eaves of the
hut, and sat down. "How dost thou like this place?" said she.
He said, "The country, methinks, is good; but I do not like
this quarrel that is come among us, for I think there is no cause
for it." "Thou art right," says she, "and I think so too; and

it is my errand to thy dwelling that I want to buy the ship of you brothers, as your ship is larger than mine, and I would break up from hence." "I will let it be so," said he, "if that will please thee." Now they parted so, and she went home, and Finboge to his bed. She went up into her berth, and with her cold feet wakened Thorvald, who asked why she was so cold and wet. She answered with great warmth, "I went to these brothers," says she, "to treat about their ship, for I want a larger ship; and they took it so ill that they struck and abused me. And thou, useless man! wilt neither avenge my affront nor thy own; and now must I feel that I am away from Greenland, but I will separate from thee if thou dost not avenge this." And now he could not bear her reproaches, and told his men to rise as fast as possible and take their weapons. They did so, and went to the tents of the brothers, and went in as they all lay asleep and seized them all, and bound them, and led them out bound, one after the other; and Freydis had each of them put to death as he came out. Now all the men were killed; but the women were left, and nobody would kill them. Then said Freydis, "Give me an axe in my hand." This was done, and she turned on those five women, and did not give over till they were all dead. Now they returned to their own huts after this evil deed; and people could only observe that Freydis thought she had done exceedingly well; and she said to her comrades, "If it be our lot to return to Greenland I shall take the life of the man who speaks of this affair; and we shall say that we left them here when we went away." Now they got ready the ship early in spring which had belonged to the brothers, with all the goods they could get, or that the ship could carry, sailed out to sea, and had a good voyage; and the ship came early in summer to Ericsfjord. Karlsefne was there still, and had his ship ready for sea, but waited a wind; and it was a common saying, that never had a richer ship sailed from Greenland than that which he steered. Freydis went home now to her house, which had stood without damage in the meantime. She bestowed many gifts on her followers that they might conceal her wickedness; and she remained now on her farm. All were not so silent about their misdeed and wickedness that something did not come up about it. This came at last to the ears of Leif her brother, and he thought this report was very bad. Leif took three men of Freydis's followers, and tortured them to speak, and they acknowledged the whole affair, and their tales agreed together. "I do not care," says Leif, "to treat my sister

Freydis as she deserves; but this I will foretell of them, that
their posterity will never thrive." And it went so that nobody
thought anything of them but evil from that time.

CHAPTER VIII. OF THORFINN KARLSEFNE AND HIS DESCEN-
DANTS.—Now we have to say that Karlsefne got ready his ship
and sailed out to sea. He came on well, and reached Norway
safely, and remained there all winter and sold his wares; and
he and his wife were held in esteem by the most considerable
people in Norway. Now in the following spring he fitted out
his ship for Iceland; and when he was quite ready, and his ship
lay outside the pier waiting a wind, there came to him a South-
country man from Bremen in Saxonland, who would deal with
him for his house-besom.[1] "I will not sell it," said he. "I
will give thee a half mark of gold for it," said the South-country
man. Karlsefne thought it was a good offer, and sold it accordingly. The South-country man went away with the house-besom,
and Karlsefne did not know what the wood was. It was massur-
wood[2] from Vinland. Now Karlsefne put to sea, and his ship
came to land north at Skagafjord, and there he put up his vessel
for the winter. In spring he purchased Glambæirland, where
he took up his abode, and dwelt there as long as he lived, and
was a man of great consideration; and many men are descended
from him and his wife Gudrid, and it was a good family. When
Karlsefne died Gudrid took the management of his estate, and
Snorre her son, who was born in Vinland. And when Snorre
was married Gudrid went out of the country, and went to the
south, and came back again to Snorre's estate, and he had built
a church at Glambæ. Afterwards Gudrid became a nun, and
lived a hermit-life, and did so as long as she lived. Snorre had
a son called Thorgeir, who was father to Bishop Brand's mother
Ingveld. The daughter of Snorre Karlsefnesson was called
Halfrid. She was mother of Runolf, the father of Bishop
Thorlak. Karlsefne and Gudrid had a son also called Biorn.
He was father of Thoruna, the mother of Biship Biorn.[3] Many
people are descended from Karlsefne, and his kin have been
lucky; and Karlsefne has given the most particular accounts
of all these travels of which here something is related.

---

[1] *Húsasnotra*, probably a carved wooden ornament for the gable.
[2] *Mǫssur*, probably maple.
[3] These three bishops were Brand Saemundarson of Holar, 1163–1202;
Thorlak Runolfson of Skalaholt, 1118–33; Bjorn Gilsson of Holar, 1147–
1163. That Brand is not here called the First (to distinguish him from
Brand Jonsson of Holar, 1263–4) may justify dating this text before 1263.

SAGA OF KING OLAF (HARALDSSON) THE SAINT [1]

CHAPTER I. OF SAINT OLAF'S BRINGING-UP.—Olaf, Harald Grænske's son, was brought up by his stepfather Sigurd Syr and his mother Aasta. Rane the Far-travelled lived in the house of Aasta, and fostered this Olaf Haraldsson. Olaf came early to manhood, was handsome in countenance, middle-sized in growth, and was even when very young of good understanding and ready speech. Sigurd his stepfather was a careful house-holder, who kept his people closely to their work, and often went about himself to inspect his corn-rigs and meadow-land, the cattle, and also the smithwork, or whatsover his people had on hand to do.

CHAPTER II. OF OLAF AND KING SIGURD SYR.—It happened one day this King Sigurd wanted to ride from home, but there was nobody about the house; so he told his step-son Olaf to saddle his horse. Olaf went to the goats' pen, took out the he-goat that was the largest, led him forth, and put the king's saddle on him, and then went in and told King Sigurd he had saddled his riding horse. Now when King Sigurd came out and saw what Olaf had done, he said, "It is easy to see that thou wilt little regard my orders; and thy mother will think it right that I order thee to do nothing that is against thy own inclination. I see well enough that we are of different dispositions, and that thou art far more proud than I am." Olaf answered little, but went his way laughing.

CHAPTER III. OF KING OLAF'S ACCOMPLISHMENTS.—When Olaf Haraldsson grew up he was not tall, but middle-sized in height, although very thick, and of good strength. He had light brown hair, and a broad face which was white and red. He had particularly fine eyes which were beautiful and piercing, so that one was afraid to look him in the face when he was angry. Olaf

---

[1] King Olaf the Saint reigned from about the year 1015 to 1030. The death of King Olaf Trygvesson was in the year 1000; and Earl Eric held the government for the Danish and Swedish kings about fifteen years.

was very expert in all bodily exercises, understood well to handle
his bow, and was distinguished particularly in throwing his spear
by hand: he was a great swimmer, and very handy, and very
exact and knowing in all kinds of smithwork, whether he himself
or others made the thing. He was distinct and acute in conversation, and was soon perfect in understanding and strength.
He was beloved by his friends and acquaintances, eager in his
amusements, and one who always liked to be the first, as it was
suitable he should be from his birth and dignity. He was called
Olaf Digre (the Thick or Great, in mind as of body).

CHAPTER IV. BEGINNING OF KING OLAF'S WAR EXPEDITION.
—Olaf Haraldsson was twelve years old when he, for the first
time, went on board a ship of war. His mother Aasta got Rane,
who was called the king's foster-father, to command a ship
of war and take Olaf under his charge; for Rane had often been
on war expeditions. When Olaf in this way got a ship and
men, the crew gave him the title of king; for it was the custom
that those commanders of troops who were of kingly descent,
on going out upon a viking cruise, received the title of king
immediately, although they had no land or kingdom. Rane
sat at the helm; and some say that Olaf himself was but a
common rower, although he was king of the men-at-arms. They
steered east along the land, and came first to Denmark. So
says Ottar Svarte, in his lay which he made about King Olaf:—

> " Young was the king when from his home
> He first began in ships to roam,
>   His ocean-steed to ride
>   To Denmark o'er the tide.
> Well exercised art thou in truth—
> In manhood's earnest work, brave youth!
>   Out from the distant north
>   Mighty hast thou come forth."

Towards autumn he sailed eastward to the Swedish dominions,
and there harried and burnt all the country round; for he
thought he had good cause of hostility against the Swedes, as
they killed his father Harald. Ottar Svarte says distinctly
that he came eastwards from Denmark:—

> " Thy ship from shore to shore,
> With many a well-plied oar,
> Eastwards across the foam is dancing,—
> Shields, and spears, and helms glancing!
> Hoist high the swelling sail
> To catch the freshening gale!

There's food for the raven-flight
Where thy sail-winged ship shall light:
Thy landing-tread
The people dread;
And the wolf howls for a feast
On the shore-side in the east."

CHAPTER V. OLAF'S FIRST BATTLE.—The same autumn Olaf
had his first battle at Sotholm, which lies in the Swedish skerry
circle.[1] He fought there with some vikings, whose leader was
Soto. Olaf had much fewer men, but his ships were larger,
and he laid his ships between some blind rocks, which made it
difficult for the vikings to get alongside; and Olaf's men threw
grappling-irons into the ships which came nearest, drew them up
to their own vessels, and cleared them of men. The vikings
took to flight after losing many men. Sigvat the scald tells of
this fight in the lay in which he reckons up King Olaf's battles:—

" The long-ship bore the royal youth
On ocean's path;
Men feared his wrath.
My verse holds memory of truth.
Where did the sea-king first draw blood?
In the battle shock
At Soto's rock:
The wolves howl over their fresh food."

CHAPTER VI. FORAY IN SWEDEN. — King Olaf steered
thereafter eastward to Sweden, and into the Lake (Mælare),
and ravaged the land on both sides. He sailed all the way up
to Sigtuna, and laid his ships close to Old Sigtuna. The
Swedes say the stone-heaps are still to be seen which Olaf had
laid under the ends of the gangways from the shore to the ships.
When autumn was advanced, Olaf Haraldsson heard that Olaf
the Swedish king was assembling an army, and also that he
had laid iron chains across Stoksund (the channel between the
Mælare lake and the sea), and had laid troops there; for the
Swedish king thought that Olaf Haraldsson would be kept in
there till frost came, and he thought little of Olaf's force, knowing he had but few people. Now when King Olaf Haraldsson
came to Stoksund [2] he could not get through, as there was a
castle west of the sound, and men-at-arms lay on the south;

[1] The belt of rocks and islets along the coast of Sweden. Snorri's
account is more elaborate than Sigvat's verse can warrant. In interpreting
the verses of Sigvat and Ottar on Olaf's early warfare, the prose biographers
allowed themselves considerable latitude in matters of detail.

[2] The present Norrström between Lake Mælare and the sea on the north
side of the ancient Stockholm.

and he heard that the Swedish king was come there with a great army and many ships. He therefore dug a canal across the flat land Agnefet out to the sea. Over all Swithiod [1] all the running waters fall into the Mælare lake; but the only outlet of it to the sea is so narrow that many rivers are wider, and after much rain or in a thaw the water rushes in a great cataract out by Stoksund, and the lake rises high and floods the land. It fell heavy rain just at this time; and as the canal was dug out to the sea, the water and stream rushed into it. Then Olaf had all the rudders unshipped, and hoisted all sail aloft. It was blowing a strong breeze astern, and they steered with their oars, and the ships came in a rush over all the shallows, and got into the sea without any damage. Now went the Swedes to their king, Olaf, and told him that Olaf the Thick had slipped out to sea; on which the king was enraged against those who should have watched that Olaf did not get away. This passage has since been called King's Sound; [2] but large vessels cannot pass through it, unless the waters are very high. Some relate that the Swedes were aware that Olaf had cut across the tongue of land, and that the water was falling out that way; and they flocked to it with the intention to hinder Olaf from getting away, but the water undermined the banks on each side so that they fell in with the people, and many were drowned: but the Swedes contradict this as a false report, and deny the loss of people. The king sailed to Gotland in harvest, and prepared to plunder; but the Gotlanders assembled, and sent men to the king, offering to pay scatt. The king found this would suit him, and he received the scatt, and remained there all winter. So says Ottar Svarte:—

> " Thou seaman-prince! thy men are paid:
> The scatt on Gotlanders is laid;
>   To guard the land
>   None raised his hand
> 'Gainst thee, nor war-shield red.
>   All men were filled with dread;
>   Eysyssel people fled;
> No man for valour is thy peer.
> Wolves fed on corpses there, I hear."

CHAPTER VII. THE SECOND BATTLE.—It is related here that King Olaf, when spring set in, sailed east to Eysyssel, [3] and landed and plundered: the Eysyssel men came down to the strand

---

[1] Swithiod, the country about Upsala, was Sweden Proper, and distinct from Gotland and other earldoms subject to Sweden. Scania belonged to Denmark.

[2] Now Söderström in Stockholm.   [3] Ösel.

and gave him battle. King Olaf gained the victory, pursued those who fled, and laid waste the land with fire and sword. It is told that when King Olaf first came to Eysyssel they offered him scatt, and when the scatt was to be brought down to the strand the king came to meet it with an armed force, and that was not what the bonders there expected; for they had brought no scatt, but only their weapons with which they fought against the king, as before related. So says Sigvat the scald:—

> " On Eysyssel's empty plain
> The king did battle once again;
> There treachery was soon revealed,
> But bonders fled from off that field.
> O mighty leader of the strife!
> Each bonder fled to save his life,
> For none would boldly make a stand
> And bide a wound from Olaf's hand."

CHAPTER VIII. THE THIRD BATTLE.—After this they sailed to Finland and plundered there, and went up the country. All the people fled to the forest, and they had emptied their houses of all household goods. The king went far up the country, and through some woods, and came to some dwellings in a valley called Herdal,—where, however, they made but small booty, and saw no people; and as it was getting late in the day, the king turned back to his ships. Now when they came into the woods again people rushed upon them from all quarters, and made a severe attack. The king told his men to cover themselves with their shields, but before they got out of the woods he lost many people, and many were wounded; but at last, late in the evening, he got to the ships. The Finlanders conjured up in the night, by their witchcraft, a dreadful storm and bad weather on the sea; but the king ordered the anchors to be weighed and sail hoisted, and beat off all night to the outside of the land. The king's luck prevailed more than the Finlanders' witchcraft; for he had the luck to beat round the Baalagaard's-side [1] in the night, and so got out to sea. So says Sigvat:—

> " The third fight was at Herdal, where
> The men of Finland met in war
> The hero of the royal race,
> With ringing sword-blades face to face.
> Off Baalagarda's shore the waves
> Ran hollow; but the sea-king saves
> His hard-pressed ship, and gains the lee
> Of the east coast through the wild sea."

[1] *Bálagarðssíða* is thought to have been the south-west coast of Finland between Turku and Helsinki, but the valley of Herdal cannot now be identified.

CHAPTER IX. THE FOURTH BATTLE IN SUDURVIK.—King Olaf sailed from thence to Denmark, where he met Thorkel the Tall,[1] brother of Earl Sigvald, and went into partnership with him; for he was just ready to set out on a cruise. They sailed southwards to the Jutland coast, to a place called Sudurvik,[2] where they overcame many viking ships. The vikings, who usually have many people to command, give themselves the title of kings, although they have no lands to rule over. King Olaf went into battle with them, and it was severe; but King Olaf gained the victory, and a great booty. So says Sigvat:—

> " A fourth time, so men say,
> He kindled battle-play;
> Thus glory, I am told,
> Is won by warriors bold.
> Yea, peace was rent in twain
> When kings met on the main,
> At Sudurvik so fell—
> Danes know that place full well."

CHAPTER X. THE FIFTH BATTLE IN FRIESLAND.—King Olaf sailed from thence south to Friesland, and lay under the strand of Kinlimma[3] in dreadful weather. The king landed with his men; but the people of the country rode down to the strand against them, and he fought them. So says Sigvat:—

> " Under Kinlemma's cliff,
> This battle is the fifth.
> Beneath Kinlemma's towering brows
> The storm had battered our strong prows;
> And down the horsemen ride
> To our ships by the water's side;
> But Olaf taught the peasant band
> To know the weight of a viking's hand."

CHAPTER XI. THE DEATH OF KING SWEND TWESKÆG [1008]. —The king sailed from thence westward to England.[4] It was

[1] Thorkel came to England in 1009 and took Canterbury in 1011. He entered the service of Ethelred in the following year and also served Canute the Great. He was banished from England in 1021.

[2] Sudurvik is no doubt Söndervik in the isle Holmland, in Ringkjöbing fjord in Jutland.

[3] *Kinnlimasíða* is a part of the coast of Old Friesland, now North Holland. Continental sources mention a viking raid up the Waal in 1009, in which Tiel was sacked and burnt. This may be the raid in which Olaf took part.

[4] The reckoning here is wrong. It was in the summer of 1013 that Swend Forkbeard seized power and drove Ethelred out; in February 1014 Swend died, and in April Ethelred returned to England. But if Olaf was a companion of Thorkel the Tall he must have reached England in 1009; Olaf's fights were part of Thorkel's campaign against the English (1009–12), not of Ethelred's struggles to regain his kingdom (1014). But Ottar's verse (p. 124) proves that Olaf did later help Ethelred.

then the case that the Danish king, Swend Forked Beard, was at that time in England with a Danish army, and had been fixed there for some time, and had seized upon King Ethelred's kingdom. The Danes had spread themselves so widely over England, that it was come so far that King Ethelred had departed from the country, and had gone south to Valland. The same autumn that King Olaf came to England, it happened that King Swend died suddenly in the night in his bed; and it is said by Englishmen that Edmund the Saint killed him, in the same way that the holy Mercurius had killed the apostate Julian.[1] When Ethelred, the king of the English, heard this in Flanders, he returned directly to England; and no sooner was he come back, than he sent an invitation to all the men who would enter into his pay, to join him in recovering the country. Then many people flocked to him; and among others came King Olaf with a great troop of Northmen to his aid. They steered first to London, and sailed into the Thames with their fleet; but the Danes had a castle within. On the other side of the river is a great trading place, which is called Sudrviki.[2] There the Danes had raised a great work, dug large ditches, and within had built a bulwark of stone, timber, and turf, where they had stationed a strong army. King Ethelred ordered a great assault; but the Danes defended themselves bravely, and King Ethelred was powerless against it. Between the castle [3] and Southwark there was a bridge, so broad that two waggons could pass each other upon it. On the bridge were raised barricades, both towers and wooden parapets, in the direction of the river,[4] which were nearly breast high; and under the bridge were piles driven into the bottom of the river. Now when the attack was made the troops stood on the bridge everywhere, and defended themselves. King Ethelred was very anxious to get possession of the bridge, and he called together all the chiefs to consult how they should get the bridge broken down. Then said King Olaf he would attempt to lay his fleet alongside of it, if the other ships would do the same. It was then determined in this council that they should lay their war forces under the bridge; and each made himself ready with ships and men.[5]

[1] The Emperor Julian fell in battle with the Persians in 363, but according to the legend the Virgin Mary sent "St. Mercurius" to kill him. See
[2] *Súðvirki*—Southwark. [Symeon of Durham, *Historic Regum*, ch. 125.
[3] On the site, probably, of the Tower of London.
[4] That is, across the bridge.
[5] London was attacked by vikings in the winter of 1009–10, but not captured. The prose account exaggerates the implications of the verses.

CHAPTER XII. LONDON BRIDGE.—King Olaf ordered great platforms of floating wood to be tied together with hazel bands, and for this he broke up wattle huts; and with these, as a roof, he covered over his ships so widely, that it reached over the ships' sides. Under this screen he set pillars so high and stout, that there both was room for swinging their swords, and the roofs were strong enough to withstand the stones cast down upon them. Now when the fleet and men were ready, they rowed up along the river; but when they came near the bridge, there were cast down upon them so many stones and missile weapons, such as arrows and spears, that neither helmet nor shield could hold out against it; and the ships themselves were so greatly damaged that many retreated out of it. But King Olaf, and the Northmen's fleet with him, rowed quite up under the bridge, laid their cables around the piles which supported it, and then rowed off with all the ships as hard as they could down the stream. The piles were thus shaken in the bottom, and were loosened under the bridge. Now as the armed troops stood thick of men upon the bridge, and there were likewise many heaps of stones and other weapons upon it, and the piles under it being loosened and broken, the bridge gave way; and a great part of the men upon it fell into the river, and all the others fled, some into the castle, some into Southwark. Thereafter Southwark was stormed and taken. Now when the people in the castle saw that the river Thames was mastered, and that they could not hinder the passage of ships up into the country, they became afraid, surrendered the tower, and took Ethelred to be their king. So says Ottar Svarte:—

> " London Bridge is broken down,—
> By thee, O warrior of renown.
>   Shields resounding,
>   War-horns sounding,
> Thou hast raised a storm of war!
>   Arrows singing,
>   Mail-coats ringing—
> Battle rages more and more! "

And he also composed these:—

> " King Ethelred has found a friend:
> Brave Olaf did his throne defend—
>   In bloody fight
>   Maintained his right,
>   Won back his land
>   With blood-red hand,
> Brought Edmund's kinsman to the throne
> His mighty forebears called their own."

Sigvat also relates as follows:—

> " At London Bridge was the sixth fight
> Where noble Olaf showed his might,
>   In England he
>   Fought valiantly.
> There the vikings hold the dyke,
> There foreign sword-blades fiercely bite,
>   There camp our men
>   On Southwark plain."

CHAPTER XIII. THE SEVENTH BATTLE.—King Olaf passed all the winter with King Ethelred, and had a great battle at Ring-mere Heath [1] in Ulfkel's land, the domain which Ulfkel Snilling at that time held; and here again the king was victorious. So says Sigvat the scald:—

> " To Ulfkel's land came Olaf bold,
> A seventh sword-thing he would hold.
> The race of Ella [2] filled the plain—
> Few of them slept at home again!
>   Ringmara heath
>   Was a bed of death:
>   Haarfager's heir
>   Dealt slaughter there."

And Ottar sings of this battle thus:—

> " Far from their ships, on Ringmere plain,
> In heaps thy warriors pile the slain;
> This tale, O king, I understood:
> That Ringmere Heath ran red with blood.
> In battle where the shields resound,
> The Englishmen crash to the ground;
> They bow before thee in the fight,
> And many more are killed in flight."

The country far around was then brought in subjection to King Ethelred; but the Thing-men [3] and the Danes held many castles, besides a great part of the country.

CHAPTER XIV. EIGHTH AND NINTH BATTLES OF OLAF.—King Olaf was commander of all the forces when they went

[1] This is the battle at Ringmere in East Anglia, mentioned by Florence of Worcester; it took place on 5th May 1010. Ulfkel is Ulfcytel, Earl in East Anglia.

[2] i.e. the English; the allusion is to King Ella of Northumbria, d. 876.

[3] The þingamenn were the warriors who formed the hired bodyguard of the Danish kings of England; the reference here must be to the followers of Swend Forkbeard. This term must not be confused with þingmenn, as used of Icelanders, Faroese, etc., which refers to all men entitled to attend a þing or Assembly, or to men who have promised their support to a particular chieftain (goði) in exchange for his help and protection in lawsuits, etc.

against Canterbury;[1] and they fought there until they took the town, killing many people and burning the castle.   So says Ottar Svarte:—

> " All in the grey of morn
>   Broad Canterbury's forced.
> Black smoke from house-roofs borne
> Hides fire that does its worst;
> Thou mad'st strong onslaught there
> 'Gainst men of noble line;
> Their lives thou didst not spare,
>   And victory was thine."

Sigvat reckons this King Olaf's eighth battle:—

> " Of this eighth battle I can tell
> How it was fought, and what befell.
>   The Scourge of Wends,
>   The Help of friends,
>   Puts forth his power
>   'Gainst fortress tower.
>   Lords of the fort,
>   Though well they fought,
>   Could not keep out
>   Olaf the Stout
> From Canterbury, that town so fair;
> The Partars now know grief and care."[2]

At this time King Olaf was entrusted with the whole land defence of England, and he sailed round the land with his ships of war.   He laid his ships at land at Nyamode,[3] where the troops of the Thing-men were, and gave them battle and gained the victory.   So says Sigvat the scald:—

> " The youthful king stained red the hair
> Of English men, and dyed his spear
> At Nyamode in hearts' dark blood;
> And where the Danes the thickest stood—
> Where the shrill storm round Olaf's head
> Of spear and arrow thickest fled,
> There thickest lay the Danish daed!
> Nine battles now of Olaf bold,
> Battle by battle, I have told."

King Olaf then scoured all over the country, taking scatt of the people, and plundering where it was refused.   So says Ottar:—

> " The English race could not resist thee,
> With money thou madest them assist thee,

[1] The siege of Canterbury began in the middle of September 1011 and lasted for twenty days.

[2] *Partar* is apparently a tribal or regional name, which has not been identified.

[3] *Nýamóða* cannot now be identified, and English sources mention no battle corresponding to this.   Here, as elsewhere, the verse records a battle of Olaf against the English, but the interpretation given in the prose is in conflict with it.

> Unsparingly thou madest them pay
> A scatt to thee in every way:
> Money, if money could be got—
> Goods, cattle, household gear, if not.
> Thy gathered spoil, borne to the strand,
> Was the best wealth of English land."

Olaf remained here for three years (1010–1012).

CHAPTER XV. THE TENTH BATTLE.—The third year King Ethelred died,[1] and his sons Edmund and Edward took the government. Then Olaf sailed southwards out to sea, and had a battle at Ringsfjord,[2] and took a castle situated beside Holl where vikings resorted, and burnt the castle. So says Sigvat the scald:—

> " Of the tenth battle now I tell,
> Where it was fought, and what befell.
> It was by Holl in Ringfjord fair
> And vikings held the fortress there:
> The people followed our brave chief,
> And razed the tower of the viking thief.
> Such rock and tower, such roosting place,
> Was ne'er since held by the roving race."

CHAPTER XVI. ELEVENTH, TWELFTH, AND THIRTEENTH BATTLES.—Then King Olaf proceeded westwards to Grislopol, and fought there with vikings at Williamsby;[3] and there also King Olaf gained the victory. So says Sigvat:—

> " The eleventh battle now I tell,
> Where it was fought, and what befell.
> At Grislopol, where chiefs were slain,
> Our young prince strode the battle-plain;
> Keen fighting raged around the town
> Which brave Earl William called his own,
> And many a tongue is quick to say
> How helms were crushed and hacked that day."

Next he fought westward on Fetlafjord, as Sigvat tells:—

> " The twelfth fight was at Fetlafjord,
> Where Olaf's honour-seeking sword
> Gave the wild wolf's devouring teeth
> A feast of warriors doomed to death."

[1] Ethelred died on 23rd April 1016.
[2] These place-names cannot be identified with certainty. According to William of Jumièges (Gesta Normanorum Ducum), some vikings led by " Olaf, King of the Norsemen," captured the castle of Dol in Brittany while fighting on behalf of Richard II of Normandy against Odo of Chartres; Holl may be a corruption of Dol.
[3] These names most probably refer to places in Spain; Spanish sources refer to viking raids in 1016; uncertainties of chronology make it possible that these are those in which Olaf took part (? 1012 or 1013). Grislupollar might be Castropol; Vilhjámsbæ (Williamsby) might be a corruption of Villamea, and Fetlafjorðr of Betanzos. The " Earl William " of the verse would then be an invention to explain a corrupt place-name.

From thence King Olaf sailed southwards to Seliopol,[1] where he had a battle. He took there a castle called Gunvaldsburg, which was very large and old. He also made prisoner the earl who ruled over the castle, and who was called Geirfinn. After a conference with the men of the castle, he laid a scatt upon the town and earl, as ransom, of twelve thousand gold shillings; which was also paid by those on whom it was imposed. So says Sigvat:—

> " The thirteenth battle now I tell,
> Where it was fought, and what befell.
> In Seliopol was fought the fray,
> And many did not survive the day.
> The king sent all his men and power,
> To Gunvaldsburg's old castle-tower;
> And a rich earl was taken there,
> Whose name was Geirfinn, I am sure."

CHAPTER XVII. FOURTEENTH BATTLE, AND KING OLAF'S DREAM.—Thereafter King Olaf steered with his fleet westward to Karlsa,[2] and tarried there and had a fight. And while King Olaf was lying in Karlsa river waiting a wind, and intending to sail up to Nörvasund,[3] and then on to the land of Jerusalem, he dreamt a remarkable dream—that there came to him a great and important man, but of a terrible appearance withal, who spoke to him, and told him to give up his purpose of proceeding to that land. " Return back to thy udal, for thou shalt be king over Norway for ever." He interpreted this dream to mean that he should be king over the country, and his posterity after him, for a long time.

CHAPTER XVIII. FIFTEENTH BATTLE.—After this appearance to him he turned about, and came to Poitou,[4] where he plundered and burnt a merchant town called Varrande. Of this Ottar speaks:—

> " Our young king, blythe and gay,
> Is foremost in the fray:
> Poitou he plunders, and his shield
> He tests in war on Tuskland's[5] field."

[1] *Seljupollar*, probably in Spain, perhaps to be identified as Guardia.
[2] Not identified; the Guadalquivir or the harbour of Cadiz have been suggested.
[3] *Norvasund* (The Narrow Sound) is the Straits of Gibraltar.
[4] Pietuland is Poitou. Verrandi is probably the town Guerande, in South Brittany, north of the mouth of the Loire (not in Poitou).
[5] Tuskland is the region of Touraine.

And also Sigvat says:—

> " Our king, whose blade is red with gore,
>   Now northwards steers
>   'Mid flashing spears,
>   And up the flowing Loire :
>   Far from the sea of Poitou's coast,
>   The town which we
>   Call Varrande
>   Was burnt by Norsemen's host."

CHAPTER XIX. OF THE EARLS OF ROUEN.—King Olaf had been two summers and one winter in the west in Valland on this cruise; and thirteen years had now passed since the fall of King Olaf Trygvesson. During this time earls had ruled over Norway; first Hakon's sons Eric and Swend, and afterwards Eric's sons Hakon and Swend. Hakon was a sister's son of King Canute, the son of Swend. During this time there were two earls in Valland,[1] William and Robert; their father was Richard earl of Rouen. They ruled over Normandy.[2] Their sister was Queen Emma,[3] whom the English king Ethelred had married; and their sons were Edmund, Edward the Good, Edwy, and Edgar. Richard the earl of Rouen was a son of Richard the son of William Long Spear who was the son of Ganger Rolf,[4] the earl who first conquered Normandy; and he again was a son of Rognvald the Mighty, earl of Möre and of Hild. From Ganger Rolf are descended the earls of Rouen, who have long reckoned themselves of kin to the chiefs in Norway, and hold them in such respect that they always were the greatest friends of the Northmen; and every Northman found a friendly country in Normandy, if he required it. To Normandy King Olaf came in autumn, and remained all winter in the river Seine[5] in good peace and quiet.

---

[1] Valland, as before noticed, means the whole west coast of France.

[2] The dukes of Normandy were called *Rúðujarlar*, Earls of Rouen, in the sagas. At this time the duke was in fact Richard II. (*d.* 1026); his son was Robert the Devil, but he had neither brother nor son named William.

[3] Sister of Richard II., not his daughter. Her sons by Ethelred were Alfred (*d.* 1036) and Edward (king 1042–66), whilst Edmund (*d.* 1016), Edwy, and Edgar were sons of Ethelred's first marriage.

[4] Ganger Rolf (*Gǫngu-Hrólfr*, Rolf the Walker) is usually identified with the Rollo who in 911 took Normandy in fief from the Frankish emperor. The settlement in Normandy was, however, predominantly Danish, and there has been much controversy over Rollo's nationality.

[5] According to William of Jumièges, it was during this stay in Normandy that Olaf became Christian and was baptized at Rouen by Archbishop Robert (Duke Richard's brother). This is intrinsically more likely than the usual Icelandic tradition that Olaf was baptized in childhood by Olaf Tryggvason (*vide* p. 58).

CHAPTER XX. OF EINAR TAMBARSKELVE. — After Olaf Trygvesson's fall, Earl Eric gave peace to Einar Tambarskelve, the son of Eindride Styrkarsson; and Einar went north with the earl to Norway. It is said that Einar was the strongest man and the best archer that ever was in Norway. His shooting was sharp þeyond all others; for with a blunt arrow he shot through a raw, soft ox-hide, hanging over a beam. He was better than any man at running in snow-shoes, was a great man at all exercises, was of high family, and rich. The earls Eric and Swend married their sister Bergliot to Einar. Their son was named Eindride. The earls gave Einar great fiefs in Orkedal, so that he was one of the most powerful and able men in Drontheim country, and was also a great friend of the earls, and a great support and aid to them.

CHAPTER XXI. OF ERLING SKIALGSSON. — When Olaf Trygvesson ruled over Norway, he gave his brother-in-law Erling half of the land scatt, and royal revenues between the Naze and Sogn. His other sister he married to the Earl Ragnvald Ulfsson, who long ruled over West Gotland. Ragnvald's father, Ulf, was a brother of Sigrid the Haughty, the mother of Olaf the Swedish king. Earl Eric was ill pleased that Erling Skialgsson had so large a dominion, and he took to himself all the king's estates which King Olaf had given to Erling. But Erling levied, as before, all the land scatt in Rogaland; and thus the inhabitants had often to pay him the land scatt, otherwise he laid waste their land. The earl made little of the business, for no bailiff of his could live there, and the earl could only come here in guest-quarters, when he had a great many people with him. So says Sigvat:—

> " Olaf the king
> Thought the bonder Erling
> A man who would grace
> His own royal race.
> One sister the king
> Gave the bonder Erling;
> And the other he gave
> To Rognvald the brave."

Earl Eric did not venture to fight with Erling, because he had very powerful and very many friends, and was himself rich and popular, and kept always as many retainers about him as if he held a king's court. Erling was often out in summer on plundering expeditions, and procured for himself means of living; for he continued his usual way of high and splendid living, although now he had fewer and less convenient fiefs than in the time of his brother-in-law King Olaf Trygvesson. Erling was one of the handsomest, largest, and strongest men; a better warrior than any other; and in all exercises he was like King Olaf himself. He was, besides, a man of understanding, zealous in everything he undertook, and a deadly man at arms. Sigvat talks thus of him:—

> " No earl or baron, young or old,
> Match with this bonder brave can hold.
> Mild was brave Erling, all men say,
> When not engaged in bloody fray;
> His courage he kept hid until
> The fight began, then foremost still
> Erling was seen in war's wild game,
> And famous still is Erling's name."

It was a common saying among the people, that Erling had been the most valiant who ever held lands under a king in Norway. Erling's and Astrid's children were these—Aslak, Skialg, Sigurd, Loden, Thore, and Ragnhild, who was married to Thorberg Arneson. Erling had always with him 90 free-born men or more; and both winter and summer it was the custom in his house to drink at the mid-day meal according to a measure,[1] but at the night meal there was no measure in drinking. When the earl was in the neighbourhood he had 300 men or more. He never went to sea with less than a fully-manned ship of 20 benches of rowers. Erling had also a ship of 32 benches of rowers, which was besides very large for that size, and which he used in viking cruises, or on an expedition; and in it there were 200 men at the very least.

CHAPTER XXII. OF THE HERSE ERLING SKIALGSSON.—
Erling had always at home on his farm 30 slaves, besides other serving-people. He gave his slaves a certain day's work; but after it he gave them leisure, and leave that each should work in the twilight and at night for himself, and as he pleased. He gave them arable land to sow corn in, and let them apply their crops to their own use. He laid upon each a certain quantity of labour to work themselves free by doing it; and there were many who bought their freedom in this way in one year, or in the second year, and all who had any luck could make themselves free within three years. With this money he bought

[1] There were silver studs in a row from the rim to the bottom of the drinking horn or cup; and as it went round each drank till the stud appeared above the liquor. This was drinking by measure.

other slaves; and to some of his freed people he showed how to work in the herring fishery; to others he showed some useful handicraft; and some cleared his outfields, and set up houses. He helped all to prosperity.

CHAPTER XXIII. OF EARL ERIC [1012].—When Earl Eric had ruled over Norway for twelve years,[1] there came a message to him from his brother-in-law King Canute, the Danish king, that he should go with him on an expedition westward to England; for Eric was very celebrated for his campaigns, as he had gained the victory in the two hardest engagements which had ever been fought in the north countries. The one was that in which the earls Hakon and Eric fought with the Jomsborg vikings; the other that in which Earl Eric fought with King Olaf Trygvesson. Thord Kolbeinsson speaks of this:—

> " A song of praise
> Again I raise.
> To Eric the bold
> The word is told,
> That Knut the Brave
> His aid would crave:
> The earl, I knew,
> To friend stands true."

The earl would not sleep upon the message of the king, but sailed immediately out of the country, leaving behind his son Earl Hakon to take care of Norway; and, as he was but seventeen years of age, Einar Tambarskelve was to be at his hand to rule the country for him.

Eric met King Canute in England, and was with him when he took the castle of London.[2] Earl Eric had a battle also to the westward of the castle of London, and killed Ulfkel Snilling.[3] So says Thord Kolbeinsson:—

> " West of London town we passed,
> And our ocean-steeds made fast,
> And a bloody fight begin,
> England's lands to lose or win.
> Blue sword and shining spear
> Laid Ulfkel's dead corpse there.
> Our Thingmen hear the war-shower sounding
> Of grey arrows from their shields rebounding."

[1] Eric, however, scarcely set out from Norway before 1014 or 1015, for Canute became king in 1014 and went to England in 1015.
[2] King Canute in the autumn of 1016 first entered London with the free consent of the burghers, not by conquest.
[3] Ulfkel Snilling fell at the battle of Assandun, 18th October 1016.

Earl Eric [1] was a winter in England, and had many battles there. The following autumn he intended to make a pilgrimage to Rome, but he died in England of a bloody flux.

CHAPTER XXIV. THE MURDER OF EDMUND.—King Canute came to England the summer that King Ethelred died,[2] and had many battles with Ethelred's sons, in which the victory was sometimes on one side, sometimes on the other. Then King Canute took Queen Emma in marriage; and their children were Harald, Hardacanute, and Gunhild.[3] King Canute then made an agreement with King Edmund,[4] that each of them should have a half of England. In the same month Henry Strion murdered King Edmund. King Canute then drove all Ethelred's sons [5] out of England. So says Sigvat:—

> " Now all the sons of Ethelred
> Were either fallen, or had fled:
> Some slain by Canute,—some, they say,
> To save their lives had run away."

CHAPTER XXV. OF OLAF AND ETHELRED'S SONS.—King Ethelred's sons came to Rouen in Valland from England, to their mother's brother, the same summer that King Olaf Haraldsson came from the west from his viking cruise, and they were all during the winter in Normandy together. They made an agreement with each other that King Olaf should have Northumberland, if they could succeed in taking England from the Danes. Therefore, about harvest, Olaf sent his foster-father Rane to England to collect men-at-arms; and Ethelred's sons sent tokens to their friends and relations with him. King Olaf, besides, gave him much money with him to attract people to them. Rane was all winter in England, and got promises

---

[1] Eric in 1016 got the earldom of Northumberland from King Canute and ruled there until his death in 1023.

[2] King Ethelred died on 23rd April 1016.

[3] Canute married Emma, the widow of Ethelred, in July 1017; Harald was not the son of Emma, but an illegitimate son of Canute by Alfiva.

[4] Edmund died on 30th November 1016. The *Anglo-Saxon Chronicle* and Florence of Worcester attribute his death to natural causes, but later sources (*e.g.* Henry of Huntingdon and Roger of Wendover) say that he was murdered by Eadric Streona, Ealdorman of Mercia, at the instigation of Canute. " Henry " (*Heinrekr*) is presumably a slip for " Eadric " (*Játrekr*).

[5] Ethelred's sons fled from England to Normandy in the winter of 1016-17, by which time Olaf had long left Normandy. Olaf's help was given to Ethelred himself when he reclaimed the kingdom in 1014, not to his sons.

from many powerful men of fidelity, as the people of the country would rather have native kings over them; but the Danish power had become so great in England, that all the people were brought under their dominion.

CHAPTER XXVI. BATTLE OF KING OLAF.—In spring King Olaf and King Ethelred's sons set out together to the west, and came to a place in England called Jungofurda,[1] where they landed with their army, and moved forward against the castle. Many men were there who had promised them their aid. They took the castle, and killed many people. Now when King Canute's men heard of this they assembled an army, and were soon in such force that Ethelred's sons could not stand against it; and they saw no other way left but to return to Rouen. Then King Olaf separated from them, and would not go back to Valland, but sailed northwards along England, all the way to Northumberland, where he put into a haven at a place called Furovald;[2] and in a battle there with the townspeople and merchants he gained the victory, and a great booty.

CHAPTER XXVII. KING OLAF'S EXPEDITION TO NORWAY.— King Olaf left his long-ships[3] there behind, but made ready two ships of burden; and had with him 220 men[4] in them, well armed and chosen people. He sailed out to sea northwards in harvest, but encountered a tremendous storm, and they were in danger of being lost; but as they had a chosen crew, and the king's luck with them, all went on well. So says Ottar:—

> " Olaf, great stem of kings, is brave—
> Bold in the fight, bold on the wave.
>   No thought of fear
>   Thy heart comes near.
> Undaunted, midst the roaring flood,
> Firm at his post each shipman stood;
>   And thy two ships stout
>   The gale stood out."

[1] *Jungufurða* has not been located, nor is any battle corresponding to this mentioned in any English sources.

[2] *Furuvald* probably refers to the Wolds of the Yorkshire and Lincolnshire coast; some manuscripts read *fyrir Valdi*, with the same meaning.

[3] There was a distinction between the long-ship, a ship of war built for coastal sailing and raids, and the broader vessels used for crossings of the open sea. The *knǫrr*, the type mentioned here, was the ocean-going merchantman in common use in the north till the thirteenth century.

[4] The " hundred " in the Saga always means the big hundred (*i.e.* 120); consequently there were at least 260 men. The reader must remember this, in every case at least where the figures are given in hundreds.

And farther he says:—

> "Thou able chief! with thy fearless crew
> Thou meetest, with skill and courage true,
>   The wild sea's wrath
>   On thy ocean path.
> Though waves mast-high were breaking round,
> Thou findest the middle of Norway's ground,
>   With helm in hand
>   On Sælö's strand."

It is related here that King Olaf came from sea to the very middle of Norway; and the isle is called Sælö where they landed, and is outside of Stad. King Olaf said he thought it must be a lucky day for them, since they had landed at Sælö [1] in Norway; and observed it was a good omen that it so happened. As they were going up in the isle, the king slipped with one foot in a place where there was clay, but supported himself with the other foot. Then said he, "The king falls." "Nay," replies Rane, "thou didst not fall, king, but set fast foot in the soil." The king laughed thereat, and said, "It may be so if God will." They went down again thereafter to their ships, and sailed to Ulvesund, where they heard that Earl Hakon was south in Sogn, and was expected north as soon as wind allowed with a single ship.

Chapter XXVIII. Earl Hakon taken Prisoner in Saudungasund by Olaf.—King Olaf steered his ships within the ordinary ships' course when he came abreast of Fialar district, and ran into Saudunga sound.[2] There he laid his two vessels one on each side of the sound, with a thick cable between them. At the same moment Hakon, Earl Eric's son, came rowing into the sound with a manned ship; and as they thought these were but two merchant vessels that were lying in the sound, they rowed between them. Then Olaf and his men draw the cable up right under Hakon's ship's keel, and wind it up with the capstan.[3] As soon as the vessel's course was stopped her stern was lifted up, and her bow plunged down; so that the water came in at her fore-end and over both sides, and she upset. King Olaf's people took Earl Hakon and all his men whom they

---

[1] The king is punning on the name of the island, *Sæla* or *Selja*, and the word *sæll*, "lucky," "blessed."

[2] Now Sauesund, east of Atleöen.

[3] The *vindáss*—windlass, capstan, winch—was used for hauling in the anchor or for raising the sailyard. This remarkable trick by which Olaf captured Hakon is also mentioned, in broadly similar terms, in the *Ágrip*, the *Legendary Saga*, and elsewhere.

could get hold of out of the water, and made them prisoners; but some they killed with stones and other weapons, and some were drowned. So says Ottar:—

> " The black ravens wade
> In the blood from·thy blade.
> Young Hakon so gay,
> With his ship, is thy prey:
> His ship, with its gear,
> Thou hast ta'en; and art here,
> Thy forefathers' land
> From the earl to demand."

Earl Hakon was led up to the king's ship. He was the handsomest man that could be seen. He had long hair, as fine as silk, bound about his head with a gold ornament.

When he sat down in the fore-hold, the king said to him, " It is not false what is said of your family, that ye are handsome people to look at; but now your luck has deserted you."

Hakon the earl replied, " It has always been the case that success is changeable; and there is no luck in the matter. It has gone with your family as with mine, to have by turns the better lot. I am little beyond childhood in years; and at any rate we could not have defended ourselves, as we did not expect any attack on the way. It may turn out better with us another time."

Then said King Olaf, " Dost thou not apprehend that thou art in that condition that, hereafter, there can be neither victory nor defeat for thee? "

The earl replies, " That is what thou only canst determine, king, according to thy pleasure."

Olaf says, " What wilt thou give me, earl, if for this time I let thee go, whole and unhurt? "

The earl asks what he would take.

" Nothing," says the king, " except that thou shalt leave the country, give up thy kingdom, and take an oath that thou shalt never go into battle against me."

The earl answered, that he would do so. And now Earl Hakon took the oath that he would never fight against Olaf, or seek to defend Norway against him, or attack him; and King Olaf thereupon gave him and all his men life and peace. The earl got back the ship which had brought him there, and he and his men rowed their way. Thus says Sigvat of him:—

> " In old Saudunga sound
> The king Earl Hakon found,
> Who little thought that there
> A foeman was so near.

> The best and fairest youth
> Earl Hakon was in truth,
> That speaks the Danish tongue,
> And of the race of great Hakon."

CHAPTER XXIX. EARL HAKON'S DEPARTURE FROM NORWAY.
—After this the earl made ready as fast as possible to leave the
country and sail over to England. He met King Canute, his
mother's brother, there, and told him all that had taken place
between him and King Olaf. King Canute received him
remarkably well, placed him in his court in his own house, and
gave him great power in his kingdom. Earl Hakon dwelt a
long time with King Canute. During the time Swend and
Hakon ruled over Norway, a reconciliation with Erling
Skialgsson was effected, and secured by Aslak, Erling's son,
marrying Gunhild,[1] Earl Swend's daughter; and the father and
son, Erling and Aslak, retained all the fiefs which King Olaf
Trygvesson had given to Erling. Thus Erling became a firm
friend of the earl's, and their mutual friendship was confirmed
by oath.

CHAPTER XXX. AASTA'S PREPARATIONS TO RECEIVE HER
SON OLAF [1014].—King Olaf went now eastward along the
land, holding Things with the bonders all over the country.
Many went willingly with him; but some, who were Earl
Swend's friends or relations, spoke against him. Therefore
King Olaf sailed in all haste eastward to Viken; went in there
with his ships; set them on the land; and proceeded up the
country, in order to meet his stepfather, Sigurd Syr. When
he came to Westfold he was received in a friendly way by many
who had been his father's friends or acquaintances; and also
there and in Folden were many of his family. In autumn he
proceeded up the country (to Ringerike) to his stepfather
King Sigurd's, and came there one day very early. As Olaf
was coming near to the house, some of the servants ran beforehand to the house, and into the room. Olaf's mother, Aasta,
was sitting in the room, and around her some of her girls. When
the servants told her of King Olaf's approach, and that he
might soon be expected, Aasta stood up directly, and ordered
the men and girls to put everything in the best order. She
ordered four girls to bring out all that belonged to the decoration
of the room, and put it in order with hangings and benches.
Two carles brought straw for the floor, two brought forward

[1] Or rather Sigrid, *vide* chap. cxl.

four-cornered tables and the drinking jugs, two bore out victuals and placed the meat on the table, two she sent away from the house to procure in the greatest haste all that was needed, and two carried in the ale; and all the other serving men and girls went outside of the house. Messengers went to seek King Sigurd wherever he might be, and brought to him his dress-clothes, and his horse with gilt saddle, and his bridle which was gilt and set with precious stones. Four men she sent off to the four quarters of the country to invite all the great people to a feast, which she prepared as a rejoicing for her son's return. All who were before in the house she made to dress themselves with the best they had, and lent clothes to those who had none suitable.

CHAPTER XXXI. KING SIGURD'S DRESS.—King Sigurd Syr was standing in his corn-field when the messengers came to him and brought him the news, and also told him all that Aasta was doing at home in the house. He had many people on his farm. Some were then shearing corn, some bound it together, some drove it to the building, some unloaded it and put it in stack or barn; but the king, and two men with him, went sometimes into the field, sometimes to the place where the corn was put into the barn. His dress, it is told, was this:—he had a blue kirtle and blue hose; shoes which were laced about the legs; a grey cloak, and a grey wide-brimmed hat; a veil [1] before his face; a staff in his hand with a gilt-silver head on it, and a silver ring around it. Of Sigurd's living and disposition it is related that he was a very gain-making man, who attended carefully to his cattle and husbandry, and managed his house-keeping himself. He was nowise given to pomp, and was rather taciturn. But he was a man of the best understanding in Norway, and also excessively wealthy in movable property. Peaceful he was, and nowise haughty. His wife Aasta was generous and high-minded. Their children were, Guttorm, the eldest; then Gunhild; the next Halfdan, Ingerid, and Harald (Hardrade). The messengers said to Sigurd, " Aasta told us to bring thee word, how much it lay at her heart that thou shouldst on this occasion comport thyself in the fashion of great men, and show a disposition more akin to Harald Haarfager's race than to thy mother's father's, Rane Narrow-nose, or Earl Nereid the Old, although they too were very wise men." The

[1] Often used by men in summer to protect the face from the stings of mosquitoes.

king replies, " The news ye bring me is weighty, and ye bring it
forward in great heat. Already before now Aasta has made
a great fuss over people who were not so near to her; and I
see she is still of the same disposition. She takes this up with
great warmth; but can she lead her son out of the business with
the same splendour she is leading him into it? If it is to proceed
so, methinks they who mix themselves up in it regard little
property or life. For this man, King Olaf, goes against a great
superiority of power; and the wrath of the Danish and Swedish
kings will be roused by these plans of his, if he persists in this
course."

CHAPTER XXXII. OF THE FEAST.—When the king had said
this he sat down, and made them take off his shoes, and put
corduvan [1] boots on, to which he bound his gold spurs. Then
he put off his cloak and coat, and dressed himself in his finest
clothes, with a scarlet cloak over all; girded on his sword, set a
gilded helmet upon his head, and mounted his horse. He sent
his labouring people out to the neighbourhood, and gathered
to him thirty well-clothed men, and rode home with them. As
they rode up to the house, and were near the room, they saw
on the other side of the house the banners of Olaf coming waving;
and there was he himself, with about 100 [2] men all well equipt.
People were gathered everywhere between the houses. King
Sigurd immediately saluted his stepson from horseback in a
friendly way, and invited him and his men to come and drink a
cup with him. Aasta, on the contrary, went up and kissed her
son, and invited him to stay with her; and land, and people, and
all the good she could do for him, stood at his service. King Olaf
thanked her kindly for her invitation. Then she took him by
the hand, and led him into the room to the high seat. King
Sigurd got men to take charge of their clothes, and give their
horses corn; and then he himself went to his high seat, and the
feast was made with the greatest splendour.

CHAPTER XXXIII. CONVERSATION OF KING OLAF AND KING
SIGURD.—King Olaf had not been long here before he one day
called his stepfather King Sigurd, his mother Aasta, and his
foster-father Rane to a conference and consultation. Olaf
began thus: " It has so happened," said he, " as is well known

[1] Corduvan was tanned leather. The untanned skin probably had been
the ordinary wear of the king. From Cordova in Spain.
[2] As usual read 120 (the long hundred) wherever hundreds are mentioned
in this saga.

to you, that I have returned to this country after a very long sojourn in foreign parts, during all which time I and my men have had nothing for our support but what we captured in war, for which we have often hazarded both life and soul; for many an innocent man have we deprived of his property, and some of their lives: and foreigners are now sitting in the possessions which my father, his father, and their forefathers for a long series of generations owned, and to which I have udal right. They have not been content with this, but have taken to themselves also the properties of all our relations who are descended from Harald Haarfager. To some they have left little, to others nothing at all. Now I will disclose to you what I have long concealed in my own mind, that I intend to take the heritage of my forefathers; but I will not wait upon the Danish or Swedish king to supplicate the least thing from them, although they for the time call that their property which was Harald Haarfager's heritage. To say the truth, I intend rather to seek my patrimony with battle-axe and sword, and that with the help of all my friends and relations, and of those who in this business will take my side. And in this matter I will so lay hand to the work that one of two things shall happen,—either I shall lay all this kingdom under my rule which they got into their hands by the slaughter of my kinsman Olaf Trygvesson, or I shall fall here upon my inheritance in the land of my fathers. Now I expect of thee, Sigurd, my stepfather, as well as other men here in the country who have udal right of succession to the kingdom, according to the law made by King Harald Haarfager, that nothing shall be of such importance to you as to prevent you from throwing off the disgrace from our family of being slow at supporting the man who comes forward to raise up again our race. But whether ye show any manhood in this affair or not, I know the inclination of the people well,—that all want to be free from the slavery of foreign masters, as soon as there is some help for the attempt. I have not proposed this matter to any before thee, because I know thou art a man of understanding, and can best judge how this my purpose shall be brought forward in the beginning, and whether we shall, in all quietness, talk about it to a few persons, or instantly declare it to the people at large. I have already showed my teeth by taking prisoner the Earl Hakon, who has now left the country, and given me, under oath, the part of the kingdom which he had before; and I think it will be easier to have Earl Swend alone to deal with, than if both were defending the country against us."

King Sigurd answers, "It is no small affair, King Olaf, thou hast in thy mind; and thy purpose comes more, methinks, from hasty pride than from prudence. But it may be there is a wide difference between my humble ways and the high thoughts thou hast; for whilst yet in thy childhood thou wast full always of ambition and desire of command, and now thou art experienced in battles, and hast formed thyself upon the manner of foreign chiefs. I know therefore well, that as thou hast taken this into thy head, it is useless to dissuade thee from it; and also it is not to be denied that it goes to the heart of all who have courage in them, that the whole Haarfager race and kingdom should go to the ground. But I will not bind myself by any promise, before I know the views and intentions of other Upland kings; but thou hast done well in letting me know thy purpose, before declaring it publicly to the people. I will promise thee, however, my interest with the kings, and other chiefs, and country people; and also, King Olaf, all my property stands to thy aid, and to strengthen thee. But we will only produce the matter to the community so soon as we see some progress, and expect some strength to this undertaking; for thou canst easily perceive that it is a daring measure to enter into strife with Olaf the Swedish king, and Canute, who is king both of Denmark and England; and thou requirest great support under thee, if it is to succeed. It is not unlikely, in my opinion, that thou wilt get good support from the people, as the commonalty always loves what is new; and it went so before, when Olaf Trygvesson came here to the country, that all rejoiced at it, although he did not long enjoy the kingdom."

When the consultation had proceeded so far, Aasta took up the word. "For my part, my son, I am rejoiced at thy arrival, but much more at thy advancing thy honour. I will spare nothing for that purpose that stands in my power, although it be but little help that can be expected from me. But if a choice could be made, I would rather that thou shouldst be the supreme king of Norway, even if thou shouldst not sit longer in thy kingdom than Olaf Trygvesson did, than that thou shouldst not be a greater king than Sigurd Syr is, and die the death of old age." With this the conference closed. King Olaf remained here a while with all his men. King Sigurd entertained them, day about, the one day with fish and milk, the other day with flesh-meat and ale.[1]

---

[1] This was, until recent times, a common way of living among the peasants and middle classes of Norway.

CHAPTER XXXIV. OF THE KINGS IN THE UPLAND DISTRICTS OF NORWAY.—At that time there were many kings in the Uplands who had districts to rule over, and the most of them were descended from Harald Haarfager. In Hedemark two brothers ruled—Rörek and Ring; in Gudbrandsdal, Gudrod; and there was also a king in Raumarike; and one had Hadeland and Toten; and in Valders [1] also there was a king. With these district-kings Sigurd had a meeting up in Hadeland, and Olaf Haraldsson also met with them. To these district-kings whom Sigurd had assembled he set forth his stepson Olaf's purpose, and asked their aid, both of men and in counsel and consent; and represented to them how necessary it was to cast off the yoke which the Danes and Swedes had laid upon them. He said that there was now a man before them who could head such an enterprise; and he recounted the many brave actions which Olaf had achieved upon his war-expeditions.

Then King Rörek says, "True it is that Harald Haarfager's kingdom has gone to decay, none of his race being supreme king over Norway. But the people here in the country have experienced many things. When King Hakon, Athelstan's foster-son, was king, all were content; but when Gunhild's sons ruled over the country, all were so weary of their tyranny and injustice that they would rather have foreign men as kings, and be themselves more their own rulers; for the foreign kings were usually abroad, and cared little about the customs of the people if the scatt they laid on the country was paid. When enmity arose between the Danish king Harald and Earl Hakon, the Jomsborg vikings made an expedition against Norway;[2] then the whole people arose, and threw the hostilities from themselves; and thereafter the people encouraged Earl Hakon to keep the country, and defend it with sword and spear against the Danish king. But when he had set himself fast in the kingdom with the help of the people, he became so hard and overbearing towards the country-folks, that they would no longer suffer him. The Drontheim people killed him, and raised to the kingly power Olaf Trygvesson, who was of the udal succession to the kingdom, and in all respects well fitted to be a chief. The whole country's desire was to make him supreme king, and raise again the kingdom which Harald Haarfager had made for himself. But

---

[1] This kind of Valders is not again mentioned.

[2] Elsewhere Snorri gives a different explanation of the motives of the Jomsborg Vikings in attacking Norway (*vide* pp. 35 ff.). The present passage is probably nearer the truth; Saxo too says that Harald Gormsson sent the Jomsvikings against Norway.

when King Olaf thought himself quite firmly seated in his kingdom, no man could rule his own concerns for him. With us small kings he was so unreasonable as to take to himself not only all the scatt and duties which Harald Haarfager had levied from us, but a great deal more. The people at last had so little freedom under him, that it was not allowed to every man to believe in what God he pleased. Now since he has been taken away we have kept friendly with the Danish king; have received great help from him when we have had any occasion for it; and have been allowed to rule ourselves, and live in peace and quiet in the inland country, and without any over-burden. I am therefore content that things be as they are, for I do not see what better rights I am to enjoy by one of my relations ruling over the country; and if I am to be no better off, I will take no part in the affair."

Then said King Ring, his brother, " I will also declare my opinion that it is better for me, if I hold the same power and property as now, that my relative is king over Norway, rather than a foreign chief, so that our family may again raise its head in the land. It is, besides, my opinion about this man Olaf, that his fate and luck must determine whether he is to obtain the kingdom or not; and if he succeed in making himself supreme king, then he will be the best off who has best deserved his friendship. At present he has in no respect greater power than any of us; nay, indeed, he has less; as we have lands and kingdoms to rule over, and he has nothing, and we are equally entitled by the udal right to the kingdom as he is himself. Now, if we will be his men, give him our aid, allow him to take the highest dignity in the country, and stand by him with our strength, how should he not reward us well, and hold it in remembrance to our great advantage, if he be the honourable man I believe him to be, and all say he is? Therefore let us join the adventure, say I, and bind ourselves in friendship with him."

Then the others, one after the other, stood up and spoke; and the conclusion was, that the most of them determined to enter into a league with King Olaf. He promised them his perfect friendship, and that he would hold by and improve the country's laws and rights, if he became supreme king of Norway. This league was confirmed by oath.

CHAPTER XXXV. OLAF GETS THE TITLE OF KING FROM THE THING.—Thereafter the kings summoned a Thing,[1] and there

---

[1] The reference to a Thing appears to have been indispensable, notwith-standing the concurrence of the small kings.

King Olaf set forth this determination to all the people, and his demand on the kingly power. He desires that the bonders should receive him as king; and promises, on the other hand, to allow them to retain their ancient laws, and to defend the land from foreign masters and chiefs. On this point he spoke well, and long; and he got great praise for his speech. Then the kings rose and spoke, the one after the other, and supported his cause, and this message to the people. At last it came to this, that King Olaf was proclaimed king over the whole country, and the kingdom adjudged to him according to law in the Uplands.

CHAPTER XXXVI. KING OLAF TRAVELS IN THE UPLANDS.— King Olaf began immediately his progress through the country, appointing feasts before him wherever there were royal farms. First he travelled round in Hadeland, and then he proceeded north to Gudbrandsdal. And now it went as King Sigurd Syr had foretold, that people streamed to him from all quarters; and he did not appear to have need for half of them, for he had nearly 300 [1] men. But the entertainments bespoken did not half serve; for it had been the custom that kings went about in guest-quarters in the Uplands with 60 or 70 men only, and never with more than 100 men. The king therefore hastened over the country, only stopping one night at the same place. When he came north to Dovrefjeld, he arranged his journey so that he came over the Fjelds and down upon the north side of it, and then came to Opdal, where he remained all night. Afterwards he proceeded through Opdal forest, and came out at Medaldal,[2] where he proclaimed a Thing, and summoned the bonders to meet him at it. The king made a speech to the Thing, and asked the bonders to accept him as king; and promised, on his part, the laws and rights which King Olaf Trygvesson had offered them. The bonders had no strength to make opposition to the king; so the result was that they received him as king, and confirmed it by oath: but they sent word to Orkedal and Skogn [3] of all that they knew concerning Olaf's proceedings.

CHAPTER XXXVII. A LEVY AGAINST OLAF IN THE DRON-THEIM LAND.—Einar Tambarskelve had a farm and house in Skogn; and now when he got news of Olaf's proceedings, he immediately split up a war-arrow, and sent it out as a token to

---

[1] *i.e.* 360 (the big hundred, as usual).
[2] Now Meldal in Upper Orkedalen.
[3] Börseskognen between Orkedal and Guldal.

the four quarters—north, south, east, west,—to call together
all free and unfree men in full equipment of war: therewith the
message, that they were to defend the land against King Olaf.
The message-stick went to Orkedal, and thence to Guldal, where
the whole war-force was to assemble.

CHAPTER XXXVIII. KING OLAF'S PROGRESS IN DRONTHEIM.
—King Olaf proceeded with his men down into Orkedal, and
advanced in peace and with all gentleness; but when he came
to Griotar[1] he met the assembled bonders, amounting to more
than 700 men. Then the king arrayed his army, for he thought
the bonders were to give battle. When the bonders saw this,
they also began to put their men in order; but it went on very
slowly, for they had not agreed beforehand who among them
should be commander. Now when King Olaf saw there was
confusion among the bonders, he sent to them Thore Gudbrand-
son; and when he came he told them King Olaf did not want to
fight them, but named twelve of the ablest men in their flock
of people, who were desired to come to King Olaf. The bonders
agreed to this; and the twelve men went over a rising ground
which is there, and came to the place where the king's army stood
in array. The king said to them, " Ye bonders have done well
to give me an opportunity to speak with you, for now I will
explain to you my errand here to the Drontheim country.
First I must tell you, what ye already must have heard, that
Earl Hakon and I met in summer; and the issue of our meeting
was, that he gave me the whole kingdom he possessed in the
Drontheim country, which, as ye know, consists of Orkedal,
Guldal, Strind district, and Strind.[2] As a proof of this, I have
here with me the very men who were present, and saw the earl's
and my own hands given upon it, and heard the word and oath,
and witnessed the agreement the earl made with me. Now I
offer you peace and law, the same as King Olaf Trygvesson
offered before me." The king spoke well and long; and ended
by proposing to the bonders two conditions—either to go into
his service and be subject to him, or to fight him. Thereupon
the twelve bonders went back to their people, and told the issue
of their errand, and considered with the people what they should
resolve upon. Although they discussed the matter backwards

[1] No longer existing. The farm was near the parsonage of Gryting in
Orkedalen.
[2] In the *Heimskringla* the name Drontheim (*þrándheim*) always refers to
the district, not the town; the latter was called Nidaros. The second
" Strind " is a textual error, and should read " Eyra district."

and forwards for a while, they preferred at last to submit to the king; and it was confirmed by the oath of the bonders. The king now proceeded on his journey, and the bonders made feasts for him. The king then proceeded to the sea-coast, and got ships; and among others he got a long-ship of twenty benches of rowers from Gunnar of Gelmin;[1] another ship of twenty benches he got from Loden of Vigg; and a third was of twenty benches from the farm of Angrar[2] in the Ness, which farm Earl Hakon had possessed, but a steward managed it for him, by name Baard White. The king had besides four or five boats; and with these vessels he went in all haste into the fjord of Drontheim.

CHAPTER XXXIX. OF EARL SWEND'S PROCEEDINGS.— Earl Swend was at that time far up in the Drontheim fjord at Steenkjar,[3] which at that time was a merchant town, and was there preparing for the Yule festival. When Einar Tambarskelve heard that the Orkedal people had submitted to King Olaf, he sent men to Earl Swend to bring him the tidings. They went first to Nidaros, and took a rowing-boat which belonged to Einar, with which they went out into the fjord, and came one day late in the evening to Steenkjar, where they brought to the earl the news about all King Olaf's proceedings. The earl owned a long-ship, which was lying afloat and rigged just outside the town; and immediately, in the evening, he ordered all his movable goods, his people's clothes, and also meat and drink, as much as the vessel could carry, to be put on board, rowed immediately out in the night-time, and came with daybreak to Skarnsund.[4] There he saw King Olaf rowing in with his fleet into the fjord. The earl turned towards the land within Masarvig,[5] where there was a thick wood, and lay so near the rocks that the leaves and branches hung over the vessel. They cut down some large trees which they laid over the quarter on the sea-side, so that the ship could not be seen for leaves, especially as it was scarcely clear daylight when the king came rowing past them. The weather was calm, and the king rowed in among the islands; and when the king's fleet was out of sight

[1] Now Gjölme near Orkedalsosen.
[2] Now Hangran in Byneset.
[3] Steenkjar is still a village at the bottom of the Trondhjem fjord, at the mouth of the large river running into it from the great lake the Snaasen Vand. No remains of the old town are to be seen.
[4] This is the sound between Inderöen and the west side of the land at the head of Trondhjem fjord.
[5] Now Mosvig, south-west of Skarnsund.

the earl rowed out of the fjord, and on to Frosta,[1] where his kingdom lay, and there he landed.

CHAPTER XL. EARL SWEND'S AND EINAR'S CONSULTATIONS. —Earl Swend sent men out to Guldal to his brother-in-law, Einar Tambarskelve; and when Einar came the earl told him how it had been with him and King Olaf, and that now he would assemble men to go out against King Olaf, and fight him.

Einar answers, "We should go to work cautiously, and find out what King Olaf intends doing; and not let him hear anything concerning us but that we are quiet. It may happen that if he hears nothing about our assembling people, he may sit quietly where he is in Steenkjar all the Yule; for there is plenty prepared for him for the Yule feast: but if he hears we are assembling men, he will set right out of the fjord with his vessels, and we shall not get hold of him." Einar's advice was taken; and the earl went to Stjordal, into guest-quarters among the bonders.

When King Olaf came to Steenkjar he collected all the meat prepared for the Yule feast, and made it be put on board, procured some transport vessels, took meat and drink with him, and got ready to sail as fast as possible, and went out all the way to Nidaros.[2] Here King Olaf Trygvesson had laid the foundation of a merchant town, and had built a king's house; but before that Nidaros was only a single house, as before related [p. 64]. When Earl Eric came to the country, he applied all his attention to his house of Lade,[3] where his father had had his main residence, and he neglected the houses which Olaf had erected at the Nid; so that some were fallen down, and those which stood were scarcely habitable. King Olaf went now with his ships up the Nid, made all the houses to be put in order directly that were still standing, and built anew those that had fallen down, and employed in this work a great many people. Then he had all the meat and drink brought on shore to the houses, and prepared to hold Yule there: so Earl Swend and Einar had to fall upon some other plan.

CHAPTER XLI. OF SIGVAT THE SCALD.—There was an Iceland man called Thord Sigvaldascald, who had been long

[1] The peninsula of Frosta on the east side of the Trondhjem fjord.
[2] The present city of Trondhjem.
[3] Lade (*Hlaðir*) lies about two miles north-east of Trondhjem; the powerful dynasty of the earls of Hlaðir took their name from it.

with Earl Sigvald, and afterwards with the earl's brother,
Thorkel the Tall; but after the earl's death Thord had become
a merchant.   He met King Olaf on his viking cruise in the west,
and entered into his service, and followed him afterwards.   He
was with the king when the incidents above related took place.
Thord had a son called Sigvat fostered in the house of Thorkel
at Apavatn,[1] in Iceland.   When he was nearly a grown man he
went out of the country with some merchants; and the ship
came in autumn to the Drontheim country, and the crew lodged
in the surrounding district.   The same winter King Olaf came
to Drontheim, as just now related by us [p. 144].   Now when
Sigvat heard that his father Thord was with the king, he went
to him, and stayed awhile with him.   Sigvat was a good scald
at an early age.   He made a lay in honour of King Olaf, and
asked the king to listen to it.   The king said he did not want
poems composed about him, and said he did not understand the
scald's craft.   Then Sigvat sang:—

> " Sinker of dark-blue ocean's steeds!
> Allow one scald to sing thy deeds;
> And listen to the song of one
> Who can sing well, if any can.
> For should the king despise all others,
> And show no favour to my brothers
> In scaldic art, yet all the same
> I still shall sing our great king's fame."

King Olaf gave Sigvat as a reward for his verse a gold ring
that weighed half a mark, and Sigvat was made one of King
Olaf's court-men.[2]   Then Sigvat sang:—

> " I willingly receive this sword—
> By land or sea, on shore, on board,
> I trust that I shall ever be
> Worthy the sword received from thee.
> A faithful follower thou hast bound—
> A generous master I have found;
> Master and servant both have made
> Just what best suits them by this trade."

Earl Swend had, according to custom, taken one half of the
harbour-dues [3] from the Iceland ship-traders about autumn;

[1] A farm and lake in Arnessysla in the south of Iceland.

[2] Sigvat became Olaf's favourite poet, and his verses are of great value
as primary records of Olaf's life and death.   Particularly important from
this point of view are the " Viking Verses," on Olaf's early battles (*vide*
chaps. vii–xviii), and the " Memorial Lay " (*Erfidrápa*), with its description of Olaf's death at Stiklestad.

[3] *Landaurar* was the tax which Icelanders had to pay when they landed in
Norway or its western tributary lands.   This tax was abolished in 1262–4
when Iceland acknowledged the Norwegian king.   *Vide* also p. 173.

for the earls Eric and Hakon had always taken one half of these
and all other revenues in the Drontheim country. Now when
King Olaf came there, he sent his men to demand that half of
the tax from the Iceland traders; and they went up to the
king's house, and asked Sigvat to help them. He went to the
king, and sang:—

> " Men say in asking I'm too bold;
> (By asking once I won red gold.)
> What now, my lord, I hope to win
> Is not red gold but merely skin.[1]
> O lavish prince, renounce thy claim
> On merchants who to Norway came;
> Remit one half of harbour-dues—
> This mighty boon is what I choose."

CHAPTER XLII. OF EARL SWEND.—Earl Swend and Einar
Tambarskelve gathered a large armed force, with which they
came by the upper road into Guldal, and so down to Nidaros,
with nearly 2000 men.[2] King Olaf's men were out upon the
Gaular ridge,[3] and had a guard on horseback. They became
aware that a force was coming down the Guldal, and they
brought word of it to the king about midnight. The king got
up immediately, ordered the people to be wakened, and they
went on board of the ships, bearing all their clothes and arms
on board, and all that they could take with them, and then
rowed out of the river. Then came the earl's men to the town
at the same moment, took all the Christmas provision, and set
fire to the houses. King Olaf went out of the fjord down to
Orkedal, and there landed the men from their ships. From
Orkedal they went up to the Fjelds, and over the Fjelds eastwards into Gudbrandsdal. In the lines composed about Klöng
Brusason,[4] it is said that Earl Eric burned the town of Nidaros:—

> " The king's half-finished hall,
> Rafters, roof, and all,
> Is burned down by the river's side;
> The flame spreads o'er the city wide."

CHAPTER XLIII. OF KING OLAF [1015].—King Olaf went
southwards through Gudbrandsdal, and thence out to Hedemark.
In the depth of winter he went about in guest-quarters; but

[1] The harbour or anchorage dues were paid in skins, or other products
of Iceland.
[2] *i.e.* 2400.
[3] *Gaularáss* is usually applied to the whole range from Guldal to Strind,
but here it means only the town hill outside Trondhjem.
[4] No more remains of this poem, nor is Klöng mentioned elsewhere.

when spring returned he collected men, and went to Viken. He had with him many people from Hedemark, whom the kings had given him; and also many powerful people from among the bonders joined him, among whom Ketel Kalf from Ringaness.[1] He had also people from Raumarike. His stepfather, Sigurd Syr, gave him the help also of a great body of men. They went down from thence to the coast, and made ready to put to sea from Viken. The fleet, which was manned with many fine fellows, went out then to Tunsberg.

CHAPTER XLIV. OF EARL SWEND'S FORCES.—After Yule, Earl Swend gathers all the men of the Drontheim country, proclaims a levy for an expedition, and fits out ships. At that time there were in the Drontheim country a great number of lendermen; and many of them were so powerful and well-born, that they were descended from earls, or even from the royal race, which in a short course of generations reckoned to Harald Haarfager, and they were also very rich. These lendermen[2] were of great help to the kings or earls who ruled the land; for it was as if the lenderman had the bonder-people of each district in his power. Earl Swend being a good friend of the lendermen, it was easy for him to collect people. His brother-in-law, Einar Tambarskelve, was on his side, and with him many other lendermen; and among them many, both lendermen and bonders, who the winter before had taken the oath of fidelity to King Olaf. When they were ready for sea they went directly out of the fjord, steering south along the land, and drawing men from every district. When they came farther south, abreast of Rogaland, came Erling Skialgsson to meet them, with many people and many lendermen with him. Now they steered eastward with their whole fleet to Viken, and Earl Swend ran in there towards the end of Lent. The earl steered his fleet to Grenmore,[3] and ran into Nessie.[4]

[1] Now Ringnes in Ottestad parish in the Stange district of Hedemarken.
[2] The lendermen appear to have been sheriffs for collecting the scatt and other revenues of the kings, and to have held the function in feu, paying for it to the king a proportion of the income of the district. The fines due to the king for misdemeanours, murders, etc., must have come through them into the royal coffers; for we find the appointment of new lendermen for every district the first act of every king on acquiring a part of the country. In his *Edda* Snorri equates the *lendr maðr* with the German Greif or English baron, but the position was not hereditary, nor was it integrated into a whole system of feudal relationships.
[3] Now Langesundfjord.
[4] *Nesjar*, "The Headlands"—*i.e.* those between Langesundfjord and the mouth of the Oslo Fjord.

CHAPTER XLV. KING OLAF'S FORCES.—King Olaf steered his fleet out from Viken, until the two fleets were not far from each other, and they got news of each other the Saturday before Palm Sunday.[1] King Olaf himself had a ship called the Carl's Head,[2] on the bow of which a king's head was carved out, and he himself had carved it. This head was used long after in Norway on ships which kings steered themselves.

CHAPTER XLVI. KING OLAF'S SPEECH.—As soon as day dawned on Sunday morning, King Olaf got up, put on his clothes, went to the land, and ordered to sound the signal for the whole army to come on shore. Then he made a speech to the troops, and told the whole assembly that he had heard there was but a short distance between them and Earl Swend. " Now," said he, " we shall make ready; for it can be but a short time until we meet. Let the people arm, and every man be at the post that has been appointed him, so that all may be ready when I order the signal to sound for casting off from the land.[3] Then let us row off at once; and so that none go on before the rest of the ships, and none lag behind, when I row out of the harbour: for we cannot tell if we shall find the earl where he was lying, or if he has come out to meet us. When we do meet, and the battle begins, let people be alert to bring all our ships in close order, and ready to bind them together. Let us spare ourselves in the beginning, and take care of our weapons, that we do not cast them into the sea, or shoot them away in the air to no purpose. But when the fight becomes hot, and the ships are bound together, then let each man show what is in him of manly spirit."

CHAPTER XLVII. OF THE BATTLE AT NESSIE.—King Olaf had in his ship 100 men armed in coats of ring-mail and in

---

[1] In 1015 it fell on 3rd April; but in 1016 it was 25th March. Snorri reckons that the battle took place in 1015, but it was really in 1016. The *Legendary Saga* says that Olaf sent messengers to Swend, urging him not to fight on so holy a day, and offering a truce until after Easter. This Snorri has omitted, since Sigvat's verses imply that Olaf took the initiative in the fight. The purpose of the *Legendary Saga* would be to clear Olaf from the blame of fighting on a day of special sanctity, when Church Law required men to keep the peace.

[2] The head probably of Charlemagne, whose name was held in great veneration. King Olaf's son Magnus was called after Charlemagne.

[3] Signals by call of trumpet, or war-horn, or lure, appear to have been well understood by all. We read of the trumpet-call to arm, to attack, to advance, to retreat, to land; and also to a Court Thing, a House Thing, a General Thing.

foreign helmets. The most of his men had white shields, on which the holy cross was gilt; but some had painted it in blue or red. He had also had the cross painted in front on all the helmets, in a pale colour. He had a white banner, on which was a serpent figured. He ordered a mass to be read before him, went on board ship, and ordered his people to refresh themselves with meat and drink. He then ordered the war-horns to sound to battle, to leave the harbour, and row off to seek the earl. Now when they came to the harbour where the earl had lain, the earl's men were armed, and beginning to row out of the harbour; but when they saw the king's fleet coming they began to bind the ships together, to set up their banners, and to make ready for the fight. When King Olaf saw this he hastened the rowing, laid his ship alongside the earl's, and the battle began. So says Sigvat the scald:—

> " Boldly the king did then pursue
> Earl Swend, nor let him out of view.
> The blood ran down on Rodi's field [1]
> When Olaf forced his foes to yield.
> Nor did the king his warriors spare
> In battle-brunt the sword and spear.
> Earl Swend his ships of war pushed on,
> And lashed their stout stems one to one."

It is said that King Olaf brought his ships into battle while Swend was still lying in the harbour. Sigvat the scald was himself in the fight; and in summer, just after the battle, he composed a lay, which is called the Nessie Song, in which he tells particularly the circumstances:—

> " In the fierce fight 'tis known how near
> The scorner of the ice-cold spear
> Laid the Charles' Head [2] the earl on board,
> All eastward of the Agder fjord."

Then was the conflict exceedingly sharp, and it was long before it could be seen how it was to go in the end. Many fell on both sides, and many were the wounded. So says Sigvat:—

> " No urging did the earl require,
> 'Midst spear and sword—the battle's fire;
> No urging did the brave king need
> The ravens in this shield-storm to feed.
> Of limb-lopping enough was there,
> And ghastly wounds of sword and spear.
> Never, I think, was rougher play
> Than both the armies had that day."

---

[1] Rodi was a legendary sea-king, so his field is the sea itself.
[2] The king's ship had a head of Charlemagne.

The earl had most men, but the king had a chosen crew in his ship, who had followed him in all his wars; and besides they were so excellently equipt, as before related, that each man had a coat of ring-mail,[1] so that he could not be wounded. So says Sigvat:—

> " I saw us, Teit, in battle's gale [2]
> Draw on our cold shirts of ring-mail.
> Soon sword on sword was shrilly ringing,
> And in the air the spears were singing.
> A helmet hid my own black hair,
> For thick flew arrows through the air.
> Right glad was I our gallant crew,
> Steel-clad from head to foot, to view."

CHAPTER XLVIII. EARL SWEND'S FLIGHT.—When the men began to fall on board the earl's ships, and many appeared wounded, so that the sides of the vessels were but thinly beset with men, the crew of King Olaf prepared to board. Their banner was brought up to the ship that was nearest the earl's, and the king himself followed the banner. So says Sigvat:—

> " ' On with the king! ' his banner's waving:
> ' On with the king! ' the spears he's braving!
> ' On, steel-clad men! and storm the deck,
> Slippery with blood and strewed with wreck.
> A different work ye have to share,
> His banner in war-storm to bear,
> From your fair girl's, who round the hall
> Brings the full mead-bowl to us all.' "

Now was the severest fighting. Many of Swend's men fell, and some sprang overboard. So says Sigvat:—

> " Into the ships our brave lads spring,—
> On shield and helm their red blades ring;
> The air resounds with stroke on stroke,—
> The shields are cleft, the helms are broke.
> The wounded bonder o'er the side
> Falls shrieking in the blood-stained tide—
> The deck is cleared with wild uproar—
> The dead crew float about the shore."

And also these lines:—

> " The shields we brought from home were white,
> Now they are red-stained in the fight:
> This work was fit for those who wore
> Ringed coats of mail their breasts before.
> Where the foe blunted the best sword
> I saw our young king climb on board.
> He stormed the first; we followed him—
> The war-birds now in blood may swim."

[1] Ring-mail was a kind of network of metal rings sewn upon a leathern or woollen shirt, like a frock or blouse; or it consisted also of rings of metal linked together.

[2] This verse is not part of the " Nessie Song " (*Nesjavísur*) but an independent stanza addressed to a friend.

Now defeat began to come down upon the earl's men. The king's men pressed upon the earl's ship, and entered it; but when the earl saw how it was going, he called out to his forecastle-men to cut the cables and cast the ship loose, which they did. Then the king's men threw grapplings over the timber heads of the ship, and so held her fast to their own; but the earl ordered the timber heads to be cut away, which was done. So says Sigvat:—

> " The earl, his noble ship to save,
> To cut the posts loud order gave.
> The ship escaped: our greedy eyes
> Had looked on her as a clear prize.
> The earl escaped; but ere he fled
> We feasted Odin's fowls with dead;—
> With many a goodly corpse that floated
> Round our ship's stern his birds were bloated."

Einar Tambarskelve had laid his ship right alongside the earl's. They threw an anchor over the bows of the earl's ship, and thus towed her away, and they slipped out of the fjord together. Thereafter the whole of the earl's fleet took to flight, and rowed out of the fjord. The scald Berse Torfeson was on the forecastle of the earl's ship; and as it was gliding past the king's fleet, King Olaf called out to him—for he knew Berse, who was distinguished as a remarkably handsome man, always well equipt in clothes and arms—" Farewell, Berse! " He replied, " Farewell, king! " So says Berse himself, in a poem he composed when he fell into King Olaf's power and was laid in prison and in fetters on board a ship:—

> " Olaf the Brave
>   A ' farewell ' gave
> (No time was there to parley long)
> To me who knows the art of song.
>   The scald was fain
>   ' Farewell ' again
> In the same terms back to send—
> The rule in arms to foe or friend.
>   Earl Swend's distress
>   I well can guess,
> When flight he was compelled to take:
> His fortunes I will ne'er forsake.
>   Though I lie here
>   In chains a year,
> In thy great vessel all forlorn,
> To crouch to thee I still will scorn:
>   I still will say,
>   No milder sway
> Than from thy foe this land e'er knew:
> To him, my early friend, I'm true."

CHAPTER XLIX. EARL SWEND LEAVES THE COUNTRY.— Now some of the earl's men fled up the country, some surrendered at discretion; but Swend and his followers rowed out of the fjord, and the chiefs laid their vessels together to talk with each other, for the earl wanted counsel from his lendermen. Erling Skialgsson advised that they should sail north, collect people, and fight King Olaf again; but as they had lost many people, the most were of opinion that the earl should leave the country, and repair to his brother-in-law the Swedish king,[1] and strengthen himself there with men. Einar Tambarskelve approved also of that advice, as they had no power to hold battle against Olaf. So they discharged their fleet. The earl sailed across Folden,[2] and with him Einar Tambarskelve. Erling Skialgsson again, and likewise many other lendermen who would not abandon their udal possessions, went north to their homes; and Erling had many people that summer about him.

CHAPTER L. KING OLAF'S AND SIGURD'S CONSULTATION.—
When King Olaf and his men saw that the earl had gathered his ships together, Sigurd Syr was in haste for pursuing the earl and letting steel decide their cause. But King Olaf replies, that he would first see what the earl intended doing,—whether he would keep his force together or discharge his fleet. Sigurd Syr said, "It is for thee, king, to command; but," he adds, "I fear from thy disposition and eagerness for power that thou wilt be slow to win loyalty from those great people, for they are accustomed of old to bid defiance to their sovereigns." There was no attack made, for it was soon seen that the earl's fleet was dispersing. The King Olaf ransacked the slain, and remained there some days to divide the booty. At that time Sigvat made these verses:—

> "The tale I tell is true:
> To their homes returned but few
> Of Swend's men, who came to meet
> King Olaf's gallant fleet.
> From the North these warmen came
> To try the bloody game,—
> On the waves their corpses borne
> Show the game that Sunday morn.
> The Drontheim girls so fair
> Their jeers, I think, will spare,
> For the king's force was but small
> That emptied Drontheim's hall.
> But if they will have their jeer,
> They may ask their sweethearts dear,
> Why they have returned shorn
> Who went to shear that Sunday morn."

[1] Swend was married to Holmfrid, the sister of the Swedish king Olaf.
[2] The district of the Oslo fjord.

And also these:—

> " Now will the king's power rise,
> For the Upland men still prize
> The king who o'er the sea
> Steers to bloody victory.
> Earl Swend! thou now wilt know
> That our lads can make blood flow—
> That the Hedemarkers hale
> Can do more than tap good ale."

King Olaf gave his stepfather King Sigurd Syr, and the other chiefs who had assisted him, handsome presents at parting. He gave Ketel of Ringaness a yacht of fifteen benches of rowers, which Ketel brought up the Glommen river and into the Mjösen lake.

CHAPTER LI. OF KING OLAF.—King Olaf sent spies out to trace the earl's doings; and when he found that the earl had left the country he sailed out west, and to Viken, where many people came to him. At the Thing there he was taken as king, and so he proceeded all the way to the Naze; and when he heard that Erling Skialgsson had gathered a large force, he did not tarry in North Agder,[1] but sailed with a steady fair wind to Drontheim country; for there it appeared to him was the greatest strength of the land, if he could subdue it for himself while the earl was abroad. When Olaf came to Drontheim there was no opposition, and he was elected there to be king. In harvest he took his seat in the town of Nidaros, and collected the needful winter provision. He built a king's house, and raised Clement's church[2] on the spot on which it now stands. He parcelled out building ground, which he gave to bonders, merchants, or others who he thought would build. There he sat down, with many men-at-arms around him; for he put no great confidence in the Drontheim people, if the earl should return to the country. The people of the interior of the Drontheim country showed this clearly, for he got no land-scatt from them.

CHAPTER LII. PLAN OF EARL SWEND AND THE SWEDISH KING.—Earl Swend went first to Sweden, to his brother-in-law Olaf the Swedish king, told him all that had happened between him and Olaf the Thick, and asked his advice about what he should now undertake. The king said that the earl should stay

---

[1] The western part of Agder between Sireaa and Otteraa.
[2] The church was situated on Strandgaden, *i.e.* Shore Street.

with him if he liked, and get such a portion of his kingdom to rule over as should seem to him sufficient; "or otherwise," says he, "I will give thee help of forces to conquer the country again from Olaf." The earl chose the latter; for all those among his men who had great possessions in Norway, which was the case with many who were with him, were anxious to get back; and in the council they held about this, it was resolved that in winter they should take the land-way over Helsingeland and Jemteland, and so down into the Drontheim land; for the earl reckoned most upon the faithful help and strength of the Drontheim people of the interior as soon as he should appear there. In the meantime, however, it was determined to take a cruise in summer in the Baltic to gather property.

CHAPTER LIII. EARL SWEND'S DEATH [1015].—Earl Swend went westward with his forces to Russia, and passed the summer in marauding there; but on the approach of autumn returned with his ships to Sweden. There he fell into a sickness, which proved fatal. After the earl's death some of the people who had followed him remained in Sweden; others went to Helsingeland, thence to Jemteland, and so from the east over the dividing ridge of the country to the Drontheim district, where they told all that had happened upon their journey: and thus the truth of Earl Swend's death was known.

CHAPTER LIV. OF THE DRONTHEIM PEOPLE.—Einar Tambarskelve, and the people who had followed him, went in winter to the Swedish king, and were received in a friendly manner. There were also among them many who had followed the earl. The Swedish king took it much amiss that Olaf the Thick had set himself down in his scatt-lands, and driven the earl out of them, and therefore he threatened the king with his heaviest vengeance when opportunity offered. He said that Olaf ought not to have had the presumption to take the dominions which the earl had held of him; and all the Swedish king's men agreed with him. But the Drontheim people, when they heard for certain that the earl was dead, and could not be expected back to Norway, turned all to obedience to King Olaf. Many came from the interior of the Drontheim country, and became King Olaf's men; others sent word and tokens that they would serve him. Then, in autumn, he went into the interior of Drontheim, and held Things with the bonders, and was received as king in each district. He returned to Nidaros, and brought there all the king's scatt and revenue, and had his winter seat provided there.

CHAPTER LV. OF KING OLAF'S HOUSEHOLD.—King Olaf built a king's house in Nidaros, and in it was a large room for his court, with doors at both ends. The king's high seat was in the middle of the room; and within sat his court-bishop, Grimkel, and next him his other priests; without them sat his councillors; and in the other high seat opposite to the king sat his marshal, Biorn, and next to him his pursuivants.[1] When people of importance came to him, they also had a seat of honour. The ale was drunk by the fire-light. He divided the service among his men after the fashion of other kings. He had in his house sixty court-men and thirty pursuivants; and to them he gave pay and certain regulations. He had also thirty house-servants to do the needful work about the house, and procure what was required. He had besides many slaves. At the house were many outbuildings, in which the court-men slept. There was also a large room, in which the king held his court-meetings.

CHAPTER LVI. OF KING OLAF'S HABITS.—It was King Olaf's custom to rise betimes in the morning, put on his clothes, wash his hands, and then go to the church and hear the matins and morning mass. Thereafter he went to the Thing-meeting, to bring people to agreement with each other, or to talk of one or the other matter that appeared to him necessary. He invited to him great and small who were known to be men of under-standing. He often made them recite to him the laws which Hakon Athelstan's foster-son had made for Drontheim;[2] and after considering them with those men of understanding, he ordered laws adding to or taking from those established before. But the Christian code he settled according to the advice of Bishop Grimkel and other learned priests; and bent his whole mind to uprooting heathenism, and old customs which he thought contrary to Christianity. And he succeeded so far that the bonders accepted of the laws which the king proposed. So says Sigvat:—

> " The king, who at the helm guides
> His warlike ship through clashing tides,
> Now gives one law for all the land—
> A heavenly law, which long will stand."

---

[1] *Gestir*, retainers of inferior rank. Their pay was half that of the " court-men " (*hirðmenn*); they were the king's messengers and executive officers, collecting dues and provisions, inflicting punishments, etc.

[2] See *Sagas of the Norse Kings*, pp. 84, 99.

King Olaf was a good and very gentle man, of little speech, and open-handed although greedy of money. Sigvat the scald, as before related [p. 147], was in King Olaf's house, and several Iceland men. The king asked particularly how Christianity was observed in Iceland, and it appeared to him to be very far from what it ought to be; for as to observing Christian practices, it was told the king that it was permitted there to eat horse-flesh, to expose infants as heathens do, besides many other things contrary to Christianity. They also told the king about many principal men who were then in Iceland. Skopte Thoraddsson [1] was then the law-speaker of the country. He inquired also of those who were best acquainted with it about the state of people in other distant countries; and his inquiries turned principally on how Christianity was observed in the Orkney, Shetland, and Faroe Islands: and, as far as he could learn, it was far from being as he could have wished. Such conversation was usually carried on by him; or else he spoke about the laws and rights of the country.

CHAPTER LVII. OF THE SWEDISH KING OLAF'S MESSENGERS, AND HIS BAILIFF ASGAUT'S DEATH [1016].—The same winter came messengers from the Swedish king, Olaf the Swede, out of Sweden; and their leaders were two brothers, Thorgaut Skarde and Asgaut the bailiff; and they had twenty-four men with them. When they came from the eastward, over the ridge of the country down into Værdal, they summoned a Thing of the bonders, talked to them, and demanded of them scatt and duties upon account of the king of Sweden. But the bonders, after consulting with each other, determined only to pay the scatt which the Swedish king required in so far as King Olaf required none upon his account, but refused to pay scatt to both. The messengers proceeded farther down the valley; but received at every Thing they held the same answer and no money. They went forward to Skogn, held a Thing there, and demanded scatt; but it went there as before. Then they came to Stjoradal, and summoned a Thing, but the bonders would not come to it. Now the messengers saw that their business was a failure; and Thorgaut proposed that they should turn about, and go eastward again. "I do not think," says Asgaut, "that we have performed the king's errand unless we go to King Olaf the Thick, since the bonders refer the matter to him." He was their commander; so they proceeded to the town (Nidaros), and took

[1] He was eight times elected Law-speaker of Iceland, 1004-30.

lodging there. The day after they presented themselves to the king, just as he was seated at table; saluted him; and said they came with a message of the Swedish king. The king told them to come to him next day. Next day the king, having heard mass, went to his Thing-house, ordered the messengers of the Swedish king to be called, and told them to produce their message. Then Thorgaut spoke, and told first what his errand was, and next how the Drontheim people of the interior had replied to it; and asked the king's decision on the business, that they might know what result their errand there was to have. The king answers, "While the earls ruled over the country, it was not to be wondered at if the country people thought themselves bound to obey them, as they were at least of the royal race of the kingdom. But it would have been more just if those earls had given assistance and service to the kings who had a right to the country, rather than to foreign kings, or to stir up opposition to their lawful kings, depriving them of their land and kingdom. With regard to Olaf the Swede, who calls himself entitled to the kingdom of Norway, I cannot tell what claims he has which could in fact be just; but well remember the skaith and damage we have suffered from him and his relations."

Then says Asgaut, "It is not wonderful that thou art called Olaf the Thick, seeing thou answerest so haughtily to such a prince's message, and canst not see clearly how heavy the king's wrath will be for thee to support, as many have experienced who had greater strength than thou appearest to have. But if thou wishest to keep hold of thy kingdom, it will be best for thee to come to the king, and be his man; and we shall beg him to give thee this kingdom in fief under him."

The king replies with all gentleness, "I will give thee an advice, Asgaut, in return. Go back to the east again to thy king, and tell him that early in spring I will make myself ready, and will proceed eastward to the ancient frontier that divided formerly the kingdom of the kings of Norway from Sweden. There he may come if he likes, that we may conclude a peace with each other; and each of us will retain the kingdom to which he is born."

Now the messengers turned back to their lodging, and prepared for their departure, and the king went to table. The messengers came back soon after to the king's house; but the door-keepers saw it, and reported it to the king, who told them not to let the messengers in. "I will not speak with them,"

said he. Then the messengers went off, and Thorgaut said he
would now return home with his men; but Asgaut insisted still
that he would go forward with the king's errand: so they
separated. Thorgaut proceeded accordingly through Strind;
but Asgaut went into Guldal and Orkekal, and intended proceeding southwards to Möre, to deliver his king's message. When
King Olaf came to the knowledge of this he sent out his pursuivants after them, who found them at the Ness in Stein,
bound their hands behind their backs, and led them down to the
point called Gaularaas, where they raised a gallows, and hanged
them so that they could be seen by those who travelled the usual
sea-way out of the fjord. Thorgaut heard this news before he
had travelled far on his way home through the Drontheim
country; and he hastened on his journey until he came to the
Swedish king, and told him how it had gone with them. The
king was highly enraged when he heard the account of it; and
he had no lack of high words. Sigvat tells of it thus:—

> " Twelve Swedish men, I've heard it said,
> Were here in Norway prisoners made;
> Olaf would mercy show to none,
> But had then hanged up every one.
> 'Tis not the first time I have known
> Those who the Swedish monarch own
> On Sigur's horse [1] ride in the sky,
> Their souls in hell, their heads hung high."

CHAPTER LVIII. KING OLAF AND ERLING SKIALGSSON RE-
CONCILED [1016].—The spring thereafter King Olaf Haraldsson calls out an army from the Drontheim land, and makes
ready to proceed eastward. Some of the Iceland traders
were then ready to sail from Norway. With them King Olaf
sent word and token to Hialte Skeggesson, and summoned him
to come to him; and at the same time sent a verbal message
to Skopte the lagman,[2] and other men who principally took part
in the lawgiving of Iceland, to take out of the law whatever
appeared contrary to Christianity. He sent besides a message
of friendship to the people in general. The king then proceeded
southwards himself along the coast, stopping at every district,
and holding Things with the bonders; and in each Thing he
ordered the Christian law to be read, together with the message
of salvation belonging thereunto, and with which many ill
customs and much heathenism were swept away at once among
the common people: for the earls had kept well the old laws

---

[1] The gallows: Sigur is Odin, who hung himself for nine days from the
World-Ash to gain magic wisdom.
[2] *i.e.* Law-speaker, *vide* note, p. 198.

and rights of the country; but with respect to keeping Christianity, they had allowed every man to do as he liked. It was thus come so far that the people were baptized in the most places on the sea coast, but the most of them were ignorant of Christian law. In the upper ends of the valleys, and in the habitations among the fjelds, the greater part of the people were heathen; for when the common man is left to himself, the faith he has been taught in his childhood is that which has the strongest hold over his inclination. But the king threatened the most violent proceedings against great or small who, after the king's message, would not adopt Christianity. In the meantime Olaf was proclaimed king in every Law Thing in the country, and no man spoke against him. While he lay in Karmt-sound messengers went between him and Erling Skialgsson, who endeavoured to make peace between them; and the meeting was appointed in Whitings Isle.[1] When they met they spoke with each other about agreement together; but Erling found something else than he expected in the conversation: for when he insisted on having all the fiefs which Olaf Trygvesson, and afterwards the earls Swend and Hakon, had given him, and on that condition would be his man and dutiful friend, the king answered, " It appears to me, Erling, that it would be no bad bargain for thee to get as great fiefs from me for thy aid and friendship as thou hadst from Earl Eric, a man who had done thee the greatest injury by the bloodshed of thy men; but even if I let thee remain the greatest lenderman in Norway, I will bestow my fiefs according to my own will, and not act as if ye lendermen had udal right to my ancestors' heritage, and I was obliged to buy your services with manifold rewards." Erling had no disposition to sue for even the smallest thing; and he saw that the king was not easily dealt with. He saw also that he had only two conditions before him: the one was to make no agreement with the king, and stand by the consequences; the other, to leave it entirely to the king's pleasure. Although it was much against his inclination, he chose the latter, and merely said to the king, " The service will be the most useful to thee which I give with a free will." And thus their conference ended. Erling's relations and friends came to him afterwards, and advised him to give way, and proceed with more prudence and less pride. " Thou wilt still," they said, " be the most important and most respected lenderman in Norway, both on account of thy own and thy relations' abilities and great

[1] *Hvitingsey* (modern Kvitingsøy), an island north-west of Tungenes.

wealth." Erling found that this was prudent advice, and that they who gave it did so with a good intention, and he followed it accordingly. Erling went into the king's service on such conditions as the king himself should determine and please. Thereafter they separated in some shape reconciled, and Olaf went his way eastward along the coast.

CHAPTER LIX. EILIF OF GOTLAND'S MURDER.—As soon as it was reported that Olaf had come to Viken, the Danes who had offices under the Danish king set off for Denmark, without waiting for King Olaf. But King Olaf sailed in along Viken, holding Things with the bonders. All the people of the country submitted to him, and thereafter he took all the king's taxes, and remained the summer in Viken. He then sailed east from Tunsberg across the fjord, and all the way east (south) to Swinesund. There the Swedish king's dominions begin, and he had set officers over this country; namely, Eilif Gautske over the north part, and Roa Skialge over the east (southern) part, all the way to the Gotha river. Roa had family friends on both sides of the river, and also great farms on Hising[1] Island, and was besides a mighty and very rich man. Eilif was also of great family, and very wealthy. Now when King Olaf came to Ranrige he summoned the people to a Thing, and all who dwelt on the sea-coast, or in the out-islands, came to him. Now when the Thing was seated the king's marshal, Biorn, held a speech to them, in which he told the bonders to receive Olaf as their king, in the same way as had been done in all other parts of Norway. Then stood up a bold bonder, by name Bryniulf Ulvalde,[2] and said, "We bonders know where the division-boundaries between the Norway and Danish and Swedish kings' lands have stood by rights in old times; namely, that the Gotha river divided their lands between the Venner lake and the sea; but towards the north the forests[3] until Eida forest, and from thence the ridge of the country all north to Finmark. We know, also, that by turns they have made inroads upon each other's territories, and that the Swedes have long had power all the way to Swinesund. But, sooth to say, I know that it is the inclination of many rather to serve the king of Norway, but they dare not; for the Swedish king's dominions surround us, both east-

[1] The large island at the mouth of the river Gotha, of which the most southerly part was Swedish.
[2] Ulvalde means "camel."
[3] *Markir:* on the Norwegian side Aremark and Øymark, and on the Swedish side Nordmark.

ward, southward, and also up the country; and besides, it may
be expected that the king of Norway must soon go to the north,
where the strength of his kingdom lies, and then we have no
power to withstand the Gotlanders. Now it is for the king
to give us good counsel, for we have great desire to be his men."
After the Thing, in the evening, Bryniulf was in the king's
tent, and the day after likewise, and they had much private
conversation together. Then the king proceeded eastwards
along Viken. Now when Eilif heard of his arrival, he sent out
spies to discover what he was about; but he himself, with thirty
men, kept himself high up in the habitations among the hills,
where he had gathered together bonders. Many of the bonders
came to King Olaf, but some sent friendly messages to him.
People went between King Olaf and Eilif, and they entreated
each separately to hold a Thing-meeting between themselves,
and make peace in one way or another. They told Eilif that
they might expect violent treatment from King Olaf if they
opposed his orders; but promised Eilif he should not want men.
It was determined that they should come down from the high
country, and hold a Thing with the bonders and the king.
King Olaf thereupon sent the chief of his pursuivants, Thore
Lange, with six men, to Bryniulf. They were equipt with their
coats of mail under their cloaks, and their hats over their helmets.
The following day the bonders came in crowds down with Eilif;
and in his suite was Bryniulf, and with him Thore. The king
laid his ships close to a rocky knoll that stuck out into the sea,
and upon it the king went with his people, and sat down. Below
was a flat field, on which the bonders' force was; but Eilif's
men were drawn up, forming a shield-fence before him. Biorn
the marshal spoke long and cleverly upon the king's account,
and when he sat down Eilif arose to speak; but at the same
moment Thore Lange rose, drew his sword, and struck Eilif
on the neck, so that his head flew off. Then the whole bonder-
force started up; but the Gotland men set off in full flight, and
Thore with his people killed several of them. Now when the
crowd was settled again, and the noise over, the king stood up,
and told the bonders to seat themselves. They did so, and then
much was spoken. The end of it was that they submitted to the
king, and promised fidelity to him; and he, on the other hand,
promised not to desert them, but to remain at hand until the
discord between him and the Swedish Olaf was settled in one
way or other. King Olaf then brought the whole northern
district under his power, and went in summer eastward as far

as the Gotha river, and got all the king's scatt among the islands. But when summer was drawing towards an end he returned north to Viken, and sailed up the Glommen to a waterfall called Sarp. On the north side of the fall, a point of land juts out into the river. There the king ordered a rampart to be built right across the ness, of stone, turf, and wood, and a ditch to be dug in front of it; so that it was a large earthen fort or burgh, which he made a merchant town of.[1] He had a king's house put up, and ordered the building of Mary church. He also laid out plans for other houses, and got people to build on them. In harvest he let everything be gathered there that was useful for his winter residence, and sat there with a great many people, and the rest he quartered in the neighbouring districts. The king prohibited all exports from Viken to Gotland of herrings and salt, which the Gotland people could ill do without. This year the king held a great Yule feast, to which he invited many great bonders of the district.

CHAPTER LX. HERE BEGINS THE HISTORY OF EYVIND URARHORN.—There was a man called Eyvind Urarhorn, who was a great man, of high birth, who had his descent from East Agder[2] country. Every summer he went out on a viking cruise, sometimes to the West sea, sometimes to the Baltic, sometimes south to Friesland,[3] and had a well-armed cutter (snække) of twenty benches of rowers. He had been also at Nessie, and given his aid to the king; and when they separated the king promised him his favour, and Eyvind again promised to come to the king's aid whenever he was required. This winter Eyvind was at the Yule feast of the king, and received goodly gifts from him. Bryniulf Ulvalde was also with the king, and he received a Yule present from the king of a gold-mounted sword, and also a farm called Vettaland, which is a very large head-farm of the district.[4] Bryniulf composed a song about these gifts, of which the refrain was:—

> " The song-famed hero to my hand
> Gave a good sword, and Vettaland."

The king afterwards gave him the title of Lenderman, and Bryniulf was ever after the king's greatest friend.

[1] Borg, which in the first half of the thirteenth century began to be called Sarpsborg. Of St. Olaf's rampart a remnant still remains.
[2] Roughly from Risör in the north to Kristiansand in the south.
[3] *i.e.* the coast between the Eider and North Holland.
[4] The farm of Vettelande in the parish of Skee in the north of Bohuslæn.

CHAPTER LXI. THRAND WHITE'S MURDER. — This winter Thrand White from Drontheim went east to Jemteland, to take up scatt upon account of King Olaf. But when he had collected the scatt he was surprised by men of the Swedish king, who killed him and his men, twelve in all, and brought the scatt to the Swedish king. King Olaf was very ill pleased when he heard this news.

CHAPTER LXII. CHRISTIANITY PROCLAIMED IN VIKEN. — King Olaf made Christian law to be proclaimed in Viken, in the same way as in the North country. It succeeded well, because the people of Viken were better acquainted with the Christian customs than the people in the north; for, both winter and summer, there were many merchants in Viken, both Danish and Saxon. The people of Viken, also, had much trading intercourse with England, and Saxony, and Flanders, and Denmark; and some had been on viking expeditions, and had had their winter abode in Christian lands.

CHAPTER LXIII. ROA'S FALL [1017]. — About spring time King Olaf sent a message that Eyvind Urarhorn should come to him; and they spake together in private for a long time. Thereafter Eyvind made himself ready for a viking cruise. He sailed south towards Viken, and brought up at the Eker Isles off Hising Isle. There he heard that Roa Skialge had gone northwards towards the island Ordost,[1] and had there made a levy of men and goods on account of the Swedish king, and was expected from the north. Eyvind rowed in by Hauge sound,[2] and Roa came rowing from the north, and they met in the sound and fought. Roa fell there with nearly thirty men; and Eyvind took all the goods Roa had with him. Eyvind then proceeded to the Baltic, and was all summer on a viking cruise.

CHAPTER LXIV. FALL OF GUDLEIF AND OF THORGAUT SKARDE. — There was a man called Gudleif Gerske,[3] who came originally from Agder. He was a great merchant, who went far and wide by sea, was very rich, and drove a trade with various countries. He often went east to Garderige (Russia), and therefore was called Gudleif Gerske (the Russian). This spring Gudleif fitted out his ship, and intended to go east in summer to

---

[1] Now Orust, a large island in Southern Bohuslæn, to the north of Hising.
[2] Now Högasund at the entrance to the north arm of the Gotha river.
[3] Gerske — viz. from Garderige — the Russian.

Russia. King Olaf sent a message to him that he wanted to speak to him; and when Gudleif came to the king he told him he would go in partnership with him, and told him to purchase some costly articles which were difficult to be had in this country. Gudleif said that it should be according to the king's desire. The king ordered as much money to be delivered to Gudleif as he thought sufficient, and then Gudleif set out for the Baltic. They lay in a sound in Gotland; and there it happened, as it often does, that people cannot keep their own secrets, and the people of the country came to know that in this ship was Olaf the Thick's partner. Gudleif went in summer eastwards to Novgorod, where he bought fine and costly clothes, which he intended for the king as a state dress; and also precious furs, and remarkably splendid table utensils. In autumn, as Gudleif was returning from the east, he met a contrary wind, and lay for a long time at the island Oland. There came Thorgaut Skarde, who in autumn had heard of Gudleif's course, in a long-ship against him, and gave him battle. They fought long, and Gudleif and his people defended themselves for a long time; but the numbers against them were great, and Gudleif and many of his ship's crew fell, and a great many of them were wounded. Thorgaut took all their goods, and King Olaf's, and he and his comrades divided the booty among them equally; but he said the Swedish king ought to have the precious articles of King Olaf, as these, he said, should be considered as part of the scatt due to him from Norway. Thereafter Thorgaut proceeded east to Sweden. These tidings were soon known; and as Eyvind Urarhorn came soon after to Oland, he heard the news, and sailed east after Thorgaut and his troop, and overtook them among the Swedish isles on the coast, and gave battle. There Thorgaut and the most of his men were killed, and the rest sprang overboard. Eyvind took all the goods, and all the costly articles of King Olaf which they had captured from Gudleif, and went with these back to Norway in autumn, and delivered to King Olaf his precious wares. The king thanked him in the most friendly way for his proceeding, and promised him anew his favour and friendship. At this time Olaf had been three years king over Norway.

CHAPTER LXV. MEETING OF KING OLAF AND EARL RAGN-VALD.—The same summer King Olaf ordered a levy, and went out eastwards to the Gotha river, where he lay great part of the summer. Messages were passing between King Olaf,

Earl Ragnvald, and the earl's wife, Ingeborg, the daughter of
Trygve. She was very zealous about giving King Olaf of Norway
every kind of help, and made it a matter of her deepest interest.
For this there were two causes. She had close kinship ties with
King Olaf; and also she could never forget that the Swedish
king had been one at the death of her brother, Olaf Trygvesson;
and also that he, on that account only, had any pretence to
rule over Norway. The earl, by her persuasion, turned much
towards friendship with King Olaf; and it proceeded so far
that the earl and the king appointed a meeting, and met at
the Gotha river. They talked together of many things, but
especially of the Norwegian and Swedish kings' relations
with each other; both agreeing, as was the truth also, that
it was the greatest loss, both to the people of Viken and of
Gotland, that there was no peace for trade between the two
countries; and at last both agreed upon a peace and still-stand
of arms between them until next summer: and they parted with
mutual gifts and friendly speeches.

CHAPTER LXVI. KING OLAF THE SWEDE; HIS DISLIKE TO
KING OLAF HARALDSSON.—The king thereupon returned north
to Viken, and had all the royal revenues up to the Gotha river;
and all the people of the country there had submitted to him.
King Olaf the Swede had so great a hatred of Olaf Haraldsson
that no man dared to call him by his right name in the king's
hearing. They called him the thick man; and never named
him without some hard by-name.

CHAPTER LXVII. BEGINNING OF THE ACCOUNT OF THEIR
RECONCILIATION.—The bonders in Viken spoke with each other
about there being nothing for it but that the kings should make
peace and a league with each other, and insisted upon it that
they were badly used by the kings going to war; but nobody was
so bold as to bring these murmurs before the king. At last
they begged Biorn the marshal to bring this matter before the
king, and entreat him to send messengers to the Swedish king
to offer peace on his side. Biorn was disinclined to do this, and
put it off from himself with excuses; but on the entreaties of
many of his friends, he promised at last to speak of it to the
king; but declared, at the same time, that he knew it would
be taken very ill by the king to propose that he should give way
in anything to the Swedish king. The same summer Hialte

Skeggeson came over to Norway from Iceland, according to the message sent him by King Olaf, and went directly to the king. He was well received by the king, who told him to lodge in his house, and gave him a seat beside Biorn the marshal, and Hialte became his comrade at table. There was good fellowship immediately between them.

Once, when King Olaf had assembled the people and bonders to consult upon the good of the country, Biorn the marshal said, " What think you, king, of the strife that is between the Swedish king and you ? Many people have fallen on both sides, without its being at all more determined than before what each of you shall have of the kingdom. You have now been sitting in Viken one winter and two summers, and the whole country to the north is lying behind your back unseen; and the men who have property or udal rights in the north are weary of sitting here. Now it is the wish of the lendermen, of your other people, and of the bonders, that this should come to an end. There is now a truce, agreement, and peace with the earl, and the West Gotland people who are nearest to us; and it appears to the people it would be best that you sent messengers to the Swedish king to offer a reconciliation on your side; and, without doubt, many who are about the Swedish king will support the proposal, for it is a common gain for those who dwell in both countries, both here and there." This speech of Biorn's received great applause.

Then the king said, " It is fair, Biorn, that the advice thou hast given should be carried out by thyself. Thou shalt undertake this embassy thyself, and enjoy the good of it, if thou hast advised well; and if it involve any man in danger, thou hast involved thyself in it. Moreover, it belongs to thy office to declare to the multitude what I wish to have told." Then the king stood up, went to the church, and had high mass sung before him; and thereafter went to table.

The following day Hialte said to Biorn, " Why art thou so melancholy, man? Art thou sick, or art thou angry at any one ? " Biorn tells Hialte his conversation with the king, and says it is a very dangerous errand.

Hialte says, " It is their lot who follow kings that they enjoy high honours, and are more respected than other men, but stand often in danger of their lives: and they must understand how to bear both parts of their lot. The king's luck is great; and much honour will be gained by this business, if it succeed."

Biorn answered, " Since thou makest so light of this business in thy speech, wilt thou go with me? The king has promised that I shall have companions with me on the journey."

"Certainly," says Hialte; "I will follow thee, if thou wilt: for never again shall I fall in with such a comrade if we part."

CHAPTER LXVIII. THE JOURNEY OF BIORN THE MARSHAL.—A few days afterwards, when the king was at a Thing-meeting, Biorn came with eleven others. He says to the king that they were now ready to proceed on their mission, and that their horses stood saddled at the door. "And now," says he, "I would know with what errand I am to go, or what orders thou givest us."

The king replies, "Ye shall carry these my words to the Swedish king—that I will establish peace between our countries up to the frontier which Olaf Trygvesson had before me; and each shall bind himself faithfully not to trespass over it. But with regard to the loss of people, no man must mention it if peace there is to be; for the Swedish king cannot with money pay for the men the Swedes have deprived us of." Thereupon the king rose, and went out with Biorn and his followers; and he took a gold-mounted sword and a gold ring, and said, in handing over the sword to Biorn, "This I give thee: it was given to me in summer by Earl Ragnvald. To him ye shall go; and bring him word from me to advance your errand with his counsel and strength. This thy errand I will think well fulfilled if thou hearest the Swedish king's own words, be they yea or nay: and this gold ring thou shalt give Earl Ragnvald. These are tokens [1] he must know well."

Hialte went up to the king, saluted him, and said, "We need much, king, that thy luck attend us;" [2] and wished that they might meet again in good health.

The king asked where Hialte was going.

"With Biorn," said he.

[1] Before writing was a common accomplishment in courts, the only way of accrediting a special messenger between kings and great men was by giving the messenger a token; that is, some article well known by the person receiving the message to be the property of and valued by the person sending it.

[2] The word here rendered "luck," *hamingja*, originally belonged to Germanic heathenism, and blended the concept of a luck-bringing spirit that protected an individual or family with that of an individual's innate power to attract success and good luck to himself. In Christian thought the first concept was assimilated to that of the guardian angel; the second came to be particularly associated with kings and great chieftains. One whose *hamingja* was very powerful was thought to be able to share it with or lend it to those under his protection.

The king said, " It will assist much to the good success of the journey that thou goest too, for thy good fortune has often been proved; and be assured that I shall wish that all my luck, if that be of any weight, may attend thee and thy company."

Biorn and his followers rode their way, and came to Earl Ragnvald's court. Biorn was a celebrated and generally known man,—known by sight and speech to all who had ever seen King Olaf; for, at every Thing, Biorn stood up and told the king's message. Ingeborg, the earl's wife, went up to Hialte and greeted him. She knew him, for she was living with her brother Olaf Trygvesson when Hialte was there: and she knew how to reckon up the relationship between King Olaf and Vilborg, the wife of Hialte; for Eric Biodaskalde father of Astrid, King Olaf Trygvesson's mother, and Bodvar father of Aalov, mother of Gissur White, the father of Vilborg, were brothers, sons of the lenderman Viking-Kaare of Voss.

They enjoyed here good entertainment. One day Biorn entered into conversation with the earl and Ingeborg, in which he set forth his errand, and produced to the earl his tokens.

The earl replies, " What hast thou done, Biorn, that the king wishes thy death? For, so far from thy errand having any success, I do not think a man can be found who could speak these words to the Swedish king without incurring wrath and punishment. King Olaf, king of Sweden, is too proud for any man to speak to him on anything he is angry at."

Then Biorn says, " Nothing has happened to me that King Olaf is offended at; but many of his disposition act, both for themselves and others, in a way that only men who are daring can succeed in. But as yet all his plans have had good success, and I think this will turn out well too; so I assure you, earl, that I will really travel to the Swedish king, and not turn back before I have brought to his ears every word that King Olaf told me to say to him, unless death prevent me, or that I am in bonds, and cannot perform my errand; and this I must do, whether you give any aid or no aid to me in fulfilling the king's wishes."

Then said Ingeborg, " I will soon declare my opinion. I think, earl, thou must turn all thy attention to supporting King Olaf the king of Norway's desire that this message be laid before the Swedish king, in whatever way he may answer it. Although the Swedish king's anger should be incurred, and our power and property be at stake, yet will I rather run the risk, than that it should be said the message of King Olaf was neglected from fear of the Swedish king. Thou hast that birth, strength of relations, and other means, that here in the Swedish land it is free to thee to tell thy mind, if it be right and worthy of being heard, whether it be listened to by few or many, great or little people, or by the king himself."

The earl replies, " It is known to every one how thou urgest me: it may be, according to thy counsel, that I should promise the king's men to support them, so that they may get their errand laid before the Swedish king, whether he take it ill or take it well. But I will have my own counsel followed, and will not run hastily into Biorn's or any other man's measures, in such a highly important matter. It is my will that ye all remain here with me, so long as I think it necessary for the purpose of rightly forwarding this mission." Now as the earl had thus given them to understand that he would support them in the business, Biorn thanked him most kindly, and with the assurance that his advice should rule them altogether. Thereafter Biorn and his fellow-travellers remained very long in the earl's house.

CHAPTER LXIX. OF THE CONVERSATION OF BIORN AND INGEBORG, TRYGVE'S DAUGHTER.—Ingeborg was particularly kind to them; and Biorn often spoke with her about the matter, and was ill at ease that their journey was so long delayed. Hialte and the others often spoke together also about the matter; and Hialte said, " I will go to the king if ye like; for I am not a man of Norway, and the Swedes can have nothing to say to me. I have heard that there are Iceland men in the king's house who are my acquaintances, and are well treated; namely, the scalds Gissur Black and Ottar Black.[1] From them I shall get out what I can about the Swedish king; and if the business will really be so difficult as it now appears, or if there be any other way of promoting it, I can easily devise some errand that may appear suitable for me."

This counsel appeared to Biorn and Ingeborg to be the wisest, and they resolved upon it among themselves. Ingeborg put Hialte in a position to travel; gave him two Gotland men with him, and ordered them to accompany him, and assist him with their service, and also to go wherever he might have occasion to send them. Besides, Ingeborg gave him twenty marks of weighed silver money [2] for travelling expenses, and sent word

---

[1] Gissur Black is otherwise unknown, save for a half-stanza ascribed to him in Snorri's *Edda*. Ottar Black later became one of Olaf's court poets, and his *Hǫfuðlausn* gives useful information on Olaf's first campaigns (*vide* chaps. iv–xxviii). He also wrote in praise of Canute (*vide* chap. clx).

[2] Weighed silver, calculated according to the actual value of the silver.

and token by him to the Swedish king Olaf's daughter, Ingigerd, that she should give all her assistance to Hialte's business, whenever he should find himself under the necessity of craving her help. Hialte set off as soon as he was ready. When he came to King Olaf he soon found the scalds Gissur and Ottar, and they were very glad at his coming. Without delay they went to the king, and told him that a man was come who was their countryman, and one of the most considerable in their native land, and requested the king to receive him well. The king told them to take Hialte and his fellow-travellers into their company and quarters. Now when Hialte had resided there a short time, and got acquainted with people, he was much respected by everybody. The scalds were often in the king's house, for they were well-spoken men; and often in the daytime they sat in front of the king's high seat, and Hialte, to whom they paid the highest respect in all things, by their side. He became thus known to the king, who willingly entered into conversation with him, and heard from him news about Iceland.

CHAPTER LXX. OF SIGVAT THE SCALD.—It happened that before Biorn set out from home he asked Sigvat the scald, who at that time was with King Olaf, to accompany him on his journey. It was a journey for which people had no great inclination. There was, however, great friendship between Biorn and Sigvat. Then Sigvat sang:—

> " With the king's marshals all have I,
>   In days gone by,
>   Lived joyously,—
> With all who on the king attend,
> And knee before him humbly bend.
> Biorn, thou oft hast ta'en my part—
>   Pleaded with art,
>   And touched the heart.
> Biorn! brave stainer of the sword,
> Thou art my friend—I trust thy word."

While they were riding up to Gotland Sigvat made these verses:—

> " Down the fjord sweep wind and rain,
>   Our stout ship's sails and tackle strain;
>   Wet to the skin,
>   We're sound within,
> And gaily o'er the waves are dancing,
> Our sea-steed o'er the waves high prancing!
>   Through Lister sea
>   Flying all free;
> Off from the wind with swelling sail,
> We merrily scud before the gale,

And reach the sound
Where we were bound.
And now our ship, so gay and grand,
Glides past the green and lovely land,
And at the isle
Moors for a while.
'Tis autumn now, and summer's gone;
'Tis now my fate that I ride on
Where horses tread
The hawthorn mead;
The noble ladies, fair and fine,
Are now to hear new deeds of mine."

One evening late they were riding through Gotland, and Sigvat made these verses:—

"The weary horse will at nightfall
Gallop right well to reach his stall;
When night meets day, with hasty hoof
He plies the road to reach a roof.
Far from the Danes, we now may ride
Safely by stream or mountain side;
But, in this twlight, in some ditch
The horse and rider both may pitch."

They rode through the merchant town of Skara,[1] and down the street to the earl's house. He sang:—

" The lovely girls, from window high,
Are swift to glance at the sparks that fly
From our horses' heels, as down the street
Of the earl's town we ride so fleet.
Spur on!—that every pretty lass
May hear our horse-hoofs as we pass
Clatter upon the stones so hard,
And echo round the paved court-yard."

CHAPTER LXXI. OF HIALTE SKEGGESON WHILE HE WAS IN SWEDEN.—One day Hialte, and the scalds with him, went before the king, and he began thus:—" It has so happened, king, as is known to you, that I have come here after a long and difficult journey; but when I had once crossed the ocean and heard of your greatness, it appeared to me unwise to go back without having seen you in your splendour and glory. Now it is a law between Iceland and Norway, that Iceland men pay landing dues [vide p. 148] when they come into Norway, but while I was coming across the sea I took myself all the landing dues from my ship's people; but knowing that you have the greatest right to all the power in Norway, I hastened hither to deliver

---

[1] On this site is the present town Skara, in Skaning barony, formerly the chief town and the oldest in West Gotland, and the seat of the earls in former times.

to you the landing dues." With this he showed the silver to the king, and laid ten marks of silver in Gissur Black's lap.

The king replies, " Few have brought us any such dues from Norway for some time; and now, Hialte, I will return you my warmest thanks for having given yourself so much trouble to bring us the landing dues, rather than pay them to our enemies. But I will that thou shouldst take this money from me as a gift, and with it my friendship."

Hialte thanked the king with many words, and from that day set himself in great favour with the king, and often spoke with him; for the king thought, what was true, that he was a man of much understanding and eloquence. Now Hialte told Gissur and Ottar that he was sent with tokens to the king's daughter Ingigerd, to obtain her protection and friendship; and he begged of them to procure him some opportunity to speak with her. They answered that this was an easy thing to do; and went one day to her house, where she sat at the drinking table with many men. She received the scalds in a friendly manner, for they were known to her. Hialte brought her a salutation from the earl's wife, Ingeborg; and said she had sent him here to obtain friendly help and succour from her, and in proof whereof produced his tokens. The king's daughter received him also kindly, and said he should be welcome to her friendship. They sat there till late in the day drinking. The king's daughter made Hialte tell her much news, and invited him to come often and converse with her. He did so: came there often, and spoke with the king's daughter; and at last entrusted her with the purpose of Biorn's and his comrades' journey, and asked her how she thought the Swedish king would receive the proposal that there should be a reconciliation between the kings. The king's daughter replied that, in her opinion, it would be a useless attempt to propose to the king any reconciliation with Olaf the Thick; for the king was so enraged against him that he would not suffer his name to be mentioned before him. It happened one day that Hialte was sitting with the king and talking to him, and the king was very merry and drunk. Then Hialte said, " Manifold splendour and grandeur have I seen here; and I have now witnessed with my eyes what I have often heard of, that no monarch in the north is so magnificent: but it is very vexatious that we who come so far to visit it have a road so long and troublesome, both on account of the great ocean, but more especially because it is not safe to travel through Norway for those who are coming here in a friendly disposition.

But why is there no one to bring proposals for a peace between you and King Olaf the Thick? I heard much in Norway, and in West Gotland, of the general desire that this peace should have taken place; and it has been told me for truth, as the Norway king's words, that he earnestly desires to be reconciled to you; and the reason I know is, that he feels how much less his power is than yours. It is even said that he intends to pay his court to your daughter Ingigerd; and that would lead to a useful peace, for I have heard from people of credit that he is a remarkably distinguished man."

The king answers, " Thou must not speak thus, Hialte; but for this time I will not take it amiss of thee, as thou dost not know what people have to avoid here. That fat fellow shall not be called king in my court, and there is by no means the stuff in him that people talk of; and thou must see thyself that such a connection is not suitable; for I am the tenth king in Upsal who, relation after relation, has been sole monarch over the Swedish, and many other great lands, and all have been the superior kings over other kings in the northern countries.[1] But Norway is little inhabited, and the inhabitants are scattered. There have only been small kings there; and although Harald Haarfager was the greatest king in that country, and strove against the small kings, and subdued them, yet he knew so well his position that he did not covet the Swedish dominions, and therefore the Swedish kings let him sit in peace, especially as there was relationship between them.[2] Thereafter, while Hakon Athelstan's foster-son was in Norway he sat in peace, until he began to maraud in Gotland and Denmark; on which a war-force came upon him, and took from him both life and land. Gunhild's sons also were cut off when they became disobedient to the Danish kings; and Harald Gormson joined Norway to his own dominions, and made it subject to scatt to him. And we reckon Harald Gormson to be of less power and consideration than the Upsala kings, for our relation Styrbiorn[3] subdued him, and Harald became his man; and yet Erik the Victorious, my father, rose over Styrbiorn's head when it came to a trial between them. When Olaf Trygvesson came to Norway and proclaimed

---

[1] According to Icelandic tradition, this series of kings ran: 1. Sigurd Ring; 2. Ragnar Lodbrok; 3. Bjorn Ironside; 4. Erik; 5. Erik Refilsson; 6. Eymund Eriksson; 7. Erik Eymundsson; 8. Bjorn the Old; 9. Erik the Victorious; 10. Olaf.

[2] Contrast *Sagas of the Norse Kings*, pp. 59 ff.

[3] Styrbjörn, Erik the Victorious' nephew, ravaged in the Baltic districts and gained Jomsborg in Vendland before he fell in battle against Eric.

himself king, we would not permit it, but we went with King
Swend, and cut him off; and thus we have appropriated Norway,
as thou hast now heard, and with no less right than if I had
gained it in battle, and by conquering the kings who ruled it
before. Now thou canst well suppose, as a man of sense, that
I will not let slip the kingdom of Norway for this thick fellow.
It is wonderful he does not remember how narrowly he made his
escape when we had penned him in in the Mælare lake. Although
he slipped away with life from thence, he ought, methinks, to
have something else in his mind than to hold out against us
Swedes. Now, Hialte, thou must never again open thy mouth
in my presence on such a subject."

Hialte saw sufficiently that there was no hope of the king's
listening to any proposal of a peace, and desisted from speaking
of it, and turned the conversation to something else. When
Hialte, afterwards, came into discourse with the king's daughter
Ingigerd, he tells her his conversation with the king. She told
him she expected such an answer from the king. Hialte begged
of her to say a good word to the king about the matter, but she
thought the king would listen as little to what she said: "But
speak about it I will, if thou requirest it." Hialte assured her
he would be thankful for the attempt. One day the king's
daughter Ingigerd had a conversation with her father Olaf;
and as she found her father was in a particularly good humour,
she said, "What is now thy intention with regard to the strife
with Olaf the Thick? There are many who complain about it,
having lost their property by it; others have lost their relations
by the Northmen, and all their peace and quiet; so that none
of your men see any harm that can be done to Norway. It
would be a bad counsel if thou sought the dominion over
Norway; for it is a poor country, difficult to come at, and the
people dangerous: for the men there will rather have any other
for their king than thee. If I might advise, thou wouldst let
go all thoughts about Norway, and not desire Olaf's heritage;
and rather turn thyself to the kingdoms in the East country,
which thy forefathers the former Swedish kings had, and which
our relation Styrbiorn lately subdued, and let the thick Olaf
possess the heritage of his forefathers, and make peace with
him."

The king replies in a rage, "It is thy counsel, Ingigerd, that
I should let slip the kingdom of Norway, and give thee in
marriage to this thick Olaf.—No," says he, "something else
shall first take place. Rather than that, I shall. at the Upsal

Thing in winter, issue a proclamation to all Swedes, that the whole people shall assemble for an expedition, and go to their ships before the ice is off the waters; and I will proceed to Norway, and lay waste the land with fire and sword, and burn everything, to punish them for their want of fidelity."

The king was so mad with rage that nobody ventured to say a word, and she went away. Hialte, who was watching for her, immediately went to her, and asked how her errand to the king had turned out. She answered, it turned out as she had expected; that none could venture to put in a word with the king; but, on the contrary, he had used threats; and she begged Hialte never to speak of the matter again before the king. As Hialte and Ingigerd spoke together often, Olaf the Thick was often the subject, and he told her about him and his manners; and Hialte praised the king of Norway what he could, but said no more than was the truth, and she could well perceive it. Once, in a conversation, Hialte said to her, " May I be permitted, daughter of the king, to tell thee what lies in my mind? "

" Speak freely," says she; " but so that I alone can hear it."

" Then," said Hialte, " what would be thy answer if the Norway king Olaf sent messengers to thee with the errand to propose marriage to thee? "

She blushed, and answered slowly but gently, " I have not made up my mind to answer to that; but if Olaf be in all respects so perfect as thou tellest me, I could wish for no other husband; unless, indeed, thou hast gilded him over with thy praise more than sufficiently."

Hialte replied, that he had in no respect spoken better of the king than was true. They often spoke together on the same subject. Ingigerd begged Hialte to be cautious not to mention it to any other person, for the king would be enraged against him if it came to his knowledge. Hialte only spoke of it to the scalds Gissur and Ottar, who thought it was the most happy plan, if it could but be carried into effect. Ottar, who was a man of great power of conversation, and much beloved in the court, soon brought up the subject before the king's daughter, and recounted to her, as Hialte had done, all King Olaf's excellent qualities. Often spoke Hialte and the others about him; and now that Hialte knew the result of his mission, he sent those Gotland men away who had accompanied him, and let them return to the earl with letters [1] which the king's daughter

[1] This seems the first notice we have in the sagas of written letters being sent instead of tokens and verbal messages.

Ingigerd sent to the earl and Ingeborg. Hialte also let them give a hint to the earl about the conversation he had had with Ingigerd, and her answer thereto; and the messengers came with it to the earl a little before Yule.

CHAPTER LXXII. OLAF'S JOURNEY TO THE UPLANDS.— When King Olaf had despatched Biorn and his followers to Gotland, he sent other people also to the Uplands, with the errand that they should have guest-quarters prepared for him, as he intended that winter to live as guest in the Uplands; for it had been the custom of former kings to make a progress in guest-quarters every third year in the Uplands. In autumn he began his progress from Sarpsborg, and went first to Vingulmark.[1] He ordered his progress so that he came first to lodge in the neighbourhood of the forest regions, and summoned to him all the inhabitants who dwelt at the greatest distance from the head-habitations of the district; and he inquired particularly how it stood with their Christianity, and, where improvement was needful, he taught them the right customs. If any there were who would not renounce heathen ways, he took the matter so zealously that he drove some out of the country, mutilated others of hands or feet, or gouged their eyes out; hung up some, cut down some with the sword; but let none go unpunished who would not serve God. He went thus through the whole district, sparing neither great nor small. He gave them teachers, and placed these as thickly in the country as he saw needful. In this manner he went about in that district, and had 300 fully-equipped men-at-arms with him; and then proceeded to Raumarike. He soon perceived that Christianity was thriving less the farther he proceeded into the interior of the country. He went forward everywhere in the same way, converting all the people to the right faith, and severely punishing all who would not listen to his word.

CHAPTER LXXIII. THE TREACHERY OF THE UPLAND KINGS. —Now when the king who at that time ruled in Raumarike heard of this, he thought it was a very bad affair; for every day came men to him, both great and small, who told him what was doing. Therefore this king resolved to go up to Hedemark, and consult King Rörek, who was the most eminent for understanding of the kings who at that time were in the country. Now when these kings spoke with each other, they agreed to send a message to

[1] The present Oslo and its surrounding district.

Gudrod, the valley-king north in the Gudbrandsdal, and likewise to the king who was in Hadeland, and bid them to come to Hedemark, to meet Rörek and the other kings there. They did not spare their travelling; for five kings met in Hedemark, at a place called Ringsaker. Ring, King Rörek's brother, was the fifth of these kings. The kings had first a private conference together in which he who came from Raumarike first took up the word, and told of King Olaf's proceedings, and of the disturbance he was causing both by killing and mutilating people. Some he drove out of the country, some he deprived of their offices or property if they spoke anything against him; and, besides, he was travelling over the country with a great army, not with the number of people fixed by law for a royal progress in guest-quarters. He added, that he had fled hither upon account of this disturbance, and many powerful people with him had fled from their udal properties in Raumarike. "But although as yet the evil is nearest to us, it will be but a short time before ye will also be exposed to it; therefore it is best that we all consider together what resolution we shall take." When he had ended his speech, Rörek was desired to speak; and he said, "Now is the day come that I foretold when we had our meeting at Hadeland, and ye were all so eager to raise Olaf over our heads; namely, that as soon as he was the supreme master of the country we would find it hard to hold him by the horns. We have but two things now to do: the one is to go all of us to him, and let him do with us as he likes, which I think is the best thing we can do; or the other is, to rise against him before he has gone farther through the country. Although he has 300 or 400 men, that is not too great a force for us to meet, if we are only all in movement together: but, in general, there is less success and advantage to be gained when several of equal strength are joined together than when one alone stands at the head of his own force; therefore it is my advice that we do not venture to try our luck against Olaf Haraldsson."

Thereafter each of the kings spoke according to his own mind, some dissuading from going out against King Olaf, others urging it; and no determination was come to, as each had his own reasons to produce.

Then Gudrod, the valley-king, took up the word, and spoke:— "It appears wonderful to me that ye make such a long roundabout in coming to a resolution; and probably ye are frightened for him. We are here five kings, and none of less high birth than Olaf. We gave him the strength to fight with Earl Swend, and with our forces he has brought the country under his power. But if he grudges each of us the little kingdom he had before, and threatens us with tortures, or gives us ill words, then, say I for myself, that I will withdraw myself from the king's slavery; and I do not call him a man among you who is afraid to cut him off, if he come into our hands here up in Hedemark. And this I can tell you, that we shall never bear our heads in safety while Olaf is in life." After this encouragement they all agreed to his determination.

Then said Rörek, "With regard to this determination, it appears to me necessary to make our agreement so strong that no one shall fail in his promise to the other. Therefore, if ye determine upon attacking Olaf at a fixed time, when he comes here to Hedemark, I will not trust much to you if some are north in the valleys, others up in Hedemark; but if our resolution is to come to anything, we must remain here assembled together day and night till this plan has been carried out."

This the kings agreed to, and kept themselves there all assembled, ordering a feast to be provided for them there at Ringsaker, and settled to a drinking bout; sending out spies to Raumarike, and when one set came in sending out others, so that day and night they had intelligence of Olaf's proceedings, and of the numbers of his men. King Olaf went about in Raumarike in guest-quarters, and altogether in the way before related [p. 179]; but as the provision of the guest-quarter was not always sufficient, upon account of his numerous followers, he laid it upon the bonders to give additional contributions wherever he found it necessary to stay. In some places he stayed longer, in others shorter than was fixed; and his journey down to the lake Mjösen was shorter than had been fixed on. The kings, after taking their resolution, sent out message-tokens, and summoned all the lendermen and powerful bonders from all the districts thereabout; and when they had assembled the kings had a private meeting with them, and made their determination known, setting a day for gathering together and carrying it into effect; and it was settled among them that each of the kings should have 300 men. Then they sent away the lendermen to gather the people, and meet all at the appointed place. The most approved of the measure; but it happened here, as it usually does, that every one has some friend even among his enemies.

CHAPTER LXXIV. THE MUTILATING OF THE UPLAND KINGS.

—Ketel of Ringaness was at this meeting [p. 150]. Now when he came home in the evening he took his supper, put on his clothes, and went down with his house-servants to the lake; took a light vessel which he had, the same that King Olaf had made him a present of, and launched it on the water. They found in the boat-house everything ready to their hands; betook themselves to their oars, and rowed out into the lake.[1] Ketel had forty well-armed men with him, and came early in the morning to the end of the lake (at Minne). He set off immediately with twenty men, leaving the other twenty to look after the ship. King Olaf was at that time at Eide (*i.e.* Eidsvold), in the upper end of Raumarike. Thither Ketel arrived just as the king was coming from matins. The king received Ketel kindly. He said he must speak with the king in all haste; and they had a private conference together. There Ketel tells the king the resolution which the kings had taken, and their agreement, which he had come to the certain knowledge of. When the king learnt this he called his people together, and sent some out to collect riding horses in the country; others he sent down to the lake to take all the rowing-vessels they could lay hold of, and keep them for his use. Thereafter he went to the church, had mass sung before him, and then sat down to table. After his meal he got ready, and hastened down to the lake, where the vessels were coming to meet him. He himself went on board the light vessel, and as many men with him as it could stow, and all the rest of his followers took such boats as they could get hold of; and when it was getting late in the evening they set out from the land, in still and calm weather. He rowed up the water with 400 men, and came with them to Ringsaker before day dawned; and the watchmen were not aware of the army before they were come into the very court. Ketel knew well in what houses the kings slept, and the king had all these houses surrounded and guarded, so that nobody could get out; and so they stood till daylight. The kings had not people enough to make resistance, but were all taken prisoners, and led before the king. Rörek was an able but obstinate man, whose fidelity the king could not trust to if he made peace with him; therefore he ordered both his eyes to be gouged out, and took him in that condition about with him. He ordered Gudrod's tongue to be cut out; but Ring and two others he banished from Norway, under oath never to return. Of the lendermen and bonders who had actually taken part in the traitorous design, some he drove

[1] The Mjösen is a lake of 60 or 70 miles in length.

out of the country, some he mutilated, and with others he made
peace. Ottar Black tells of this:—

" The giver of rings of gold,
　The army leader bold,
　　In vengeance springs
　　On the Hedemark kings.
Olaf, the bold and great,
　Repays their foul deceit—
　　In full repays
　　Their treacherous ways.
He drives with steel-clad hand
The small kings from the land,—
　　Greater by far
　　In deed of war.
The king who dwelt most north
Tongueless must wander forth:
　　All fly away
　　In great dismay.
King Olaf now rules o'er
What five kings ruled before—
　　To Eida's [1] bound
　　Extends his ground.
No king in days of yore
E'er won so much before:
　　God strengthens thee
　　With victory."

King Olaf took possession of the land these five kings had
possessed, and took hostages from the lendermen and bonders
in it. He took money instead of guest-quarters from the
country north of the valley district, and from Hedemark; and
then returned to Raumarike, and so west to Hadeland. This
winter his stepfather Sigurd Syr died; and King Olaf went to
Ringerike, where his mother Aasta made a great feast for him.
Olaf alone bore the title of king now in Norway.

CHAPTER LXXV. OF KING OLAF'S HALF-BROTHERS.—It is
told that when King Olaf was on his visit to his mother Aasta,
she brought out her children and showed them to him. The
king took his brother Guttorm on the one knee, and his brother
Halfdan on the other. The king looked at Guttorm, made a
wry face, and pretended to be angry at them; at which the
boys were afraid. Then Aasta brought her youngest son, called
Harald, who was three years old, to him. The king made a wry
face at him also; but he looked the king in the face without
regarding it. The king took the boy by the hair, and plucked
it; but the boy seized the king's whiskers, and gave them a
tug. "Then," said the king, "thou wilt be revengeful, my

[1] Eidskog, the great forest on the border between Norway and Sweden.

kinsman, one day." The following day the king was walking with his mother about the farm, and they came to a playground, where Aasta's sons, Guttorm and Halfdan, were amusing themselves. They were building great houses and barns in their play, and were supposing them full of cattle and sheep; and close beside them, in a clay pool, Harald was busy with chips of wood, sailing them in his sport along the edge. The king asked him what these were; and he answered, these were his ships of war. The king laughed, and said, "The time may come, kinsman, when thou wilt command ships."

Then the king called to him Halfdan and Guttorm; and first he asked Guttorm, "What wouldst thou like best to have?"

"Corn land," replied he.

"And how great wouldst thou like thy corn land to be?"

"I would have the whole ness that goes out into the lake sown with corn every summer." On that ness there are ten farms.

The king replies, "There would be a great deal of corn there." And, turning to Halfdan, he asked, "And what wouldst thou like best to have?"

"Cows," he replied.

"How many wouldst thou like to have?"

"When they went to the lake to be watered I would have so many that they stood as tight round the lake as they could stand."

"That would be a great housekeeping," said the king; "and therein ye take after your father."

Then the king says to Harald,[1] "And what wouldst thou like best to have?"

"House-servants."

"And how many wouldst thou have?"

"O! so many I would like to have as would eat up my brother Halfdan's cows at a single meal."

The king laughed, and said to Aasta, "Here, mother, thou art bringing up a king." And more is not related of them on this occasion.

CHAPTER LXXVI. OF THE DIVISION OF THE COUNTRY, AND OF THE LAWS IN SWEDEN.—In Sweden it was the old custom, as long as heathenism prevailed, that the chief sacrifice took place in Goe month[2] at Upsala. Then sacrifice was offered for peace,

---

[1] Harald (Hardrade—the Severe), afterwards king of Norway.
[2] Goi month included part of February and of March.

and victory to the king; and hither came people from all parts of Sweden. The Assembly of all Swedes was also held there then, and a market and meeting for buying, which continued for a week: and after Christianity was introduced into Sweden, the Things and fairs were held there as before. After Christianity had taken root in Sweden, and the kings would no longer dwell in Upsala, the market-time was moved to Candlemas,[1] and it has since continued so, and it lasts only three days. There is then the Swedish Thing also, and people from all quarters come there. Sweden is divided into many parts. One part is West Gotland, Vermeland, and the Marks, with what belongs to them;[2] and this part of the kingdom is so large that the bishop who is set over it has 1100 churches[3] under him. The other part is East Gotland, where there is also a bishop's seat, to which the islands of Gotland and Oland belong; and forming all together a still greater bishopric.[4] In Sweden itself (Swithiod) there is a part of the country called Sudermanland, where there is also a bishopric.[5] Then comes Westmanland, or Fiathryndaland, which is also a bishopric.[6] The third portion of Sweden proper, or Swithiod, is called Tiundaland; the fourth Aattundaland; the fifth Sioland, and what belongs to it lies eastward along the coast. Tiundaland is the best and most inhabited part of Swithiod, or Sweden proper, under which the other kingdoms stand. There Upsala is situated, the seat of the king and arch-bishop; and from it Upsala-Ode, or the domain of the Swedish kings, takes its name. Each of these divisions[7] of the country has its Lag-thing, and its own laws in many parts. Over each is a lagman (or Law-speaker), who rules principally in affairs of the bonders; for that becomes law which he, by his speech, determines them to make law: and if king, earl, or bishop goes through the country, and holds a Thing with the bonders, the lagmen reply on account of the bonders, and they all follow their

[1] 2nd February; the change would be to prevent the market from falling in Lent. The Candlemas Fair at Upsala continued to be held until the end of the nineteenth century, but Snorri is mistaken in thinking that a General Thing was still held there in his own times.
[2] Nordmarka and Dalsland.
[3] The See of Skara embraced West Gothland, Dalsland, and Vermeland. In the thirteenth century the number of the churches was about 630 (not 1100, i.e. 1320).
[4] The See of Linköping embraced East Gothland with Kalmar-len, Njudung, Finnveden, Öland and Gotland. In the year 1500 it contained 486 churches. Snorri has omitted the county of Værend with its See.
[5] The See of Strengnes. [6] Vesteraas.
[7] Snorri supposed that the bishoprics and lagmen districts were the same. But such was not the case.

lagmen; so that even the most powerful men scarcely dare to come to their Al-thing without regarding the bonders' and lagmen's law. And in all matters in which the laws differ from each other, Upsala-law is the directing law; and the other lagmen are under the lagman who dwells in Tiundaland.

CHAPTER LXXVII. OF THE LAGMAN THORGNY.—In Tiundaland there was a lagman who was called Thorgny, whose father was called Thorgny Thorgnyson. His forefathers had for a long course of years, and during many kings' times, been lagmen of Tiundaland. At this time Thorgny was old, and had a great court about him. He was considered one of the wisest men in Sweden, and was Earl Ragnvald's relation and foster-father.

CHAPTER LXXVIII. MEETING OF EARL RAGNVALD AND THE KING'S DAUGHTER INGIGERD [1018].—Now we must go back in our story to the time when the men whom the king's daughter Ingigerd and Hialte had sent from the east came to Earl Ragnvald [p. 178]. They relate their errand to the earl and his wife Ingeborg, and tell how the king's daughter had oft spoken to the Swedish king about a peace between him and King Olaf the Thick, and that she was a great friend of King Olaf; but that the Swedish king flew into a passion every time she named Olaf, so that she had no hopes of any peace. The earl told Biorn the news he had received from the east; but Biorn gave the same reply, that he would not turn back until he had met the Swedish king, and said the earl had promised to go with him. Now the winter was passing fast, and immediately after Yule the earl made himself ready to travel with sixty men, among whom were the marshal Biorn and his companions. The earl proceeded eastward all the way to Swithiod; but when he came a little way into the country he sent his men before him to Upsala, with a message to Ingigerd the king's daughter to come out to meet him at Ullerager, where she had a large farm.[1] When the king's daughter got the earl's message she made herself ready immediately to travel with a large attendance, and Hialte accompanied her. But before he took his departure he went to King Olaf, and said, "Continue always to be the most fortunate of monarchs! Such splendour as I have seen about thee I have in truth never witnessed elsewhere, and wheresoever

---

[1] Ullerager was a district on the west side of the Fyrisaa near the present Upsala, whilst Old Upsala was further north in Vaxhalda. The Thing-place of Ullerager was near the present Bondkyrka in Upsala.

I come it shall not be concealed. Now, king, may I entreat thy favour and friendship in time to come? "

The king replies, " Why art thou in so great a haste, and where art thou going? "

Hialte replies, " I am to ride out to Ullerager with Ingigerd thy daughter."

The king says, " Farewell then: a man thou art of understanding and politeness, and well suited to live with people of rank."

Thereupon Hialte withdrew.

The king's daughter Ingigerd rode to her farm in Ullerager, and ordered a great feast to be prepared for the earl. When the earl arrived he was welcomed with gladness, and he remained there several days. The earl and the king's daughter talked much, and of many things, but most about the Swedish and Norwegian kings; and she told the earl that in her opinion there was no hope of peace between them.

Then said the earl, " How wouldst thou like it, my cousin, if Olaf king of Norway were to pay his addresses to thee? It appears to us that it would contribute most towards a settled peace if there was relationship established between the kings; but I would not support such a matter if it were against thy inclination."

She replies, " My father disposes of my hand; but among all my other relations thou art he whose advice I would rather follow in weighty affairs. Dost thou think it would be advisable? " The earl recommended it to her strongly, and reckoned up many excellent achievements of King Olaf's. He told her, in particular, about what had lately been done; that King Olaf in an hour's time one morning had taken five kings prisoners, deprived them all of their governments, and laid their kingdoms and properties under his own power. Much they talked about the business, and in all their conversations they perfectly agreed with each other. When the earl was ready he took leave, and proceeded on his way, taking Hialte with him.

CHAPTER LXXIX. OF EARL RAGNVALD AND THE LAGMAN THORGNY.—Earl Ragnvald came towards evening one day to the house of Lagman Thorgny. It was a great and stately mansion, and many people stood outside who received the earl kindly, and took care of the horses and baggage. The earl went into the room, where there was a number of people. In the high seat sat an old man; and never had Biorn or his companions seen a man so stout. His beard was so long that it lay upon his knee, and was spread over his whole breast; and the man moreover was gay and lively. The earl went forward and saluted him. Thorgny received him joyfully and kindly, and bade him go to the seat he was accustomed to take. The earl seated himself on the other side, opposite to Thorgny. They remained there some days before the earl disclosed his errand, and then he asked Thorgny to go with him into the conversing room. Biorn and his followers went there with the earl. Then the earl began, and told how Olaf king of Norway had sent these men hither to conclude a peaceful agreement. He showed at great length what injury it was of to the West Gotland people that there was hostility between their country and Norway. He further related that Olaf the king of Norway had sent ambassadors, who were here present, and to whom he had promised he would attend them to the Swedish king; but he added, "The Swedish king takes the matter so grievously that he will not hear of anyone speaking in favour of it. Now so it is, my foster-father, that I do not trust to myself in this matter; but am come on a visit to thee to get good counsel and help from thee in the matter."

Now when the earl had done speaking Thorgny sat silent for a while, and then took up the word. "Ye have curious dispositions who are so ambitious of honour and renown, and yet have no prudence or counsel in you when you get into any mischief. Why did you not consider, before you gave your promise to this adventure, that you had no power to stand against King Olaf? In my opinion it is not a less honourable condition to be in the number of bonders, and have one's words free, and be able to say what one will, even if the king be present. But I must go to the Upsala Thing, and give thee such help that without fear thou canst speak before the king what thou findest good."

The earl thanked him for the promise, remained with Thorgny, and rode with him to the Upsala Thing. There was a great assemblage of people at the Thing, and King Olaf was there with his court.

CHAPTER LXXX. OF THE UPSALA THING.—The first day the Thing sat, King Olaf was seated on a stool, and his court stood in a circle around him. Right opposite to him sat Earl Ragnvald and Thorgny in the Thing upon one stool, and before them the earl's court and Thorgny's house-people. Behind their stool stood the bonder community, all in a circle around them. Some stood upon hillocks and heights, in order to hear the better. Now when the king's messages, which are usually handled in the Things, were produced and settled, the marshal Biorn rose beside the earl's stool, and said aloud, " King Olaf sends me here with the message that he will offer to the Swedish king peace, and the frontiers that in old times were fixed between Norway and Sweden." He spoke so loud that the Swedish king could distinctly hear him; but at first, when he heard King Olaf's name spoken, he thought the speaker had some message or business of his own to execute; but when he heard of peace, and the frontiers between Norway and Sweden, he saw from what root it came, and sprang up, and called out that the man should be silent, for that such speeches were useless. Thereupon Biorn sat down; and when the noise had ceased Earl Ragnvald stood up and made a speech.

He spoke of Olaf the Thick's message, and proposal of peace to Olaf the Swedish king; and that all the West Gotland people sent their entreaty to Olaf that he would make peace with the king of Norway. He recounted all the evils the West Gotlanders were suffering under; that they must go without all the things from Norway which were necessary in their households; and, on the other hand, were exposed to attack and hostility whenever the king of Norway gathered an army and made an inroad on them. The earl added, that Olaf the Norway king had sent men hither with the intent to obtain Ingigerd the king's daughter in marriage.

When the earl had done speaking Olaf the Swedish king stood up and replied, and was altogether against listening to any proposals of peace, and made many and heavy reproaches against the earl for his impudence in entering into a peaceful truce with the thick fellow, and making up a peaceful friendship with him, and which in truth he considered treason against himself. He added, that it would be well deserved if Earl Ragnvald were driven out of the kingdom. The earl had, in his opinion, the influence of his wife Ingeborg to thank for what might happen; and it was the most imprudent fancy he could have fallen upon to take up with such a wife. The king spoke long and bitterly, turning his speech always against Olaf the Thick. When he sat down not a sound was to be heard at first.

CHAPTER LXXXI. THORGNY'S SPEECH. — Then Thorgny stood up; and when he arose all the bonders stood up who had before been sitting, and rushed together from all parts to listen to what Lagman Thorgny would say. At first there was a great din of people and weapons; but when the noise was settled into silent listening, Thorgny made his speech. "The disposition of Swedish kings is different now from what it has been formerly. My grandfather Thorgny could well remember the Upsala king Eric Eymundsson, and used to say of him that when he was in his best years he went out every summer on expeditions to different countries, and conquered for himself Finland, Leifland, Courland, Esthonia, and the eastern countries all around; and at the present day the earth-bulwarks, ramparts, and other great works which he made are to be seen. And, moreover, he was not so proud that he would not listen to people who had anything to say to him. My father, again, was a long time with King Biorn, and was well acquainted with his ways and manners. In Biorn's lifetime his kingdom stood in great power, and no kind of want was felt, and he was gay and sociable with his friends. I also remember King Eric the Victorious, and was with him on many a war-expedition. He enlarged the Swedish dominion, and defended it manfully; and it was also easy and agreeable to communicate our opinions to him. But the king we have now got allows no man to presume to talk with him, unless it be what he desires to hear. On this alone he applies all his power, while he allows his scatt-lands in other countries to go from him through laziness and weakness. He wants to have the Norway kingdom laid under him, which no Swedish king before him ever desired, and therewith brings war and distress on many a man. Now it is our will, we bonders, that thou King Olaf make peace with the Norway king, Olaf the Thick, and marry thy daughter Ingigerd to him. Wilt thou, however, reconquer the kingdoms in the east countries which thy relations and forefathers had there, we will all for that purpose follow thee to the war. But if thou wilt not do as we desire, we will now attack thee, and put thee to death; for we will no longer suffer law and peace to be disturbed. So our forefathers went to work when they drowned five kings in a morass at the Mora-thing,[1] and they were filled with the same insupportable pride thou hast shown toward us. Now tell us, in all haste, what resolution thou wilt take." Then the whole public approved, with clash of arms and shouts, the lagman's speech.

The king stands up and says he will let things go according

---

[1] An emendation of *Múlaþing*, which is unknown. *Móraþing* was an old assembly-place near Upsala where the Swedes once chose their kings.

to the desire of the bonders. "All Swedish kings," he said, "have done so, and have allowed the bonders to rule in all according to their will." The murmur among the bonders then came to an end; and the chiefs, the king, the earl, and Thorgny talked together, and concluded a truce and reconciliation, on the part of the Swedish king, according to the terms which the king of Norway had proposed by his embassadors; and it was resolved at the Thing that Ingigerd, the king's daughter, should be married to Olaf Haraldsson. The king left it to the earl to make the contract feast, and gave him full powers to conclude this marriage affair; and after this was settled at the Thing, they separated. When the earl returned homewards, he and the king's daughter Ingigerd had a meeting, at which they talked between themselves over this matter. She sent Olaf a long cloak of fine linen[1] richly embroidered with gold, and with silk points.[2] The earl returned to Gotland, and Biorn with him; and after staying with him a short time, Biorn and his company returned to Norway. When he came to King Olaf he told him the result of his errand, and the king returned him many thanks for his conduct, and said Biorn had had great success in bringing his errand to so favourable a conclusion against such animosity.

CHAPTER LXXXII. OF KING RÖREK'S TREACHERY [1018].—
On the approach of spring King Olaf went down to the coast, had his ships rigged out, summoned troops to him, and proceeded in spring out from Viken to the Naze, and so north to Hordaland. He then sent messages to all the lendermen, selected the most considerable men in each district, and made the most splendid preparations to meet his bride. The wedding feast was to be in autumn, at the Gotha river, on the frontiers of the two countries. King Olaf had with him the blind king Rörek. When his wound was healed, the king gave him two men to serve him, let him sit in the high seat by his side, and kept him in meat and clothes in no respect worse than he had kept himself before. Rörek was taciturn, and answered short and cross when any one spoke to him. It was his custom to make his foot-boy, when he went out in the daytime, lead him away from people, and then to beat the lad until he ran away. He would then complain to King Olaf that the lad would not serve him. The King changed his servants, but it was as before; no servant would hold it out with King Rörek. Then the king appointed a man called

---

[1] *Pell* (from Latin *pallium*), a word applied to various rich fabrics.
[2] More accurately " silken ribbons " (*silkireimar*), perhaps for garters.

Swend to wait upon and serve King Rörek. He was Rörek's relation, and had formerly been in his service. Rörek continued with his habits of moroseness, and of solitary walks; but when he and Swend were alone together, he was merry and talkative. He used to bring up many things which had happened in former days when he was king. He alluded, too, to the man who had, in his former days, torn him from his kingdom and happiness, and made him live on alms. " It is hardest of all," says he, " that thou and my other relations, who ought to be men of bravery, art so degenerated that thou wilt not avenge the shame and disgrace brought upon our race." Such lamenting he often brought out. Swend said they had too great a power to deal with, while they themselves had but little means. Rörek said, " Why should we live longer as mutilated men with disgrace? I, a blind man, may conquer them as well as they conquered me when I was asleep. Come then, let us kill this thick Olaf. He is not afraid for himself at present. I will lay the plan, and would not spare my hands if I could use them, but that I cannot by reason of my blindness; therefore thou must use the weapons against him, and as soon as Olaf is killed I can see well enough that his power must come into the hands of his enemies, and it may well be that I shall be king and thou shalt be my earl." So much persuasion he used that Swend at last agreed to join in the deed. The plan was so laid that when the king was ready to go to vespers, Swend stood on the threshold with a drawn dagger under his cloak. Now when the king came out of the room, it so happened that he walked quicker than Swend expected; and when he looked the king in the face he grew pale, and then white as a corpse, and his hand sunk down. The king observed his terror, and said, " What is this, Swend? Wilt thou betray me? " Swend threw down his cloak and dagger, and fell at the king's feet, saying, " All is in God's hands and thine, king! " The king ordered his men to seize Swend, and he was put in irons. The king ordered Rörek's seat to be moved to the second bench.[1] He gave Swend his life, and he left the country. The king appointed a different lodging for Rörek to sleep in from that in which he slept himself, and in which many of his court-people slept. He set two of his court-men, who had been long with him, and whose fidelity he had proof of, to attend Rörek day and night; but it is not said whether

---

[1] *i.e.* the long bench, which was opposite that on which the king's high seat was. Rörek had formerly been sitting on the bench on which Olaf's seat was.

they were people of high birth or not. King Rörek's mood
was very different at different times. Sometimes he would sit
silent for days together, so that no man could get a word out
of him; and sometimes he was so merry and gay, that people
found a joke in every word he said. Sometimes his words were
very bitter. He was sometimes in a mood that he would drink
them all under the benches, and made all his neighbours drunk;
but in general he drank but little. King Olaf gave him plenty
of pocket-money. When he went to his lodgings he would often,
before going to bed, have some stoups of mead brought in, which
he gave to all the men in the house to drink, so that he was
much liked.

CHAPTER LXXXIII. OF LITTLE FINN.—There was a man
from the Uplands called Finn the Little, and some said of him
that he was of Finnish [1] race. He was a remarkably little man,
but so swift of foot that no horse could overtake him. He was
a particularly well exercised runner with snow shoes, and shooter
with the bow. He had long been in the service of King Rörek,
and often employed in errands of trust. He knew the roads in
all the Upland hills, and was well known to all the great people.
Now when King Rörek was set under guards on the journey
Finn would often slip in among the men of the guard, and
followed, in general, with the lads and serving-men; but as
often as he could he waited upon Rörek, and entered into
conversation with him. The king, however, only spoke a word
or two with him at a time, to prevent suspicion. In spring,
when they came a little way beyond Viken, Finn disappeared
from the army for some days, but came back, and stayed with
them a while. This happened often, without any one observing
it particularly; for there were many such hangers-on with the
army.

CHAPTER LXXXIV. OF THE MURDER OF SOME OF KING
OLAF'S COURT-MEN.—King Olaf came to Tunsberg before Easter
(6th April 1018), and remained there late in spring. Many
merchant vessels came to the town, both from Saxon-land and
Denmark, and from Viken, and from the north parts of the
country. There was a great assemblage of people; and as
the times were good, there was many a drinking meeting. It
happened one evening that King Rörek came rather late to his

[1] The Laplanders are called Finns in the sagas.

lodging; and as he had drunk a great deal, he was remarkably merry. Little Finn came to him with a stoup of mead with herbs in it, and very strong. The king made every one in the house drunk, until they fell asleep each in his berth. Finn had gone away, and a light was burning in the lodging. Rörek waked the men who usually followed him, and told them he wanted to go out into the yard. They had a lantern with them, for outside it was pitch dark. Out in the yard there was a large closet standing upon pillars, and a stair to go up to it. While Rörek and his guards sat there they heard a man say, " Cut down that devil; " and presently a crash, as if somebody fell. Rörek said, " These fellows must be dead drunk to be fighting with each other so: run and separate them." They rushed out; but when they came out upon the steps both of them were killed: the man who went out the last was the first killed. There were twelve of Rörek's men there, and among them Sigurd Hit, who had been his banner-man, and also little Finn. They drew the dead bodies up between the houses, took the king with them, ran out to a boat they had in readiness, and rowed away. Sigvat the scald slept in King Olaf's lodgings. He got up in the night, and his footboy with him, and went to the closet. But as they were returning, on going down the stairs Sigvat's foot slipped and he fell on his knee; and when he put out his hands he felt the stairs wet. " I think," said he, laughing, " the king must have given many of us tottering legs to-night." When they came into the house in which light was burning the footboy said, " Have you hurt yourself that you are all over so bloody? " He replied, " I am not wounded, but something must have happened here." Thereupon he wakened Thord Foleson, who was standard-bearer, and his bedfellow. They went out with a light, and soon found the blood. They traced it, and found the corpses, and knew them. They saw also a great stump of a tree in which clearly a gash had been cut, which, as was afterwards known, had been done as a stratagem to entice those out who had been killed. Sigvat and Thord spoke together, and agreed it was highly necessary to let the king know of this without delay. They immediately sent a lad to the lodging where Rörek had been. All the men in it were asleep; but the king was gone. He wakened the men who were in the house, and told them what had happened. The men arose and ran out to the yard where the bodies were; but, however needful it appeared to be that the king should know it, nobody dared to waken him.

Then said Sigvat to Thord, " What wilt thou rather do, comrade,—waken the king, or tell him the tidings ? "

Thord replies, " I do not dare to waken him, and I would rather tell him the news."

Then said Sigvat, " There is much of the night still to pass, and before morning Rörek may get himself concealed in such a way that it may be difficult to find him; but as yet he cannot be very far off, for the bodies are still warm. We must never let the disgrace rest upon us of concealing this treason from the king. Go thou, Thord, up to the lodging, and wait for me there."

Sigvat then went to the church, and told the bell-ringer to toll for the souls of the king's court-men, naming the men who were killed. The bell-ringer did as he was told. The king awoke at the ringing, sat up in his bed, and asked if it was already the hour of matins.

Thord replies, " It is worse than that, for there has occurred a very important affair. Rörek is fled, and two of the court-men are killed."

The king asked how this had taken place, and Thord told him all he knew. The king got up immediately, ordered to sound the call for a meeting of the court, and when the people were assembled he named men to go out to every quarter from the town, by sea and land, to search for Rörek. Thore Lange took a boat, and set off with thirty men; and when day dawned they saw two small boats before them in the channel, and when they saw each other both parties rowed as hard as they could. King Rörek was there with thirty men. When they came quite close to each other Rörek and his men turned towards the land, and all sprang on shore except the king, who sat on the aft seat. He bade them farewell, and wished they might meet each other again in better luck. At the same moment Thore with his company rowed to the land. Finn the Little shot off an arrow, which hit Thore in the middle of the body, and was his death; and Sigurd, with his men, ran up into the forest. Thore's men took his body, and transported it, together with Rörek, to Tunsberg. King Olaf undertook himself thereafter to look after King Rörek, made him be carefully guarded, and took good care of his treason, for which reason he had a watch over him night and day. King Rörek thereafter was very gay, and nobody could observe but that he was in every way well satisfied.

CHAPTER LXXXV. OF RÖREK'S ASSAULT.—It happened on Ascension-day (15th May 1018) that King Olaf went to high mass, and the bishop went in procession around the church and conducted the king; and when they came back to the church the bishop led the king to his seat on the north side of the choir. There Rörek sat next to the king, and concealed his countenance in his upper cloak. When Olaf had seated himself Rörek laid his hand on the king's shoulder, and felt it.

" Thou hast fine clothes on, cousin, to-day," says he.

King Olaf replies, " It is a festival to-day, in remembrance that Jesus Christ ascended to heaven from earth."

King Rörek says, " I understand nothing about it, so as to hold in my mind what ye tell me about Christ. Much of what ye tell me appears to me incredible, although many wonderful things may have come to pass in old times."

When the mass was finished Olaf stood up, held his hands up over his head, and bowed down before the altar, so that his cloak hung down behind his shoulders. Then King Rörek started up hastily and sharply, and struck at the king with a long knife of the kind called ryting;[1] but the blow was received in the upper cloak at the shoulder, because the king was bending himself forwards. The clothes were much cut, but the king was not wounded. When the king perceived the attack he sprang upon the floor; and Rörek struck at him again with the knife, but did not reach him, and said, " Art thou flying, Olaf, from me, a blind man? " The king ordered his men to seize him, and lead him out of the church, which was done. After this attempt many hastened to King Olaf, and advised that King Rörek should be killed. " It is," said they, " tempting your luck in the highest degree, king, to keep him with you, and protect him, whatever mischief he may undertake; for night and day he thinks upon taking your life. And if you send him away, we know no one who can watch him so that he will not in all probability escape; and if once he gets loose he will assemble a great multitude, and do much evil."

The king replies, " Ye say truly that many a one has suffered death for less offence than Rörek's; but willingly I would not darken the victory I gained over the Upland kings, when in one morning hour I took five kings prisoners, and got all their kingdoms: but yet, without having to be the murderer of any of them, as they were all my kinsmen. As yet I can scarcely see whether Rörek puts me in the necessity of killing him or not."

It was to feel if King Olaf had armour on or not, that Rörek had laid his hand on the king's shoulder.

[1] Dagger or sheath-knife.

CHAPTER LXXXVI. KING RÖREK'S JOURNEY TO ICELAND [1019-1020].—There was an Iceland man, by name Thorarin Nefiolfsson, who had his relations in the north of the country. He was not of high birth, but particularly prudent, eloquent, and agreeable in conversation with people of distinction. He was also a far-travelled man, who had been long in foreign parts (*i.e.* in Norway). Thorarin was a remarkably ugly man, principally because he had very ungainly limbs. He had great ugly hands, and his feet were still uglier. Thorarin was in Tunsberg when this event happened which has just been related, and he was known to King Olaf by their having had conversations together. Thorarin was just then done with rigging out a merchant vessel which he owned, and with which he intended to go to Iceland in summer. King Olaf had Thorarin with him as a guest for some days, and conversed much with him; and Thorarin even slept in the king's lodgings. One morning early the king awoke while the others were still sleeping. The sun had newly risen in the sky, and there was much light within. The king saw that Thorarin had stretched out one of his feet from under the bed-clothes, and he looked at the foot a while. In the meantime the others in the lodging awoke; and the king said to Thorarin, " I have been awake for a while, and have seen a sight which was worth seeing; and that is a man's foot so ugly that I do not think an uglier can be found in this merchant town." Thereupon he told the others to look at it, and see if it was not so; and all agreed with the king. When Thorarin observed what they were talking about, he said, " There are few things for which you cannot find a match, and that may be the case here."

The king says, " I would rather say that such another ugly foot cannot be found in the town, and I would lay any wager upon it."

Then said Thorarin, " I am willing to bet that I shall find an uglier foot still in the town."

The king:—" Then he who wins shall have the right to get any demand from the other he chooses to make."

" Be it so," said Thorarin. Thereupon he stretches out his other foot from under the bed-clothes, and it was in no way handsomer than the other, and moreover wanted the big toe. " There," said Thorarin, " see now, king, my other foot, which is so much uglier; and, besides, lacks the big toe. Now I have won."

The king replies, " That other foot was so much uglier than

this one by having five ugly toes upon it, and this has only four; and now I have won the choice of asking something from thee."

"The sovereign's decision must be right," says Thorarin; "but what does the king require of me?"

"To take Rörek," said the king, "to Greenland, and deliver him to Leif Ericsson."

Thorarin replies: "I have never been at Greenland."

The king:—"Thou, who art a far-travelled man, wilt now have an opportunity of seeing Greenland, if thou hast never been there before."

At first Thorarin did not say much about it; but as the king insisted on his wish he did not entirely decline, but said, "I will let you hear, king, what my desire would have been had I gained the wager. It would have been to be received into your body of court-men; and if you will grant me that, I will be the more zealous now in fulfilling your pleasure." The king gave his consent, and Thorarin was made one of the court-men. Then Thorarin rigged out his vessel, and when he was ready he took on board King Rörek. When Thorarin took leave of King Olaf, he said, "Should it now turn out, king, as is not improbable, and often happens, that we cannot effect the voyage to Greenland, but must run for Iceland or other countries, how shall I get rid of this king in a way that will be satisfactory to you?"

The king:—"If thou comest to Iceland, deliver him into the hands of Gudmund Eyolfsson,[1] or of Skopte the lagman,[2] or of some other chief who will receive my tokens and message of friendship. But if thou comest to other countries nearer to this, do so with him that thou canst know with certainty that King Rörek shall never return alive to Norway; but do so only when thou seest no other way of doing whatsoever."

When Thorarin was ready for sea, and got a wind, he sailed outside of all the rocks and islands, and when he was to the north of the Naze set right out into the ocean. He did not immediately get a good wind, but he avoided coming near the land. He sailed past Iceland to the south, close enough to get a sight of it, and onwards west around the land out into the Greenland ocean. There he encountered heavy storms, and drove long about upon the ocean; but when summer was coming

---

[1] Gudmund the Mighty of Modruvellir in the north of Iceland.

[2] Icelandic had two words for "Law-speaker"—*lǫgsǫgumaðr* and *lǫgmaðr*; the former applied to Icelanders, the latter to Swedes and Norwegians or to Icelanders of the later, Norway-dominated, period. "Lagman" is an Anglicized form of the latter term, and its use here is misleading.

to an end he landed again in Iceland in Breida fjord. Thorgils
Areson [1] was the first man of any consequence who came to him.
Thorarin brings him the king's salutation, message, and tokens,
with which was the desire about King Rörek's reception.
Thorgils received these in a friendly way, and invited King Rörek
to his house, where he stayed all winter. But he did not like
being there, and begged that Thorgils would let him go to
Gudmund; saying he had heard some time or other that there,
in Gudmund's house, was the most sumptuous way of living in
Iceland, and that it was intended he should be in Gudmund's
hands. Thorgils let him have his desire, and conducted him
with some men to Gudmund at Modrovald. Gudmund received
Rörek kindly on account of the king's message, and he stayed
there the next winter. He did not like being there either;
and then Gudmund gave him a habitation upon a small farm
called Kalfskind,[2] where there were but few neighbours. There
Rörek passed the third winter, and said that since he had laid
down his kingdom he thought himself most comfortably situated
here; for here he was most respected by all. The summer after
Rörek fell sick, and died; and it is said he is the only king whose
bones rest in Iceland. Thorarin Nefiolfsson was afterwards
for a long time upon voyages; but sometimes he was with
King Olaf.

CHAPTER LXXXVII. BATTLE IN ULFREKSFJORD. — The
summer that Thorarin went with Rörek to Iceland, Hialte
Skeggeson went also to Iceland, and King Olaf gave him many
friendly gifts with him when they parted. The same summer
Eyvind Urarhorn went on an expedition to the West sea, and
came in autumn to Ireland, to the Irish king Konofogor. In
autumn Einar earl of Orkney and this Irish king met in Ulfreksfjord,[3] and there was a great battle, in which Konofogor [4] gained
the victory, having many more people. The earl fled with a
single ship, and came back about autumn to Orkney, after losing
most of his men and all the booty they had made. The earl
was much displeased with his expedition, and threw the blame
upon the Northmen, who had been in the battle on the side of
the Irish king, for making him lose the victory.

[1] He lived at Reykholar on the northern side of the Breidefjord in the
west country.   He was alive in 1024.
[2] On the west side of Eyjafjord in the north of Iceland. There is a
burial mound near by which is said to be Rörek's.
[3] *Ulfreksfjorðr* is in Ireland, and is probably to be identified with Lough
Larne.   (See *Orkneyinga Saga*, chap. xv.)
[4] This is the Norse form for Conchobhar; he has not been identified.

CHAPTER LXXXVIII. KING OLAF PREPARES FOR HIS BRIDAL JOURNEY.—Now we begin again our story where we let it slip— at King Olaf's travelling to his bridal [p. 191], to receive his betrothed Ingigerd the king's daughter. The king had a great body of men with him, and so chosen a body that all the great people he could lay hold of followed him; and every man of consequence had a chosen band of men with him distinguished by birth or other qualifications. The whole were well appointed, and equipt in ships, weapons, and clothes. They steered the fleet eastwards to Konghelle; but when they arrived there they heard nothing of the Swedish king, and none of his men had come there. King Olaf remained a long time in summer at Konghelle, and endeavoured carefully to make out what people said of the Swedish king's movements, or what were his designs; but no person could tell him anything for certain about it. Then he sent men up to Gotland to Earl Ragnvald, to ask him if he knew how it came to pass that the Swedish king did not come to the meeting agreed on. The earl replies, that he did not know. " But as soon," said he, " as I hear, I shall send some of my men to King Olaf, to let him know if there be any other cause for the delay than the multitude of affairs; as it often happens that the Swedish king's movements are delayed by this more than he could have expected."

CHAPTER LXXXIX. OF THE SWEDISH KING'S CHILDREN.— This Swedish king, Olaf Ericsson, had first a concubine who was called Edla, a daughter of an earl of Vendland, who had been captured in war, and therefore was called the king's slave-girl. Their children were Eymund, Astrid, and Holmfrid.[1] Further- more he and she had a son, who was born the day before St. Jacob's-day (25th July 1007 or 1009). When the boy was to be christened the bishop called him Jacob, which the Swedes did not like, as there had never been a Swedish king called Jacob. All King Olaf's children were handsome in appearance, and clever from childhood. The queen was proud, and did not behave well towards her stepchildren; therefore, the king sent his son Eymund to Vendland, to be fostered by his mother's relations, where he for a long time neglected his Christianity. The king's daughter, Astrid, was brought up in West Gotland, in the house of a worthy man called Egil. She was a very lovely girl: her words came well into her conversation; she was merry, but

[1] The manuscripts are defective; in the next sentence " she " must mean the Queen, not Edla, for Jacob was legitimate (vide p. 216).

modest, and very generous. When she was grown up she was often in her father's house, and every man thought well of her. King Olaf was haughty and harsh in his speech. He took very ill the uproar and clamour the country people had raised against him at the Upsala Thing, as they had threatened him with violence, for which he laid the chief blame on Earl Ragnvald. He made no preparation for the bridal, according to the agreement to marry his daughter Ingigerd to Olaf the king of Norway, and to meet him on the borders for that purpose. As the summer advanced many of his men were anxious to know what the king's intentions were; whether to keep to the agreement with King Olaf, or break his word, and with it the peace of the country. But no one was so bold as to ask the king, although they complained of it to Ingigerd, and besought her to find out what the king intended. She replied, " I have no inclination to speak to the king again about the matters between him and King Olaf; for he answered me ill enough once before when I brought forward Olaf's name." In the meantime Ingigerd, the king's daughter, took it to heart, became melancholy and sorrowful, and yet very curious to know what the king intended. She had much suspicion that he would not keep his word and promise to King Olaf; for he appeared quite enraged whenever Olaf the Thick was spoken of as " king."

CHAPTER XC. OF THE SWEDISH KING OLAF'S HUNTING.—
One morning early the king rode out with his dogs and falcons, and his men around him. When they let slip the falcons the king's falcon killed two black-cocks in one flight, and three in another. The dogs ran and brought the birds when they had fallen to the ground. The king ran after them, took the game from them himself, was delighted with his sport, and said, " It will be long before the most of you have such success." They agreed in this; adding, that in their opinion no king had such luck in hunting as he had. Then the king rode home with his followers in high spirits. Ingigerd, the king's daughter, was just going out of her lodging when the king came riding into the yard, and she turned round and saluted him. He saluted her in return, laughing; produced the birds, and told her the success of his chase.

" Dost thou know of any king," said he, " who made so great a capture in so short a time? "

" It is indeed," replied she, " a good morning's hunting, to have got five black-cocks; but it was a still better when, in one morning, the king of Norway, Olaf, took five kings, and subdued all their kingdoms."

When the king heard this he sprang from his horse, turned to Ingigerd, and said, " Thou shalt know, Ingigerd, that however great thy love may be for this man, thou shalt never get him, nor he get thee. I will marry thee to some chief with whom I can be in friendship; but never can I be a friend of the man who has robbed me of my kingdom, and done me great mischief by marauding and killing through the land." With that their conversation broke off, and each went away.

CHAPTER XCI. OF OLAF THE NORSE KING'S COUNSELS.— Ingigerd, the king's daughter, had now full certainty of King Olaf's intention, and immediately sent men to West Gotland to Earl Ragnvald, and let him know how it stood with the Swedish king, and that the agreement made with the king of Norway was broken; and advising the earl and people of West Gotland to be upon their guard, as no peace from the people of Norway was to be expected. When the earl got this news he sent a message through all his kingdom, and told the people to be cautious, and prepared in case of war or pillage from the side of Norway. He also sent men to King Olaf the Thick, and let him know the message he had received, and likewise that he wished for himself to hold peace and friendship with King Olaf; and therefore he begged him not to pillage in his kingdom. When this message came to King Olaf it made him both angry and sorry; and for some days nobody got a word from him. He then held a House-Thing with his men, and in it Biorn arose, and first took the word. He began his speech by telling that he had proceeded eastward last winter to establish a peace, and he told how kindly Earl Ragnvald had received him; and, on the other hand, how crossly and heavily the Swedish king had accepted the proposal. " And the agreement," said he, " which was made, was made more by means of the strength of the people, the power of Thorgny, and the aid of the earl, than by the king's good will. Now, on these grounds, we know for certain that it is the king who has caused the breach of the agreement; therefore we ought by no means to make the earl suffer, for it is proved that he is King Olaf's firm friend. The king wishes now to hear from the chiefs and other leaders of troops what course he should adopt: Whether he should go against Gotland, and maraud there with such men as we have got; or is there any other course that appears to you more advisable? " He spoke both long and well.

Thereafter many powerful men spoke, and all were at last agreed in dissuading from hostilities. They argued thus: "Although we are a numerous body of men who are assembled here, yet they are all only people of weight and power; but, for a war expedition, young men who are in quest of property and consideration are more suitable. It is also the custom of people of weight and power, when they go into battle or strife, to have many people with them whom they can send out before them for their defence; for the men do not fight worse who have little property, but even better than those who are brought up in the midst of wealth." After these considerations the king resolved to dismiss this army from any expedition, and to give every man leave to return home; but proclaimed, at the same time, that next summer the people over the whole country would be called out in a general levy, to march immediately against the Swedish king, and punish him for his want of faith. All thought well of this plan. Then the king returned northwards to Viken, and took his abode at Sarpsborg in autumn, and ordered all things necessary for winter provision to be collected there; and he remained there all winter with a great retinue.

CHAPTER XCII. SIGVAT THE SCALD'S JOURNEY EASTWARDS. —People talked variously about Earl Ragnvald; some said he was King Olaf's sincere friend; others did not think this likely, and thought it stood in his power to warn the Swedish king to keep his word, and the agreement concluded on between him and King Olaf. Sigvat the poet often expressed himself in conversation as Earl Ragnvald's great friend, and often spoke of him to King Olaf; and he offered to the king to travel to Earl Ragnvald's, and spy after the Swedish king's doings, and to attempt, if possible, to get the settlement of the agreement. The king thought well of this plan; for he oft, and with pleasure, spoke to his confidential friends about Ingigerd, the king's daughter. Early in winter Sigvat the scald, with two companions, left Sarpsborg, and proceeded eastwards over the Marks [1] to Gotland. Before Sigvat and King Olaf parted he composed these verses:— [2]

> " Sit happy in thy hall, O king!
> Till I come back, and good news bring:
> The scald will bid thee now farewell,
> Till he brings news well worth to tell.
> He wishes to the helmed hero
> Health, and long life, and a full flow

[1] *Vide* note 3, p. 163.
[2] This sequence of strophes is known as *Austrfaravísur*, " Verses on a Journey to the East."

Of honour, riches, and success—
And, parting, ends his song with this.
The farewell word is spoken now—
The word that to the heart lies nearest.
And yet, O king! before I go,
One word on what I hold the dearest.
I fain would say, ' O! may God save
To thee, the bravest of the brave,
The land which is thy right by birth! '—
This is my dearest wish on earth."

Then they proceeded eastwards towards Eida,[1] and had difficulty in crossing the river in a little cobble; but they escaped, though with danger: and Sigvat sang:—

" On shore the crazy boat I drew,
Wet to the skin, and frightened too;
For truly both were folly then:
To go on, or turn back again.
Hell take that boat, that mockery,
That worst craft I did ever see!
The crossing was with peril fraught,
Yet ended better than I thought."

Then they went through the Eida forest,[2] and Sigvat sang:—

" A hundred miles through Eida wood,
We trudged along, in weary mood;
And this indeed was not the first
Of hardships for us, nor the worst.
With many a grumble, many a groan,
Full thirteen leagues we trudged right on;
And every king's man of us bore
On each foot-sole a bleeding sore."

They came then through Gotland, and in the evening reached a farm-house called Hof.[3] The door was bolted so that they could not come in; and the servants told them it was holy there, and they could not get admittance. Sigvat sang:—

" Now up to Hof in haste I hie,
And round the house and yard I pry.
Doors are fast locked—but yet within,
Methinks, I hear some stir and din.
I peep, with nose close to the ground,
Below the door, but small cheer found.
My trouble with few words was paid—
' 'Tis holy time,' the house-folks said.
Heathens! to shove me thus away!
I' the foul fiend's claws may you all lay."

Then they came to another farm, where the good wife was

---

[1] The river of the Eida Forest (Eidskog).
[2] The forest that lay along the border between Norway and Sweden.
[3] Unidentified; the modern Store Hof is not on the right road.

standing at the door, and told them not to come in, for they were busy with a sacrifice to the Elves.[1]   Sigvat sang of it thus:—

> " ' Thou rash fool, enter not, I pray! '
> Thus to me did the old wife say;
> ' For all of us are heathens here,
> And I for Odin's wrath do fear.'
> The ugly witch drove me away,
> Like scared wolf sneaking from his prey,
> When she told me that those within
> Held sacrifice to the elvish kin."

Another evening they came to three bonders, all of them of the name of Olvir, who drove them away.   Sigvat sang:—

> " Three of one name,
> To their great shame,
> The traveller late
> Drove from their gate!
> Now much I fear
> That each Olvir
> Will drive from his home
> The guests that come."

They went on farther that evening, and came to a fourth bonder, who was considered the most hospitable man in the country; but he drove them away also.   Then Sigvat sang:—

> " Then on I went to seek night's rest
> From one who was said to be the best,
> The kindest host in the land around,
> And there I hoped to have quarters found.
> But, faith, 'twas little use to try;
> For not so much as raise an eye
> Would this huge wielder of the spade:
> If he's the best, it must be said
> Bad are the rest, and the scald's praise
> Cannot be given to churls like these.
> How much I longed for Aasta's bower,
> Beyond the Eida Forest far,
> When we, king's men, were even put
> Lodging to crave in a heathen's hut.
> I knew not where the earl to find:
> Four times driven off by men unkind,
> I wandered now the whole night o'er,
> Driven like a dog from door to door."

Now when they came to Earl Ragnvald's, the earl said they must have had a severe journey.   Then Sigvat sang:—

> " The message-bearers of the king
> From Norway came his words to bring;
> And truly for their master they
> Hard work have done before to-day.

[1] The *álfar*, " elves," were probably originally spirits of the dead; they were thought of as living in mounds and affecting the seasons and the fertility of crops.

> We did not seek to spare our pain,
> When sent by Norway's great chieftain,
> Yet Eida's forest ways are rough,
> So eastwards we went slow enough.
> I praise thee, earl—but men of thine
> (So lavish, generous and fine)
> Should not have turned me from their doors
> When towards thee I took my course."

Earl Ragnvald gave Sigvat a gold arm-ring, and a woman said, "He had not made the journey with his black eyes for nothing." Sigvat sang:—

> " My coal-black eyes
> Are of Iceland's guise;
> They have lighted me
> Across the sea
> To gain this golden prize:
> These feet of mine,
> O lady fine,
> Undaunted trod
> An ancient road;
> It is an unknown place
> To warriors of thy race."

When Sigvat came home to King Olaf he went into the hall, and, looking around on the walls, he sang:—

> " When our men their arms are taking
> The raven's wings with greed are shaking;
> When they come back to drink in hall
> Brave spoil they bring to deck the wall—
> Shields, helms, and pantzers,[1] all in row,
> Stripped in the field from lifeless foe.
> In truth no royal hall comes near
> Thy splendid hall in precious gear."

Afterwards Sigvat told of his journey, and sang these verses:—

> " O king's court-guards, I bid you hear
> About our journey and our cheer.
> Our ships in autumn reach the sound,
> But long the way to Swedish ground.
> With joyless weather, wind and rain,
> And pinching cold, and feet in pain—
> With sleep, fatigue, and want oppressed,
> No songs had we—we scarce had rest."

And when he came into conversation with the king he sang:—

> " When first the mighty earl I met,
> No word of thine did I forget,
> O king, but gave thy message all.
> Often I spoke in his own hall

---

[1] Laing had in mind " a complete suit of plate-armour," but the original has only *brynjar*, the usual word for shirts of ring-mail.

With Rognvald, that gen'rous man,
And never, since my life began,
Have I known one in whom I heard
More loyal zeal in every word.
The earl, thy friend, bids thee, who art
So mild and generous of heart,
His servants all who here may come
To cherish in thy royal home;
And thine who may come to the east
In Ragnvald's hall shall find a feast—
In Ragnvald's house shall find a home—
At Ragnvald's court be still welcome.
When first I came the people's mind
Incensed by Eric's son I find;
For he has stirred them by his word
To treachery against their lord.
But Rognvald ('tis truth I tell)
Has served thee loyally and well;
His help will strengthen and increase
Thy realm, if thou and he keep peace.
The earl is wise, and understands
The need of peace for both the lands;
And he entreats thee not to break
The present peace for vengeance' sake! "

It was early in winter that Sigvat the scald, with two companions, left Sarpsborg, and proceeded eastward over the moors to Gotland; but they often met with poor reception on their journey. One evening he came to three peasants, who drove them all out of their houses; and Sigvat the scald composed his song " The Travellers to the East " on this expedition. At last Sigvat arrives at Earl Ragnvald's, and was long entertained kindly and well in his house. The earl heard by letters sent by Ingigerd, the king's daughter, that ambassadors from King Jarisleif [1] were come from Russia to King Olaf of Sweden to ask his daughter Ingigerd in marriage, and that King Olaf had given them hopes he would agree to it. About the same time King Olaf's daughter Astrid came to Earl Ragnvald's court, and a great feast was made for her. Sigvat soon became acquainted by conversation with the king's daughter, and she knew him by name and family; for Ottar the scald, Sigvat's sister's son, had long had intimate acquaintance with King Olaf the Swedish king. Among other things talked of, Earl Ragnvald asked Sigvat if the king of Norway would not marry the king's daughter Astrid. " If he will do that," said he, " I think we need not ask the Swedish king for his consent." Astrid, the king's daughter, said exactly the same. Soon after Sigvat returns home, and comes to King Olaf at Sarpsborg a little before

[1] Jaroslav the Wise, son of Vladimir (Valdemar) the Great, was Grand Duke of Novgorod 1016–54.

Yule. He immediately tells King Olaf the news he had heard; and at first the king was much cast down when he heard of King Jarisleif's suit, and he said he expected nothing but evil from King Olaf; but wished he might be able to return it in such a way as Olaf should remember. A while afterwards the king asks Sigvat about various news from Gotland. Sigvat spoke a great deal about Astrid, the king's daughter; how beautiful she was, how agreeable in her conversation; and that all declared she was in no respect behind her sister Ingigerd. The king listened with pleasure to this. Then Sigvat told him the conversation he and Astrid had had between themselves, and the king was delighted at the idea. "The Swedish king," said he, "will scarcely think that I will dare to marry a daughter of his without his consent." But this speech of his was not known generally. King Olaf and Sigvat the scald often spoke about it. The king inquired particularly of Sigvat what he knew about Earl Ragnvald, and "if he be truly our friend," said the king. Sigvat said that the earl was King Olaf's best friend, and sang these verses:—

> "The mighty Olaf should not cease
> With him to hold good terms and peace;
> For this good earl unwearied shows
> He is thy friend where all are foes.
> Of all who dwell by the East Sea
> So friendly no man is as he:
> At all their Things he takes thy part,
> And is thy firm friend, hand and heart."

CHAPTER XCIII. EARL RAGNVALD AND ASTRID'S JOURNEY TO NORWAY [1019].—After Yule, Thord Skotakoll, a sister's son of Sigvat, attended by one of Sigvat's footboys, who had been with Sigvat the autumn before at Gotland, went quite secretly from the court, and proceeded to Gotland. When they came to Earl Ragnvald's court, they produced the tokens which Olaf himself had sent to the earl, that he might place confidence in Thord. Without delay the earl made himself ready for a journey, as did Astrid, the king's daughter; and the earl took with him 100 men, who were chosen both from among his court-men and the sons of great bonders, and who were carefully equipt in all things, clothes, weapons, and horses. Then they rode northwards to Sarpsborg, and came there at Candlemas (2nd February 1019).

CHAPTER XCIV. OF KING OLAF'S MARRIAGE.—King Olaf had put all things in order in the best style. There were

all sorts of liquors of the best that could be got, and all other
preparations of the same quality. Many people of consequence
were summoned in from their districts. When the earl arrived
with his retinue the king received him particularly well; and
the earl was shown to a large, good, and remarkably well-
furnished house for his lodging; and serving-men and others
were appointed to wait on him; and nothing was wanting, in
any respect, that could grace a feast. Now when the entertainment had lasted some days, the king, the earl, and Astrid had a
conference together; and the result of it was, that Earl Ragnvald
contracted Astrid, daughter of the Swedish king Olaf, to Olaf
king of Norway, with the same dowry which had before been
settled that her sister Ingigerd should have from home. King
Olaf, on his part, should give Astrid the same bride-gift that had
been intended for her sister Ingigerd. Thereupon the feasting
was prolonged, and King Olaf and Queen Astrid's wedding was
drunk in great festivity. Earl Ragnvald then returned to
Gotland, and the king gave the earl many great and good gifts
at parting; and they parted the dearest of friends, which they
continued to be while they lived.

CHAPTER XCV. THE AGREEMENT WITH THE KING OF NORWAY
BROKEN BY OLAF OF SWEDEN.—The spring thereafter came
ambassadors from King Jarisleif in Novgorod to Sweden, to
treat more particularly about the promise given by King Olaf
the preceding summer to marry his daughter Ingigerd to King
Jarisleif. King Olaf talked about the business with Ingigerd,
and told her it was his pleasure that she should marry King
Jarisleif. She replied, " If I marry King Jarisleif, I must have
as my bride-gift the town and earldom of Ladoga." The Russian
ambassadors agreed to this, on the part of their sovereign.
Then said Ingigerd, " If I go east to Russia, I must choose the
man in Sweden whom I think most suitable to accompany me;
and I must stipulate that he shall not have any less title, or in
any respect less dignity, privilege, and consideration there, than
he has here." This the king and the ambassadors agreed to, and
gave their hands upon it in confirmation of the condition.
" And who," asked the king, " is the man thou wilt take with
thee as thy attendant? "
" That man," she replied, " is my relation Earl Ragnvald."
The king replies, " I have resolved to reward Earl Ragnvald
in a different manner for his treason against his master in going
to Norway with my daughter, and giving her as a concubine

to that thick fellow, who he knew was my greatest enemy. He shall be hanged for this this summer."

Then Ingigerd begged her father to be true to the promise he had made her, and had confirmed by giving his hand upon it. By her entreaties it was at last agreed that the king should promise to let Earl Ragnvald go in peace from Sweden, but that he should never again appear in the king's presence, or come back to Sweden while Olaf reigned. Ingigerd then sent messengers to the earl to bring him these tidings, and to appoint a place of meeting. The earl immediately prepared for his journey; rode up to East Gotland; procured there a vessel, and, with his retinue, joined Ingigerd, and they proceeded together eastward to Russia. There Ingigerd was married to King Jarisleif; and their children were Valdemar,[1] Visivald,[2] and Halte the Bold.[3] Queen Ingigerd gave Earl Ragnvald the town of Ladoga, and earldom belonging to it. Earl Ragnvald was there a long time, and was a celebrated man. His sons and Ingeborg's were Earl Ulf and Earl Eyliff.

CHAPTER XCVI. HISTORY OF THE LAGMAN EMUND.—There was a man called Emund of Skara, who was lagman of West Gotland, and was a man of great understanding and eloquence, and of high birth, great connection, and very wealthy; but was considered deceitful, and not to be trusted. He was the most powerful man in West Gotland after the earl was gone. The same spring that Earl Ragnvald left Gotland the Gotland people held a Thing among themselves, and often expressed their anxiety to each other about what the Swedish king might do. They heard he was incensed because they had rather held in friendship with the king of Norway than striven against him; and he was also enraged against those who had attended his daughter Astrid to Norway. Some proposed to seek help and support from the king of Norway, and to offer him their services; others dissuaded from this measure, as West Gotland had no strength to oppose to the Swedes. "And the king of Norway," said they, "is far from us, the chief strength of his country very distant; and therefore let us first send men to the Swedish king to attempt to come to some reconciliation with him. If that fail, we can still turn to the king of Norway." Then the bonders asked Emund to undertake this mission, to which he agreed;

---

[1] Vladimir, born in 1020, but died in 1052 before his father.
[2] Vsevolod, born 1030, Grand Duke 1078–1093.
[3] Halte is unknown. There were also four more sons and three daughters.

and he proceeded with thirty men to East Gotland, where there were many of his relations and friends, who received him hospitably. He conversed there with the most prudent men about this difficult business; and they were all unanimous on one point,—that the king's treatment of them was against law and reason. From thence Emund went into Sweden, and conversed with many men of consequence, who all expressed themselves in the same way. Emund continued his journey thus, until one day, towards evening, he arrived at Upsala, where he and his retinue took a good lodging, and stayed there all night. The next day Emund waited upon the king, who was just then sitting in the Thing surrounded by many people. Emund went before him, bent his knee, and saluted him. The king looked at him, saluted him, and asked him what news he brought.

Emund replies, " There is little news among us Gotlanders; but it appears to us a piece of remarkable news that Atle from the Dales,[1] up in Vermeland, whom we look upon as a great sportsman, went up to the forest in winter with his snow-shoes and his bow. After he had got as many furs [2] in the fjelds as filled his hand-sledge [3] so full that he could scarcely drag it, he returned home from the woods. But on the way he saw a squirrel in the trees, and shot at it, but did not hit; at which he was so angry that he left the sledge to run after the squirrel: but still the squirrel sprang where the wood was thickest, sometimes among the roots of the trees, sometimes in the branches, sometimes among the arms that stretch from tree to tree. When Atle shot at it the arrows flew too high or too low, and the squirrel never jumped so that Atle could get a fair aim at him. He was so eager upon this chase that he ran the whole day after the squirrel, and yet could not get hold of it. It was now getting dark; so he threw himself down upon the snow, as he was wont, and lay there all night in a heavy snow-storm. Next day Atle got up to look after his sledge, but never did he find it again; and so he returned home. And this is the only news, king, I have to tell."

The king says, " This is news of but little importance, if it be all thou hast to tell."

Emund replies, " Lately something happened which may well

[1] There is a pun here on *dælskr* " from the Dales " and *dælskr* " foolish "; vide p. 214.
[2] Squirrel skins.
[3] *Skíð-sleði*, a small sledge on ski-shaped runners, which can be dragged by hand over the snow.

be called news. Gaute Toveson went with five war-ships out of the Gotha river, and when he was lying at Eker Island there came five large Danish merchant-ships there. Gaute and his men immediately took four of the great vessels, and made a great booty without the loss of a man; but the fifth vessel slipped out to sea, and sailed away. Gaute gave chase with one ship, and at first came nearer to them; but as the wind increased, the Danes got away. Then Gaute wanted to turn back; but a storm came on so that he lost his ship at Lesö, with all the goods, and the greater part of his crew. In the meantime his people were waiting for him at Eker; but the Danes came over in fifteen merchant-ships, killed them all, and took all the booty they had made. So but little luck had they with their greed of plunder."

The king replied, " That is great news, and worth being told; but what now is thy errand here? "

Emund replies, " I travel, sire, to obtain your judgment in a difficult case, in which our law and the Upsala law do not agree."

The king asks, " What is thy appeal case? "

Emund replies, " There were two noble-born men of equal birth, but unequal in property and disposition. They quarrelled about some land, and did each other much damage; but most was done to him who was the more powerful of the two. This quarrel, however, was settled, and judged of at a General Thing; and the judgment was, that the most powerful should pay a compensation. But at the first payment, instead of paying a goose, he paid a gosling; for an old sow he paid a sucking pig; and for a mark of stamped gold only a half mark, and for the other half mark nothing but clay and clay; and moreover threatened, in the most violent way, the people whom he forced to receive such goods in payment. Now, sire, what is your judgment? "

The king replies, " He shall pay the full equivalent whom the judgment ordered to do so, and that faithfully; and further, three-fold to his king; and if payment be not made within a year and a day, he shall be cut off from all his property, his goods confiscated, and half go to the king's house, and half to the other party." [1]

Emund took witnesses to this judgment among the most considerable of the men who were present, according to the laws

---

[1] Here Snorri confuses Norwegian and Swedish law; the former divided fines into half-shares between the king and the plaintiff, but the latter into three shares—for king, plaintiff, and men of the district.

which were held in the Upsala Thing. He then saluted the king, and went his way; and other men brought their cases before the king, and he sat late in the day upon the cases of the people. Now when the king came to table, he asked where Lagman Emund was. It was answered, he was home at his lodgings. "Then," said the king, "go after him, and tell him to be my guest to-day." Thereafter the dishes were borne in; then came the musicians with harps, fiddles, and musical instruments; and lastly, the cup-bearers. The king was particularly merry, and had many great people at table with him, so that he thought little of Emund. The king drank the whole day, and slept all the night after; but in the morning the king awoke, and recollected what Emund had said the day before: and when he had put on his clothes, he let his wise men be summoned to him; for he had always twelve of the wisest men who sat in judgment with him, and treated the more difficult cases; and that was no easy business, for the king was ill pleased if the judgment was not according to justice, and yet it was of no use to contradict him. In this meeting the king ordered Lagman Emund to be called before them. The messenger returned, and said, "Sire, Lagman Emund rode away yesterday as soon as he had dined." "Then," said the king, "tell me, ye good chiefs, what may have been the meaning of that law case which Emund laid before us yesterday?"

They replied, "You must have considered it yourself, if you think there was any other meaning under it than what he said."

The king replied, "By the two noble-born men whom he spoke of, who were at variance, and of whom one was more powerful than the other, and who did each other damage, he must have meant us and Olaf the Thick."

They answered, "It is, sire, as you say."

The king:—"Our case was judged at the Upsala Thing. But what was his meaning when he said that bad payment was made; namely, a gosling for a goose, a sucking pig for a sow, and clay and dirt for half of the money instead of gold?"

Arnvid the Blind replied, "Sire, red gold and clay are things very unlike; but the difference is still greater between king and slave. You promised Olaf the Thick your daughter Ingigerd, who, in all branches of her descent, is born of kings, and of the Upland Swedish race of kings, which is the most noble in the North; for it is traced up to the gods themselves. But now Olaf has got Astrid; and although she is a king's child, her mother was but a slave-woman, and besides of Vendish race. Great difference, indeed, must there be between these kings, when the one takes thankfully such a match; and now it is evident, as might be expected, that no Northman is to be placed by the side of the Upsala kings. Let us all give thanks that it has so turned out; for the gods have long protected their descendants, although many now neglect this faith."

There were three brothers:—Arnvid the Blind, who had a great understanding, but was so weak-sighted that he was scarcely fit for war; the second was Thorvid the Stammerer, who could not utter two words together at one time, but was remarkably bold and courageous; the third was Freyvid the Deaf, who was hard of hearing. All these brothers were rich and powerful men, of noble birth, great wisdom, and all very dear to the king.

Then said King Olaf, " What means that which Emund said about Atle from the Dales? "

None made any reply, but the one looked at the other.

" Speak freely," said the king.

Then said Thorvid the Stammerer, " Atle, quarrelsome, greedy, ill-tempered; of the Dales, foolish."

Then said the king, " To whom are these words of reproach and mockery applied? "

Freyvid the Deaf replied, " We will speak more clearly if we have your permission."

The king:—" Speak freely, Freyvid, what you will."

Freyvid took up the word, and spoke. " My brother Thorvid, who is considered to be the wisest of us brothers, holds the words ' Atle ' and ' quarrelsome,' ' Dales ' and ' foolish ' to be the same thing; for it applies to him who is weary of peace, longs for small things without attaining them, while he lets great and useful things pass away as they came. I am deaf; yet so loud have many spoken out, that I can perceive that all men, both great and small, take it ill that you have not kept your promise to the king of Norway; and, worse than that, that you broke the decision of the community as it was delivered at Upsala Thing. You need not fear either the king of Norway, or the king of Denmark, or any other, so long as the Swedish army will follow you; but if the people of the country unanimously turn against you, we, your friends, see no counsel that can be of advantage to you."

The king asks, " Who is the chief who dares to betray the country and me? "

Freyvid replies, " All Swedes desire to have the ancient laws, and their full rights. Look but here, sire, how many chiefs are sitting in council with you. I think, in truth, we are but six whom you call your councillors: all the others, so far as I know, have ridden forth through the districts to hold Things with the people; and we will not conceal it from you, that the message-token has gone forth to assemble a Retribution-thing.[1] All of us brothers have been invited to take part in the decisions of this council, but none of us will bear the name of traitor to the sovereign; for that our father never was."

Then the king said, " What counsel shall we take in this dangerous affair that is on our hands? Good chiefs, give me counsel, that I may keep my kingdom, and the heritage of my forefathers; for I cannot enter into strife against the whole Swedish force."

Arnvid the Blind replies, " Sire, it is my advice that you ride down to Aaros [2] with such men as will follow you; take your ship there, and go out into the Mælare lake; summon all people to meet you; proceed no longer with haughtiness, but promise every man the law and rights of old established in the country; keep back in this way the message-token, for it cannot as yet, in so short a time, have travelled far through the land. Send, then, those of your men in whom you have the most confidence to those who have this business on hand, and try if this uproar can be appeased."

The king says that he will adopt this advice. " I will," says he, " that ye brothers undertake this business; for I trust to you the most among my men."

Thorvid the Stammerer said, " I remain behind. Let Jacob your son go with them, for that is necessary."

Then said Freyvid, " Let us do as Thorvid says: he will not leave you in time of danger, and I and Arnvid must travel."

This counsel was followed. Olaf went to his ships, and set out into the Mælare lake, and many people came to him. The brothers Arnvid and Freyvid rode out to Ullerager, and had with them the king's son Jacob; but they kept it a secret that he was there. The brothers observed that there was a great concourse and war-gathering, for the bonders held the Thing night and day. When Arnvid and Freyvid met their relations

---

[1] *Refsiping*—a Thing for punishment by penalty or death for crimes and misdemeanours.

[2] Aaros—the river-mouth; the present Upsala at the mouth of the Fyrisaa.

and friends, they said they would join with the people; and many agreed to leave the management of the business in the hands of the brothers. But all, as one man, declared they would no longer have King Olaf over them, and no longer suffer his unlawful proceedings, and overweening pride which would not listen to any man's remonstrances, even when the great chiefs spoke the truth to him. When Freyvid observed the heat of the people, he saw in what a bad situation the king's cause was. He summoned the chiefs of the land to a meeting with him, and addressed them thus:—" It appears to me, that if we are to depose Olaf Ericsson from his kingdom, we Swedes of the Uplands should be the leading men in it; for so it has always been, that the counsel which the Upland chiefs have resolved upon among themselves has always been followed by the men of the rest of the country. Our forefathers did not need to take advice from the West Gotlanders about the government of the Swedes. Now we will not be so degenerate as to need Emund to give us counsel; but let us, friends and relations, unite ourselves for the purpose of coming to a determination." All agreed to this, and thought it was well said. Thereafter the people joined this union which the Upland chiefs made among themselves, and Freyvid and Arnvid were chiefs of the whole assemblage. When Emund heard this he suspected how the matter would end, and went to both the brothers to have a conversation with them. Then Freyvid asked Emund, "Whom, in your opinion, should we take for king, in case Olaf Ericsson's days are at an end? "

Emund:—" Him whom we think best suited to it, whether he be of the race of chiefs or not."

Freyvid answers, " We Uplanders will not, in our time, have the kingdom go out of the old race of our ancestors, which has given us kings for a long course of generations, so long as we have so good a choice as now. King Olaf has two sons; one of whom we will choose for king, although there is a great difference between them. The one is noble-born, and of Swedish race on both sides; the other is a slave-woman's son, and of Vendish race on the mother's side."

This decision was received with loud applause, and all would have Jacob for king.

Then said Emund, " Ye Upland Swedes have the power this time to determine the matter; but I will tell you what will happen:—some of those who now will listen to nothing but that the kingdom remain in the old race, will live to see the day when they will wish the kingdom in another race,[1] as being of more advantage."

Thereupon the brothers Freyvid and Arnvid led the king's son Jacob into the Thing, and saluted him with the title of king; and the Swedes gave him the name of Onund, which he afterwards retained as long as he lived. He was then ten or twelve years old. Thereafter King Onund took a court, and chose chiefs to be around him; and they had as many attendants in their suite as were thought necessary, so that he gave the whole assemblage of bonders leave to return home. After that ambassadors went between the two kings; and at last they had a meeting, and came to an agreement. Olaf was to remain king over the country as long as he lived; but should hold peace and be reconciled with King Olaf of Norway, and also with all who had taken part in this business. Onund should also be king, and have a part of the land, such as the father and son should agree upon; but should be bound to support the bonders in case King Olaf did anything which the bonders would not suffer.

CHAPTER XCVII. MEETING OF RECONCILIATION BETWEEN THE KINGS, AND THEIR GAME AT DICE.—Thereafter embassadors were sent to Norway to King Olaf, with the errand that he should come with his retinue to a meeting at Konghelle with the Swedish kings, and that the Swedish kings would there confirm their reconciliation. When King Olaf heard this message, he was willing, now as formerly, to enter into the agreement, and proceeded to the appointed place. There the Swedish king also came; and the relations, when they met, bound themselves mutually to peace and agreement. Olaf the Swedish king was then remarkably mild in manner, and agreeable to talk with. Thorstein Frode [2] relates of this meeting that there was a farm in Hising which had sometimes belonged to Norway, and sometimes to Gotland.[3] The kings came to the agreement between themselves that they would cast lots by the dice to determine who should have this property, and that he who threw the highest should have the farm. The Swedish king threw two sixes, and said King Olaf need scarcely throw. He replied, while shaking the dice in his hand, " Although there be two sixes

---

[1] The last of the old line of Swedish kings was Olaf's son Eymund (*vide* p. 200); after his death (*c.* 1055), his son-in-law Earl Steinkel was chosen king.

[2] An unknown chronicler.

[3] The two most southerly parishes on Hising Isle (Lundby and Tuve) in ancient times belonged to Gotland, the other four belonged to Norway.

on the dice, it would be easy, sire, for God Almighty to let them turn up in my favour." Then he threw, and had sixes also. Now the Swedish king threw again, and had again two sixes. Olaf king of Norway then threw, and had six upon one dice, and the other split in two, so as to make seven eyes in all upon it; and the farm was adjudged to the king of Norway. We have heard nothing else of any interest that took place at this meeting; and the kings separated having reached agreement with each other.

EVERYMAN'S LIBRARY AND EVERYMAN PAPERBACKS: A Selection

indicates the volumes also in paperback: for their series numbers in Everyman Paperbacks add 1000 to the EML numbers given.

BIOGRAPHY

ESSAYS AND CRITICISM

FICTION

2

HISTORY

LEGENDS AND SAGAS

POETRY AND DRAMA

RELIGION AND PHILOSOPHY

SCIENCES: POLITICAL AND GENERAL

TRAVEL AND TOPOGRAPHY